EDDIE'S WAKE

A Novel

C. A. PETERSON

Outskirts Press, Inc.
Denver, Colorado

Outskirts Press, Inc.
http://www.outskirtspress.com

ISBN: 978-1-4327-0960-0

Outskirts Press and the "OP" logo are trademarks belonging to Outskirts Press, Inc.

PRINTED IN THE UNITED STATES OF AMERICA

In memory of my father,
John Schulz:
Fisherman, Woodsman, Teacher.

In Gratitude

Where does one start? Writing *Eddie's Wake* has been a labor of love; not just mine but that of the many people who supported me. I wish to thank my teacher and mentor, author Carol Davis Luce, for her direction and encouragement. She was undaunted by my bad writing habits, patient in making suggestions and kind in correcting my work. I also want to thank my classmates from *Writers' Online Workshops* who offered feedback on the early drafts of *Eddie's Wake*. Thanks to Bob Sitze, Anne Basye and all the others who organized and presented the ELCA *Advanced Writers Workshop 2003: Writing for the Church,* as well as to the other participants. Thank you to all the friends and family members who read *Eddie's Wake* in its various drafts, especially Nancy Peterson Anderson and Amy Hessel, whose critiques were invaluable. My deep gratitude to Dave Aldrich of Aldrich Design for producing a stunning book cover, better than I could have imagined! Many thanks are due to Paul and Florence Peterson for their moral and financial support and for saying *the story is sterling* even while it still needed plenty of polishing. Thanks to my mother, Dorothy Schulz, for sharing her memories of growing up and for always being there for me. Most of all, a heartfelt thank you to my husband, Tom: for giving me the best place in the house to write, for supporting me when I took time off to work on *Eddie's Wake*, for being patient with me when I didn't like his critiques, but most of all for his love. I shudder to imagine what my life would be like without him.

Set me as a seal upon your heart, as a seal upon your arm;

for love is strong as death, passion fierce as the grave.

Its flashes are flashes of fire, a raging flame.

Many waters cannot quench love, neither can floods drown it.

If one offered for love all the wealth of one's house,

it would be utterly scorned.

Song of Songs 8:6-7

Chapter 1

Love Strong as Death
October, 1928 Tomos Bay, Wisconsin

The way his flannel pajamas bunched up around his knees that morning as he dozed, the blood-red linoleum of the kitchen floor, the smell of wet wool and fish mingled together, the feeling of cold air on his bare feet as it swept through the house: these were the things that chiseled themselves into his memory as his world tilted and came crashing down around him.

Thirteen years old and a seventh grader at Holy Angels School, Karl Stern had to stay home for the day, sick again. October was only half gone, but he'd already missed three days of school because of the wheezy cough he came down with every fall. His mother, Maggie, blamed it on the damp lake air that settled over Tomos Bay whenever the weather turned colder. Since the kitchen was the warmest place in the house, his father set up the rollaway cot between the cupboards and the table before leaving for work that morning. There Karl's mother could watch over him while she took care of her other housework.

Wrapped up in his blanket with his feet dangling off

the end of the cot, Karl dozed and dreamed about the summer just past, when his father, Eddie, had finally given him real work to do on his fishing boat. Karl liked to think he was truly helpful and needed, and in the dream, he was; his young, strong muscles casting and hauling nets, sorting fish and throwing back the ones that were too small, keeping the boat on course when his father had something else to do. But just as his father said *Good job, son,* Karl heard a ruckus on the boat and someone calling for his mother. When the voices came closer, he awoke to the sound of a frantic commotion on the front porch. Bleary eyed, he got up and stood at the kitchen door in his bare feet and wrinkled pajamas.

Before his mother crossed the living room, the front door burst open and hit the inside wall, cracking the gray plaster behind it. The framed picture of Saint Andrew that hung there bounced once and crashed to the floor, face down, its glass shattering into a thousand pieces. Eddie's partner, Will Denver, and their crewman, Rob Holstrom, each tripped on the threshold, nearly dropping Eddie's limp, wet body. The many layers of waterlogged wool, the long underwear, heavy jacket, sweater, and two shirts underneath it all added to the load Will and Rob had to carry. Panting, they laid Eddie on the worn gray and maroon rug.

Maggie spit out the question Karl wanted to ask. "Is he dead?"

His heart began to beat the way it did when he raced his pals around the schoolyard and down the block after school.

"No, but he will be if we don't get him warm right away."

His mother took charge. "Rob, get some wood from

outside and stoke up the kitchen stove, then go feed the furnace. Will, help me get these wet clothes off him. Karl, move your things off the cot. We have to get him into the kitchen where it's warm."

Too stunned to move, Karl watched with dread as his mother and Will fought with swollen, nearly frozen buttons and buttonholes. His pounding heart reached down and clutched at his stomach.

"Karl, go get my sewing scissors, and bring the quilt and the featherbed from our room. Hurry!"

Karl jumped and did as he was told, grabbing the scissors, racing through the house, nearly tripping on the bedding as he brought it from his parents' bedroom. He gave the scissors to his mother and took the quilt and featherbed into the kitchen, where he removed his pillow and book, but left his blanket for his father. Back in the living room, he watched his mother cut every button from his father's sodden, smelly clothing while Will helped peel it off, layer after layer. Finally freed of it all, Eddie Stern looked like a corpse lying there, even though his chest moved up and down ever so slightly.

"We need the quilt out here, Karl."

Karl ran to get it from the cot.

Rob returned as Maggie and Will wrapped Eddie's icy body in the quilt. Now the two men carried him easily into the kitchen, where Maggie pushed the table away and pulled the cot close to the wood stove. There they laid him, cocooned in the quilt and featherbed. Karl thought this would certainly revive him.

After Karl's mother sent Rob for Dr. Lyman, Will told them about the black ice that covered the deck when they arrived that morning; treacherous, invisible ice, slick as all get out. "No one saw what happened; we didn't even realize he'd fallen in. When we found him, he was already going under." He turned away from Karl and Maggie, pulled out a handkerchief and blew his nose. He didn't turn around again for a long time.

The fishermen had a saying: *if you fall in, swim to the bottom because it's warmer there.* You might as well give up the fight and die quickly. The northernmost and deepest of the five Great Lakes, Lake Superior's average temperature is 40 degrees, cold enough to suck the life right out of a body even in summer. Yet Will and Rob refused to let Eddie go. Together they outweighed him, but holding on and trying to pull him in stretched their muscles and their determination. Rob slipped and almost fell in himself and Will hit his head hard enough on the railing that he had a goose egg before they got Eddie on deck, drenched, freezing and waxy as death.

When Karl and Will came back from hanging Eddie's wet clothing in the basement, Maggie lay on the cot with his father, all wrapped up in the featherbed next to him. Maybe the warmth of her body next to his would help; for a moment, Karl had the impulse to climb in, too. His mother held his father's hands close to her heart and kissed his face—something he'd seen her do a hundred times.

"Eddie, can you hear me? Open your eyes; you don't have to say anything, just open your eyes so I know you're still here. Please? Can you do that; can you open your eyes for me?"

When his eyes fluttered open, Maggie cried out. "Oh, there you are! I love you, Eddie, I love you..." She kissed his cold, motionless face again and again; she brought his stiff, white fingers to her mouth and kissed each one of them, too. "We'll get you warmed up, don't worry..."

She lay still, staring into his blank eyes. "Eddie... Ed*ward*... Eddie? Where are you?" Her words wobbled;

her voice rose in panic. "You don't know me, do you? You can't see me, can you?"

In the pit of his clutched up stomach, Karl knew how this was going to end.

Late that night, after the priest had been there and Grandma O'Keefe, Aunt Kathleen and Uncle Melvin had come and gone; after his sisters, Lizzie and Anna were asleep; after Dr. Lyman had come and gone a second time; Karl woke up and crept through the darkness and down the stairs. A dim light spilled through the kitchen door, a beacon to his father's sickroom.

His mother sat on the floor next to the cot where his father still lay, his face now flushed with fever. She'd propped up his head with three pillows and covered him with only a light blanket. The familiar smell of Eddie Stern's sweat filled the kitchen; his tall, sturdy body seemed shrunken from its dousing in the cold lake. Every few minutes he coughed weakly.

Maggie still wore the faded green house dress she had on yesterday, green like a sick, stormy sea. Her long hair fell around her shoulders, its reddish flecks brought to life by the lamplight. Karl thought she looked like a young girl, her arm across his father, her head resting between his upper arm and his chest.

"Mama?"

Maggie raised her head. "Karl, what are you doing out of bed? Where are your slippers?" Deep shadows filled the curves beneath her eyes and her puffy eyelids drooped, half open, half closed.

"I woke up and couldn't go back to sleep. How's Daddy?"

"He took in too much lake water. Dr. Lyman said his heart isn't beating very well."

"Is he going to die?"

"I think so."

Karl's brow wrinkled, his throat suddenly tight. "No!" He wanted it to be yesterday at this time, he wanted to be able to warn his father to watch out for ice on the deck.

"Come here, sit with me." His mother pulled the blanket he'd left for his father onto the floor, making a place for him to sit between her and the cot. She wrapped him in the blanket and then in her arms, smoothing his curly blond hair away from his face. They sat without talking for a long time as she rocked him and he cried. She had no words or wisdom for him, only the strength of a sorrow shared.

"I wanted to be his partner on the boat. I wanted to work with him. I wanted to be just like him." Karl pulled away and looked into his mother's eyes.

Maggie smiled a little. "You two have been squabbling an awful lot lately, so you'd better tell him, Karl, you'd better tell him everything you want him to know before it's too late."

"Do you think he can hear us?"

"I don't know for sure. Just *believe* he can, and tell him everything." She stood up and rubbed the back of her neck. "I'm going to change out of these clothes and look in on the girls. You stay here and talk to him." She kissed the top of Karl's head and disappeared up the stairs.

All alone with his father, at first Karl felt foolish, like he was talking to himself, but it didn't take long before he remembered all the things the two of them had done together. He talked about the sunburn they'd both had after the first day on the lake last summer.

"But that didn't matter, 'cause it was the best summer of my whole life."

He talked about their wrestling matches and told him how proud he felt when Eddie quit letting him win, laughed and said, "But I still hate losing." Karl remembered the day they'd gone out to the woods to see the huge sugar maple that Eddie climbed as a boy, and how they'd made plans to tap the tree for syrup next spring. "I can almost taste it, Daddy, you *have* to get well."

Karl buried his face in his father's blankets, crying. He said, "I love you" again and again. He kissed Eddie's bearded cheek the way he did when he was still small enough to be swooped up in his father's arms and lifted high into the air. And he whispered over and over again, "Please don't go, Daddy. God, please, don't let him die, please. He has to get well. I'll never be bad or talk back ever again, just let him live. Please!"

The next morning, Karl's mother sent his sisters off to school after telling them to kiss their Daddy goodbye. She told them he was very sick, but didn't say he'd probably die before the end of the day. Karl stayed home again even though he'd stopped coughing; his father stopped coughing, too, but for him it was not a good sign.

Maggie's sister, Kathleen, and her husband, Melvin Straus, came back again, arriving at the same time as Dr. Lyman. He listened to Eddie's chest and shook his head. It would only be a few hours at most. Maggie didn't even look upset when she asked Uncle Melvin to go back for Father Cunningham. While they waited, Karl helped the doctor move Eddie and the cot from the kitchen to the living room, not far from the place on the rug that was still wet from his soaked clothing. He remembered the powerful weight of his father on top of him the other day as they laughed and wrestled in the back yard. Now he seemed as light as air.

The priest came and gave Eddie Stern last rites. As he prepared to leave, he took Maggie's hand. "Margaret, I'm so sorry," he said. "We'll talk more later."

Karl followed the priest out the door. "Father?" For the first time he noticed that they were exactly the same height. Although Father Cunningham outweighed him by quite a bit, Karl had no reason to be afraid of him.

"Yes, Karl." They stood on the same cement steps Eddie crossed on his way to work only yesterday; the same steps Will and Rob crossed to bring him home again, only yesterday.

"Why didn't you pray for him to get well and live like you did before? Sister said, 'ask and you shall receive.' She said Jesus said so. Why didn't you ask God to make my father well again? Why couldn't you pray for a miracle?" Karl's voice broke and his eyes filled up. "I mean no disrespect, Father, but I have to know."

Father Cunningham sighed. "You're asking a hard question, son. We pray for him to be in paradise with God. What better life could there be than that?"

"But I want him here!" Karl cried, unashamed.

The priest put both of his hands on Karl's shoulders and looked directly into his watery eyes. They stood man to man. "Of course you do, we all do, especially your mother, but in cases like this, there are no miracles and we have to accept that death is inevitable. Now you listen to me, Karl. Your mother's the one we have to be concerned about now. You're old enough to understand that. No more of those tears. You're the man of the house; she needs you to be strong. She's depending on you to help her."

"I'll try, Father." He wiped his eyes with his sleeve.

"You can do it if you try hard enough. I'll see you again soon. Take care of your mother and your sisters."

Father Cunningham hurried down the street toward Holy Angels Church. Well, if the priest wouldn't pray for a miracle, he would. "Please, God, please, make him well. Please, don't let him die. Please, *please.*" He didn't bother to cross himself or pray to Jesus or even to the Virgin Mary. He knew he should have worked harder on the prayer, but he couldn't do any better than that.

Dr. Lyman opened the front door. He spoke gently. "You'd better come in, son, your mother's asking for you."

Maggie knelt by the cot, holding Eddie's hand, dry eyed and remarkably calm. She looked up at Karl and held out her other hand to him. "Come here, now. He's going."

He knelt with his mother. "Nooo."

"Shh! Shh! Say goodbye."

"Goodbye, Daddy." He touched his father's beard and wondered if he'd ever be able to grow one like that. He tried not to cry, but it was no use. His mother's arm tightened around his shaking shoulders.

The weak rise and fall of his father's chest stopped completely. Dr. Lyman listened with his stethoscope, and looked from Karl to Maggie before shaking his head. He removed the earpieces. "I'm sorry, Margaret."

"God help us all," Aunt Kathleen whispered. She turned to stop the mantel clock. A heavy silence blanketed the house for a moment.

Maggie kissed her husband's forehead and glanced up at Uncle Melvin for an instant. He smiled slightly and winked at her. She looked away, stood and turned to the doctor so quickly that she lost her balance, steadying herself when he took her hand. "Thank you for everything, Doctor."

"Margaret, dear... Send for me if there's anything you need."

"We'll be fine."

Uncle Melvin smiled, showing off his gold dental work. "I'll take care of things, John, don't worry."

After Dr. Lyman left, Maggie took charge, like she had yesterday. "Kathleen, go get mother. Melvin, you and Karl go for the undertaker. I'll stay with Eddie."

"You can't be alone, Margaret." Uncle Melvin sounded kind, an odd thing for him. "Let me go to your mother's; Kathleen should stay with you."

"No. I want everyone out. Now. Leave. Please."

His mother's calm insistence scared Karl.

Aunt Kathleen wiped her eyes. "Maggie, you really— I'll stay with you; you should have someone—"

"No, I want everyone out of the house. Everyone. Go."

Aunt Kathleen hurried out the door without her coat and had to come back in to get it before she started her walk to Grandma O'Keefe's house. Uncle Melvin got into his car and lit a cigarette, his left arm dangling from the window. Karl found his jacket and started to leave, but went back to hug his mother.

"Go, now." Her voice wobbled again.

As soon as Karl closed the door his mother locked him out. Two steps down and he heard a long, animal-like wail coming from inside the house, coming from *her*. With the fine hairs on his neck standing straight up, he climbed into the car and looked out the back window at their tan, shingle sided house. "Mama," he whispered.

"Now, Karl, I know this isn't easy for you," said Uncle Melvin as he drove toward town. "Turn around and act like a man, come on, son. You know you *are* the man of the family now, don't you? Do you know what that means?"

Karl shook his head, swallowing hard. Uncle Melvin was trying to be nice to him and he desperately needed kindness from someone.

"It means you have to take responsibility for your mother and your sisters. It means you have to be strong for them. You'll only bring shame on your father's name if people see you like this. Crying is for women, they're weak. You're better than that."

Karl looked out the window at the houses and stores they passed. He saw people sweeping sidewalks, mailing letters, walking dogs, doing ordinary, everyday things; they looked like people who didn't have a care in the world. He wished he were one of them. Tears ran down his cheeks, he couldn't help it.

They weren't even close to Hill's Funeral Parlor, but Uncle Melvin pulled off the road. He turned to Karl and smiled. "Listen, son, you don't have a daddy anymore to take charge of you, so I'll have to do it for him." He still spoke with that syrupy voice. He lit another cigarette. "Look at me, boy."

Obediently, Karl faced his uncle, wiping his eyes with the sleeve of his jacket.

"If I ever see so much as one more tear from you, or hear anything about you carrying on like a girl, I will use my belt to *make* you into a man. That's a promise. For your own good. For your daddy. D'you understand?"

Karl set his jaw, pressed himself tight against the door, and looked out the window again, his hands balled into fists. He wished Uncle Melvin hadn't taken the day off from his job at the bank to "help" the family.

Uncle Melvin slammed his open hand on the dashboard and yelled. "I said *do you understand me?*"

Karl jumped. "Yessir." He understood completely.

Chapter 2

Eddie's Wake

"Margaret, do you have a black dress?"

Maggie stared out the window, watching the hearse drive away as if it carried a load much greater than the shrunken body of her husband. How could he be so careless? How could he leave her like this?

"You'll need a black dress, a proper one."

She felt herself sinking into a dark and lonely hole, far from the simple, ordinary life she knew with Eddie Stern. She hoped she told him she loved him when he left for the boat yesterday morning, but she couldn't remember saying it. On the chance that this was only a nightmare, she reached out for him in their warm bed, then pulled her hand back, feeling stupid. She squeezed her eyes shut. No, it really happened. He was gone.

She hated to cry in her mother's presence; even so, Maggie couldn't prevent the tears from coming. Outside, rain pelted the earth with fat, hard drops. Her bare fingers couldn't get rid of the tears any more than she could stop the rain.

"Margaret, are you listening to me?"

A warm hand touched her shoulder. "Here, honey." Her sister, Kathleen, put a fine Irish linen hanky in her hand. "Don't you worry, not one little bit. We're going to take good care of you; you won't want for a thing."

"I'll always want for Eddie." Maggie daubed at her eyes and returned the pretty hanky. "Thank you, Kathleen. You're very sweet."

"No, you keep it." Kathleen pressed it back into Maggie's hand. "Come have a cup of tea. It'll take the chill off."

Maggie allowed herself to be led like a child. She sat at the dining room table that once belonged to Eddie's mother. She wrapped her icy hands around the teacup her mother handed her.

"What about that dress, Margaret? You need a proper black dress. We'll have to find one for you."

She didn't answer. Why did her mother always have to champion such meaningless details?

"Did you hear me?"

Maggie stared at the wall, at the crucifix that also came from Mother Stern's house. "I'm not wearing black. Eddie didn't like women to wear black."

"You'll cause a stir. People will talk about you."

"I don't care."

"Appearances are everything, Margaret." Melvin leaned against the door jam. "If you don't wear black, men will forget you're in mourning."

Maggie glanced up. When she saw the way his eyes wandered down from her face, she turned away, pulling her sweater close and crossing her arms over her breasts. She didn't have to see Melvin's face to imagine the tilt of his head, his pout, as he went on.

"And we wouldn't want that, now, would we, dear?"

"See, Melvin knows I'm right," said her mother. "I'll bring my dress and you can use it until you find time to make your own. Edward won't know the difference now."

Maggie sighed. "No, Mother, I don't suppose he will."

Someone rapped on the door twice. Maggie flew out of her chair when Will Denver and his wife, Bernie stepped inside, all wet from the rain. They shared no greetings, but Maggie stood face to face with Will, looking into his eyes, seeing in them the same pain that must be showing in her own.

"He's gone, then?" Will choked on the words.

Maggie nodded and fell into his arms weeping, both of them, clinging to one another despite the wet.

"Ah, love, we passed the hearse an' knew it had to be Eddie." Bernie rested one hand on each of them, lightly rubbing Maggie's back in a circle.

"Margaret!" Her mother's voice sliced through this small comfort. "Is that something you want your son to be watching?"

Will moved away, reached into his pocket for his handkerchief and took off his wet jacket.

"It's all right, Mrs. O'Keefe," said Bernie. "Eddie 'n Will are like brothers."

"*Were*, Bernice, they *were* like brothers."

Jumping at the intensity of Melvin's voice, Karl raced up the stairs. The bathroom door banged shut and the lock turned. Maggie went after him, but the men's voices followed her.

"What kinda thing is that to say in front of the boy, Straus?"

"He'd better face the truth."

"An' you think you're the one to take care o' that?"

"I'm his uncle. He's my responsibility, now."

"Over my dead body!"

Maggie turned around and shouted at them. "Stop it, both of you! We don't need any of that today." Her neck muscles tightened and her head began to pound.

Karl retched in the bathroom.

"Karl." Maggie tried to turn the knob. "Come on, baby, unlock the door. Please?"

He retched again. "I'm sick."

"Let me in."

He groaned and the toilet flushed.

"Karl, right now." The lock turned. Maggie opened the door and found him on the floor, as white as the sink. "Oh, you poor dear... Are you finished? Can you get up?"

He nodded and started to cry.

Filled with pity, Maggie wiped his face with a cool cloth. She'd lost her best friend and lover, but Karl lost his father, the compass and rudder of his life. "Come, lie down and rest for a bit. You didn't get much sleep last night, did you?"

"I guess not."

She led him into her own room and settled him on her bed, remembering how she used to bring baby Karl to bed with her and Eddie when he'd exhausted himself from coughing.

"Mama, I'm so scared."

She sat on the side of the bed and held him. "Me, too. It's going to be hard, but we have to believe everything will be all right. We have to have faith. We've got each other and Will and Bernie. They'll help us. Everything will be all right."

Karl relaxed in her arms, surprising Maggie; scaring her, too. How could he so easily accept her word when she had no idea if she could keep it? "Lie down and try to sleep for a while."

He leaned back on Eddie's pillow and she covered him with a blanket, rubbing his arm until his eyes closed and his breathing became deep and even. As she watched Eddie's boy, she thought she ought to pray, but could find no words. What would become of them?

"It doesn't fit, Mother, can't you see that? Please let me take it off." Maggie hung onto the bed post while her mother tightened the laces of the whale-boned corset that went under her black mourning dress.

"If you hadn't been eating so much of your own baking, this would fit you." Isabelle O'Keefe tied the corset. "Now stand up straight."

Maggie obeyed. Every rib hurt, making it nearly impossible to breathe.

Her mother pulled the freshly starched dress over Maggie's head. "It's too short, but I can't fault you for that, you're taller than I am." She began slipping buttons into buttonholes from the waist all the way up to the high collar.

"It's choking me. No one will notice if you don't button them all."

But Isabelle kept fastening the buttons, jerking Maggie's head back. Maggie wondered how long she'd be able to stand wearing this thing.

"There." Isabelle buttoned the top button. "Let me look at you." She stood back and squinted. "No rouge, you're in mourning."

"I don't *have* any rouge." Maggie had to breathe in shallow gasps, which made her voice sound soft and raspy.

"Mother, you're more worried about me being a proper widow than about me losing Eddie. Don't you care?" Tears filled her eyes. She didn't need much from her mother; a loving look, a gentle word or even a kind hand on her shoulder would mean so much.

Isabelle looked into her daughter's eyes for a long time before speaking. Maggie guessed she must be trying to think of what to say.

"I'm very sorry about your loss, Margaret, but life goes on. It's important to do things the proper way. That's why I'm here—to help you do things right."

Feeling fragile in both body and spirit, Maggie descended the stairs to the living room, where Mr. Hill had arranged Eddie's open coffin in front of the fireplace. Dressed in their Sunday best, Lizzie and Anna sat on the davenport like little dolls, motionless, bewilderment painted on their faces. Six-year-old Anna cried and couldn't understand why her Daddy didn't wake up when she talked to him. Lizzie, ten, explained it to her, exasperated, but later hid under her bed, crying, refusing to come out until Maggie lay down on the floor to hold her hand. Karl, in his white shirt and too-short black pants, wandered around with his hands in his pockets until Isabelle gave him the job of arranging the extra chairs Melvin brought over from her house. Melvin sat in Eddie's easy chair, waiting for Kathleen to bring him coffee and a plate of finger sandwiches.

Will and Bernie arrived, laden with Bernie's baked goods and extra cups and saucers. Will stopped to see Eddie and almost dropped the basket he held in his hand. Maggie took it from him and sent it to the kitchen with Karl.

Will took off his hat and played with its brim while he looked at his friend. He didn't speak for a long time. "I can't say as he looks peaceful, exactly, but he looks better than he did wet." When his eyes got teary, Maggie put her hand on his arm.

"It's all right, Will."

"No, this is terrible. Nothing will ever be the same again." His shoulders shook.

When she saw Will crying, Anna started to cry, too, but Maggie couldn't lift her or even bend to her because of the corset. "It's all right, honey. Karl, please come take care of your sister."

Before Karl could get there, Melvin scooped Anna off the davenport. "Come, come, my little sweetheart, I'll take good care of you from now on."

Anna screamed, "No, I want my Daddy!" She wiggled and cried, trying to escape Melvin's hold.

Will backed away from the coffin. "Straus!"

Melvin handed her to Karl. He ran his hands over his hair and laughed softly. "Oh, she'll get used to me."

Maggie felt her stomach crawl into her throat.

Before she could say anything to Anna, Father Cunningham arrived for prayers. He brought with him a brown-robed monk with sad eyes, Eddie's older brother, gone from Tomos Bay since Eddie was Karl's age.

"George?"

"Hello, Margaret." Without looking in the coffin, he took both her hands. "Father called the Abbey. I'm so sorry—for all of us."

"I didn't think you would come."

"He's my brother. You're my family."

Anna wiggled away from Karl and clung to Maggie's skirt, still crying.

"Anna, this is your Uncle George."

"No more uncles!"

Melvin laughed. George bent and offered his hand to his brother's youngest, but she hid behind Maggie and refused to say hello.

Isabelle came from the kitchen. "Where are your manners, young lady?"

Anna startled at her Grandmother's sharp voice, crying even louder, terrified. Maggie wanted to sit on the davenport and hold her, but her mother's corset wouldn't let her bend. Father Cunningham sent Karl to gather everyone for prayers; Bernie's kind hands took Anna and held her on her lap, soothing her with whispers and kisses. George finally stood before his brother, crossed himself and reached into the folds of his robe for a rosary, which he placed in Eddie's weather-worn hands.

"This belonged to Papa," he whispered.

Melvin muttered an obscenity, Father Cunningham glared at him. When Kathleen took too long in the kitchen, Melvin bellowed that Father didn't have all night. Lizzie covered her ears, Will's fists tightened, Karl stared out the window.

While Father prayed, Maggie looked from face to face, her eyes finally resting on her husband's. *Look what you've started, Eddie.*

Bernie offered to take Lizzie and Anna to her house for the night and Maggie agreed, knowing they wouldn't be able to bear much more of this. People came and went all evening, paying their respects to Eddie and offering condolences to Maggie: fishermen with wives who looked at Eddie with undisguised fear; women from Holy

Angels, the Sisters who taught the children at school, Dr. Lyman and his wife, some of Isabelle's friends and a few of Maggie's cousins who lived in Ashland. Maggie appreciated them coming, but wished everyone would go away so she could take off her mother's dress and corset. She resented the way it kept her from taking care of the girls, the way it threatened to suffocate her, the way it made her move like a wooden doll.

After most everyone went home, Karl helped Kathleen clear the cups and saucers from the dining room table without being asked. Maggie's heart swelled with love and pride. She thanked him in front of everyone. He smiled at her, but Melvin ruined things by scolding her for allowing Karl to do women's work.

"There's no such thing as women's work or men's work," said George. "All honest work is blessed in God's eyes."

"Well, blessed or not, no boy should be allowed to do that."

Karl fumbled with a cup and saucer and dropped them to the floor, breaking them. His face turned red and he hurried to clean up the mess, but not before Melvin came near.

"Look what you did, you idiot! You should be more careful." He raised his arm to strike, but lowered it when George bent to help Karl.

"When did you become so cruel, Melvin?" asked George.

"Cruel? I'm doing my duty. He's my responsibility now."

"No, he's not." Maggie tried to raise her voice, but couldn't get enough air. Nobody heard her.

Karl backed away, turned, and ran up the stairs,

taking them two at a time. A door slammed shut. Two footsteps pounded above, followed by a loud crash. He must have thrown himself on the bed again, knocking the bed slats askew, sending the mattress and the springs to the floor.

"What's gotten into him?" Maggie's mother clicked her tongue and scowled.

"Have a heart, Mother."

Melvin hitched up his trousers, his hands remaining on his belt. "I'll handle this."

"No you won't." Maggie started for the stairs but Melvin was already at the top, stomping his way down the hall, barging into Karl's room. "Leave him alone," she gasped as she hurried after him.

"Get up, you sissy!" Melvin grabbed Karl by the collar of his shirt. Karl sobbed and sniffed and tried to wipe his face with his sleeve. Melvin pushed the boy against the wall. "If you don't start acting like a man, I'll have to take over around here. Is that what you want?"

Even without the corset, there wasn't enough air in the world to let Maggie scream as loud as she wanted to. "Get away from my son!"

Will bounded up the stairs and into the room, almost knocking Maggie over. "You have no business, Straus!"

Melvin took a step backward and unbuckled his belt, pulling it from his belt loops. "I warned him. This is my responsibility. I'm his only male relative."

George followed Will, beads of sweat strung across his red face. "Keep your pants on, Melvin. I'm blood, and I say let him be."

Melvin dropped the belt and swung his fist at George. George ducked but tripped on the bed frame, hitting his cheekbone against the edge of Karl's desk.

Karl moved along the wall until he was next to Maggie.

Will picked up the belt and swung it slightly. "I know him better'n either one of you; he's like my own boy. Eddie would say I know what's best!" He stomped his foot like a child.

The shouting escalated, each man claiming the right to discipline Karl. Maggie, hot with anger, picked up a bed slat and slammed it against Karl's desk.

"My dead husband is downstairs and you are acting like bad children." Angry tears sprung from her eyes. "You are behaving badly, *badly!* Get out of my house! All of you!" She tried to catch her breath. "Karl, wait in my room and shut the door."

Karl stepped over the broken bed frame and fled. Still holding the bed slat, Maggie glared at the men. "Go!"

George stopped at the door. "But Margaret, who will sit with you tonight?" Sadness drew his eyes downward and softened his voice. He tilted his head like Eddie did when he was earnest about something. His cheek bled.

She almost allowed him to stay; she wanted to clean up his wound. "My son is here. We will sit together."

The three men filed out and down the stairs. Maggie heard the front door open and close twice. She dropped the piece of wood and crossed the hall to her own room.

Karl sat on the edge of her bed in the dark, his head in his hands. "I'm sorry, Mama. I know I'm the cause of all this."

Maggie turned on the lamp and closed the door. "No you're not. Please—I need your help." She turned around. "Start with the buttons."

"What?"

"I can't breathe in this corset. Unbutton them."

"All of them?"

"Yes. Do it!"

As the buttons came loose, Maggie held the dress up in the front. "Good. Now the corset."

"Mama, I shouldn't be doing this."

"I have to get this thing off."

Karl fumbled with the knot, but couldn't pick the taut cord from the eyelets. "It's too tight, I can't."

"Get my scissors and cut it."

He'd almost finished freeing her when Isabelle rapped on the door. "Margaret! What's going on in there?" She opened the door without waiting for an answer and gasped.

Maggie held the corset and the dress to her chest. Although her ribs still hurt, she could breathe again. "Thank you, Karl. Thank you very much. Now go see if you can put your bed back together."

Karl eyed his grandmother and hurried past her.

"Margaret, you're a grieving widow, but this is scandalous. Your son shouldn't see you like this. And look what he did to my corset!"

"I told him to." She slipped into her housecoat, leaving Isabelle's black dress where it fell on the floor. "Take that thing home. I never want to see it again."

"Shame on you, *shame* on you!"

Maggie sat down and buried her face in her hands, weeping. "Go home, Mother. This has been a terrible night. I want to be alone. You people are no comfort at all."

In huff, Isabelle gathered up her dress and corset and left. Maggie heard the front door open and close. A car started and the sound of its engine disappeared into the distance.

Maggie turned off all but one lamp in the living room.

With her hair braided for bed and in her nightgown, housecoat and slippers, she stood before Eddie, remembering how she'd lain next to him on the cot trying to warm his cold body, wondering what it would be like to lie next to him now. Karl came downstairs in his pajamas with a blanket and pillow. Together they sat on the davenport, exhausted from the evening, but too troubled to sleep. They said the Rosary and took turns remembering things about Eddie Stern, sometimes crying, but often laughing, too.

At nearly midnight, Will came to the door, saying that Bernie bawled him out and sent him back to apologize. His arrival lifted their spirits. Maggie said he didn't need to apologize and Karl agreed. He brought his tools so he and Karl could fix the bed frame.

While they worked on Karl's bed, Maggie put on the tea kettle and set out leftover bread and honey. Soon George knocked on the door and Maggie welcomed him, too. She'd known him since childhood, for as long as she'd known Eddie.

"Father Cunningham heard my confession and sent me back to sit with you. I'm sorry for my behavior, Maggie."

"Eddie missed you, George; he always missed you. You were his hero. You must have known that."

George nodded, his sad eyes moist.

"But you never answered his letters. Or remembered his birthday. It would have meant so much to him."

"I am *truly* sorry. I missed so much of his life. It's just that I..." He looked away from her, the corners of his mouth pulling down.

Maggie made him a cold compress for his bruised cheek.

When he could speak again he said, "Maybe I could do

something for Karl to make up for it."

"Eddie would like that."

The four of them sat together through the night, Karl leaning on Maggie, dozing. They talked and remembered and laughed and cried and sometimes sat in silence. A dreary dawn brought an end to their communion when Mr. Hill came to take Eddie to the church.

Maggie stood at the coffin, burning the sight of her husband's face into her mind. She kissed his cold lips and held her hand over his heart, exactly where she used to rest her head as he slept. "I'll love you forever, my dearest."

Her knees weakened and buckled as Will helped the undertaker carry him out of the house for the last time. Tight and painful sobs overcame her, yet she felt strangely detached, as if she were watching all this from far away. George and Karl, one on either side, tenderly lifted her and helped her to the door so she could watch the hearse drive away. Will stood in the street with both hands over his heart.

"There goes a good man," said George.

"The best in all the world," whispered Karl.

Maggie rested her weary head on George's shoulder. "What have you done to us, Eddie?"

George touched his head to hers. "God rest his soul."

Chapter 3
Passion Fierce as the Grave

"*R*equiem *aeternam dona ei, Domini, et lux perpetua luceat ei. Requiescat in pace. Amen.*" Father Cunningham made the sign of the cross over the coffin. He closed his book and stepped carefully across the dirt to where Karl's mother stood. Even so, the bottoms of his shiny black shoes became caked with mud. "I'm sorry about Edward, Margaret, but I know you'll feel better as soon as things get back to normal."

Maggie moved her wet handkerchief to her left hand and held out her right to him. "Thank you, Father."

Father Cunningham took it for a moment before turning to Karl, who stared down at his father's coffin. "Karl, I'll see you and your sisters in school. Remember what I told you."

Karl quickly glanced up at him before returning his gaze to the hole, swallowing hard. "Yes, Father." He began to cough.

Without another word, the priest turned back toward Holy Angel's Church, hiking up his cassock to keep any more mud from collecting along its hem.

It had rained steadily for the past three days, a cold rain announcing the change of seasons. Even though the downpour had slowed to a fine mist that morning, it made the cemetery grounds spongy; it squished through the grass and under the feet of anyone foolish enough come outside. It deepened the gray of crosses and headstones; it darkened the brownstone walls of the church and the rectory, it soaked the trunks of trees to a black-brown color. Nothing looked like it was supposed to.

The small group of mourners surrounded Eddie Stern's grave: Karl next to his mother, near the head of the grave, Will on her other side with Anna between them, clinging to her coat. Uncle George stood next to Karl, squeezing his shoulder. Lizzie stood with Bernie, at the foot of the grave, but made her way to Karl and slipped her hand into his. He'd never say so, but it made him feel a little better so he didn't push her away. Across from Karl's mother, Grandma hid deep beneath her big black umbrella; to her right Aunt Kathleen dabbed her eyes and held on to Uncle Melvin's arm. They were all silent for nearly a minute after Father Cunningham left them.

Karl stared hard at the little group of mourners. *So this is it, we just leave him here and go home?* His heavy heart anchored him to this place; he wanted to stay, even in the rain.

Isabelle took charge, bossing everyone around, as usual. "Melvin, Margaret and I will ride with you and Kathleen. William, how many can you fit into your truck?" Everyone was invited to Grandma's house for lunch.

Will looked miserably at Isabelle, as if he didn't understand a word she said, his sagging, tired eyes lined in red.

"We can take the girls, Mum." Bernie answered. She'd grown up in Liverpool, England, and called all older women *Mum*.

"Karl you'll have to walk with George," ordered Grandma.

Karl coughed again. Maggie turned and felt his forehead. "Let Karl take my place, Mother. I'd rather walk anyway."

"I want to go with Will, Mama."

"Then you come with us, Margaret." Grandma O'Keefe had to be in charge of everything.

Maggie sighed. "No, I want to stay here for a while."

"We can't leave you alone, girl."

"Why not?"

Will finally spoke. "I'll stay with Maggie, Mrs. O'Keefe. Bernie can drive the truck and we'll be along in a little while."

"You ride with us, Karl."

"I'm staying with them, Grandma." He was not getting back in Uncle Melvin's car if he could help it.

"George?"

"Thank you, Mrs. O'Keefe, but I'm not ready to leave, either."

Isabelle clicked her tongue and turned to leave. "Oh, for heaven's sake, you'll all catch your death and we'll be back here again before you know it. Melvin, let's go. Bernice, you can follow to our house." Isabelle and her entourage were almost to Melvin's car before Bernie turned to Maggie.

"If it's all right with you, Love, I'd like to take the girls home with me. It would do 'em good to play with Billy and Ned after all they been through, and the boys have been askin' for 'em. My Mum is prob'ly wore out from watchin' 'em by now, so I need to be gettin' home."

"Please, Mama?" "Please?" The girls adored five-year-old Billy and three-year-old Ned.

"Are you sure, Bernie?"

"O' course I'm sure; you know I love havin' your girls come to visit."

The two women embraced. Maggie kissed her daughters and Will helped them into the truck. Bernie took the keys from him and held him for a long minute, whispering in his ear. Will watched her drive away, motionless.

"Karl, come here," called Maggie. "See, this is your Grandma Stern's grave."

It wasn't far from where they were standing. The gravestone said *Eleanor Burktold Stern, 1859 – 1918.*

George followed. "Do you remember her?"

"I think so; I think I remember playing with her on her bed. She called me *little bear* or something."

Maggie laughed a little. "No, you were her *little berry boy*. She had a basket full of strawberries once, and she cut some of them into tiny pieces so you could have a taste. Well, you gobbled them up and surprised everyone by saying clear as day, '*More, more!*' She got so excited about you talking that she gave you more than anyone else. You couldn't get enough berries and your Grandma Stern couldn't get enough of you."

Karl noticed tears in his mother's eyes.

"She was a wonderful lady."

"Yes, indeed," said Uncle George.

"I still miss her." Maggie bent over and touched her gravestone.

Karl looked around. "Where's Grandpa Stern?"

"They buried him at the asylum before they even wrote to say he was dead. That always bothered your father."

Uncle George crossed himself.

"What happened to him? Did you know him, Mama?"

"Before he got sick everyone knew him. He owned

the newspaper, edited and wrote for it. A good man, but no one wanted him around after..." Maggie looked across the cemetery. "Come here, I want to show you where my father is buried."

Karl didn't protest when his mother took his hand as if he were still a little boy, although he hoped none of his classmates could see him from the school. Uncle George stayed behind at Grandma Stern's grave; Will went back to Eddie's. Karl and Maggie stopped at a stone marked with the words *Michael Liam O'Keefe 1862–1917*.

"Do you remember your Grandpa O'Keefe?"

"He smelled like peppermint."

Maggie smiled. "He always had candy for the children. He was one of the town constables, but he loved to have fun, too." The smile disappeared. "He got shot by a drunk when he tried to break up a fight on St. Patty's Day." She sighed. "After that, we never celebrated again."

"Oh. I didn't know."

Maggie crouched down and traced her father's name. "Oh, Daddy," she whispered. "Eddie's gone, too. Who will help me now?" Tears ran down her face again.

"Mama, don't you think we should be going?" Karl held out his hand to help her. She took it and stood up, looking toward his father's grave.

"Oh, no, they can't bury him yet!" She ran across the soggy grass, still holding on to Karl, dragging him with her. Uncle George stared into the hole, shaking his head. Two other men in work clothes had come, too, one with a shovel in his hand. The other one went running to an old wooden shed behind the church.

"Where's Will?"

The soggy earth had caved in along one side of the hole, collapsing under Will's feet, taking him down, depositing him between the coffin and the dirt wall. He knocked the edge of Eddie's coffin when he fell, tilting it slightly and leaving it askew. He had nothing to grab hold of to help him climb out; the coffin was the only solid thing.

"If you get on top of it, maybe I could pull you up with the shovel," shouted the gravedigger.

"I can't, my foot is already buried in the mud."

"Can't you give it try, Will?" Uncle George stood wringing his hands like a woman. Karl wondered why he wasn't doing anything useful.

"Just go for more help, will you?"

Karl got close enough to see Will's face. His eyes went wild with fear, his voice rough. "Get away, boy, you wanna come down here, too?"

Karl didn't say, "yes," but inside he thought it might not be so bad. He turned to the grave digger. "What if I get down on the ground and you hold onto my legs, and I grab him? We can pull him. Maybe we could get him on the coffin; then he could climb out."

"No, Karl, you get away from there!" Maggie screamed, her voice raspy with hysteria.

"Listen to your mother, boy." Uncle George took his arm.

Karl pulled away. "Mama, we gotta get him out." He took off his jacket and gave it to her.

"No, Karl, don't, please."

"Karl!" Uncle George locked eyes with him.

Karl saw his father's eyes in his uncle's; he had to look away so he wouldn't start crying. Determined to help Will, he had to focus. His senses sharpened; he felt his heart pound and his blood course to every corner of his body. "I *have* to help."

Will shouted from the grave. "No, you *don't!*"

"I'll be safe," answered Karl, "nothing's going to happen, don't worry."

The second, older man returned, huffing and puffing. "There's nothin' in there," he said, between breaths. "No rope, nothin' but spiders and old school desks."

"We're gonna let the boy help, Ralph. What's your name, son?" The man spoke with a southern drawl, too slow for this emergency.

"Karl. It's my daddy in there."

"Karl's gonna lay over the edge while we hold 'im, and he'll grab his daddy and—"

"My daddy's in the box."

"Can you hurry it up, it's wet down here." Will sounded like he was crying.

Small drops began to fall; seconds later, the heavens gushed and spewed cold rain.

"See, now, Karl's gonna take hold of—what's your name?

"It's *Will!* Come on now, *do* something!"

"Calm down, there, Will. If we can get Will on the coffin, maybe he can climb out."

"Get me outta here, *please.*"

Karl wondered if his father had been as scared as Will when he fell into the water.

"You be careful with my son," cried Maggie. She'd taken cover under a nearby tree. Uncle George went with her, his arm around her shoulders.

Karl got down in the mud. The men each held one of his legs. He scooted himself forward until his whole torso hung over the edge of the grave. He could feel the ground squish down beneath him, but he had his eyes on Will. He stretched his arms out and so did Will. Their hands met, each held on to the other's forearm.

"Can you push against anything?"

"It's nothin' but mush in here."

"Hold on," he said to Will, then called to the gravediggers. "Pull!" The two men dragged his legs away from the grave. Karl felt his shirt pull out of his trousers; he felt the skin of his bare belly drag against the soft earth even though they'd only moved a few inches.

"Lord have mercy, what in heaven's name is going on here?" Father Cunningham had returned.

"Can you pray for us, Father?" asked Karl.

"But do it while you go find a long board, or a ladder," said Ralph.

"I'll have to find the custodian, he knows where—"

"Hurry!"

"Come on, try it again." This time Karl didn't let the men do all the work, but pulled Will with his own arms, too. They ached and burned and trembled with the effort, the same way they did when he helped Will and his father drag in the huge nets filled with fish, but it was worth it. Will began to move.

"What's happening down there?"

"Just keep—pulling!" Karl had little breath for talking.

Will moved some more, got one knee up on Eddie's coffin, then the other. The earth crumbled to fill the space he left.

"Stop!"

Still holding on to Karl, Will tried to stand on the top of the box, but slipped. Steadfast, Karl kept his hold on him. He could hear his mother fretting and crying and Uncle George trying to calm her.

"I'm going to try it again," said Will.

"Whatever you do, don't let go of me." Karl's resolve strengthened; his father might be dead and in the grave, but he wasn't about to let Will die, too.

Will pulled out of the mud and knelt on the coffin, but when he tried to stand, the whole thing shifted and sank a few inches as the earth began to swallow Eddie. Will slipped again and as he did, Karl slid forward, his whole torso going back into the hole.

"Hold on to him, will you?" His mother's voice raised in panic.

"Yes, Ma'am, we ain't gonna let go of him, don't you worry."

Will straddled the coffin like it was a horse, all the while holding on to Karl so he resembled a warrior on horse-back coming back from battle, arms raised in victory. "I think I should let go so I can hang on to the box."

"All right, one hand at a time, my left, your right." Carefully, they both let go and remained motionless for a second. Will slowly withdrew his hand and put it on Eddie's coffin. They let go of the other hand and Will put it on the coffin, too. He lay forward, arms and legs wrapped around the coffin of his best friend, his right cheek resting on the wood.

"Help me up, fellas." As Karl slid back, a hunk of mud cascaded into the grave from the place where he'd been. "Are you all right, Will?"

"I'm fine, except I'm getting *buried alive!*"

Karl sat up and rolled his shoulders. His fair hair was flattened from the rain and mud. "Don't worry; nobody's leaving here without you. At least *I'm* not." He turned to look at his mother and Uncle George.

"I know, Karl," Will spoke so quietly that only Karl could hear him. "But if it doesn't work out, tell Bernie I love her, will you?"

"Tell her yourself, here comes Father Cunningham

with a ladder." Karl smiled.

The priest struggled and dragged a ten foot ladder across the wet grass. Uncle George was finally moved to action and went to help him. Father's nice black suit was dusty from the storeroom and now wet from the rain, and his shiny black shoes were getting as wet and muddy as everyone else's. "The custodian is out sick today, but I found it on my own." Obviously pleased with himself, Father Cunningham grinned.

The grave diggers took the ladder. After surveying the situation again, they slid it into the hole, angled across the top of Will and the coffin, and did their best to stabilize its bottom in the mud.

"All right, ah—Will. It's up to you now. We'll hold 'er steady from up here, and you just reach over and climb onto the ladder an' we'll pull you out, nice and easy."

"Oh, God," said Will quietly. When he took hold of the ladder, his movement shifted the coffin again. Quickly, he twisted his body around and threw his leg over. One of the rungs cracked under his weight, so he stepped higher. "Go!"

The men had to jerk the ladder to get it loose from the mud before they could pull it, tilting it lower and lower. Will rode it like a sled on the snow. There were cheers from the men, from Karl and even from Maggie and George as he rose up from Eddie's grave. He lay on the ladder for a moment, still clinging to the sides.

"Come on, you can get out of the mud, now." Once more, Karl held out his hand to him.

Will stood up and hugged him, hard, tears in his eyes. When he could speak, he said, "Your daddy would be so proud of you, boy, so proud."

"I only did what he would do." Karl's throat tightened.

"Aw, Will..." He hid his face against his father's friend and allowed himself to cry, but only a little. The rain came harder, washing off some of the mess.

"He's still here, Karl." Will put his muddy hand over Karl's heart.

Karl coughed and pulled away. "Sure, he is."

Ralph broke in. "We need to finish our job here, folks, if you don't mind, before that monster fills up with water. And you should get outta this rain."

Will shook hands with Ralph and his partner, thanking them, then turned to Father Cunningham without extending his dirty hand. "And you, too, Father, thank you for bringing the ladder."

George held his hand out to Karl. "Son, when I look at you, I see Eddie Stern, in every way. Come visit me at St. Aidan's, maybe you can even come to our school when you're a little older. I'd like to know you better."

Karl didn't know what to say. Why hadn't Uncle George done more to help? "You're leaving already?"

"My train leaves at three. I need to wash up before I go."

Maggie stepped out from under the tree. "Good bye, George."

He took her hand. "I'll try to do better from now on, Maggie."

"Of course." She turned to Karl. She touched his dirty cheek, and took his hand again, leading him as close to the grave as she dared. Will stood back.

"Good-bye, Eddie. I will always love you."

Karl painted this one last image of his father into his memory. His eyes filled with tears again, but they couldn't erase the picture. He looked up to let the rain wash them away. With Will at his side, he followed his mother away from the grave and out of the cemetery. None of them looked back.

Chapter 4

617 Blight Street

As she walked home from the corner, Maggie shivered and pulled her green woolen shawl tight around her shoulders. Even at seven-thirty in the morning, it promised to be one of those rare, windless autumn days when warm sunlight bathed the earth from a sapphire sky. But she knew it was only a tease before the bitter winds of winter came for good, and she was already cold.

She'd pulled back her fair red hair and fastened it with the ivory scrimshawed combs Eddie gave her as an engagement present. Her hazel eyes, upturned slightly at their outer edges, usually gave the impression of good cheer, but today they failed her. Misery colored her eyes, while lack of sleep drew dark circles underneath.

Eddie's funeral mass and burial was on Monday and she'd kept her children home with her again on Tuesday, but by Wednesday morning she knew they needed to do something normal again. So she walked them to the corner, hugged and kissed them all and waved them off to Holy Angels'.

From across the street and a few doors down, Maggie

stopped and looked at her house—her house and Eddie's. Nearly identical to every other cheaply built house in the neighborhood, 617 Blight Street had two stories with a black roof and tan shingles for siding. Once upon a time, it seemed that the people who lived inside didn't have a care in the world, but now...

Like all the others, 617 Blight Street had a small front porch, little more than a stoop, really, but large enough to seat two people on a nice evening. As Maggie started up the steps, she tried to remember the last time she and Eddie sat out in the evening air. A long time ago, they used to sneak outside as often as they could while their babies slept and the house was quiet. Why had they stopped?

Maggie hurried inside. She poured a cup of lukewarm tea and sat down with it at the rarely used dining room table. What did it matter if the breakfast dishes didn't get washed until noon?

She thought about the day she and Eddie moved into the house. They'd lived with Eddie's mother, Eleanor, for nearly a year, the child inside Maggie growing week by week. As the time for the birth drew near, Mother Stern helped them find a place of their own, paying the first month's rent as a housewarming gift. When moving day arrived, Maggie and Eddie didn't have much to do, since a bed, a small chest of drawers, and a few dishes were all they could claim as their own; only these necessities, and the cradle that once rocked Eleanor's two babies.

But the house didn't stay bare for long. While Maggie carefully unpacked the dishes her Grandma O'Keefe had given her, someone knocked on the door and handed Eddie a letter from his mother giving them nearly all her worldly possessions. A horse drawn wagon heaped high with Eleanor's furniture waited in front of the house.

Maggie remembered the bewildered look on Eddie's face when he read the letter and her own awe and sense of gratitude for such a lavish gift.

Mother Stern kept only her own bed, bureau, and a small kitchen table with four chairs. From moving day until her death three years later, Eleanor lived between her bedroom and the kitchen. It saddened both Eddie and Maggie to see the way she'd given up on life; her only joy seemed to be little Karl. Maggie still missed her mother-in-law, who died the day after Lizzie—*Elizabeth Eleanor*—was born, ten years ago last May.

Maggie looked into the living room, at the worn burgundy davenport that fit so perfectly against the east wall under the high windows. It almost matched the red flowers on the faded carpet. She crossed the room, touched the upholstery with her fingertips, and sat down, trying to remember its place in Mother Stern's parlor.

Eleanor's marble-topped table stood under the front window, topped with her green double-globed lamp. An artist with a perfect hand had painted the globes with great sweeping strokes, forming a pink rose on the bottom globe and a rosebud on the top. Once it took kerosene to light the lamp, but Mother Stern had it wired for electricity as a birthday gift to Maggie. Turn the switch once to light the bottom globe, once more to light the top, a third time to light them both and again to turn it all off. In summer, when Eddie and Will stayed out on the water overnight, Maggie left the small light burning all night long as a beacon to bring them home. She loved the lamp, as she loved the small captain's clock they found among the treasures on the wagon. A wedding gift from Eddie's father, Karl, to Eleanor, the clock sat on the mantle above the fireplace at 617 Blight Street. When they decided to put it there, it never occurred to her that it would mark the moment of Eddie's death.

Only five days had passed since Will and Rob laid Eddie in the middle of the living room floor, on the gray carpet with the faded red flowers. Eddie's heavy clothing, wet with lake water, left a dark spot, almost in the shape of his body. It remained wet, and Maggie wanted it to stay that way, for its drying would only take him further and further away from her. She got down on her knees to touch it, to see if it had dried any, but instead she watered it with her tears.

Later that day, at supper time, Uncle Melvin and Aunt Kathleen came to visit. Karl had to go for extra chairs while his mother cleared places for them to sit down, poured coffee and set out more cookies. As soon as he and his sisters finished eating, she sent them upstairs to do their homework.

Usually Karl would have complained about being dismissed when company came, but not tonight. Up in his room he tried hard to focus on his history assignment, but it was no use. The voices below disturbed him; especially his mother's. He left his room, careful to avoid creaky floorboards, and stood as still as death at the top of the stairs, not even breathing. He strained to hear the voices coming from the kitchen.

"Listen, you've got three mouths to feed and no income. Do you have any idea if Ed left anything in the bank for you?"

"Nobody ever called him 'Ed' when he was alive, and we're not going to start now, Melvin."

"All right, did Eddie—Ed*ward*—leave you any money?"

"I don't know yet, but I'm not worried. They had a good season this year."

"A good season doesn't mean they made a profit."

"This is none of your business, Melvin."

"Maggie, please, dear, he's only trying to help." Karl could almost see Aunt Kathleen lean toward his mother as she spoke.

"*We're* only trying to help, Kathleen. Now Margaret, you know we have lots of room at our house, plenty of space for you and your kids." Uncle Melvin made a lot of money from his job at the bank. He and Aunt Kathleen lived in a big house on the nicer side of town. "You'll have a roof over your heads and food on the table. And someone like me to keep your kids in line, especially Karl. He needs a father."

Karl shuddered.

"He needs his *own* father," said Maggie.

Karl knew from the sound of her voice that she was about to cry.

"Of course, he does. But face it, you can't make it on your own. You might as well admit that right now and save yourself a whole pack of trouble."

"I appreciate your offer..."

Karl bit his lower lip, silently beseeching his mother: "Say no, please, say no; don't make us live with *him*, Mama, please!"

Lizzie came out of her room. "It's rude to eavesdrop, Karl. I'm gonna tell on you."

Karl whipped around at the sound of her footsteps and put his finger on his lips. She came closer.

"Shh! No, listen to them," he whispered.

Lizzie stood still.

"You don't have anyone else, Margaret."

"I appreciate your offer, but no. We'll stay here, in our own home. I'll get work—"

"Now what can *you* do other than wipe noses and scrub floors?"

"I can take in laundry. I could do a lot of things."

Uncle Melvin laughed. "Sure you can." A chair scraped on the kitchen floor. Heavy footsteps came toward the stairs.

"Quick, to your room." The two turned and rushed into the girls' bedroom. Lizzie sat down at the little table where she'd been doing her arithmetic and Karl followed and pretended to help her. Uncle Melvin went into the bathroom and peed like a horse.

Anna's pencil moved up and down on the paper as she practiced making the letters "G" and "H." She smiled at her big brother, revealing gaps where her lower teeth should be. "Karl, will you help me, too?"

The bathroom door opened.

"Sure. See, you just do this."

Uncle Melvin came to the bedroom door. "You shouldn't be in your sisters' room, Karl."

"I—I'm helping with their homework. Mama is busy and they asked for help."

"Get back to your room and mind your own business. If the girls need help, I can do it." Melvin undid his belt, hiked his pants up, and tightened it over his big belly.

Karl's heart began to beat hard when he saw his uncle go for his belt. He looked at Lizzie with wide eyes, then hurried past Melvin and down the hall. He sat down at his desk and strained to hear.

"Okay, honey, now what do you need help with?"

"It's all right, Uncle Melvin, Karl answered my question."

Karl heard Melvin's footsteps move into his sisters' room. Lizzie shrieked, Melvin laughed. Karl stood up, shaking.

"Just a little love pinch. Next time I'll have one for you, too, Annie."

"It's An-*na* and, no you *won't!*" Anna stomped her foot on the floor.

"My, you're a feisty one!" Melvin laughed again as he went clomping down the stairs. "Think about it, Margaret," he hollered from the living room. "Sooner or later you'll come to me for help, so why not save face and move in with us now, before you have to come begging? Come on, Kathleen, it's late, time to go. "

The front door opened and closed, two car doors slammed and the sound of the engine faded away.

Karl hurried back into the girls' cramped room and made his way around the furniture to where Lizzie stood, her hands over her mouth. The bed his sisters shared took up most of the floor space, leaving room for only a little homework table and a dresser. Lizzie's face was red.

"What happened?" Karl asked. "What'd he do?"

Anna answered. "He pinched her on the bottom. Daddy would *never* do that!"

Lizzie burst into tears. Karl stood next to her. He felt stupid because he didn't know what to say. "It's okay, Liz, they went home." He patted her arm, and then pulled his hand back, embarrassed.

Anna ran out of the room. "Mama, Lizzie's crying!"

Maggie came rushing up the stairs. "What's going on?" Before she got to the door, Lizzie ran into her arms, sobbing. "What happened, baby? Did Uncle Melvin say something bad to you?"

Karl remembered that Father Cunningham said he was

supposed to take care of his mother and sisters. "Mama, he pinched her."

"*Hard*—on her bottom," said Anna. "And I saw it!"

A lump formed in Karl's throat. He swallowed to get rid of it. "I'm sorry I didn't stop him. I'm really sorry, Liz."

"He told her it was a *love* pinch, Mama, and next time he'd have one for me, too."

Lizzie cried and clung to her mother. "Make him stay *a-waay* from me!"

"All right, everyone calm down. It's okay, he's gone home. Karl, go find the ice bag and chop a little from the ice box and bring it here for your sister. Lizzie, let me see what he did to you."

Karl found the ice bag in the bathroom and the pick in the kitchen drawer. The ice man had come that day, so a new block of ice sat next to a smaller, more melted one. He attacked the little one, imagining that it was Uncle Melvin's head.

"You bloody—" Karl knew what word he wanted to use, but he also knew he didn't dare say it. He kept on stabbing at the block of ice until he'd made many more chips than he needed to fill the bag. He trembled and his knees shook.

"Karl, what are you doing?"

He hadn't heard his mother come down the stairs. He pulled away from the icebox and turned to her, panting, holding the ice pick like a dagger.

Her voice was calm and gentle. "Give me the ice pick, honey."

He coughed as tears of fear and rage ran down his

cheeks. "Are you going to make us live with *him*?"

"No, not if I can help it. Now give me the ice pick."

Slowly, he handed it to her.

"Put some of those chips in the ice bag and take it up to Lizzie. Not all of them, just a few. Then go wash your face."

"Mama?" His voice wavered.

"I'll be up in a minute."

Karl climbed the stairs and heard the milk bottles rattle inside the icebox when his mother slammed the door. In the bathroom, he turned on the faucet and leaned over the sink. He watched the water run from the tap down into the drain, losing himself in the noise it made. Water had killed his father—water and the cold. He wished he could stab another block of ice; he'd hate water for the rest of his life.

"Oh, that's ridiculous," he said out loud. He plunged his cupped hands into the stream and brought them up to his face three, four, six, seven times. He wished he could make time go backwards to before his father slipped on that ice and ask him how he was supposed to protect his mother and Lizzie and Anna from Uncle Melvin. And how on earth could he do it if they had to live with him? He shuddered.

His mother knocked on the door. "Are you all right?"

"Yeah." He turned off the water, dried his face and opened the door.

"We're in here, Karl."

Karl went to his sisters' room and stood in the doorway, feeling like an intruder. His mother sat on the bed, her arm around Lizzie's shoulders. Both sisters wore faded flannel nightgowns; Lizzie looked flushed and sleepy. Karl realized how like their mother she was and how they were both beautiful. Neither deserved Uncle Melvin's nastiness.

"Come sit with us." Maggie put out her other arm for him and he went to sit next to her. Gently she rubbed his back. Anna wiggled her way onto Karl's lap.

"Now I want you all to hear this. I don't know how we're going to get by, but you don't have to worry, I'll figure it out. I don't want to live with Uncle Melvin any more than you do, especially after tonight. I'll do my best so we can stay here. But we all may have to make some sacrifices. Are you willing to do that, will you help when I ask you to?"

The girls nodded.

"I'll do anything, Mama, anything." Karl meant what he said.

"Good. We're in this together." His mother pulled all three of them closer. "We've got each other. We're still a family. Now let's say prayers."

Chapter 5

The Only Way

After Maggie tucked the girls in and kissed them goodnight—Lizzie twice—she looked in on Karl. He'd made his bed that morning by throwing his Grandma Stern's patchwork quilt over the jumble of sheets and blankets without smoothing anything out. Dirty socks littered the floor, papers covered the top of the dresser, and an undershirt hung from a drawer. Maggie knew he spent more time studying than keeping his room neat, so she rarely scolded him for being disorderly. Tonight, though, she sensed a greater disorder within Karl himself. She sat down on his bed.

"What else did Uncle Melvin do to make you so angry? Did he say something to you? Did he hurt you?"

"No." Karl looked down at his history book.

"Why don't I believe you?"

"I dunno."

"It's more than what he did to your sister, isn't it?"

Maggie waited but Karl didn't answer.

"Uncle Melvin did a bad thing to Lizzie, and he made it even worse by laughing about it, but you couldn't have stopped him. I don't want you thinking this was your fault."

Karl looked up at her. His words came out in a rush. "I'm supposed to be taking care of you and Lizzie and Anna. I should have been able to stop him, but he made me—I was helping them with their homework and he said I shouldn't be in their room and he made me leave and I heard Lizzie yell but I—"

Maggie got up and went to him. She held his face in her hands. "Karl." His hazel eyes went liquid, like the mysterious edge of a pond in September, green and brown; the edge where matters of life and death are simple and expected. With an arm around his shoulders and the other still on the side of his face, she drew him in and held him. "It's all right."

Karl sobbed once and gasped for air. "I miss Daddy! Uncle Melvin wouldn't have pinched Lizzie if Daddy was here." Karl looked up and pulled away from her. His white-blonde curls were matted against his head. He needed a haircut. "Mama, I will do anything, *anything*, but please don't make us live with him. Please? I'll quit school as soon as I finish eighth grade and I'll go to work so we have some money, and I'll work Saturdays and all summer, too. I'll give up my room so you can rent it out and I'll sleep on the davenport. But please, don't make us..." He took a breath. "He likes to hurt people. I *hate* him."

"Hate is poison, Karl. If you hate him, it's like drinking poison and you could turn into a bully, too. Don't hate, don't ever hate." Maggie took his face in her hands again. "Anyway, what did I just tell you?" A lump rose in her own throat, but she fought it. "Didn't you hear me? I will do everything I can so we can stay here. And so you can stay in school. Your Daddy has big dreams for you to finish high school and go to college; he knows how smart you are."

"If we have to live with Uncle Melvin just so I can go to school, I'd rather quit and go to work."

"Let me worry about this. I'll let you know when I need your help. I promise, I will." She kissed him goodnight. "I'm so proud of you. You're a good son and a good brother. Try to get some sleep, now."

Karl stood up and put his long arms around his mother. He clung to her almost like Lizzie had. "Goodnight, Mama."

Maggie got ready for bed, lit a candle on the bed table, closed her door, and turned off the light. In her flannel nightgown and wrapped in a blanket, she got down on her knees and started to pray. The braided rug underneath her did little against the cold.

First, her rosary. She prayed to Mary, begging with words, then only with her heart. "Holy Mother... Pray for us..." After a while, she dozed, her head nodded and rested on the mattress, before waking and praying some more. "Deliver us from evil, deliver us from Melvin..." Maggie groaned, remembering the day Melvin gave Kathleen her engagement ring. He said he didn't want Maggie to feel left out, so he had a present for her, too. When she opened the box to find an expensive cameo brooch, her father made her give it back, saying she was much too young for such a gift. Later, when Daddy wasn't home, Melvin gave it back to her. *Our little secret* he called it. He told her someday she could come and live in his big house, too, just like Kathleen.

Maggie trembled, remembering the day he started

touching her when she was barely fourteen. She remembered that awful Sunday afternoon when her mother sent her out to pick raspberries for supper, how Melvin followed her and tried to show her what married people did. She burst into tears, feeling again the heat of the sun against her bare skin where he tore her dress trying to get what he wanted; feeling the sting of the raspberry canes scraping across her cheek. She remembered how her father came running when he heard her scream, his revolver in his hand, his face red with fury. She held her stomach, remembering her mother's sharp words, blaming her for tempting Melvin, banishing her to her room.

Now with her father and Eddie both dead, she knew Melvin would come after her again. She sobbed into the blankets, finally dozing again, still on her knees. Her desperate praying and weeping went on for hours.

As she hovered in that place between sleep and waking, Maggie felt a warm hand on her shoulder. Before she could turn to tell Karl to go back to bed, for she thought he had come to comfort her, she heard Eddie's voice. "Rosie... Rosie, you know I love you. It ended too soon; can you forgive me?"

Maggie's heart raced. Eddie called her *Rosie* when they were alone; no one else in the world knew about the pet name. "Eddie, is it really you?"

"You have to sell the boat, Maggie, it's the only way."

"Don't leave me again. Please? I miss you so much."

Maggie looked around the room, trying to see him. The candlelight flickered, making shadows dance on the wall, but she didn't see Eddie.

"I'll always be in your dreams, Rosie."

The candle's flame went out in a little puff of air. The sweet smell of warm beeswax filled every corner of the room. Missing him, wanting him, Maggie got up off her stiff knees, crawled in between the covers, and fell asleep clutching his pillow.

The gray walls of the house reflected Maggie's mood in the weeks following Eddie's death, while the world outside turned brown and dead with the passing of the season. Without him, she knew the bleak winter would take forever to let go and turn to spring. She missed him more than she ever thought possible, but the moments of forgetting hurt even more. She'd worry about Karl's sullen anger and think, *Eddie should handle this.* She'd fret about Lizzie's nightmares or Anna wetting the bed again, and want to talk to Eddie about these things, too.

Then she'd remember. No more homecomings after two or three days out on the water, no more late night talks and laughter with one or both of them propped up on their elbows in bed. She'd feel foolish and embarrassed for forgetting, afraid she might be going off the deep end, like Eddie's father. Each time it happened, the pain came fresh and new and her heart bled all over again. She thought nobody else would understand this, so she added it to the other burdens she carried alone in silence.

Maggie knew she needed to think about money, but her sorrow and fear kept her paralyzed for weeks. She hadn't paid the November rent yet, the shelves were nearly bare, and the pile of coal in the basement grew smaller every day. She didn't feed the furnace while the children were at school, but she knew she'd need a little heat once winter came in earnest. Finally, nearly a month after Eddie died, she forced herself go to the bank to see how much money he'd left them. She found about what she'd expected: enough to pay November's rent, order some coal, go to the market and keep a few dollars in reserve for un-expected expenses. If everyone stayed healthy, the money might last until Thanksgiving. Then what?

A few days later, Will Denver brought the ledger book from the *Stern and Denver Fishery* to show Maggie. Will grieved Eddie's death as deeply as she did. Eddie used to say he and Will must somehow share the same brain, each knowing what the other would say or do almost before he said or did it. They'd been a perfect team; they trusted one another with the boat and the business, their families and even their own lives. They had a true partnership, a once in a lifetime friendship, and Will was lost without Eddie. Maggie's heart went out to him.

Will and Maggie sat in the kitchen with a teapot be-tween them while the girls slept upstairs and Karl did his homework. Will opened the ledger book. They *had* made a healthy profit this year, but they'd spent some of the money on nets and supplies for next season. Because Will paid for most of Eddie's funeral, there was far less cash available than Maggie hoped. She knew it should all go to Will. She tried to hide her panic.

"Now, all of that is Eddie's, I mean yours."

"I can't take any more money from you, Will." She hugged her arms across her chest, hoping he wouldn't see her shake.

"What else are you gonna do?"

"I don't know," she whispered. Silence hung heavy between them. "Wait, I have an idea." Maggie hurried up-stairs and opened the cedar chest. At the bottom, beneath some summer clothes, her heavy woolen sweater and the treasures of her life with Eddie, she found a small blue velvet jewelry box. She lifted the lid and shuddered at the sight of the pink cameo brooch with four small diamonds set in gold filigree.

Downstairs, she handed the box to Will. "I'll take what's in the account if you take this and sell it so you have some money to put away for next spring."

Will looked inside. "I can't take this. If Eddie gave it to you, he meant for you to have it."

"Eddie didn't give it to me. He didn't even know I had it."

"If it's a family heirloom, you should give it to one of your girls."

"It's not."

"Where'd it come from, if you don't mind my asking?"

Maggie looked away. "Melvin Straus gave it to me before he married my sister, for reasons that were... less than pure. I was only fourteen. I never wore it. It's why he thinks I should—" She turned back. "I've always regretted having it. Don't ask me to explain any more, just take it, please."

"You sure? You could use the money."

"Please take it. It's my way of making sure the fishing goes on, one way or another. It's what Eddie would want." Maggie looked into her cup and tried to decide how much she should tell him about Eddie's visit to her.

"Listen, Will, I know what I'm going to say to you is hard news, and maybe you'll think I'm crazy." She looked up at him. "Eddie came to me one night and told me to sell the boat. I heard the words in his own voice, and I felt his hand on my shoulder. It was real. It was him." She started to cry. "I miss him so much."

Will's eyebrows went up when he heard what Maggie said. "I don't think you're crazy." He lowered his voice and leaned toward her, across the table. "I've been dreaming about him, too, a couple times a week, at least. He's been trying to tell me to do something with the boat, getting impatient, you know, like he used to. I can never figure it out."

She put her hand on his arm.

"Last night he told me to sell the boat, but I told him I couldn't. We argued like mad men. We never argued before, not once." His voice tightened. "I'm not sellin' the boat... but I can't manage it alone, either."

"Can you find another partner? Do you know anybody?"

"I dunno. Who could replace him?"

"That's up to you. Eddie's right, though. The boat is all we have."

Will raised his voice a little as he pulled his arm away from her hand. "Well, I'm *not* gonna ask my mother for money so I can buy Eddie's half from you, and I'm *not* gonna to sell the boat to anyone else! I didn't bury our dream in the ground with 'im and I'm not gonna let go of it now."

"But I need money," Maggie said gently. "I have children to feed. My only other choice is to move in with Melvin and Kathleen and he's—"

"A skunk, I know, you don't have to tell me." Will stood up and put his jacket on, pulled his hat out of his pocket. "I have to go, it's late. Bernie's waiting up. I'll figure something out. Don't worry, I won't let you starve." He went as far as the dining room, came back and kissed Maggie on the cheek. "Thanks for the tea."

"Anytime, Will." She touched his hand. "Tell Bernie *hello*."

Karl sat on the steps listening to Will and his mother, angry with both of them. He waited until Will closed the door before he showed up in the kitchen, pretending to look for something to eat. He opened the icebox and spoke into it, as if his mother were inside. "You can't sell the boat, Mother."

"What?" Maggie finished washing the cups and saucers and turned off the faucet.

Karl slammed the icebox shut. "I said, you can't sell the boat!" This time he raised his voice.

Maggie turned around. "You were listening to us?"

"I couldn't help it. You can't sell the boat, it's Daddy's. And it's my future, you know."

"Mind your own business, Karl."

He crossed his arms in defiance. "I *won't* let you sell it."

"You aren't in charge of this."

"You can't sell it!" Karl stomped his foot like when he was little.

"If I don't sell the boat, we'll have to move in with Uncle Melvin. Is that what you want?"

"I want the boat!" He felt his throat get tight.

"You said you'd do anything so we wouldn't have to live with him. I said there might have to be some sacrifices. This is one of them."

"Daddy would want you to keep it for me so I could work on it next summer and after I'm done with school—"

"You are *not* going back to work on that boat. Ever. It

killed your father."

"What if I told you I had a dream and Daddy told me to keep the boat?" Karl mocked both Will and his mother.

Maggie took one step toward him and put her hands on her hips. "How *dare* you! Up to bed with you, this instant. You don't need anything to eat. If you're not careful, you won't get any breakfast, either. Go."

Karl saw more tears in his mother's eyes, turned around and stormed up the stairs. He'd seen his mother cry almost every day, and he found it nearly impossible to behave like the man he supposed to be when she acted like this.

The tightness in his own throat came every day, too, and some days it stayed with him from the time he woke up until the time he went to bed, but he discovered he could keep the tears away if he got angry. So he made himself angry with his father for not being more careful, angry with Uncle Melvin for threatening him and for hurting Lizzie; angry with Father Cunningham for not praying for his father to live. He got mad at his teachers for telling him lies—lies like "ask and you shall receive."

He got mad at all his friends, too. For the first few weeks, his classmates would suddenly stop talking and stare at him whenever he came near. He felt like he'd become a curiosity, a freak. Were they afraid *their* fathers might die if he got too close to them, like death was catching or something? Were they waiting to see him cry? Some of the girls tilted their heads and furrowed their brows when he walked by. *Poor Karl.* Well, he didn't want their pity.

Jimmy Rusch and Elmer Klein, his best friends since first grade, began avoiding him, too, "forgetting" to save a place for him at the lunch table so he'd have to eat with the fifth and sixth graders. Aw, who needed friends like that, anyway?

Karl got mad at Lizzie and Anna, too, for acting like sissy girls. He was angry with his mother for crying all the time, and now, for talking about selling the boat. And now he was mad at Will, too, for conspiring with her.

But most of all, heaven forbid, Karl raged against God for not listening and answering his prayer; for letting—no, *making*—his father die. His whole world was falling apart and there was nothing he could do about it.

Chapter 6

High Time

After his third trip from the back porch in the early morning darkness, Jacob Denver finished loading the huge pile of packages and baskets into the panel truck he'd borrowed from the mill and closed it's door. The train would have been so much easier, he thought, and safer this time of year, and he would have taken it except that his mother, Theresa, brought all this stuff for him to deliver to his brother, Will. He shook his head when he saw the measure of her largesse for his brother's family. "Good grief, Mother, they're not starving."

Jacob went back into his house for gloves and a hat and the lunch his housekeeper packed for him, and locked the door. He could think of a dozen things he'd rather do on the day before Thanksgiving than drive from Wakelin to Tomos Bay, but he'd been talking on the telephone with his younger brother nearly every day since the middle of October, and each call disturbed him more than the last. The first three had come from Will, distraught over Eddie Stern's near drowning, devastated by his death, terrified by his own fall into Eddie's grave. After that, Jacob made it a point to call him every day, each time thinking he'd surely sound better, each time hearing the same dismal tone in his voice. Will usually brought his family to Wakelin at Thanksgiving, taking the train at his mother's insistence and at her expense. This year, when he told Jacob he didn't have the heart to come, Jacob invited himself to Tomos Bay. He wanted to look into his brother's eyes to see if he could find any of the cheerful old Will there, to see if he could coax him out of hiding. Like a stone in his shoe, Jacob found his brother's sadness discomforting.

The long drive north went smoothly, and although patches of snow covered the ground in places, the roads were clear and the sun shone. From Wakelin, Wisconsin, Jacob drove north and west along the Chicago and Northwestern Railroad, past lake after lake in what once was a forest thick with white pine. At Carson Village he turned due north, skirting the state of Michigan at Hurley, and from there drove west into the sun along the south shore of Lake Superior. Tomos Bay clung to the eastern limits of Ashland like a jealous little sister.

Jacob stopped twice along the way to check the white pine seedlings he planted two springs ago, caressing the soft needles of this one or that. He loved the way they felt: supple, tender, pliable enough to survive the heavy snows to come. Jacob's grandfather had amassed a huge fortune for himself in lumber and Jacob's father, Henry, followed in his footsteps, clear-cutting the land, ignoring the wounds they made in the rapidly dwindling forests. Once they'd finished with it, their generations sold it to unsuspecting immigrants who soon found it unsuitable for farming.

Even before Henry died, Jacob decided it was up to him to atone for the sins of his forebears. He bought up acre upon acre of stump-studded, rocky property and endured his father's ridicule for making such foolish investments. Jacob paid a fair price to the immigrants, employed some of them and began to restore the great pine forest by planting new trees wherever he could. It would be many years, however, before the land looked anything like a forest again.

The sun hung low in the west when Jacob arrived in Tomos Bay. After stopping at the butcher shop to buy the turkey for tomorrow's dinner, he pulled up to Will's dark brown shingle-sided house. Carrying the wrapped turkey like a baby, he knocked on the front door. Two little faces topped with brown hair peeked out from behind the living room curtains; Jacob heard their whoops and hollers through the closed door. *Here we go.*

"Mummy, Mummy, Uncle Jacob is here!" Four year old Billy opened the front door. His grin reached from ear to ear.

Little Neddie squealed. "Unka-Jakup! Unka-Jakup!"

"Well, well, well, happy Thanksgiving, boys!" Jacob tried to sound like a jolly, fun loving uncle.

"Izat a baby, Unka-Jacup?"

"No it's a turkey; *gobble-gobble-gobble!*"

"*Gobba gobbagobba! Gobba gobbagobba!*" Neddie mimicked, laughing.

"Where's your mother?"

"I'm right here." Bernie came out of the kitchen and met Jacob at the door. He leaned across the turkey and kissed her cheek. She smiled. "It's good to see you, Jakey.

Go put that thing in the sink so we can clean it."

Billy and Ned danced around Jacob's feet as he tried to walk, almost tripping him twice. "*Gobba-gobbagobba! Gobba-gobbagobba!*" Their loud laughter already annoyed him. He hoped he wouldn't have to listen to this for two days straight.

Bernie laughed, too. "Do you have other things to bring in? I'm sure these two little turkeys could give you a hand. Go put your jackets on, boys."

Billy jumped up and down with excitement. "Presents from Grandma!" The boys scrambled joyously for their jackets and waited for Jacob by the front door.

Jacob pulled his driving gloves off and put them in his pocket. "When does Will get home?"

"Should be here any time now."

"C'mon, Uncle Jacob!" shouted Billy.

Jacob crossed the living room as the little boys burst out the door and raced to his truck. He set them to work carrying baskets of bread and cookies and other unbreakable items, finally giving them the packages with their names on them. When Jacob came in with his own heavy load, the boys were running back and forth from the living room to the kitchen in happy chaos, showing their mother every little thing Grandma Denver had sent for them. Once again, they got underfoot and nearly tripped him. Jacob wondered how many times they'd knocked his brother over.

Safely in the kitchen, Jacob gave Bernie her package, took off his coat, and sat down. "For you, *Bernice*." He imitated his mother's voice.

"Oh, my, she doesn't always have to do this."

"No, she doesn't, but it makes her happy. She'd love to have you closer so she could do it all the time."

Bernie frowned and shook her finger at him. "Now don't you go pressuring Will about that, Jacob. He's got enough on his mind these days. Say, could you lend me a hand and chop those onions for the stuffing?"

"I guess so." Jacob detested raw onions, but he rolled up his sleeves and washed his hands. "So how is he?"

"How do you think?" Bernie poured boiling water into the teapot. "One day he blames himself for not gettin' Eddie outta the water sooner and the next he blames himself for not lettin' him go to the bottom of the lake. He frets about Maggie and the kids, an' he has bad dreams most every night. The only thing he's feelin' these days is pain, missin' Eddie, thinkin' about what's gonna happen to that boat. He goes down to the marina every day and stares at it, tryin' to figure out how he can sell Eddie's share and still keep his own. *Who wants to buy half a fishin' business?* he says. He's gotta get that thing outta the water before winter, or come spring it won't be worth anything." Suddenly she tilted her head and smiled. "Say, maybe *you* could help 'im. Gettin' that boat ready for winter is a two man job, and Rob's already gone south to build houses. What do ya think?"

Jacob had only sliced and chopped half of the first onion, but his eyes already burned and watered, sending tears running down his face. "I'll help if he asks me, but I'm not going to push myself on him." He looked away from the cutting board and sniffed. "Would you be so kind as to get the handkerchief from my coat pocket, Bernice?"

Bernie chuckled and found the handkerchief. "Big man like you cryin' over a little onion, what's this world comin' to?" She handed it to him and watched as he wiped his eyes. "Your brother needs a push, Jakey. If you ask me, he needs a kick in the pants, but I'm not the one to do it."

"Why doesn't he buy it?"

"What? The boat? You think we're made 'o money? The foundry job pays well, but not that well."

"He could call Mother, she'd be happy to help him out. He has a right to some of the Denver money." Will's stubbornness irritated Jacob.

"Good Lord, Jacob, you of all people should know that's the last thing he'd do. He'll find some other way to keep the boat. And keep Maggie and her kids from the poor house, even if it means they move in with us."

"William, William, your heart is huge, but so is your pride." Jacob stopped and wiped his eyes again. "He's a true Denver, in spite of himself."

Bernie laughed. "Don't you *dare* let 'im hear you say that."

The back door opened and Will came in. The odor of dust, metal and sweat surrounded him.

"Your brother's here, Love. Wash up and come have a nice cuppa tea."

Will hung his hat and coat on a peg by the back door and plodded up the steps. His hands and face were dark with dust from the foundry where he worked during the winter. He kissed Bernie and handed her his lunch pail, and greeted his brother without stopping on his way through the kitchen. "Well, well, I see we have a new kitchen maid. The job suits you, Jacob." The clip of his words made clear Will's displeasure at having him there.

"Happy Thanksgiving, William."

"Sure thing."

"*Gobba gobbagobba*, Daddy!" The little boys ran after him as he climbed the stairs, but Will didn't even acknowledge them.

Bernie shook her head. "Sorry. He's been this way for weeks."

"This is how he acted the year he ran away."

"Well, I sure hope he's not fixin' to run from me."

Will trudged back into the kitchen and sat down heavily, slouching over in his chair. "Well, now, Jacob, how are things down there in lumber-land? Any big sales lately?" Bernie filled his cup.

"Mother says hello. She sent you cookies. She made them herself."

Bernie put them out on the table.

Jacob eyed his brother and asked, "How *are* you?" as if he didn't already know.

"Tired as an old mule." His drawn face and sagging eyes verified Will's words.

"You're cranky as an old mule, too."

"What's that supposed to mean?"

"You've been home ten minutes and you haven't had a nice thing to say to anyone, that's what. How about a little cheer?"

"Right." Will faked a laugh, then sobered. "So, are you going to give me the message now or later?"

"When do you want it?"

"Couldn't we skip it for once?"

"I promised Mother: she misses you and you'd make her happy if you came back to Wakelin. You'd have a good job and—"

"I'd be sneezing sawdust for the rest of my life. I'd have to do whatever she asks, and *you'd* be my boss. No offense, but no thanks, Jacob. There's people here depending on me. Tell her you mentioned it, and the answer is same as always."

"Well, don't say you aren't wanted." Between his

brother and the commotion his two nephews made, Jacob wasn't enjoying his visit, not one whit.

Later, stretched out on his attic mattress, Jacob looked up at the roof boards and thought about Will's unhappiness. Jacob hated seeing him like this.

He rolled over, blew out the lantern he'd brought with him, and pulled the covers over his head, savoring the quiet. All evening long, the two little versions of his brother played big turkey after little turkey, then little turkey after big turkey, laughing and running wildly through the house, calling *Gobba gobbagobba!* Will spoiled their exuberance when he shouted at them to stop, making Billy cry and sending Neddie off to hide in his mother's skirts. Jacob appreciated having things settle down, but he'd never seen his brother be so rough with his sons. It reminded him too much of Henry Denver. He wanted the happy Will back.

Suddenly, a scene from long ago erupted from Jacob's memory. He might have been about Billy's age, Will a couple years younger, not much more than a toddler. They were laughing and running around on the big front porch of their house in Wakelin because making noise and running inside were strictly forbidden. He remembered his father coming to the door to call them in for dinner. The brothers obeyed immediately, as they'd been taught, but their father swatted Willie hard on the backside as he went in the door, hard enough to make him cry. When Jacob hesitated, afraid he'd hit him, too, his father laughed and tousled his hair. "Come on in for dinner, Jack."

He opened his eyes to make the memory go away, but it refused to budge. He was the oldest, the strongest, the son with the hefty lumberjack physique, the one who loved the smell of wood and sawdust. With great pride, Henry called him *Jack* whenever Theresa, who did not approve of nicknames, couldn't hear him.

Will, on the other hand, couldn't stand the noise of the mill, hated the dust and couldn't for the life of him pull a saw the way his father wanted him to. Henry Denver had no special name for this son, the one who most resembled him, with his slight build and eyes that squinted whenever something displeased or upset him. Henry had nothing but disgust for this miserable little nobody.

Jacob used to feel guilty about how he'd fallen into his father's ways, about how superior he'd acted toward Will as they grew up, about how smug he'd been about all the special favors he received that Will had not. But when Will fell in love, married Bernie and was finally happy, Jacob allowed himself believe that everything was all better for him, the past forgiven and forgotten.

As he sucked in the cold attic air, the guilt returned. He had to admit he owed his brother and it was high time he paid up.

Chapter 7

We Gather Together

Maggie smelled it the moment Karl called her. "Mama, I think your pies are burning!" She scrambled down the stairs, grabbed her potholders, and flung open the oven door. A blast of hot air and smoke hit her face, blinding her for an instant, but, thank God, it was only from the bubbling juices burned to a black, gooey mess on the sides of the pans. She took the pies out of the oven and set them on the dish drainer to cool, then opened the kitchen window a crack.

Maggie had been distracted by the letter she received yesterday from her Aunt Mary; rereading it when she should have been minding the pies. Isabelle's older sister from Duluth, Minnesota, Aunt Mary had a special love for her nieces. When Kathleen and Maggie were girls she sent them sweet cards and lavish gifts for birthdays and Christmas; even now, they delighted whenever they received mail from her. Her letters were chatty and ordinary, but special, filled with simple, everyday wisdom. Maggie found them to be especially comforting these days, not because of anything she wrote, but because she imagined

Aunt Mary's voice as she read them. In this latest letter, she wrote to tell Maggie she'd be coming to Tomos Bay for Thanksgiving dinner at Melvin and Kathleen's. It was the only reason Maggie wanted to go.

As Maggie and her children walked to her sister's house, she worried about how to keep them safe from Melvin. The girls chattered about school; Karl scowled.

"Mama," he said, "do we really have to go to Uncle Melvin's? I mean, after what he did to Lizzie—"

"It's a holiday, and they're the only family we have. Besides, my Aunt Mary will be there." Maggie didn't want Karl to know how unsettled she was. "I don't think Melvin will try anything today, but still, I think it would be best if you all stay in the same room with me or Aunt Mary or my cousin, James."

"Who's he?" asked Lizzie.

"Aunt Mary's son. His daughter, Amanda, will be there, too; she's fourteen."

Anna giggled. "Ohh, a girlfriend for Karl."

"Uh-uh. We're related, you know." Karl sounded aggravated, but his eyes twinkled. The girls kept teasing him, and for once, he played along.

Melvin and Kathleen Straus lived in the fancy part of town where the houses were either built of wood or real brick, not shingles made to look like brick. At the dead end of a boulevard lined with young elm trees, their boxy house seemed small and out of place compared to the grand homes around it, even though it was a palace compared to 617 Blight Street. Blooming flowers adorned the spacious yard in summer and specially chosen shrubs added winter beauty, but the wrought iron fence around it reminded Maggie of a prison.

Melvin worked at Tomos Bay Savings and Loan and earned a large enough salary to afford such a place. He started years ago as a vault clerk, was promoted to teller, then became a loan officer, which allowed him to join the Rotary Club in Ashland. He attended weekly luncheon meetings, participated in community service events and promoted charitable causes. Maggie suspected he chose his good deeds to increase his chances of being hailed in the newspaper. Her mother kept each article in a scrapbook and brought them to family gatherings.

When he came home at night, though, Melvin left his charity at the back door. Kathleen kept house for him, cooked for him and did every little thing he asked her to do; she rarely went anywhere except to the market or to Mass on Sundays and Holy Days. Maggie knew she owned two good dresses, but Kathleen seldom wore either one of them because Melvin reprimanded her harshly if she spilled a drop of coffee or a bit of butter on them.

Melvin and Kathleen's brick house was three stories tall, capped with a red tile roof. Inside, the ceilings measured at least eleven feet from the floors: living room, dining room, kitchen, parlor, and library below with four generous bedrooms and a full attic above. Maggie remembered how once upon a time Kathleen dreamed of filling the house with children, but after eighteen years of marriage, she had none.

A deep porch extended the width of the house; at its center stood a heavy wooden door with leaded glass windows. With the basket of her slightly over-done pies in hand, Maggie rang the bell and the four of them waited.

Kathleen came to the door, smiling. "Happy Thanksgiving, everyone; come in, come in."

The aromas of roast turkey and duck, mixed with baked sweet potatoes and fresh bread, lured them in. Even though Eddie didn't like Melvin, Maggie remembered how he looked forward to each Thanksgiving when he'd have his annual taste of roast duck. Melvin spent his fall weekends hunting, bringing home birds for Kathleen to clean, since he couldn't stomach doing it himself. That bothered Eddie, but not enough to keep him from relishing every bite. Maggie argued with him about it last year; now she'd clean the bird herself if it meant Eddie would come back and eat it.

Kathleen's voice called her back to the present. "Karl, you can take your coats and put them on the bed in the guest room. Maggie, give me your basket and go say hello to Aunt Mary, she's been waiting for you."

The old woman sat in a wingback chair by the window, near the warm radiator. A girl with glasses and bobbed hair sat next to her on a footstool, reading a book. Aunt Mary's hair—now faded to pure white—had once been reddish blond, like Isabelle, Kathleen, and Maggie's, but the family resemblance ended there. The years had softened and rounded her face and body until she and Isabelle looked nothing alike. She wore a deep blue dress with a square collar hanging like an ivory bib in front of her. Even though the dress reminded Maggie of a pilgrim costume and made her want to laugh, Aunt Mary's love and kindness made her the most beautiful thing in the house.

"Margaret, dear." She held out her arms to Maggie, who gladly filled them.

The older woman gently stroked Maggie's cheek with the back of her hand. "It's a crying shame, what happened to Edward, and at such a young age. You poor thing."

Trying to ignore the lump in her throat, Maggie turned to the girl. "You must be Amanda; my how you've grown. Lizzie, Anna, this is your cousin, Amanda."

"Hi." Amanda looked at the girls before returning to her book.

Karl stood in the doorway watching, his left hand behind him, latched on to his right elbow. Maggie could tell he was nervous. "And this is my son, Karl."

"Hello." This time Amanda didn't look up at all.

Lizzie and Anna giggled. Maggie shook her head at them.

"Margaret, you have such beautiful children. Come here, all of you. My goodness, Karl, nobody will ever forget what your Daddy looked like because you are so much like him. You should be proud. Elizabeth, what a beautiful young lady you are, just like your mother; and Anna, you must be an angel from heaven." The old woman clasped her hands in front of her heart then reached into her pocket and brought out three pieces of peppermint candy. "Shh," she put her finger up to her lips and whispered. "Don't tell your grandma I gave you candy before dinner."

How could anyone not love Aunt Mary?

Melvin appeared in the doorway. "Karl, go up to the spare room and bring down those four old chairs and put them around the table." He didn't even say hello.

Karl looked at Maggie, who nodded at him. He hurried out of the room, tripping on his own two feet.

"For land's sake, Karl, be careful coming down the stairs, you wouldn't want to fall on those chairs and break them, now, would you? They're valuable antiques. Margaret, your sister could use your help in the kitchen."

"And a Happy Thanksgiving to you, too, Melvin." Maggie got up and started toward the kitchen, then turned back. "You girls stay and visit with Aunt Mary and Amanda. Tell them about your sewing projects; Aunt Mary used to be a seamstress."

But before Maggie reached the kitchen she heard Melvin's sticky sweet voice. "There's a surprise for you girls up in the guest room. Amanda, you, too; come see what we have for you."

She whipped around. "Not until after dinner, Melvin. They should be helping in the kitchen. Come, girls."

"I thought you said they could stay with me and visit!" called Aunt Mary.

Kathleen came from the kitchen carrying a large bowl of steaming sweet potatoes. "Dinner will be on the table in two minutes. Maggie, would you fill the water glasses, please?"

Maggie remembered how much Eddie loved sweet potatoes, too. "Of course."

Anna and Lizzie followed her into the kitchen. "Can we help, Aunt Kathleen?"

Isabelle's cackling voice sliced through Maggie's hopes for a pleasant Thanksgiving. "There you are, Margaret! Isn't it just like you to come late and get out of the work? Girls, you go find your places at the table and stay out of the way."

"I apologize, Kathleen. The girls and I will wash the dishes for you." Maggie filled the water pitcher and took it into the dining room. Lizzie and Anna followed behind her like little ducklings.

When the table was covered with the bounty of Kathleen's food and everyone had a place to sit, Melvin stood up. "Since today is Thanksgiving, I'm asking each of you to name one thing you're thankful for." He turned to Kathleen. "You start, dear."

"Well," she cleared her throat. "I'm thankful for my family, and that you all came today." She glanced up at Melvin. "And for Melvin, of course."

Melvin pretended to scold her. "You named three things, Kathleen, see how lucky you are?"

Isabelle was thankful for her daughters and Melvin; James was thankful for his mother and Amanda; Amanda said she didn't know—everything; Karl said he was thankful his mother hadn't burned the apple pies, which made everyone laugh. The girls both said they were thankful for their mother; Maggie said she was thankful for her children; and Aunt Mary got teary-eyed and said, "I thank God for every one of you, my dear family."

Melvin was last. "I'm thankful that I make enough money so I can give some to the church and some to help the poor." Then he spouted forth a long and pious sounding prayer, filled with flowery and vacant words. Before it ended, he prayed, "And please bring our dear Margaret to her senses so she and the children will come live with us and fill this house with the happy voices of children. Amen."

Maggie felt her face burn. "I'm not going to change my mind."

"Margaret, you stupid girl, you don't know a good thing when you see it." Isabelle shook her head. "Sooner or later, you'll change your mind; mark my words, you'll have to. Now start the potatoes. Pass to the left, everyone."

Maggie looked down at her hands. Tears fell onto her lap while her neck muscles tightened, a prelude to one of her nasty headaches. Aunt Mary, seated to her left, slid her hand across Maggie's shoulders and pulled her close.

Isabelle clicked her tongue. "Oh, stop babying her.

Pass the dressing, Melvin needs some dressing."

"Someone ought to be taking care of her, and here you're doing nothing but hounding the poor girl. Good heavens, Isabelle, have you forgotten what it feels like?" Aunt Mary's husband, Raymond, died last spring.

"Of course we want to take care of her, but she won't let us." Melvin spoke with food in his mouth. He shoveled it in even as the dishes were being passed. "Now stop your blubbering, Margaret, and eat your dinner; your mother and sister worked long and hard to make this meal."

From across the table, Maggie saw the muscles in Karl's jaw tighten. Her own stomach clutched. She handed the bowl of potatoes to Aunt Mary without putting any on her own plate. "Excuse me." She put her napkin next to her plate and stood up. Lizzie and Anna stared at her, eyes wide. "I'm all right."

Melvin wiped his greasy hands on his napkin and bellowed. "Then sit down and eat your dinner!"

"Let the lady go, Melvin," said James; *dear* James, the gentle and quiet one who usually watched the world go by without adding any comments of his own. "Don't you have any manners?"

Maggie wanted to kiss him. "Excuse me." She left the dining room and hurried up the stairs to the bathroom, hands shaking as she turned the lock behind her. Overwhelmed by a dreadful sense of danger, she turned on the faucet, yet even the warm water running over her hands brought no comfort.

After a few minutes Kathleen knocked on the door. "Maggie? Let me in, honey, it's okay."

"Where's Melvin?"

"He's still eating. He wants you to come back to the table."

Maggie knew she'd have to, sooner or later.

"Please let me in."

Slowly, she turned the lock and opened the door a crack. Kathleen stood there all by herself in her faded blue dress and white apron with its little yellow flowers. Maggie opened the door and let her in.

"Come here." Kathleen opened her arms to her sister. "I've wanted to do this ever since Eddie died, but he wouldn't let me; he said it would make you soft."

In the big white-tiled bathroom with the extra large claw foot tub, Maggie clung to her sister and cried.

Kathleen kept her voice low, speaking into Maggie's ear. "I'm sorry Melvin's behaving so badly today. We only want what's best for you and the children."

Maggie pulled away and looked her sister in the eye. "I won't bring them to live here. He scares them. And I couldn't stand watching what he does to you, I'm sorry."

Kathleen took both Maggie's hands in hers. "You know I'd love to have you here with me, but do whatever you can to stay in your own home. Only don't tell him I said so."

"I won't." Maggie noticed a purple tinge on Kathleen's neck, near where her collar ended. She touched it; almost imperceptibly, Kathleen winced. "What happened?"

"Nothing."

"You've got a bruise. What did he do to you?"

The sisters looked in the mirror together. They looked very much alike, except that Kathleen looked very much older than her 35 years. "You're imagining things, Maggie, I'm fine."

"No, you *aren't* fine."

"Look," Kathleen whispered, turning away from the

reflected Maggie to the real Maggie. "I married him; I wanted to, even though Daddy didn't trust him. It pleased Mother and got me out of her house. I made promises to him before God and everyone. This is my home now, he is my husband, I'm supposed to be loyal to him and love him. I'm not saying he hits me, and I'm not saying he doesn't. Please, let it go. I'll tell you when I need your help." She spoke out loud again. "Wash off your face and come down to dinner, Maggie. Aunt Mary is here, remember?"

Maggie rubbed the back of her neck.

"Are you getting a headache?"

"I think so."

Kathleen opened the medicine chest and took out a bottle of white pills. "Here, take one of these, it will help."

"What are they?"

"Aspirin. They work; I should know." She took a clean handkerchief from the drawer in the wash stand, unfolded it and poured some pills into the center, carefully wrapping them. She handed the package to Maggie. "Put these in your pocket and take them home with you." She opened the door. "I'll tell them you're on your way down."

"Kathleen? Thank you."

Kathleen turned and looked at her. "Come down to dinner, will you, please, for me?" There was no mistaking the fear in her eyes.

When they returned to the table, Melvin snapped his attention away from James. His voice turned rough again. "It's about time, *lay-deez!*" Maggie saw Lizzie and Anna jump. Aunt Mary put her hand on Maggie's when she sat down. After that, everyone but Melvin ate in silence. Even so, he ate more and faster than anyone else.

After the meal was over and Maggie's pies devoured, Melvin reminded the girls about the surprise that awaited them in the guest room. Kathleen smiled. "I know you'll like it, and you can play with it whenever you come to visit."

"You can play with it all the time when you live here," corrected Melvin. "Go show them, Kathleen. James, let's go to the den, I've got some Cuban cigars. You, too, Karl."

"No, thanks, I'll help with dishes."

"I told you before, no boy's gonna do woman's work in my house. You're coming with us."

Karl looked at Maggie again. She met his eyes and glanced at James and back again, nodding once. "No cigars for Karl, Melvin." Karl hesitantly followed.

Isabelle, Aunt Mary, Kathleen, Maggie, and the girls went upstairs to find the surprise: a doll house, complete with furniture and people. The rooms resembled those in Melvin and Kathleen's house, with six wooden figurines: two women, one man, two girls and an older boy. The girls laughed with delight; Maggie felt sick and recoiled. Lizzie and Anna had never seen anything like it; they'd certainly never had such an elaborate toy of their own. They said, "thank you" over and over again. Even Amanda said she liked it.

Kathleen smiled broadly. "Well, you three are excused from dish duty today. Have fun, now." The women returned to the kitchen to clean up from dinner while Aunt Mary sat in the parlor and put her feet up.

As Maggie went in and out of the dining room carrying dishes, she heard the girls giggling upstairs. She smiled.

It had been a long time since she'd heard her daughters laugh. After a while, though, the laughter stopped. As she stood at the foot of the stairs wondering if she should go up, Melvin came down, buckling his belt, belching cigar smoke, and rubbing his belly. Maggie's heart raced.

"They're having a good time up there, Margaret. They'll have a good time every day when you come to live here. "

Suddenly, wild laughter erupted from the guestroom. She forced a smile and said, "Excuse me, Melvin." She started up the stairs, calmly, so he wouldn't follow her, even though she wanted to take them two at a time.

Amanda, Lizzie and Anna were laughing so hard they could barely talk. As soon as Amanda saw Maggie, though, she stopped and looked out the window.

"What's so funny?" asked Maggie.

"Uncle Melvin has fur in his pants," giggled Anna.

"What?"

"He forgot to button his pants when he came out of the bathroom," Lizzie blushed. "All this black fuzz was sticking out. I don't think he had any underwear on."

"Did he touch you, Lizzie, did he touch any of you? What else did you see, anything?" Panic rose in her throat, her neck muscles tightened again.

"He made a bad stink in the bathroom." Lizzie held her nose, giggling.

"Did he touch you? Tell me! Did he come in the room? Did he hurt you?"

"He came in to say hello, but he didn't touch anyone," replied Lizzie.

Amanda turned away from the window. "I think he's a pig, Aunt Maggie."

Maggie's hands shook; it took every ounce of energy

she had to refrain from screaming. "Lizzie and Anna, pick up the dolls and get your coats on, we're going home, right now."

"But Mama, we're having fun," whined Anna.

"Sorry, it's getting late, time to go." Maggie took her own coat and Karl's from the bed and hurried down to the den. "Karl, it's time to go, come on."

Karl took his coat and waited for her to thank Kathleen. Lizzie and Anna come down the stairs, all bundled up in their coats, hats and mittens. The three of them stood together by the front door.

Maggie wanted to leave without talking to Melvin again, but he stepped out of his den with a cigarette dangling from his mouth.

"Going so soon, Margaret? If you lived here, you wouldn't have to go out in the cold, would you?" He laughed and went away.

Maggie shuddered. Suddenly, she remembered Aunt Mary. She found her in the parlor, sleeping in the chair, snoring softly. She crouched down and touched the old woman's hand. "Good bye, Aunt Mary, we're going home."

The old woman opened her eyes. "Not already? I wanted to chat with you."

"I'm sorry; I have to take my children home." She leaned over and kissed her beloved aunt.

Mary sat up. "What's going on? Something's happened; tell me."

"I can't." Maggie looked over her shoulder. "Ask Amanda, ask her in private. Where are you staying tonight?"

"With your mother."

"Thank God. Keep an eye on Amanda while you're

in this house. Make sure she doesn't get left alone with Melvin." Maggie kissed her again.

"Wait; let James drive you, it's getting dark."

Maggie gave directions as they got into the car. Her cousin had little to say until he heard the girls chattering in the back seat.

"I guess Uncle Melvin isn't so mean, after all," said Anna. "He bought us a dollhouse. Maybe it wouldn't be so bad if we had to live with him."

"No, Anna! He's so stupid; he doesn't even know to button his pants before he comes out of the bathroom."

Anna giggled. "Remember that fur? Maybe he's really a bear or something."

"He's a bear, all right," Karl said under his breath.

"He should wear underwear like real people do," said Lizzie. "I don't want to live with an animal like him."

"That's enough, girls." Maggie turned around.

James glanced at her. "What are they talking about?"

"Here's our street, we're down the block. There."

As James pulled up to 617 Blight Street, Maggie gave her key to Karl. "You three go on in, I want to talk to Uncle James for a minute."

They watched as the children went up the walk together and let themselves into the house.

"Now tell me what they were talking about."

"It seems Melvin came out of the bathroom with his pants open and stopped in to say hello to the girls while they were playing."

"What? What did they see?"

"Just—fur, I guess. Watch out for him. A few weeks ago, he pinched Lizzie on her—well, where he shouldn't have touched her."

"Good God, Margaret, and I left my daughter there?"

"She's fine; your mother is watching her."

"I've got to get back!"

"Thanks for the ride, James." Maggie's feet had barely touched the ground when her cousin made a sharp U-turn in the middle of the street and sped off. Rubbing her neck, she watched him drive away."

Later on, after she'd tucked the girls safely into bed, Maggie put on a sweater, took another one of Kathleen's pills and sat in Eddie's easy chair, her feet on the ottoman. When she closed her eyes, her mind wandered to days gone by, to her wedding night with Eddie on the boat; to the silliness of trying to make love on those skinny benches he called "beds." In the dream he kissed her lips, his hands moving all over her body. She smiled and touched his cheek then saw Melvin's face. No! She started awake, her heart pounding. Karl stood over her, shaking her shoulder.

"Mama, wake up. Aunt Mary and James are here to see you."

"Oh, my, I didn't even hear you knock." Maggie stood up too fast and tottered slightly.

"Hello, dear. Karl, take these packages and put them in your ice box, will you please? Your Aunt Kathleen sent you some leftovers."

Maggie regained her composure. "Here, let me take your coats. Would you like some tea?"

James kept his coat on. "I'm not staying, Margaret. I came in to apologize for being so short with you."

"I don't blame you at all. How is Amanda?"

"She's fine. She's with Aunt Isabelle and they're wait-ing for me to play anagrams. I'll come back before nine, Mother."

"Thank you, dear."

After Maggie hung her aunt's coat on a peg by the front door, she went into the kitchen to put water on to boil. Aunt Mary followed her.

They found Karl looking through the packages of leftovers. "No pie, Mama, but there's lots of meat and a bunch of bones."

"Those are for soup. Aunt Mary, we can sit in the din-ing room, it's much nicer out there."

"No, it's warm and cozy in here, this is fine." Karl pulled out a chair for her. She sat down and looked up at him. "Did you find the bread, Karl? Are you hungry?"

"I'm always hungry."

"Then why don't you make yourself a sandwich? With your mother's permission, of course."

"As long as he cleans up after himself and leaves some for our dinner tomorrow."

He grinned. "Thanks, Aunt Mary."

"You are very welcome, but you should thank your Aunt Kathleen." She smiled sweetly. "Now, dear, I have some things to discuss with your mother. Would you be so kind as to leave us so we might talk in private?"

He nodded. "Can I take this up to my room, Mama?"

"*May I.* Yes, just don't leave anything for the mice."

"Karl, you are a fine young man," said Aunt Mary. "I know you'll go far in life. Be sure to listen to your mother, she is very wise."

"Yes, Ma'am. Goodnight."

Karl started out of the kitchen; Maggie caught up with him in the dining room. "No eavesdropping tonight," she kept her voice low. "You'll be in big trouble if I find you sitting on the steps listening. Do you understand?"

"She a nice old lady, Mama, I'll stay upstairs, I promise." He leaned over and kissed her. "Goodnight, O Wise Woman." He bowed a little, smiling.

Maggie smiled back. It was something Eddie would have said. "Sleep well."

Aunt Mary poured tea into the china cups Maggie had taken from the cupboard. "I came to see how you are getting along—really. You seem to be having a hard time of it, and your mother isn't making it any easier."

"She thinks we would be better off living with Melvin and Kathleen."

"And you don't think it's a good idea?"

"No I *don't*." She didn't intend to sound so vehement. "I mean, if I didn't have the children, maybe. The problem is Melvin." Maggie couldn't get comfortable in her chair. She pulled it in to the table, then backed it out again. "Did Amanda tell you what he did today?"

"Yes. Is there more?"

"He frightens my children. He pinched Lizzie on her behind; he said or did something to Karl that Karl won't talk to me about. They wouldn't be safe in his house." She got up for the sugar bowl. "Sugar, Aunt Mary? Cream?"

"I don't need anything, Margaret, thank you; now, sit. What else?"

"It's Kathleen." Maggie sighed and sat down. "She gets bruises. She had one on her neck today."

"Under her collar."

Maggie nodded. "She wouldn't tell me what happened, she wouldn't even admit to having it. I know he hurts her. Sometimes we go weeks without seeing her. He tells us she's sick."

"Does your mother know about this?"

"She thinks Melvin is a saint; she's so proud her daughter married a banker. She won't see Kathleen's suffering, and if we go to live there, she won't see our suffering, either. In fact, she thinks people deserve whatever befalls them." Maggie choked up, remembering the black mourning dress. "Whenever we need her help or comfort, all she can do is scold us." She looked away.

Aunt Mary put her hand on Maggie's. "Do you have another way to support your family? Money? Anything?"

Maggie tried to sound hopeful. "I'm taking in a little laundry. Eddie's partner is trying to find someone to buy our share of the boat, and when he does, we'll have enough for a while. I know how to be thrifty, we'll manage."

Aunt Mary reached for her purse. She opened it and pulled out a thick envelope. "This is for you. I brought it so you could make a nice Christmas for your children, but it seems you need it to keep body and soul together." She gave it to Maggie. "Open it."

The envelope held five and ten dollar bills. Maggie gasped.

"There are seventy-five dollars and I will send you more when I get home."

Maggie had never seen so much money at one time. "How can I ever thank you?"

"Listen to me: if Melvin threatens any of you, you have a home with me; Kathleen, too. I will send James for you—in the dead of night, if necessary."

"This is our home, Aunt Mary." Eddie's still here with me, she thought. "But thank you. You don't know what this means to me."

"Then promise me one thing, Margaret," Aunt Mary's voice hardened with a touch of Isabelle's impatience.

"Under *no* circumstances are you to move into Melvin Straus' home. Let me help you, instead. Promise me!"

"I promise," whispered Maggie. She had the impulse to cross herself and kneel at the old woman's feet. For the first time in a long time, the joy of love in her heart far outweighed its pain."I promise."

Chapter 8

Brothers

Jacob pushed himself away from the table. "This is one of the best Thanksgiving dinners I've tasted in a long time, Bernie, but I don't have room for another bite."

"Aw, Jakey, I could fix you fish tails in sawdust and you'd say that!" Bernie laughed.

"That's because my brother married a fine cook." Jacob looked at Will, hoping he'd say something nice to her. He'd been grumping around all morning.

Will got up and kissed his wife. "Thanks for the meal, Bern; you out did yourself again." He rubbed his belly and looked at his brother. "How about a walk, old man?"

"I might consider it if you'd rephrase the question."

"Come on, Jacob, I need some air."

Bernie had her sisters to help her and didn't seem to mind having the men leave for a while. "We'll clean up a bit and save the pie for later; you two have a nice walk."

Jacob pulled on his coat, buttoning it as he stood on the doorstep. "You know, you're a lucky man, brother. As far as I'm concerned, Bernie's the best. I envy you."

"You envy *me*? Now that's a first."

"No, it's not. I hope I'm as lucky as you someday." He pulled on his fine leather driving gloves. "So, which way to the marina?"

"Why?"

"I want to see your boat."

"Oh, I dunno... Why spoil a nice day?"

"What are you talking about?"

"I don't want to look at her today."

"Come on, we can walk by and you can point it out to me. It's been a long time since I've seen it."

"Oh, for land's sake, all right."

The two walked toward the bay without saying anything. Grim faced, Will stopped when the lake came into view. "There she is. See it?"

Jacob shielded his eyes with his right hand as he squinted into the cold sunshine. The loneliness of the place saddened his heart. The *Maggie O'Keefe* floated all alone at the dock, bobbing in the water as if she didn't know the other boats were gone. The sound of waves splashing on waves seemed lonely, too; even as a stranger, Jacob missed the clamor of bells, the calling from one boat to another. Even the expected fishy-seaweed smell was barely discernable. Jacob cleared his throat. "She's as pretty as ever, Will, but why is she still—"

"She isn't in storage 'cause I haven't had the money or the help or the will to do it, a'right?" He glared at Jacob. "There, are you satisfied? Your brother's a lazy sloth."

"Well, I planned to go home tomorrow, but I could stay another day or two and give you a hand. It would be fun." Jacob forced a smile and turned to face his brother.

"There's nothin' fun about it, it's hard work! Anyway,

you don't know the first thing about it." Will spit out his words, refusing to meet Jacob's eyes.

"I imagine you could teach me. I'm a quick learner."

Will didn't say anything for a few seconds. He looked at Jacob, then at the *Maggie O'Keefe*, then back again. "You'd do that?"

"You're my brother."

Forlorn, Will looked out at the boat again. "The problem is, I don't have money to hire Swenson to pull it out."

"I thought you had a good year."

"We did, but I gave all the money to Eddie's wife. She couldn't pay the undertaker and needed coal and groceries, so I... He didn't leave her much except his share of the boat and she's got three kids to feed. Now I have to find a buyer for his half, a new partner for me." He swallowed. "Or sell the whole thing and be done with it. I'm thinking it might be easier that way."

"You don't really want to do that, do you?" Jacob realized what a good and generous man his brother was. "You've put too much into this business to let it go."

"Business? It's just a fishing boat."

"You make your living off it for half the year, don't you? You have customers, don't you? It's a business. Don't sell it. We'll work something out."

Will squinted at his brother. Their eyes locked. "I'm not interested in any of your lumber money, Jacob."

"I know. I know that quite well."

Will looked at the boat again. "If you're gonna stay, you'd better make sure you've got plenty of warm clothes. And blankets. Be ready when I get home after work tomorrow. We'll have an early supper then go down to the boat. We should be there before dark."

"You want to spend the night down there? We'll freeze!" Jacob wondered what he'd gotten himself into. "We'd be smarter to start out early on Saturday, wouldn't we?"

"It's not about bein' smart. It's about tradition, Eddie's and mine. We always spend the last night of the season on the boat. If I'm going to hold on to this *business,* as you call it, I'm holding on to the traditions, too. Are you still in?"

"If you can do it, I can do it."

Will grunted and turned for home. "We better get back; they're waiting pie for us."

When Will came home from work the next night, Bernie had hot turkey stew waiting. She served it up with thick slabs of bread and leftover pumpkin pie. The two brothers loaded Will's truck with everything Bernie thought they'd need: coffee, bread, eggs and sausage for breakfast; a change of clothes for each of them, and twice as many blankets as they'd planned on taking. "You'll need 'em tonight—unless you plan on keepin' each other warm."

When they got to the marina, Will opened his door and looked at Jacob. "You stay here while I go make sure the dock isn't covered with ice."

"Let me carry things down to the dock for you."

"No!" Will raised his voice. "You stay where you are and wait for my signal. From now on, I'm the boss; got that, Jacob? Do what I tell you or you'll end up in the drink like Eddie. Understand?" He got out of the truck, muttering. "Good Lord, what would I tell Mother?" He pulled his wool cap down over his ears and slammed the door.

Jacob watched his brother. Although the air was still,

Will walked like he was fighting the wind—or some other unseen force. At the dock, he swung his foot lightly across the boards, checking for ice. He moved with a smooth and careful grace; in the waning daylight he looked like a dancer performing ritual moves to placate the hungry, freezing sea.

The dance ended and Will reached over and pulled down a set of steps from the deck of the *Maggie O'Keefe*. Before boarding, he appeared to examine the deck rail, then unlocked the cabin door and disappeared inside. Soon light shone through the row of round windows on the side of the boat. Jacob expected Will to return and signal him to start unloading, but he sat waiting for at least fifteen minutes with no sign of him; he knew because he checked his pocket watch twice.

While he waited, Jacob tried to imagine the tragedy that wrecked such havoc on his brother. He felt a twinge of jealousy, wondering if his own death would have the same impact on Will as Eddie Stern's had. Except for his mother and Hilde, his housekeeper, he didn't think his death would matter much to anyone.

Suddenly the truck door opened and Will hollered, "You sleepin' in there, Jacob? Didn't you see me wave?"

"No and no. May I come out now?"

"Give me a hand with this stuff; I thought you came along to help."

Jacob jumped out of the truck and took a load of blankets and food from Will. When he started down to the dock, Will yelled at him.

"Wait! Lemme go first!"

Jacob stopped, stepped aside and let Will pass. He wondered how long he'd have to take this.

"I'll go first, and you can hand things in to me; then

you'll have both hands free when you board."

"Whatever you say."

Will put his load down on the dock and carefully climbed the steps. He disappeared into the cabin, then reappeared with a kerosene lantern, which he set on the deck, away from the steps. It cast enough light so Jacob could see the broken rail along the edge of the boat and a couple of places near the water line where the paint was scraped thin. The *Maggie O'Keefe* had been left alone too long, he thought.

But once Will finally allowed him to board and enter the cabin, he liked what he saw. The galley kitchen with its two burner gas stove had coffee perking away on top; a kerosene lamp cast light and warmth from its place on the wall above a small built-in table. Built-in benches framed the table on three sides; two other cushion-covered benches ran along either wall of the cabin, each about three feet wide where the hull of the boat was widest, narrowing down to less than two feet at either end. Underneath the benches were hinged storage cabinets, whitewashed, but scuffed and dirty. Highly varnished pine paneled the walls, light brown and shiny, with dark knots scattered along the boards like watchful eyes. Jacob smiled at the small braided rug inside the door, knowing their mother would approve of such a homey touch.

"Put the blankets on those benches then come have a cup of coffee to warm up."

Jacob complied. Will took two mugs out of the cupboard and filled them with thick, strong coffee. Jacob shivered when he sat down on the cold bench. "I don't suppose you have a heater."

"Just the stove. This isn't first class accommodations like you're used to; I warned you this wouldn't be—what did you call it? Fun?"

"Other than the lack of heat, it's a nice place."

"Sure it is. You don't have to be polite on my account."

"Come on, Will; I've already had enough of that chip on your shoulder."

"No head in here, either. I'm going out to take a piss." Will shut the door hard behind him.

Jacob sipped the hot coffee and began to get warm. He took out his pocket watch. Six-thirty. If things kept on the way they'd been going, this was going to be a very long night, not to mention the whole day tomorrow. He heard Will pacing out on the deck, back and forth, back and forth. Worried, Jacob pulled his stocking cap down over his ears and went out.

Will crouched at the fractured railing. When he looked up, the pained expression on his face reminded Jacob of the day he threw his clothes in a bag and stormed out the door, looking to go as far away from Wakelin as he could. This time, though, Jacob saw their father, Henry, in Will's slim, wiry build, in the set of his mouth, in the dark moustache and beard, in the squint of his eyes, in the way his shoulders sagged.

"This is the place," Will said. He ran his hand back and forth across the twisted and splintered wood of the railing, a neglected wound that cried out for tending.

"What?"

"This is where he slipped. We wouldn't have known he fell in except for this. If I close my eyes, I can still see him tryin' to tread water with all those clothes on." Will sucked in a lot of air, let it out again, then looked down into at the lake. He'd been wounded that day, too.

Jacob put his hand on his brother's shoulder, about to

encourage him to come back inside to get warm, but Will stood and whirled around in one movement, his fist colliding hard with Jacob's jaw. Stunned, Jacob reeled backward, hitting his head on the cabin wall, his feet slipping out from under him. He lay sprawled on the deck, his head cradled in a coil of thick rope.

"Don't you ever touch me like that again, d'you hear me?" Will stood over Jacob, cussing him out with wave after wave of accusations, droplets of spit spewing from his mouth as he yelled. "How dare you touch me like that, like you cared! You didn't care when he took you off on trips and left me home. When you busted your bike, he told you to take mine, and then you threw it in the lake when the tires went flat from your riding on the railroad tracks. Did you get in trouble? Nooo! You both laughed about it! You didn't care then, why should you care now?" He stopped to catch his breath.

"I'm sorry, Will."

"Shut up and listen, you sonofa—bastard! Neither one of you ever had time for my little birthday, but when your birthday came, la-dee-da, he'd make a big party with the men from the mill and I had to show up and kiss your ass. You acted like royalty and he treated you like a prince! And now the best friend I ever had on this earth is gone and you have the gall to act like you care! Big important Miss-ter Denn-ver, *sir*, how nice of you to get down off your high horse and pretend like you care about your poor little brother. You jack-ass, you!" He kicked at the coil of rope; Jacob flinched.

Will's tirade went on and on in the darkness, pelting Jacob with a hailstorm of words the likes of which he'd never heard coming from Will's mouth. Bewildered, he'd thought these things were bygones, over and done, water under the bridge between them, but as the words flew from Will's mouth, Jacob learned the truth. He lay mute in the cold night air and took it.

Suddenly, Will stopped his rant and stomped into the cabin, letting the door bang as it closed behind him. Jacob sat up and rubbed his jaw. He felt like going back to Wakelin without saying another word to his brother, but the cabin door jerked open again and Will stuck his head out, still gruff as a bear.

"Get in here, Jacob." He shut the door.

Jacob stayed where he was.

The door flew open a second time. "I'm not going to hit you again. I got somethin' for you."

The rapidly swelling tissues on the side of his face made Jacob's words come out slow and thick. "A gun? You think I'm going let you to finish the job?"

"No gun. I'm not gonna hurt you."

"Right." Jacob stood up and rubbed his neck. When the stars quit flying around behind his eyelids, he cautiously went back into the cabin, intending to stay as far away from Will as he could.

On his knees rummaging through the storage area below one of the beds, Will had his back to Jacob. "Finish your coffee, you're gonna need your cup."

Jacob took his cup outside and threw the cold coffee over the rail, then came back in.

"Here it is." Triumphantly Will held up a bottle filled with brown liquid. "Sit down, Jacob, I've got somethin' for what ails you."

Jacob sat down at the table. "Is that what I think it is?"

"Yep."

"I thought you were the good Methodist. Where'd you

get it?"

"It's Eddie's. He always had a bottle on board, to toast the new season and to end the old. Well, tonight we're going to drink to his memory and empty this bottle."

"Where'd he get it?"

"I don't know and I don't care, but I can't keep it, and I'll be damned if I'm going to dump it in the lake." He pulled the cork with his teeth and spit it at the wall. "We won't be needin' that again." He poured into the mugs, handing one to his brother. "Drink up, Jacob."

Jacob lifted his mug to his lips.

"No, wait." Will raised his mug high. "To Eddie Stern, the best friend a man could ever have, like a brother. Rest in peace, old boy, I sure do miss ya."

He choked on the last words. Jacob saw his eyes glisten. Will sipped, then downed the rest of the whiskey in one swallow. "Ahh!" He set the mug down hard on the table.

Jacob raised his mug and started to drink the way Will had, but stopped midswallow. His eyes watered, too, but not from emotion. His throat stung and his stomach burned. "What *is* this?"

Will laughed. "You never had whiskey?"

"No, I haven't."

"Well, it's about time. What kind of a lumberjack are you, anyway?"

Will seemed pleased to have one up on him and that irritated Jacob.

"I never knew you to be a drinking man, William. What would Mother say? What would Bernie say?" As soon as the words were out of his mouth, he realized how righteous and uppity he sounded.

"Neither one of 'em needs to know about it, you hear

me?" He squinted at Jacob. "Anyway, it's only twice a year I do this," he pointed the mouth of the bottle at Jacob, "and now you're my accomplice." He poured more into his own mug. "Sip it, it goes down easier."

Jacob took a little swallow. Once he got used to the taste, he felt the whiskey warm and relax him. His arms and legs felt loose and heavy. He sighed and hung his head. "You're absolutely right about everything you said out there. I'm as guilty as he was." Surprised to find himself owning up to the truth, Jacob took another sip, then emptied the mug. "I'm really sorry, Will." He held it out so Will could refill it.

"Aw, you weren't as bad as him. You just never stood up for me; you never did anything to stop him; you never even said anything good about me."

"He terrified me."

"Will laughed. "You? The golden boy? You lie."

"After I saw how he treated you… If I didn't measure up, what would he do to me?"

"You think he'd kick your ass? You're crazy. You coulda robbed a bank and he woulda congratulated you for it."

"Cut it out."

"That bastard." Will spat the words with disgust, then swallowed from his mug.

"Can I ask you something?"

"What?"

"Did he hit you? Did he beat you? 'Cause he told me he did. And he said he'd do the same to me and worse if I didn't do what he wanted."

Will laughed bitterly and shook his head. "You expect me to believe that?"

"It's true. So did he hit you?"

"No. Worse."

"What?"

"He ignored me. I didn't exist. If he'd beat me, I'd know I meant somethin' to him. But, no, you were all the son he needed, always showin' you off like you were the prince of England or somethin'! I wanted that. I tried to please him; I wanted him to be proud of me, too, but he never once said, 'good job, son.' Hell, he never even called me *son*." Will gulped from his mug. "I couldn't do anything right, and the harder I tried, the worse it got." He paused. "Mother liked me, though. They used to fight about me."

"I remember." Jacob took another drink.

"I finally gave up. Might as well act the part. God, I hated working at that mill of his!"

"I know. Can't blame you for getting out."

"So what happened after I left?"

"He spent the whole day searching. By the time he checked the train station, you were long gone and nobody could remember seeing you. He acted crazy, *mad*. He woulda beat you if he found you. I stayed as far away from him as I could. When he told Mother you'd gone, she let him have it." Jacob sipped at his whiskey. "I'd never seen her like that before or since. She made it sound like he killed you. He didn't yell or fight her back, though."

"Yeah?"

"She wouldn't talk to him for weeks, threw him out of their bedroom. I don't know how long he slept in the spare room, months, maybe. But the next day he acted like nothing happened, business as usual. After that, I hated him as much as I loved him."

Will poured more into each mug. "A toast. To our *won-der-ful* family."

They hit their mugs together, and drank. "Another toast," said Jacob. "To brothers. Eddie or me. Whichever."

His lips felt like they did when he'd been out in the cold too long, thick and stiff. They clinked and drank.

"What do you mean *Eddie*?"

"You said *To Eddie Stern, the best friend a man could ever have, like a brother.* You sure act like you lost one."

Will rested his forehead in the palm of his left hand. "Oh, God!" He leaned over and buried his face in his elbow, still for a moment before his body shook with sobs.

Not wanting to feel his brother's fist again, Jacob kept his hands to himself. Anyway, when he turned his head the whole cabin spun in crazy angles, so he tried not to move.

"You have no idea what it's like." Will's voice come from under his elbow, muffled and whiney.

At first irritated then mad as a hornet, Jacob stared at his brother until he lifted his head and reached in his pocket for his handkerchief. In his drunken blur, Jacob leaned and brought his face close to Will's. "What's'at you say?"

"Huh? Oh. You have no idea—"

"You think *you're* the only one who ever went through this?"

"I'm sorry, Jacob, I forgot. Jacob?"

"Forget it." Jacob set his mug down with a smack. "Fill it up. *Brother.*" Tentatively he got up, afraid his legs wouldn't work. He went for the door.

"Where're you going?"

"Out."

"Use the bucket; you're too drunk to piss over the rail."

"Aye, aye, Cap'n." Jacob attempted a salute, but almost lost his balance.

"I hate that!"

"Sorry." Now Jacob slammed the door.

Outside, in clearer air, Jacob breathed in, deeply. Tiny

snowflakes drifted softly in the darkness. He exhaled, fighting with himself, angry that he'd remembered his own pain, doing his best to shove it back into the corners of his heart. He stood still by the bucket for a long time, watching the snowflakes disappear into the dark lake. In the cold air, he could focus his thoughts.

The cabin door opened with a nasty squeak.

"You still out there, Jacob?"

"Yep."

"Whaddaya doin'?"

"Thinkin'."

"Well, quit your thinkin' and get back in here and help me finish off this bottle."

Jacob stumbled through the door. He took one of the blankets from the bench, wrapped up in it and sat back down, across from his brother. "Aw-right. Here's what I propose." He took a drink. "You need a partner. I need to make amends. Tell me how much."

"Whaddarya talkin' about?"

"I'm offering to buy Eddie's share. Be your partner."

Will threw his head back and laughed. "You're gonna quit lumber to fish?"

"No. But I can keep you in biz-ness. Hire the derrick and get this nice little ship outta the water." Jacob patted the top of the table. "I'll pay for it."

"I said I don't want your damn lumber money! Didn't ya hear me?" The volume of Will's voice doubled.

"It's biz-ness, you fool. I'll be your partner. It means I share the profits. I share the expenses, but I get half the profits. Or whatever."

"I need a partner on the boat."

"Hire one. What about the boy?"

"Eddie's boy? Karl? His mother wouldn't let him set

foot off dry land."

"Find someone else, then. Whaddaya say?"

"I dunno, Jacob. It's that lumber money."

Jacob closed his eyes and saw red. "Listen to me." He opened them again and set his jaw before he spoke. "I *owe* you." He slapped his hand on the table, making the remaining whiskey jump and slosh back and forth in the bottle. "The Denver money belongs to you, too. Like it or not, you're still a Denn-ver!" His words slurred.

"Don't remind me." Will looked away.

"You're still my brother, Will-yam, for God's sake; the only brother I have." He waited for Will to turn back. "Let me do this, you *pig-headed idiot!* It's biz-ness. An invesst-ment. We can do it up all legal."

Will sat still for a minute, then spoke so softly Jacob barely heard him. "Y'sure?"

"You wanna keep the boat?"

"Yeah."

"Then I'm sure." Jacob held out his hand.

"Well. Awright, then." Will smiled a lopsided, drunken smile. "You got yourself a fishin' boat." He held his hand out to Jacob, but they couldn't connect. Will started to giggle. "Brother, we are *soused!*"

Jacob laughed, too. "One more toast."

Will emptied the bottle into the two mugs. They held them high in the air.

"To this fine little ship. To the *Maggie O'Keefe*."

"No, Jacob. To brothers. You and me." They hit the mugs together and drank the last of the whiskey down.

Chapter 9

Bleak Midwinter

Karl opened his eyes, punched his pillow and rolled over, staring into the darkness. He couldn't sleep, thinking about Uncle Melvin leaving his pants open and parading in front the girls. Thank God his sisters were too young to understand. Thank God they thought it was stupid and funny. Thank God they weren't scared to death by it, although maybe they should have been. And how dare he pinch Lizzie like that?

Karl's eyes closed again and he started to drift off. His body relaxed until he heard a confused jumble of Uncle Melvin's warnings. *Karl, be careful, for land's sake... Don't you fall on those chairs and break 'em, boy, or I'll take you behind the garage and use my belt... I'll make you into a man, and that's a promise... For your own good... For your Daddy... With my belt... Don't you fall on those chairs and break 'em, do you hear me? They're valuable antiques, boy, valuable antiques... I said, mind your own business.*

He started awake, out of breath, his heart banging in his chest. When Uncle Melvin sent him up to the spare room for the extra chairs before Thanksgiving dinner, he took the first two he found and carefully carried them down to the dining room. When he went back for the others, he saw a third chair, but couldn't find the fourth. Thinking it might be in the closet, he opened the door. What he saw and smelled filled him with disgust.

An ordinary walk-in closet, not more than five feet deep and width of the room, it reeked of urine soaked wood, like the backside of an outhouse where guys peed on the wall. The dirty gray walls might have been less noticeable if Aunt Kathleen had hung coats or dresses on the clothing rod, but the tangle of empty wire hangers couldn't hide a thing.

Karl guessed right about extra chairs being in the closet; there were two, but nobody could use either of them. One sat underneath the clothing rod, its caning stained and torn. Half the spindles attaching the seat to its high back were broken into splinters and three legs were askew. The whole thing looked like it would collapse if anyone sat on it.

He found the second chair in the corner, all smashed up. He stepped into the closet, bent over and picked up a piece from one of the legs. A nail protruded from its edge, the wood was streaked and caked with something dark. The instant he realized it was blood, he jerked his hand away, letting it fall to the wood floor. Stupid. What if someone heard? He stood absolutely still, holding his breath. Common sense told him to get out and look somewhere else for the fourth chair, but he couldn't ignore this.

As he took one more step, something crunched under his shoe; he looked down and saw shards of broken glass. Near the farthest corner of the closet, on a small shelf sat a broken bottle, jagged edges jutting dangerously from its perfect, unbroken neck. Lengths of rope hung tossed over three hooks; belts and dirty old handkerchiefs hung from others. This must be some kind of torture chamber.

Karl stepped out of the closet, closed the door soundlessly behind him, and took a deep breath, appreciating anew the aroma of roasting turkey and sweet potatoes. That's when he saw the fourth chair on the opposite side of the bed, covered with a pile of faded quilts. He put the quilts on the bed and took both chairs out of the room, stopping in the hallway to look back at the closet door. A key hung on a nail near the top of the molding. He wondered if he should go back and lock it and steal the key so he could throw it into the lake. For the rest of the day he thought about it, but in the end, he was too chicken.

Hours later, safe in his own bed, in his own house, Karl could still smell the overpowering stench of the closet. He felt a chill start in his chest that moved outward to his hands and feet. He wanted to tell his mother what he saw, he felt like he had to, but she'd been smiling when she came in to say goodnight, and he didn't want to spoil whatever made her happy. Maybe he should wait and tell her when she already felt bad about something else, but, no, that would only make things worse for her. Anyway, what would *she* be able to do about it?

Before the snow fell deep and heavy, Jimmy and Elmer invited Karl to stay after school for a game of basketball. Karl thought they wanted to be friends again, so he figured they'd understand why he couldn't stay.

"Sorry, fellas, I have to go home and help Mama."

Elmer laughed so hard he couldn't talk, but Jimmy exploded. "What is wrong with you? You used to go home late all the time, you never cared if you caught it from her before. I thought we were pals."

"Yeah, that's what I thought, too."

"So what's wrong? You turning into a pansy?"

"Come on, have a heart. My mother's still pretty upset about my father. Besides, there's chores to do, and I'm supposed to—"

"*Go home and help my Mama!*" Jimmy raised his wrists, letting his hands flap around while he pinched his knees together and pretended to walk like a girl. Suddenly he stopped. "Aww, see if we care! You never were good at basketball anyway, ya 'old clod!"

Elmer stopped laughing long enough to add his own ridicule. "We always knew you were a sissy, Stern. There's other guys who wanna play, we don't need you, so get outta here, you little mama's boy." He shoved Karl, who lost his balance and fell back against the playground fence.

After that, it was all over between them. Jimmy and Elmer and any other boys they could find snickered whenever Karl went by, whispering "Mama's boy" just loud enough for him to hear, but not the teachers. In the classrooms, they stuck their feet out between the desks and tripped him, and laughed when the sisters would look up and scold Karl for causing such a commotion. Karl decided he had no reason to have friends anymore.

Every Sunday afternoon between Thanksgiving and Christmas, Uncle Melvin showed up to talk to Karl's mother, trying to convince her to change her mind and move her family into his house. Each time he came, Karl excused himself to do homework, but instead of going to his room, he sat at the top of the stairs, listening.

He thought of his sisters, glad they were spending every Sunday afternoon in December at the school's *Christmas Club,* making gifts with the Sisters.

The first week, Aunt Kathleen came with Uncle Melvin, so Maggie poured coffee and offered cookies. Uncle Melvin started out sweetly, "Come on, Margaret, you *know* it would be best for *all* of you. Kathleen wants you to come, too, isn't that right, dear?"

"I'd love to have her, but I think we should let Maggie decide for herself, Melvin. She knows what's best for her—"

"What're you talking about?" Uncle Melvin laughed. "You're as foolish as she is." He laughed some more. "*She knows what's best,* that's the funniest thing I've heard all day! You two have more hanging on your chests than you have in your heads, and that's not saying much since neither one of you has much up front. Ha, ha, ha!"

Karl wanted to go down and punch Uncle Melvin in the nose, but he heard his mother tell him to leave. Kathleen could stay, but Melvin had to go. Of course, Melvin ordered her to put on her coat and get in the car.

Karl dreamed about the closet that night.

The second Sunday, Uncle Melvin came alone, saying that Aunt Kathleen didn't feel well. Karl's mother wouldn't listen to any talk about moving into the Straus residence, but wrapped a few pieces of cake for him to take home for Aunt Kathleen. Karl sat on the steps and rolled his eyes. He imagined Melvin stuffing his mother's chocolate cake into his mouth as he drove home. Didn't she know Aunt Kathleen wouldn't get one bite of it?

The following week was awful for Karl. In addition

to daily chapel services, Father Cunningham led Mass for the whole school each Friday morning. Father began his sermon by saying that the Holy Christmas season is the time to give of ourselves, since God gave of Himself when he sent his Only Begotten Son to be our Lord. He gave examples of people who gave of themselves, like the women from the parish who went to visit the sick every week and the Sisters who loved and taught the pupils from Holy Angels, and all those who brought their offerings to church with glad and generous hearts. Father looked at Lizzie, and then at Karl, and started talking about a fine Christian man named Mr. Straus, who gave a great deal to the church. Jesus surely lived in the heart of this man, said Father Cunningham, because he wanted to do even more. Mr. Straus offered to give a home to some poor, needy relatives who were, at that *very* minute, cruelly refusing his generous kindness in the same way sinful mankind cruelly refused God's generosity by crucifying His only Begotten Son, Jesus, the Savior.

Karl felt his face burn, but he kept his eyes fixed on Father Cunningham. He tried to appear indifferent to the priest while ignoring his own anger and pain, like the Greek Stoics his class studied. After Father finished his lecture, Lizzie looked back toward Karl, but jerked around again when her teacher snapped her fingers sharply. Their eyes never met.

After communion, Karl passed the pew where Jimmy and Elmer sat. He assumed they wouldn't trip him because they were in church, but suddenly, Elmer extended his leg into the aisle. Before Karl could step high or to the side to avoid it, his foot caught Elmer's leg and down he went, face first, hitting his elbow on the back of the pew. A titter spread across the rows where the seventh and eighth graders sat, but it stopped immediately when the school principal, Sister Mary Anthony, appeared in the aisle. She bent over, grabbed his collar and dragged him to his feet, popping two buttons from his shirt. The bread stuck in the back of his mouth and he began to choke on it. As he hacked and coughed and tried to breathe, she boxed his ears and pushed him onto the last pew in the back, leaving him all alone. Even as she humiliated him in front of the whole school, Karl marveled at the strength of this tall, skinny old woman.

"After the benediction—to the sacristy, young man!" She whispered so loud Karl thought even the priest could hear her.

While removing his vestments, Father Cunningham let him have it.

"How old are you now, Karl?"

"Thirteen."

"Real-ly?" He undid the long row of buttons running down the front of his cassock, but didn't take it off. He leaned over the chair where Karl sat, his hands on its arms, the black tent of his cassock confining the young offender. "Then why do you want to play on the floor like a two year old?"

"Father, I—"

"You distracted your classmates from their prayers. In fact you even got a laugh out of them. You must be quite proud of yourself."

"No, I—"

"You never did this sort of thing before your father died, what's wrong with you? I'll tell you what's wrong.

You wanted me to pray for him to live and I didn't, so you blame his death on me—correct?"

"No, Father."

"And you get your revenge by mocking me, mocking the Lord. Correct?"

"No, Father. Would you please listen to me?"

Father Cunningham frowned. "Speak." He moved away, took off the cassock and hung it in the closet.

Karl cleared his throat, still raw from all the coughing. "Father, I tripped and fell, that's what happened. I'm very sorry."

"According to your teachers you seem to be tripping a lot lately. You've become the class clown, I hear." The priest looked in the mirror, took a comb from his back pocket and ran it over his thinning gray hair.

"No, Father, it's not like that."

"You want attention, now you'll get it." He looked away from the mirror and back at Karl. "Since you seem to like the floor so much, you will come tomorrow with a bucket and rags, and you will spend the day scrubbing the whole sanctuary floor. Sister Mary Anthony will give you plenty of attention while you're on your knees. You'll start after early Mass, in fact, I expect you here for Mass; seven o'clock sharp. Now go to class and get out of my sight. It's time for my breakfast."

"Yes, Father."

But as he stood up to leave, Father Cunningham stopped him. "One more thing, Mr. Stern. Tell your mother she's a fool for refusing your Uncle's offer. Not only do you people need the money, *you* need the discipline of a real man."

Back at home, Karl said nothing of the sort to his mother. He only told her what happened at Mass because he had to scrub the church floors the next day.

Karl got to Holy Angels at five minutes to seven the next morning and sat in the back pew with his bucket, scrub brush and rags. The only people who came to this Mass were the Sisters and a few old women from the neighborhood. Afterward, he waited for Sister Mary Anthony at the sanctuary door, but everyone seemed to have disappeared. He went to the janitor's closet and filled his bucket with warm water. When he came out, Sister Anne, his history and geography teacher—his *favorite* teacher—was waiting for him. She held a bucket, too.

"Hello, Karl. It looks like we're going to be spending the day together."

"I thought Father said it would be Sister Mary Anthony."

"You're disappointed?" She smiled at him, a little twinkle in her eye.

"No, I meant—"

"Father has a way of committing us to things without consulting us. Sister Mary Anthony has gone to Duluth. Her niece is getting married this afternoon. So I told him I would supervise you, instead. Where should we begin? We've got a lot of ground to cover."

"Sister, *I'm* supposed to do this."

"And I'm supposed to stand over you with a ruler, but we're not going to do it that way. Now, should we start in the front or the back?"

They decided to get the floor nice and shiny in the front where Father Cunningham would notice it the most. He would start listening to confessions at three o'clock and they had to be finished by then. If they ran out of time, at least the unfinished part would be in the back where he might overlook it.

Karl took Sister Anne's bucket to fill it for her. He'd started the day with nothing but bad and angry feelings, but having her there instead of Sister Mary Anthony made him want to cry. He ran the water a long time, trying to swallow the lump in his throat.

"Karl?" Sister said from in the hall. "We've got a lot to do."

He filled her bucket and came out. "Sorry, Sister." She tried to take it from him, but he wouldn't let her carry it. He walked on ahead of her, looking down.

"Stop, Karl. Now." She spoke sharply. "Please put the buckets down and look at me."

Sister Anne, barely five feet tall and a little on the heavy side, had sparkling eyes and a gentle smile. Every so often, Karl noticed gray hairs poking out from the sides of her wimple, so he thought she might be as old as his grandmother, maybe even older. Sister Anne couldn't be intimidating to him if she tried, but he always did what she told him to do because he liked her.

"Let me tell you that I think this whole thing is terribly unfair to you. I've been watching those other boys fall into the devil's trap of kicking someone when he's down because it makes them feel big and powerful."

"But Father Cunningham—"

"Even adults fall into that trap. Even sisters and priests, sometimes even our own family members do it. But I want you to believe me when I say I am not going to do that to you."

She put her warm hand on his arm. The lump in Karl's throat won out; his eyes filled with tears. Quickly, he wiped his eyes with his sleeve, and looked around to make sure they were alone.

"Please don't tell, Sister," he whispered.

"Tell what?"

"That I..."

"That you cried?"

Karl nodded and put his index finger up to his lips. "Shh! Please? Father Cunningham said I'm supposed to be strong, and Uncle Melvin said he'd take his belt after me if he heard about me crying."

"Oh, for heaven's sake. No, I will *not* tell. That's another example of kicking someone when he's down. Remember, your uncle can't see what you do *all* the time... but you should be careful all the same. Now, let's get busy."

They started washing the smooth stone floor near the altar. Karl felt funny being so close to the place where Father Cunningham turned the bread into the Body of Christ, especially when he saw a serpent carved into the stone floor.

"Sister," he whispered, "what's this snake doing here?"

She stopped scrubbing for a moment. "It stands for Satan."

"What?"

"Genesis 3:15. *And I will put enmity between thee and the woman, and between thy seed and her seed; it shall bruise thy head, and thou shalt bruise his heel.* The Lord's words to the serpent in the garden when Adam and Even first sinned. The seed of the woman—the Blessed Mother—is Christ, who defeated evil when he gave his life in sacrifice for our sins. The serpent on the floor stands for Satan. The priest stands on its head when he celebrates Mass."

"Oh. I never noticed it before."

"Most people don't, and if they do, they don't know what it means. You'll see another carving over in the alcove, near the votives. That one shows Mary standing on the serpent. We had a stone cutter in the parish a long time ago. You'll find his carvings all over the building. They were his gift to the church."

Karl thought about Uncle Melvin, an evil snake, for sure. Father Cunningham must not realize it. He tried to imagine Father standing on Melvin's head, but couldn't.

They kept scrubbing. When the water in the buckets got dirty, Karl would empty them and refill them with clean warm water while Sister Anne rested. As they worked, she explained many things to him, things he'd been looking at all his life and never even wondered about. In the baptistery, she told him that the font had eight sides because Easter was considered the eighth day of creation, when Christ made all things new. The same thing happens when a person is baptized. She told him the names of the angels in the big stained glass window above the altar, and she told him stories about the saints on the side windows.

In the back, near the confessional booth, light shone through a stained glass window of a woman kneeling before Jesus. You couldn't see her face because she was bent over wiping his feet with her long reddish hair. Karl remembered hearing the Bible story read somewhere.

"That woman was a prostitute, wasn't she?"

"Yes, but she repented and the Lord forgave her. So she kissed his feet and cried, wiping her tears away with her hair. This window is by the confessional because this is where we come to repent." With difficulty, Sister Anne got up off her knees. "We need a break. I have some soup for our lunch. I'm going to the kitchen to warm it up."

"My mother sent a sandwich for me, Sister."

"You need something hot, too; you've been working awfully hard." They'd washed the floors in the chancel of the church, the center aisle and both side aisles. "I'm afraid you are going to have to wash under the pews by yourself, Karl. I don't think I could crawl around underneath them like you can. And I am worn out. But I'll stay and keep you company."

"Thank you, Sister."

While they were eating Sister Anne's split pea soup, she said, "I've been doing all the talking this morning. Now it's your turn. Tell me, other than the nastiness going on here at school, how are you and how are things at home?"

"I'm okay."

"You seem to have a lot on your mind these days."

"Yeah. I mean, yes, I do."

"How is your mother doing?"

"All right, I guess, but everyone in the family wants us to move in with Uncle Melvin and Aunt Kathleen and we don't want to, so my mother is a little nervous."

"Why does that make her nervous?"

"I don't know if I should talk about it."

"You can trust me, Karl; I'm not going to repeat anything you say unless you give me permission to do so."

He couldn't imagine giving a teacher permission for *anything*. He looked into Sister Anne's eyes and believed her. "Uncle Melvin keeps coming over and bothering us. We don't like him because he picks on people."

"How?"

"Well, he pinched Lizzie for no reason, where... He shouldn't have touched her there, Sister. She got really upset about it. And at his house there's this, this—and he said next time he'd have a *love pinch* for Anna, too, but she said she'd step on his foot if he tried." He laughed, remembering the way she stomped her little foot.

Sister Anne laughed with him. "That Anna, she is something special, isn't she? Well, you all are. Your mother, too." Sister Anne had been Maggie's first grade teacher.

"Thank you for the soup, Sister, but I think I'd better get back to work now."

"Yes, indeed. I'll clean up here and be along in a few minutes."

As Karl began washing the floors under the front pews, Mrs. Buckley, the music teacher and church organist, arrived to practice her music. Sister Anne came a few minutes later and sat down on the fourth pew from the front. When Karl looked at her, she smiled and put her finger up to her lips. He smiled back, nodded, and went back to work.

Sometimes the music sounded fierce, sometimes dissonant, but mostly it felt to Karl like it came from some other world. Even as he crawled and scrubbed, he felt it take him a whole world away from Elmer and Jimmy and Father Cunningham and Uncle Melvin, to a place beyond their hurting him. *Maybe time would stop for a while if I could hide here under the pews* he thought. *I could rest, and when I came out everything would be all right again.* But Karl knew things didn't work that way. His father was the only one with the power to chase away all the bad things that were happening, and he was dead. Even though he thought about this a lot, he didn't feel like crying anymore. Maybe it was because Sister Anne cared about him.

When he went for more clean water, he found her slouched over in the pew, leaning on the side, resting her head on her arm. It scared him until he saw her breathe deeply, rhythmically. She'd fallen asleep. He went on working, making sure not to disturb her.

The whole church began to smell fresh and clean and Karl imagined sending all the bad things in his life down the drain when he dumped the dirty water in the sink. Heaven must be like this: peaceful, with beautiful music and someone who truly cared keeping a steadfast watch over him. It was the first comfort he'd felt since his father died. He smiled, knowing that's not what Father Cunningham had in mind.

Sister Anne woke up when Mrs. Buckley stopped playing. Karl finished, too, except for the floor underneath Sister.

"I'm afraid I haven't been much company for you this afternoon, Karl. I apologize."

"Oh, yes, you were. I liked having you here even if you were napping."

She smiled at him. "Thank you."

"Thank *you*, for everything. I'll see you tomorrow." He started to leave then turned back. "Sister, you are the only reason I can stand to come here."

"Oh, dear, Karl. People can be so evil, but God is good, God is *always* good."

"I'd like to believe that. Anyway, *you're* not evil, you're good."

Father Cunningham came in the door, wearing his cassock, carrying a little black book. "Leaving so soon, Karl? Did he finish, Sister?"

"Yes, he did, and you may inspect it. He did a fine job. You may go, Karl. Remember what I said. God is good,

God is *always* good."

"Yes, Sister. Good-bye, Father."

But the priest didn't answer. He was too busy inspecting the floor as he went to the confessional.

Chapter 10

Huge

On Sunday, Uncle Melvin came alone again, saying Aunt Kathleen wouldn't be well enough to leave the house for some time. He said she needed a woman to take care of her, and who better than her own sister? Besides Karl was in big trouble and needed the discipline of a man. "He has a bad attitude toward school and the Church, and it's getting worse by the day. If you don't do something soon, he'll burn in hell. Is that what you want? If you move in with us, I could adopt him and your girls, be their new father and give them a solid future, on earth and in the hereafter. What do you say?"

"Go home, Melvin."

"You know you need my money... and some of this..."

Karl heard noises from his mother, like she was struggling; a slap, then her furious voice.

"Melvin Straus, don't you ever put your hands on me again!"

"*Damn!*" Uncle Melvin laughed. "You're all grown up and now you're twice the woman your sister is. *Damn!*"

"Out—get *out* of here!"

"I'll be back, sweetheart."

"*Leave!*"

The door slammed, the lock turned, and Karl hurried back to his room. His mother stormed up the steps, went into the bathroom, locked the door and threw up. When he sat down at his desk, he realized he'd pulled his hands into fists again. Yesterday's peace faded like a ghost in the air.

He heard her crying and couldn't take it anymore. He got up and knocked on the door.

"Are you all right in there, Mama? Do you need anything?"

She didn't answer. Karl got madder by the second.

"Mother! What did he *do* to you?" He didn't mean to yell so loud.

"Just a minute, Karl."

He heard the faucet run while she brushed her teeth. She spit over and over while he stood in front of the door like a pop gun, all cocked and ready to blow. Maggie finally opened the door, her mouth contorted.

"Are you okay?"

"I think so. You were listening, weren't you?"

Karl nodded. "I'm sorry I didn't come down and punch him in the nose! What did he do to you?" He lifted his fists. His mother covered them with her hands and gently pushed them down until his arms hung at his sides.

"Settle down, now. Melvin—" She looked at the wall and not at Karl. "He kissed me and touched me like only Daddy was allowed to—only a husband." She stepped back into the bathroom to spit and rinse her mouth again. "Are you almost finished with your homework?"

"Yes," he lied.

"Get your coat; we're going to Will and Bernie's."

"Don't you think you should rest a few minutes?"

"No, I need to get out of here." Her voice trembled.

"Mama, you're scaring me."

"I'm scared, too, but we're going to hold our ground. After what he did, under no circumstances will we move in with them." She went back to the sink to spit and rinse her mouth again. "Ever."

Karl let his mother hold on to his arm as they walked. She seemed a little unsteady and every time she heard a car come from behind she would look over her shoulder and lean in a bit closer to him. On the surface, Karl felt calmer, but his anger and dread went beyond trembling hands and a pounding heart. They went deeper now, into a cave he dug for them in the core of his being. Maybe he could store them there and they wouldn't bother him anymore. He wondered if he should tell her about Uncle Melvin's closet. No, she was already upset enough. Besides, what happened today practically guaranteed they wouldn't move in with him.

Bernie welcomed them with open arms, happy to see them, as always. She bustled around the kitchen, filling the tea kettle and setting some sweets out on a plate for them. Will came up from the basement when he heard their voices.

Will looked at Maggie and furrowed his brow. "What's wrong?"

Tears puddled in her eyes and spilled onto her cheeks.

Karl answered. "It's Uncle Melvin. He keeps bothering

us, and today he hurt her."

"How?" asked Will. "Do you need a doctor?"

She shook her head and cried, all slouched over like an old woman.

Bernie came and put her arms around her. "Now sit down and tell us what happened, Love. Do you want Karl and Will to go downstairs so you can tell me in private?"

"No. Karl already knows." She wiped her eyes. "I've always felt safe in our house. Until today."

"Uncle Melvin came over and said I'm going to burn in hell if he doesn't adopt us."

"Oh, for pity's sake," Bernie sat down. "What, now he thinks he's the Lord God A'mighty?"

Maggie shivered. "He came without Kathleen and kissed me on the mouth with his big sloppy... He had his hands all over me and he twisted my arm and... He said he was coming back, too."

"I shoulda taken a swing at him!" Karl punched his left palm with his right fist. He looked at his mother. "I'm supposed to watch out for you and I messed up again. I'm sorry, Mama."

Will shook his finger at Karl. "Listen to me, boy— you're no match for him. He weighs double what you do and thinks he has the law in his pocket. Don't you try fighting him, 'cause you'll lose." He turned to Maggie. "You shouldn't be alone. You're staying here tonight."

Karl remembered his homework. "No, we can go home. I'll sleep downstairs on the davenport; I can take care of him if he comes back."

"What did I just tell you? Don't you do *anything* to him!"

"What am I supposed to do if he comes back, stand by

and watch him hurt my family some more?"

"You're not the one to fight this. If you try, believe me, it will backfire on you. Stay out of it."

Will's gruffness didn't scare Karl. Even though they were arguing, Karl wished he could be their father. He'd be much better at it than Uncle Melvin could ever be.

"Willie, it would be awright with me if you spent the night at Maggie's." Bernie touched Will's hand. "I'll make up a bedroll for you and you could go to work from there in the morning. That way Maggie and the kids can get a good night's sleep, knowin' Melvin would have to face you first if he came back."

"Sure, I could do that. What do you say, Maggie?"

"Thanks, but you should be with your own family."

"My Mum is just a call away, and I have cousins who would come if we needed help. But we're not the ones with trouble, Love. You are."

"This isn't your problem." Maggie started to cry again.

"It is, too, my problem." Will leaned across the table and took Maggie's hands. "Listen, now, if it'd been me in the drink and Eddie was still here, he'd be taking care of my family—that's the way we were." He leaned back in his chair. "I've been thinking, we need to get you a telephone so you can call for help when you need it."

"I can't afford a telephone."

"Let me worry about it."

"Will..."

"I'm setting it up for you tomorrow, no more discussion."

"Karl!" Billy came swooping into the kitchen, just up from his nap. "Play with us!"

Neddie came behind him, rubbing his eyes. "Hi, Karl.

Play horsie?"

Karl couldn't help smiling. "All right, for a few minutes, I think we're leaving soon."

"Horsie!"

The two little boys each took an arm and dragged Karl
into the living room. He laughed and gave them rides on
his back, walking, trotting, and even bucking. Like yesterday, as he crawled around under the pews, he felt like he'd
escaped to another world where things were simple and
happy. If there really *was* a heaven, he thought, it would
have to be like this, full of laughter and innocence and
little boys who liked him and wanted to play with him.

Karl didn't bother with his bedtime prayers that night.
When he tried to imagine Jesus standing on Uncle Melvin's
head, like the priest standing on the serpent, he could only
hear Father Cunningham's voice saying Jesus *surely* lived in
Mr. Straus' heart. If that was true, he didn't want anything
to do with Jesus or God. Ever.

On Monday, Will came by with a man Karl had never
met before. He was shorter than Karl, hefty and muscular,
with a round face, a brown moustache and only a little
hair on the top of his head. One arm curled around a
bedroll while the other held a lunch pail.

Maggie hurried from the kitchen, drying her hands
on a dishtowel. Will introduced them to David Johansen,
his coworker and friend from the foundry. Mr. Johansen
would spend the night on their davenport, like Will did
the night before.

"I have men lined up for every night this week," he
told Maggie, "they're all men you can trust, you have my
word on it. They'll keep watch for you. And we'll all come

back next week, too, if you need us. Would you be able to fill their lunch buckets?"

"This is an awful lot to ask of people who don't even know me, Will."

"Will told us what happened." Mr. Johansen stood with his feet far apart, arms bent at the elbows and hands curved into loose fists. "If it was our wives or daughters or sisters, we'd want someone to help them. It's the right thing to do."

Karl smiled a little and nodded to his new ally. He still thought *he* should be the one sleeping downstairs. Well, maybe. Maybe not. He didn't know what he would do if Uncle Melvin came around again. Will was probably right; he shouldn't try to fight him.

Karl's mother reached out for Mr. Johansen's lunch pail. "I'll take care of this for you."

The next night, Mr. Wallis came; and on Wednesday it was Mr. Berg, the grocer; on Thursday their mailman, Mr. Curtis, stayed; and Friday it was Oskar Anderson, who docked his boat next to the *Maggie O'Keefe* in the summer. Melvin never showed up, although Karl saw him drive by the house shortly after Mr. Curtis arrived on Thursday. He felt his heart race, waiting for him to pull off the road and get out of the car, but he drove on without stopping. After that, Karl let go of the idea he could somehow protect his mother. He saw her relax as soon as the guardian of the night walked in the door, so he relaxed, too.

With Christmas just over a week away, Maggie began decorating the house while Karl and his sisters were in school.

"How can we have Christmas without Daddy?" he asked after he put the afternoon coal in the furnace.

"Christmas comes no matter what else happens, Karl. It's a Holy Day, we should at least acknowledge it. Besides, your sisters are looking forward to it."

"Mama, we can't afford—"

She smiled. "Aunt Mary gave me some money so we could have a nice Christmas. So, we're going to have a nice Christmas, with a few surprises. I think we should go out and find a tree on Saturday. What do you think?"

"Who's gonna put it up?"

"You are. You're strong enough, and I know you're tall enough to decorate the top. I'll help. We can do it together."

"But Daddy won't be here!" He whined like a one of the girls.

"Listen, Karl." Maggie finished arranging the little wooden nativity on the mantle. She put the baby Jesus in the wobbly matchstick manger and turned to him. "It doesn't matter if we have a tree or not; either way your father won't be here. So I've decided to make the best of it. It's what he would tell us to do."

So on Saturday, Karl, his mother and his sisters dragged a little fir home from the nursery at the edge of town. They laughed and had a good time in the snow, even Karl. They passed Elmer and Jimmy hanging around outside the drugstore on the way home. The boys snickered and threw a snowball when Karl went by, but he didn't care about them anymore.

Bringing the tree home made Karl realize he didn't have gifts for his mother or for his sisters. Later on, when Will came to keep watch, he asked him for advice.

"You wanna make something for them?"

"I dunno. What could *I* make?"

Will looked around for Maggie and went on when he heard her upstairs with the girls. "I've been doing some woodworking, and I have a few extra boards. Have you ever seen a woodburning?"

"You mean a fire?"

Will threw his head back and laughed. "No, no, it's where you burn designs and words into wood with a special tool. I can show you how to do it and you can make pictures for them to hang on the wall. It shouldn't take too long and they'd be nice presents."

"I'm not very good at art, Will."

"Well, then, you could burn words into the wood instead."

"What would I write?"

"You'll have to come up with that yourself. Bring your mother over tomorrow afternoon—Melvin usually comes then, doesn't he? She can have tea with Bernie and we can work on the presents. Maybe you'll miss his weekly visit."

The next day, Karl and his mother walked to Will and Bernie's. The ladies laughed and giggled about something while they had tea; Karl thought his mother sounded a whole lot better than she did a week ago.

In the basement, Will made Karl sand his three pine squares until they were like velvet on all sides, then showed him how to use the drill to make holes for hanging. With a pencil, Karl wrote on the wood so he'd have a pattern to go by once he was ready to burn. It took two or three tries before he had anything worth making permanent, but when he did, he liked the power he felt as he dragged the red hot stylus over the wood. He liked the smell of burning wood, too. It helped him forget about the bad stuff he'd been shoving into his cave.

He decided to make name plaques for the girls to hang in their room, like the one in Sister Mary Anthony's office. For his mother, he wrote three words he'd seen on an embroidery hanging in Bernie's kitchen: *Home Sweet Home*. None of them were fancy, but he liked the way they turned out. Will kept them in his basement, saying he'd have Bernie tie some ribbons on to dress them up.

They left Will's house a bit later than they'd planned, so they had to hurry to the school to meet Lizzie and Anna, then rush home because they expected Mr. Johansen before dark. When they arrived, light already shone through the windows of 617 Blight, and Melvin's Model T stood out front like it belonged there.

"Mama, he's in the house," said Karl.

Anna took his hand.

"Oh, for pity's sake, how did he get in? I locked both doors."

Karl wished for a huge foot to come down from heaven to squash Uncle Melvin, he even prayed for it, sort of. He heard laughter and knew it came from down the block, but he imagined all of heaven laughing at them.

Lizzie reached for Maggie. "I'm scared, Mama."

"Just stay with me. Come on, everyone. It is our house, after all."

The front door opened without the key. Inside, Grandma O'Keefe sat on the davenport, her face pinched into a sour frown; Uncle Melvin had made himself comfortable on the easy chair.

"Where have you been?" Grandma's Irish upbringing came out every time she got angry like this, her brogue becoming shrill the louder she talked. Karl found it almost

A. PETERSON

unbearable to listen to her.

"What are you two doing in my house?" Maggie replied. "I locked the doors."

"You gave me a key once, remember?" Grandma held it out in the palm of her hand. "We came to see you, and when you weren't here, I let us in."

"I'd like it back, please. Give me the key." Maggie reached for it, her mother snapped her hand closed and held it against her chest.

"No." Grandma smiled slightly when she said it.

Uncle Melvin stood up. "You kids get upstairs and do your homework. We have something to discuss with your mother."

Maggie nodded. "Go on, girls."

Anna and Lizzie hurried to gather their things and ran up the stairs, looking over their shoulders, wide-eyed.

Karl didn't move. "I'm not going anywhere unless my mother tells me to."

Melvin went for his belt buckle. "Upstairs!"

"No, Karl, stay here. And leave your belt on, Melvin. Whatever you and Mother have to say to me, you can say in front of him."

Karl stood next to his mother. He balled his hands into fists.

Melvin produced an envelope filled with money from his jacket pocket. "Where did you get all this?"

"It's none of your business." Maggie reached for it. Melvin snatched it away. "Give it back!"

"Not until you tell us how you got it, Margaret."

"You tell me how *you* got it. How dare you go through my things!"

"We didn't have to go through anything," said Grandma. "We found it on the mantel, behind the clock. Where *on*

128 —

earth did you get that kind of money?"

"I don't have to tell you."

Maggie reached for the envelope again and Melvin grabbed her forearm and twisted it, while holding the envelope away from her in his other hand. Karl's rage rose high from the cave where he'd hidden it a week ago. He felt his face burn. He lunged for the envelope and took it.

Melvin released Maggie's arm and took a quick step toward Karl as if to strike him, and backed away just as fast. "Keep your whore money. It's nothing but filthy lucre."

Karl stepped toward Melvin with his fists up. "Be careful what you call my mother."

"Get away from him, Karl." Never had he seen his mother's eyes burn so hot with her anger. Karl did what she said. "What on earth are you talking about?"

Grandma stood up. "My good friend Mrs. Schmidt has been keeping an eye on you." Mrs. Schmidt lived next door, but she'd never been much of a neighbor. "She came to visit me yesterday and said she's seen strange men coming and going from here at all hours. Never in my life did I think one of my daughters would sell herself for money. I'm ashamed of you, Margaret!"

Someone knocked on the door. Karl opened it and let Mr. Johansen in. Nobody spoke.

The man looked around the room, from one face to another. "Excuse me, Mrs. Stern, am I interrupting something?"

"How *dare* you take advantage of my daughter with her children present?" Grandma looked over her glasses at Mr. Johansen.

"Come in, Mr. Johansen; take off your coat." Maggie started to laugh, like she'd heard a good joke. "Mother, this is David Johansen. Mr. Johansen, this is my mother, Isabelle O'Keefe. And this is my brother-in-law, Melvin Straus. They think I'm a prostitute."

The way his mother laughed scared Karl.

Mr. Johansen put down his bedroll and stood the same way he did the first time he came, ready to fight. "I can assure you that the lady is doing nothing of the sort. Will Denver has arranged for a man to be here every night, to protect her and her children from the likes of you, Mr. Straus."

"Very interesting," said Melvin. "Will Denver is a panderer. What next?"

"If you're not selling yourself, explain the money, Margaret." Grandma's voice cackled like an old hen.

Mr. Johansen moved slowly until he stood at Maggie's other side, the three of them in a line: the boy, his mother and the night watchman. Karl put his arm around his mother's shoulders. Her eyes flashed in anger, her muscles tensed and she began to shake. She didn't answer.

Melvin took over. "You're nearly beyond hope, Margaret, but I'm here to rescue you and your children from such a corrupt life as you have chosen. Unless I help you now, you'll take your children down the road to eternal perdition. Karl, go pack your things and tell your sisters to do the same. You're coming home with me."

"We are not on the way to *eternal perdition* and I will not hand my children over to you or to anyone else."

Mr. Johansen stepped up close to Melvin. His arms were thick with muscle, his body stocky and strong. "It's time for you to leave, sir, and please take Mrs. O'Keefe with you. Now."

Grandma snatched her coat from the peg by the door. "Come on, Melvin. Enough of this. Maybe we should send the law to see what's going on here."

"Good i-dea." Melvin turned on his heel and went out the door with a smirk on his face. "I think I'll call the sheriff as soon as I get home."

Grandma followed him, scowling.

Karl expected his mother to collapse into a heap on the floor crying, but she went to the door and locked it. With tears still in her eyes, she laughed crazy again. "A lot of good that's going to do!"

Karl could see her hands shake.

"Mrs. Stern, until you can get your landlord to change the locks, we need to put some kind of bolt on the doors, something you can only open from the inside."

"I know, I'll ask Will tomorrow."

"No, you need them tonight. I have some bolts in my workshop at home. If I could use your telephone, I'll call Will and ask him to get my son to bring them over with my tools. We can install them yet tonight."

The telephone. Karl had forgotten all about it. It came on Wednesday; Will asked them to rush the job.

"Oh, I can't trouble everyone like that!"

"Mama, Will would be mad if you didn't call him. This is why he got you the telephone."

Maggie handed her coat to Karl. "All right. I'm going to fix some supper. Please tell them to plan on eating with us." She turned, muttering to herself. "Why on earth would all these people care about us?"

For Karl, the encounter with his Grandma and Uncle Melvin was awful beyond telling. Before he fell asleep that night, he replayed the terrible scene in his head. "Jesus, I waited for your foot to crush Uncle Melvin, but you didn't come." He sighed and shoved his disappointment down into his cave.

Then, for some reason, he remembered Mr. Johansen's work boots sitting by the back door. They were worn, they were dirty—and they were huge.

Chapter 11

Pardoned and Rebuked

That week in school, Karl watched where he stepped, especially in the lunchroom, especially in church. Elmer, Jimmy, and now some of the other boys kept stretching their legs out in front of him in the classrooms, but he was cautious enough not to trip, not even once.

The problem was, he looked like a buffoon with all his stepping over and stepping sideways. Now he didn't have to fall on his face to make his classmates laugh. His teachers quit frowning at him and started threatening him with the ruler if he didn't stop acting like a clown. Except for Sister Anne. She sent Elmer, Johnny and two other boys to Sister Mary Anthony with a note. When they came back to school the next day, they all had bruised knuckles, which they compared and bragged about at recess.

After the knuckle rapping, the taunting stopped and Karl relaxed. But on Friday, the last day of school before Christmas, it started up again, in the church, during Mass. Like last time, Elmer slid his leg out as Karl passed by, tripping him and making him stumble. This time, though, Karl didn't fall, and this time, he didn't keep quiet about it.

"Stop it. Just *stop!*" Everyone heard him, and everyone heard his voice crack on the word *stop*. As he went by, he scooped up his books from where he'd been sitting but didn't bother with his coat. He bolted down the rest of the aisle with the slapping of Sister Mary Anthony's shoes following him, to the vestibule with the sound of Father Cunningham trying to maintain order in the sanctuary, out the door with its heavy slamming behind him. He did not look back. Everything he'd stored in his cave screamed furiously to get out, but he kept walking, pretending he didn't hear Sister Mary Anthony calling him.

"Karl Stern, you come back here, this instant!"

As he turned toward home, he started to shiver. The wind blew snow at him, hard little pellets, nothing beautiful or soft about it. Without his coat, the walk home felt longer than it really was, but he didn't care. Let it be his penance. He had enough of that school, those people, that church.

Finally, Karl rounded the corner onto his own street. He went to the back door and turned the knob. It was locked. He banged on the window, but his mother didn't answer. He scurried around to the front, but that was locked, too. He followed his own tracks to the back door again, rattled the knob, knocked, and pounded. Where did she go? He picked up a big hunk of snow with his bare hands and hurled it against the fence. "Dammit!" For once, he said it out loud.

He brushed a patch of snow off the back stoop and sat down, folding his arms against his chest, drawing his legs in close to the rest of his body for warmth. He rested his forehead on his knees and cried, finally letting the cave empty itself. How did life get so horrible?

Snow began to fill the space between the collar of his

shirt and his neck; it settled in his hair, too, without melting. He wheezed and coughed. He had no idea how long he'd been there. Maybe he should forget about breathing, close his eyes and never wake up.

He wheezed again but stifled the cough when he heard the sound of a car stopping, a door slamming shut and someone pounding on the front door.

"Margaret! Answer this door!" Uncle Melvin, who else?

From the back stoop, Karl looked for the tracks he'd left in the snow. They were gone; the wind had erased them. He sat still, trying hard not to breathe or cough.

"Let me in, Margaret. I have a message for Karl from Father Cunningham."

"He's in school." His mother was in the house all along. Why didn't she hear *him* pounding?

"He is *not* in school. He left Mass in a huff after making a big fuss again. Where is he?"

"I don't know."

"I don't believe you."

"He's not here."

"Let me come in and look."

"No!"

"Well, I suppose he'll turn up sooner or later," said Melvin. "He left school without his coat."

"What? When?"

"Father called me as soon as the Mass was over. Your son is in trouble, *big* trouble. I've been driving around looking for him for almost an hour and I need to go back to work. Are you sure he isn't in there?"

"Yes, I'm sure."

"Well, I have some words for that boy. He needs a piece of my belt, and he's going to get it. You obviously can't control those children of yours, so I'll have to do it for you. I'll be back after work, and he'd better be here."

Karl heard Melvin get back into the car and waited until the car drove away and turned the corner. Coughing, he picked up his books and pounded on the back door. "Let me in, Mama, please!"

His mother looked out the window, slid the bolts and turned the lock. The door flew open. "Good Lord, Karl. How long have you been out here?"

He stepped inside, onto the back landing. "Didn't you hear me?" His cough overcame him and he couldn't say anything else, but it didn't matter. The house felt warm. He started brushing snow off his shirt.

"Never mind, take it all off. What on earth were you thinking? You're going right into the tub." She turned and hurried up the stairs. Karl heard the squeak of the faucet as she ran his bath water.

Still coughing, he took off the damp shirt and pants and left them where they fell. He started up the stairs in his underwear, hugging his arms to his chest. His mother stood at the top, looking worried. "Don't worry, Mama, I'm only a little cold." His teeth chattered uncontrollably.

"Get in the tub; you can talk to me through the door."

The bath water felt like you could cook potatoes in it. Karl slid his foot in and pulled it back, yelling. "Owww! This water is boiling hot!" He coughed some more.

"It only feels that way because you're so cold. Get in slowly."

After a few minutes, he'd immersed every part of his body except for his head. He started to feel sleepy.

"Karl? What happened?"

"They did it again. In church."

"Did what? Who?"

"Elmer Klein tripped me during Mass, only this time I didn't take it."

"Oh, no. What did you do?"

"I yelled at him."

"During Mass?"

"Uh-huh."

"Oh, Karl... You're not making it any easier for me to fight Melvin."

"I'm sorry, but I'm sick of taking the blame for what they do." He coughed. "I never want to go back there again."

"Why did you leave your coat?"

"Sister Mary Anthony almost..." He forgot what he was going to say.

"Don't fall asleep in there."

"I'm not."

"You shouldn't have run off without your coat. Why—"

"I needed my books... for my... homework. If I took my coat, too, she would have caught me. I'm never going back to that stupid place."

"Are you warm yet?"

"Yeah."

"Then dry off and come out of there. I'll bring your father's bathrobe."

Karl got out of the tub and dried off. His mother opened the door a crack and handed him the robe. He wrapped the brown flannel around himself, closed his eyes and buried his face in the sleeve, breathing in without coughing. The robe still held the scent of his father, and once inside Karl, the smell went searching for a place to land. The cave was nearly empty, so he stored it there, his longing for Eddie Stern filling it to overflowing.

When he came out of the bathroom, his mother touched his face and put her arms around him. "You smell like your father."

Karl nodded. "Yeah, it's the robe."

"I know." She stepped away from him. "I should be deciding how to punish you, but I don't have the heart. Think about what you've learned from all this and we'll talk about it later. Now get yourself into bed and keep warm. I'll check on you in a few minutes."

"Uncle Melvin said he was coming back."

"Don't worry; I'll take care of it. Go to sleep."

When Karl's head hit the pillow, there was nothing, blessed nothing; no dreams or voices or sweating—nothing. He didn't open his eyes till hours later, when Lizzie woke him up.

"Karl? You know what happened at lunch today?"

"Umm. What time is it?"

"We just got home. Guess what happened." She smiled triumphantly.

"I dunno, Liz, what happened?" Karl sat up, coughed and rubbed his eyes.

"Sister Mary Anthony caught Elmer and Johnny teasing Michael Grady." A pudgy, pimply sixth grader, Michael didn't have many friends. "They made him trip and fall with his lunch tray. Food went everywhere, and they laughed like nobody's business. At first, Sister scolded Michael for not being more careful and sent him to the broom closet for a mop, but then you know what? All the girls in seventh grade stood up and told Sister what they saw. First Susan and Rebecca stood up—I think they like you, Karl—then pretty soon all the girls in your class were standing up at their tables. And Ella told Sister that those boys tripped you, too, and that they even did it in church. The girls weren't afraid of Sister or Elmer or Johnny or anyone!"

"Really?"

"Yeah, and then Sister made Elmer and Johnny clean up the mess and apologize to Michael in front of everyone, then they got the ruler in front of everyone, too."

"Well, the ruler didn't stop 'em last time."

"I know, but then she made a big speech and made us all late to our classes. She said there would be no more spiteful teasing or tripping of anyone at Holy Angels, and if there was, the guilty boys or girls would suffer more than the victims. She said that kind of behavior was hardly in the spirit of Christmas and it certainly wasn't pleasing to God, and that she never wanted to see it happen again. She's going to make those *hooligans* apologize to you in chapel, in front of everyone, on the first day after vacation."

Karl shook his head. "This is all a story isn't it?"

"No, it's not. Elmer and Johnny had to spend the afternoon in Sister's office doing assignments and they missed the Christmas party. And guess what else?"

"What?"

"Sister sent home a note for you and cupcakes from the party."

"And your coat!" Anna came running in with Karl's coat and jumped on his bed.

"You mean she's not mad at me anymore? I'm not in trouble?"

"She wouldn't have sent you cupcakes if she was mad, Karl. She even smiled when she gave them to me. And you know what else? All the girls like you, now. You're famous at school."

"I am not."

"Yes, you are! Yes, you are!" Anna started bouncing the bed. Karl grabbed her and tickled her.

"Mama says you can have a cupcake if you come down to the kitchen. Sister sent four; do you think we could have one, too?"

"Yeah, sure. Go on and let me get dressed."

The girls ran down the stairs. "Mama, he said he would share!"

Karl got out of bed and stubbed his toe on the desk chair. "Oww!" It hurt, which meant he wasn't dreaming this. He put on clean clothes and tried to imagine Sister Mary Anthony scolding Elmer and Johnny. He tried to imagine her smiling, too, but instead he saw her standing on their heads, like the Holy Mother on the serpent.

Maggie smiled when Karl came into the kitchen. She felt his forehead. "No fever. I thought you'd have one, the way you've been coughing. How do you feel?"

"Fine. Hungry."

"Well, sit down." She poured him a glass of milk and set one of the cupcakes in front of him. "I think you should read the note first." She handed it to him.

"I don't want to even think about school or church for a while."

"You should read it."

He unfolded the piece of stationery. It said *Holy Angels Catholic School* on the top. Sister Mary Anthony had perfect handwriting. He read out loud.

Dear Karl,
I am writing to tell you that I am sorry you were punished because of what others did to you. It was unfair, and I'm sorry that I allowed myself to become part of it.

I hope that you will find it in your heart to forgive me, your other teachers, and Elmer and Jimmy. From now on, I want you to know that you can come to us with your problems or if other students torment you. We will do our best to listen and try to understand.

None of your teachers assigned homework for over vacation, but they gave me a list of the class assignments you missed today so you can catch up before school starts again week after next. They are written on the other side of this paper.

I did not like seeing you leave today without your coat, and I hope you don't catch cold for your time off. I sincerely wish you and your family a Blessed and Merry Christmas.
Sister Mary Anthony

Karl folded the note and put it in his shirt pocket. He looked up and saw his mother and Lizzie and Anna all grinning at him.

"Well, go on, you two, eat your cupcakes. Mama, your stew sure smells good. When's supper?"

"Oh, not for a while yet."

As she got up to stir the pot, the front door rattled and opened. She stepped into the dining room. "Melvin! How did you get in here?"

"The door's unlocked. Where's that boy of yours? I've got some business with him."

"It's been taken care of."

"Is that right?" He came into the kitchen. "So you're having a party?"

"I said it's been taken care of. You can go home."

The idea of all the girls standing up for Michael Grady made Karl feel brave—or maybe foolhardy. He stood up to Uncle Melvin, who was already unbuckling his belt.

"I didn't do anything wrong."

"You call making a ruckus at such a holy time as mass *nothing wrong?* You call being truant from school *nothing wrong?* You showed disrespect toward Father Cunningham and contempt before the Lord. You should be ashamed of yourself. Get downstairs, boy. It's time I taught you a lesson!"

"No." Karl crossed his arms and stood his ground.

Maggie tried to step in between him and Uncle Melvin. "Keep your hands off him; this is none of your business!"

Enraged, Uncle Melvin smacked her across the face with the back of his hand, his shirt pulling out of his pants in the front as he flung his arm at her. "Don't you tell me what to do, you pathetic bitch!" He hit her with such force that she stumbled and fell against the corner of the cupboards, hitting the right side of her head above her ear. Lizzie screamed. In seconds, blood ran down Maggie's neck, onto her collar, all over her blue dress.

Karl grabbed a dishtowel and rushed around the table, tripping on the leg of a chair. "Mama?" Seeing all that blood made him feel sick. He swallowed and tried to wipe it from her cheek.

Uncle Melvin grabbed him from behind. "*You* shut up!"

"Get out, Melvin!" Maggie winced and leaned her head on her hand. "I don't need any more of your help. Please, just go home." She sounded weary.

"Not until I take care of this." Melvin shoved Karl down the stairs, kicking his calves and the backs of his knees to make him go faster. "Move it."

Karl heard his sisters crying.

"You two go on up to your room," said his mother. "Don't worry, it'll be all right."

At the bottom of the stairs, Melvin threw Karl onto the coal pile next to the furnace. The coal shifted when Karl landed and his hands sunk in up to his wrists. When Melvin reached down and ripped open his shirt, Karl kicked him in the stomach. The sensation of his shoe connecting with Melvin's flabby gut felt immensely satisfying, better than Thanksgiving dinner, better than his mother's apple pie.

Karl started to get up, but Melvin doubled over for only a second before he came back after him like a savage beast. Karl could have sworn that the pupils of his eyes burned red. Sweat glistened on his greasy brow.

"Why, you little—" In one move, Melvin thrust Karl back onto the coal pile, flipped him over on his stomach and tore the rest of his shirt off. As the coal scraped his bare chest, Karl saw the note from Sister Mary Anthony go flying with the remains of his shirt.

Melvin clenched his teeth and roared, his voice gravelly. "You will respect your elders, give the Lord the honor due His name, and stop breaking the rules." With each demand, Melvin kicked Karl hard in the ribs with his fine wing-tipped shoes. "You're a Stern and you deserve eternal suffering, starting this very minute!"

For a reason he couldn't understand, Karl wasn't afraid when the belt started coming down on his bare shoulders and back; on his still clothed buttocks and legs. He looked at the gray block walls and the dirt floor and Sister Mary Anthony's note and didn't even count how many times Melvin hit him. He didn't cower or fight, he just lay there face down on the coal pile like he didn't feel a thing. *Hah! I can take this!*

Melvin became angrier and more vicious. "Ohh, you!" He ground his teeth and switched the belt around so the buckle became the instrument of torture. He whipped the belt harder and faster than before, grunting each time the leather and metal hit Karl's tender skin. Still, Karl didn't cry out or beg for mercy or even flinch.

Hoping to catch Melvin by surprise, Karl suddenly rolled over, put his hand out, caught the buckle and jerked it hard. "Enough!" For once, his voice didn't crack.

Melvin lost his footing, then regained it. Their eyes locked. They held the belt taut between them, both of them motionless for an instant before Melvin yanked the belt away. "Haven't I taught you anything, you little miscreant?" He dropped the belt and hit Karl in the face with his fist, slamming the other side of his head against the furnace.

Even though it hurt like anything, Karl still pretended he didn't care. Involuntarily, his eyes closed; he forced them open when he heard a scuffle. Will stood on the bottom step, his left elbow around Melvin's neck, his right hand pushing the handle of a wooden spoon into Melvin's ribs. Karl recognized it as the spoon from the stove.

"I'm not afraid to use this, Straus!" Will jabbed the spoon handle harder; Melvin winced.

Karl wanted to laugh, but it hurt too much.

"Okay, okay, let up, you're choking me."

"Oh. Sorry." Will pulled his elbow tighter. "Can you get up, Karl?"

Karl tried but the room spun around. "Give me a minute."

There were hurried footsteps upstairs and an unfamiliar voice. "Where are they?"

"In the basement."

A police officer appeared on the steps. Will hauled Melvin over so the officer could get past. "How's the boy?"

"I'm okay."

The officer seemed surprised. "Melvin Straus?" He put him in handcuffs, and went to see about Karl.

He reached out his hand. When Karl took hold of it and tried to stand up again, everything moved at crazy angles. "Nope, not yet."

"Good grief! Stay put, son, you need a doctor." He called up the stairs. "He needs a medic; see if they have anyone they can call."

"We've already called the doctor for his mother."

The officer smiled at Will. "Nice piece you got there, sir."

"What? Oh, this?" Will held up the spoon and laughed. "It was handy." He moved away from Melvin and went to Karl, still stretched out on the coal.

Karl grinned at Will. "Aww, Will, you're swell; you were *greeaat...*" He started to shiver. Will took off his jacket and put it on top of him. "Warrrm. Thanks. I'll take you for a father any day."

Will pushed a lock of Karl's hair away from his eyes and frowned. "Your mother isn't going to like this. You're a mess."

Melvin looked at Karl. "You're all right, now, aren't you, boy? You know I meant no harm." He turned to the officer. "He needs discipline."

"That looks more like assault than discipline, Mr. Straus. You got his mother pretty good, too."

"Oh, I didn't mean to hurt her either; she's family, my wife's sister."

"How's my mother?" Karl tried to sit up again.

Will held him down. "Don't worry; Doc Lyman is on his way over."

"But is she okay?" It hurt to shout, but he needed

an answer.

Her voice came from the kitchen, tight and strained. "I'm all right, Karl, it's only a little cut and a bump. How are you? How is he, Will?"

"Don't worry, Mama."

"He's going to be a little colorful, but I think he'll be all right."

"Melvin Straus, you are under arrest."

"You must not know who I am." Melvin smiled. "I'm only doing my duty; they're family." Suddenly he changed his tone, pleading, sounding like he might cry. "The boy's papa is dead, what a pity... I was only trying to help, officer."

"You can tell the judge all about it."

While the officer led Melvin up the stairs and out of the basement he whimpered and complained. "If you let me go, I won't ever do this again. I promise." He shouted, "*I promise, Karl!*"

Karl heard the weak little apology Melvin gave his mother. "I'm sorry Margaret; it was an accident. You know that, don't you? You know how much I care about you and the kids."

"Let's go, Straus." More footsteps. The front door opened and closed.

The other officer said they'd be back later to take their statements.

"Please, I want to see my son."

"Sit down, now. You're not so steady on your feet."

"I can take care of her until Dr. Lyman gets here, sir." Lizzie sounded like a grown up.

"Did you know my sister called for help?" In his head, Karl could see Anna's toothless grin. He smiled.

"You can be very proud of her."

"We learned how to use the telephone in school," said Lizzie. "Girls can stand up for people, you know."

"Yes, indeed, they can. Look, I think your doctor is here."

Although Karl could make out Dr. Lyman's voice talking to his mother, he couldn't understand what they said. He closed his eyes for a second.

"Karl?"

He opened them to see Doc Lyman towering over him.

The doctor crouched down, pushed his glasses up the bridge of his nose and shone a light in Karl's eyes, then looked at both sides of Karl's face. "Great God Almighty, what kind of beast is he?" Dr. Lyman helped him sit up. "Careful, now." When he saw Karl's back he cursed, something Karl never heard him do before.

"I'm okay, Doc. It's only a few bruises."

"No, you're *not* okay. You've got a nasty bump on the noggin and your back is torn to shreds. It's going to take all night to clean you up. What'd you do to make him so mad?"

"It's a long story. When can I have my supper?" Karl realized he hadn't eaten since breakfast.

"Not now."

Will and Dr. Lyman each took an elbow and lifted Karl to his feet. He wobbled a little, before steadying himself. "I'm all right, I can walk by myself."

"Not on your life." Dr. Lyman stubbornly held his elbow. "Will, put your jacket over his shoulders so Margaret doesn't see this until I get it cleaned up."

Karl felt a victorious rush of excitement even though he was the one who got beat up. "You know, I'm not afraid of Melvin anymore."

"I don't know how wise that is, Karl," warned Will.

"Aw, he's nothin' but an old windbag."

"Then that was quite a windstorm."

Karl reveled in his relief until he saw his mother. She still sat in the kitchen, pale, holding the bloodied dish-towel against her head. The cupcakes sat uneaten on the table; milk covered the floor, and someone had moved the stew off the stove.

A dark half moon curved under her right eye. She lifted her head slightly. "Oh, no, Karl, look at you!"

Karl shrugged himself away from Will and Doc Lyman and stumbled over to her. "Look at *you!* He's a monster, Mama; you shoulda stayed out of his way."

Maggie smiled a little and touched his swelling face with her free hand. "Didn't you hear what your sister said? *Girls can stand up for people, you know.*"

After he put stitches in Maggie's head, it took Dr. Lyman over two hours to clean the mess of blood, dirt and coal from Karl's back. Pick, wash, pat dry, swab with iodine, over and over. Will stayed the whole time, holding a lamp over Doc Lyman's shoulder, yacking away about anything and everything, obviously trying to distract Karl from this continuing torture. On his stomach, in his own bed, in his own room, Karl felt far less brave than he had in the basement. This time he did cry out, again and again, clawing at anything he could reach. Sweat from his forehead and chest wet his pillow and bed sheets.

Dr. Lyman wouldn't allow Maggie to come into Karl's room, but they could hear her fretting in the hallway.

"Margaret, go sit down, you're making the boy nervous."

"When can I have some of your stew, Mama? I'm starving."

"I'll go warm it up for you."

He heard her going down the stairs and let out a long sigh. "I want my cupcake, too."

Doc Lyman called after her. "Put on the stew then *sit down!*" He turned to Karl. "Good thinking, son." He pushed his wire rimmed glasses up the bridge of his nose with his left hand and went back to work.

"Hurry up, will you? This hurts like heck."

"It's going to hurt for a while, I'm afraid. Now be still so I can finish and go home to my own supper."

Will went home and sent Bernie over to stay the night and help out. Dr. Lyman said he wanted both Karl and his mother to be awakened every hour, just in case. Karl didn't know what *just in case* meant, but he wasn't sure he wanted to know. They were both to rest for the next twenty-four hours, but they were allowed to go to Grandma's for Christmas Eve dinner and to Midnight Mass if they felt up to it. Bernie slept in Maggie's room and set and reset the alarm clock all night, getting up to shake Karl's shoulder every few minutes. Karl hated having this happen at Christmas, the first Christmas without his father. He wished he could turn back the clock to last year.

At breakfast, Maggie said they would not be going to Grandma O'Keefe's for dinner that night. "Christmas Eve or not, she's already angry with me, and if Melvin is out of jail, he'll probably be there, too."

"Listen, Love," said Bernie, "your Mum should see what he did to the both of you." Karl had blue and purple bruises on both sides of his face; the bruise under Maggie's eye had deepened and the hair over her ear was cut off, black stitches in its place. "Maybe it would help Kathleen. Maybe she'd admit he hurts her, too."

Karl wondered if he should tell about the closet. What if Uncle Melvin hurt her and locked her up in that stinky trap?

"Do you think they could have let him out yet?" Maggie asked.

"I don't know." Bernie got up to clear the table. "Somebody would have gone to get him, don'cha think?"

Lizzie ran to the front window. "His car's gone, Mama."

Stunned, no one said a word for a few seconds.

His mother sounded like she could cry. "I thought he'd be locked up until Monday."

"This is what I think." Karl sat up as straight as he could. "Uncle Melvin wants us to be afraid of him. If we go to Grandma's and to church, we'll be telling him that he doesn't scare us anymore." Everyone looked at him. His heart started to race. "Mama, I have something to tell you, but I don't think Lizzie and Anna should hear it."

"Girls, go on upstairs and put some fresh sheets on Karl's bed. Don't come down until I call you."

"I'm old enough to hear, Mama." Lizzie whined. "I called the police, remember?"

"Please, take Anna and go upstairs. If it's something I think you should know about, I will tell you."

Lizzie pouted. "C'mon, Anna." The girls stomped off.

"What is it, Karl?"

He waited until he could hear his sisters in his room, then told his mother and Bernie what he found in Melvin's closet, everything, including how it smelled like pee.

Maggie and Bernie looked at each other.

"Do you think Uncle Melvin locks Aunt Kathleen up in there?"

"I don't know what to think, but we have to find a way to ask her." Maggie stood up, slowly. "It's decided, then. We're going to Grandma's for Christmas Eve dinner, like we always do. I'll call and tell her we're still coming."

Chapter 12

Snakes & Angels

Karl spent most of Christmas Eve day on his bed, lying on his stomach. Wearing clothes hurt, sitting in a chair hurt, moving much of anything hurt. Once his mother got over the shock of seeing what Melvin had done to his back, she smoothed on some ointment and covered it with a clean undershirt for a bandage. That made it felt some better.

At five o'clock, Will came by to give them a ride to Grandma's. She met them at her back door and acted happy to see them; she even smiled and said, "Merry Christmas, everyone!" The aromas of clove-studded ham and her special Irish potato dish overcame the smell of bleach that usually permeated her house.

Beyond the steamy kitchen with its white walls, pine cupboards and checkerboard linoleum floor was the dining room. The table was set with Grandma's good dishes on a red tablecloth; an arrangement of holly and evergreen sat in the center with candlesticks on either side that matched the creamy color of the dishes. A deep blue flowered rug covered the floor, marred by a path worn from the kitchen to the stairway. A small Christmas tree adorned the corner of the living room, decorated with the same gold paper chain that Grandma had on her Christmas trees for as long as Karl could remember.

Aunt Kathleen had come without Melvin. She looked like she'd been crying a lot. She was nice to them, too, but then she always was. Before dinner, while Karl sat alone in the parlor looking through the family photo album, she came and sat with him.

"Look, there, that's your mother when she was about your age, and there's me."

"This is *your* wedding?"

"Yes. I married at a young age, but he was much older and had a good job, so my mother approved and convinced my father to allow it." She talked about this like it was someone else's life.

"Oh." Next to Aunt Kathleen stood a tall, thin groom with lots of hair. Karl wondered if Melvin's nasty streak had started yet. In the picture they both looked happy.

"Karl," the corners of Aunt Kathleen's mouth pulled down as she put her hand on his arm. "I want you to know how sorry I am for the pain Uncle Melvin has caused you and your mother."

"That's okay, Aunt Kathleen, it's not your fault. He just got too mad."

"Yes, he does that."

"Does he hurt you?"

She paused. "Yes, he does. Sometimes."

"Does he do terrible things to you and lock you in that closet?" She didn't answer, so he went on. "You know, the closet in the spare room. On Thanksgiving, he told me to bring four chairs down but I could only find three in the room, so I looked in the closet."

Aunt Kathleen looked away, then back at Karl. Her voice did not waver, even though she spoke quietly. "You must forget you ever saw that."

"I can't. It gives me nightmares."

"Making a fuss about it would only make things worse for me. Forget what you saw. "

"How can I, when I dream about it all the time?"

"Well, before you go to sleep, make good wishes for me, and pray for my safety and don't be afraid. But please, forget about the closet."

"I told my mother about it."

"I know you did. I told her the same thing. If you care about me, you will forget about it."

"You let him do things to you?"

"No more than you did. Please, Karl, it's Christmas, let's talk about something else."

"Where is he now? I don't want him coming over to our house anymore."

"He's at home. Father Cunningham brought him home around midnight. He's supposed to stay away from you and your mother, but he's allowed to go to church tonight, being that it's Christmas Eve and all. I'll eat dinner with you and go home early to be with him."

"Is he... Is he mad at you, like he was mad at us? 'Cause I don't want him hurting you on Christmas."

"Uncle Melvin's been nice to me ever since he came home. Father Cunningham must have had a talk with him, and he always listens to Father, so I think he'll behave himself for a while. He even brought me flowers and a Christmas present."

Karl noticed the string of pearls around her neck. "Is that what he gave you?"

She smiled but her eyes were sad. "Yes, it is. Aren't

they lovely?"

Maggie wondered at the change in her mother's attitude. Was it simply a little Christmas cheer, or did she feel bad about what Melvin had done to them? Did she finally understand what Kathleen had been living with all this time; did she understand why she didn't want to bring her children to live with them? Whatever the reason, Maggie decided to accept the change as the gift it was, even if it only lasted the evening.

Maggie knew her mother was working hard to keep the conversation around the table cheerful. In Eddie and Melvin's absence, she gave Karl the honor of asking the blessing, and then complimented him for doing "such a *wonderful* job." She didn't act cranky at all; she acted like nothing had happened, but Maggie noticed her glancing at Karl every so often while they ate. Nobody else mentioned what Melvin did, either, so they talked about ordinary, insignificant things, like favorite foods and what Isabelle's mother used to bake at Christmastime; about cookies and gifts and oh, had anyone seen the church since it was decorated, because it looked absolutely beautiful.

After dinner, Isabelle gave each of the children an orange and two shiny nickels and Kathleen gave them thick pads of drawing paper, with colored pencils for Karl and crayons for the girls. Kathleen also had an extra gift for Karl: two new, store bought shirts, one in blue flannel and the other a white dress shirt.

"One is for the shirt you ruined when you saved Will Denver," she said, "and one for the shirt Melvin ruined yesterday. Merry Christmas, Karl."

He smiled, but to Maggie it seemed forced. "Uh—you

didn't have to do this, Aunt Kathleen. But thank you."

"We hope you'll let bygones be bygones."

"Yeah... well, thank you."

Maggie thought it was too much to ask of Karl; for heaven's sake, let him heal up first. She watched him re-fold the shirts and put them back in the box. He winced as he stood up, but leaned over and kissed Kathleen on the cheek.

She beamed and took his hand. "Oh, you sweet boy!" Still smiling, Kathleen turned to Maggie. "Now, Magpie, I have something special for you, too." She took a small jewelry box from her pocket. "This is from Melvin. He picked it out all by himself when he bought my pearls. He says it's a peace offering."

Maggie opened the box. The pink cameo brooch was nestled in black velvet, setting off the four diamonds and gold filigree. The room took a step sideways, then swirled around her. "Oh, my." She held her handkerchief over her mouth. "Kathleen, this is too expensive, I can't—"

Her mother took the box. "Oh, my goodness, would you look at that?" She smiled as she held it out for the children to see. "Wasn't that nice of him?"

She tried to give the box back, but Maggie pretended not to see it. Maggie stood up, hoping she looked calm, hoping her voice didn't reveal her panic. "Kathleen, come help me make up a plate for Melvin before you go. Mother, you take it easy and visit with the children, you've already worked too hard today."

"Why, thank you, Margaret." She turned to the children. "Would you three like to play dominoes?"

Kathleen followed Maggie to the kitchen. Angry, she closed the kitchen door and whispered. "What is wrong with you?"

Maggie shook all over. "I can't accept that, you have to take it back."

"Why? He feels bad about what happened, he wants to make it up to you."

"It's the same brooch he tried to give me when he asked you to marry him. When he gave you your ring. The brooch Daddy wouldn't let me keep."

"That was years ago; how can you possibly remember what it looked like?"

"Because," Maggie had to sit down before her knees failed her. "He gave it back to me when Daddy wasn't home. He said it was *our little secret.*" Remembering the other things he'd said and done, she started to cry even though she tried not to. "I've had it all this time."

"Then how—"

"I gave it to Will after Eddie died. He gave me all the money from last season, so I told him to sell it, so he'd have start up money for spring."

"I still don't understand why you can't keep it."

"Because he... I can't tell you why. Take it back to him."

"Please, Maggie, don't insult him. Don't get him all upset again. Let me pretend I have a nice husband, a man who loves me, even if it doesn't last. Could you give me that?"

"I can't wear it, Kathy."

"I don't care what you do with it; just don't send it back to him."

They looked into each other's eyes for a moment. Maggie knew Kathleen suffered under Melvin's hand, but she'd never noticed the deep pain and exhaustion that had set in around her eyes, across her wrinkled brow and through the lines that curved from her nose to her chin.

She could see that Kathleen died a little every day. One day, she'd be gone.

Maggie wiped her eyes and reached for her sister's hand. "He'll be here for you soon. What should we put on his plate?"

Kathleen still whispered. "I'm sorry for everything, Magpie, I'm so sorry."

"Shh, that's enough. He likes a lot of ham, doesn't he? And potatoes? I'll wrap some extra so you have leftovers, too, there's plenty here."

"He'd like that." Kathleen looked out the window. "Can you hurry? He's waiting."

On Christmas Eve, Holy Angels Church stood out like a jewel in an otherwise dreary neighborhood. The stained glass windows glowed from the inside out, making all the saints and angels that Sister Anne had told Karl about come alive with color and light. Candles burning in quart jars lined the walkways and surrounded the life-sized nativity in the yard. Inside, to the left of the altar, stood a Christmas tree, so tall it nearly touched the high, vaulted ceiling. Wreaths adorned the walls and lighted votives sat on window sills and on posts attached to the pews and all around the statue of the Blessed Virgin.

Karl and his family arrived early for midnight mass because Grandma liked to sit near the front. He looked around for Elmer and Jimmy, afraid at first to go in, vigilant about where he put his feet, but when he saw them with their parents, he sighed with relief. They stared at him when they saw him come in; they stared at his mother, too.

Uncle Melvin and Aunt Kathleen came in and sat

one row ahead of them on the other side of the aisle. Melvin looked like a puppy dog who'd been beaten with a newspaper for wetting in the house; he met Karl's eyes for a second then quickly averted his. Aunt Kathleen held onto his arm, and he let her genuflect and move into the pew first, like a gentleman. Karl wondered how long that would last.

Mrs. Buckley started playing the same music Karl heard her practicing a couple of weeks ago. He sat still, closed his eyes and tried to go back to the floating, heavenly place he'd found while scrubbing under the pews, but the skin on his back and shoulders felt like it was on fire and his head hurt. He hoped Father Cunningham wouldn't be too long winded tonight.

The Choir of Sisters chanted some psalms and sang *alleluia*, and the Children's Choir sang *gloria something something*. After everyone stood up when Father read the Christmas story, the adult choir sang a ragged and squeaky anthem that made Grandma cry. She sat next to him, on his left, with Lizzie on his right, her eyes at half mast, like she could fall asleep any minute. Karl hoped she wouldn't decide to lean on him.

Father Cunningham preached and talked and preached some more about how the spirit of Christmas giving should go on all year round, not only in December. Blah, blah, yack, yack, blah, blah, blah. Karl had trouble paying attention to anything he said. He looked at his mother, who held Anna's head on her lap as she slept. She smiled at him, but he saw her tears. She missed Daddy; Karl knew because he did, too. He felt drowsy and wished he could close his eyes like Anna.

Then, when they got to the part of the Mass where Father Cunningham stood on the serpent's head, Karl saw a snake rise out of the stone floor under Father's shiny shoes, black, thick, with a pale underbelly and a strange hood around its head. It looked like the picture of a cobra in his science book—deadly poisonous! He blinked and it disappeared, but then it came back, growing and getting longer and longer and winding itself around the priest's legs and in and out of his vestments and around his middle and along his arms as they moved and blessed and made the sign of the cross. Karl blinked and it was gone, blinked again and it slithered onto the altar, circled the candles and the tabernacle and the big missal and everything. His heart went wild, his face burned, and his knees trembled. He looked around to see if anyone else looked as terrified as he felt, but everyone seemed fine, normal. He wanted to escape, but didn't dare.

The snake raised its head and locked its red-hot eyes onto Karl's. It flicked its tongue and showed its fangs, but Father went on with the Mass, like he didn't even see it. Karl couldn't take his eyes away, couldn't even blink anymore, so mesmerized was he by the serpent's wicked stare. Those red eyes found the cave he'd dug inside himself and went in, stirring up everything he'd hidden there. They bored through to his heart and into his soul. Karl's choked on the lump in his throat, wheezed, and coughed. "My God," he thought, "it's got me!" He broke out in a sweat and felt the floor shift beneath him.

Father lifted the host and the little bell chimed and the snake looked at the priest and reared its head. Suddenly, it dried up and cracked into a hundred pieces, disintegrating first to dust, then to a fine powder that blew away to nothing when Father moved his arms.

Karl knees buckled and his world went black. Helpless,

he felt big hands grab him from behind, under his arms, like a person would pick up a baby. They lowered him to sit on the pew and quickly pushed his head down to his knees. His heart raced and dark silence engulfed him.

He knew nothing at all after that until the sharp smell of ammonia pierced his consciousness. He tried to get away from it, but it followed him wherever he went until he finally opened his eyes. Two men he'd never seen before hovered over him; one big, like a giant, with wild gray hair and the other with dark hair. When Karl tried to sit up, the man with the gray hair pushed his shoulder back down and held him. He heard beautiful music, and he tried to say so, but the man held his finger to his lips.

Oh, yeah. He was in church.

Slowly, they allowed him to sit up. He looked around, confused. People stared at him. He remembered the cobra. "Did you see the snake?" he whispered to the dark haired man, who squinted his eyes, and felt his forehead like his mother did when she thought he had a fever.

"I gotta get outta here." He stood up and started down the aisle. His knees went rubbery on him and the air became thick and hard to suck into his lungs. He fought his way past his mother and grandmother, who stood by watching, horrified; past the rows and rows of worshipers seated behind them; out the door and into the drafty vestibule. The two men followed and found a bench where they made him lie down.

"What's your name, son?" asked the dark haired man.

"Karl. Stern."

"Well, Karl Stern, that wasn't a very smart thing to do."

"I had to get out!" Karl nearly shouted.

"Why?" The man with the gray hair was gruff and

almost as loud as Karl.

"Shhh," warned the other man. "They're still busy in there."

"Didn't you see it? The cobra? It came out of the floor and went up Father Cunningham's legs and arms and onto the altar." The men stared at Karl without answering. "It had red eyes, and—"

"There wasn't no snake, boy."

"But I saw it!"

"Sorry, Karl," said the dark haired man. "You saw something that wasn't there."

He groaned and hung his elbow over his eyes. A door opened; he turned to see his mother coming toward him. He covered his eyes again. "Please don't tell her I'm seeing things, okay? I'll be fine." He wondered if his Grandpa Stern saw snakes that weren't there when he went insane.

The dark haired man drove Karl and his family home. He carried the sleeping Anna into the house and up to her room. Karl mumbled his thanks as he dragged himself up the stairs, but his mother made up for it by calling the men *angels of mercy.*

He awoke when she looked in on him a little while later. "We've had a tough few days, Karl." She smiled and sat on the bed. "But I think your father sent two angels to take care of us tonight. I have a feeling things are going to be better from now on."

"I sure hope so."

"Good night." She kissed his forehead and stood up. "Sweet dreams." She closed the door behind her.

Karl rolled onto his side, where it didn't hurt so much. Angels, huh? Then how come he saw the devil?

Chapter 13

Noel

Christmas Day fell on Sunday, but none of them went to Mass, for which Karl was most grateful. Even though she got up early, his mother let him sleep late, but once Anna woke up, everyone else was awake, too. They gathered around the Christmas tree in their pajamas to see if Santa had come.

Each of them found one of Eddie's socks filled with pencils and candies, a new pair of their own socks, with hair ribbons for the girls and with a new comb for Karl. His mother reached behind the davenport and produced more gifts for the children. She gave Lizzie and Anna each a doll with doll clothes she'd sewn for them and the little china tea set she and Aunt Kathleen played with when they were young. Lizzie smiled and said, "Ohh, thank you so much, Mama!" but Anna climbed on her mother's lap and covered her with hugs and kisses.

Karl waited patiently, hoping there would be a gift for him, too, and his mother did not disappoint him. She gave him a heavy package, wrapped in brown paper. It felt like a book. He tore off the paper and found the first volume of the *Encyclopedia Britannica.*

"Do you know what it is?"

"It's part of an encyclopedia, we have a set at school." He smiled. "Is this really for me?"

"Yes, it is. And the other volumes are already in your room."

"Mama, I know these are too expensive..."

"Do you like it?"

"Well, yes, but—"

"If you look on the inside cover, you will see that they belonged to my cousin, James. He bought a newer set and asked me if I thought you would like this one."

"This is swell, thanks. I'll have to write James a letter and thank him, too. Maybe if I read every volume, I'll know everything."

His mother laughed. "By the way, Karl, I forgot to tell you that Will left a package when he came the other night. It's under my bed."

"Oh, yeah." He started for the stairs.

"No, Karl. Lizzie, go get the package for your brother."

Lizzie went but Karl complained. "Come on, Mama, I could have gone, I'm fine."

"You were not fine last night. I intend to keep you quiet today. After breakfast it's back to bed with you."

"But I'm okay!"

Lizzie returned with the package. Karl tore off the brown paper and found the three wood burnings Will helped him make. Anna's was on top. "Merry Christmas, Annie. This is to put on your wall, in case you ever forget who you are. Lizzie, here's yours." The girls both laughed and thanked him. Karl wondered if he should have made one for himself, so he'd remember his name after he'd gone crazy.

He handed the last one to his mother. "Merry Christmas, Mama. I hope you like it."

"*Home Sweet Home*," she read. "Oh, Karl." She came to hug him and began to weep.

"I'm sorry; I didn't want to make you cry. Please, stop, it's Christmas."

She moved away and wiped her eyes with one of his father's handkerchiefs. "This *is* a sweet home; it's sweet because you and your sisters make it that way. Thank you, Karl. I will always treasure this, always. Where do you think I should hang it?"

"Bernie has one in her kitchen."

She smiled. "I'll have Will hang it for me when they're here later."

"I could do it for you."

"No, you can't, not today. Now, girls, you go get dressed; Karl, you come in the kitchen and keep me company while I cook the oatmeal."

Karl started for the basement.

"Where are you going?"

"To feed the furnace."

"I already did it. Sit down at the table and tell me what happened to you last night." She measured the oats into a pan, covered them with a mixture of water and milk and stirred them before putting them on the stove.

"I passed out, I guess. It was too stuffy in there."

"I know you, Karl, and I know there's more to it than that."

He didn't answer. He didn't want to scare her, not today.

"What, Karl?"

"I sort of had this—this bad dream."

"You weren't asleep."

He lied to her. "I know, but while I was out, I had this bad dream."

"Can you tell me about it?"

"No."

"You were afraid, I could tell."

"Yeah, I guess so."

"After everything that's happened to us over the past few weeks, what could be so awful that you can't tell me?"

"I can't talk about it now."

"Later maybe?"

"I dunno, maybe."

After breakfast, Maggie sent Karl back to bed and gave the girls each a job to help get ready for their company. Karl took out the drawing pad and the colored pencils Aunt Kathleen gave him and sat in bed sketching. He didn't understand why, but he felt compelled to set down on paper what he'd seen the night before. He tried to draw the cobra, but couldn't quite get its hood and its eyes right, so he went to the box of encyclopedias sitting under the window and opened the "C" volume. Inside, he found a picture of a cobra. He looked away from it, shaking.

"Stupid," he said to himself. "This one can't see you." He forced himself to look at it again, paying attention to the proportions of the eyes to the head, the head to the hood. Back in bed, he started over and once finished, felt quite pleased with himself. With the colored pencils, he filled in the black back and tan belly and then—although it made his heart race when he did it—he used red in the cobra's eyes. He turned the page and started over, this time making the snake smaller, with its mouth wide open and drops of venom hanging from its fangs. Above the snake, he drew a bare foot coming down from heaven, hovering over its head, ready to crush it.

Karl heard Lizzie and Anna in their room, so he closed the cover on the drawing pad, slid it under his bed and picked up the encyclopedia and pretended to read it. He knew his sisters and mother would make a big fuss if they saw his drawings so he decided they were for his eyes only. If he truly was going insane, he figured he was entitled to do something a little strange, but he sure hoped he wouldn't spend next Christmas in the asylum, like his Grandpa Stern.

If anyone could make Christmas jolly and merry, it was Will and Bernie and their two little boys. Lizzie and Anna were happy to see them because Bernie would take over helping their mother in the kitchen and they could play with Billy and Ned. Maggie was happy, since Bernie always brought laughter and cheer along with her. And Karl was glad to see all of them: Billy and Ned, who thought he was some kind of hero; Bernie, who made a big fuss over him; and Will, who sat out in the living room with him and waited for dinner.

After they'd eaten Maggie's roasted chicken with mashed potatoes and gravy and the leftover oyster stew Bernie brought from their Christmas Eve celebration, Will announced that desert would have to wait since he had a few surprises. He made everyone sit by the Christmas tree while he went out to his truck. Billy and Ned hopped around with excitement, and Bernie smiled like she knew a wonderful secret, too. Will came in with three wrapped packages; two of them looked alike.

"I thought we agreed a long time ago to leave gift giving to the families and just have fun on Christmas Day," said Maggie.

"That we did, but this year is an exception. It was my idea, Maggie, so don't be upset with Will."

"I'm not, it's just—" Maggie smiled when Lizzie came and whispered in her ear. "All right, go get them."

Lizzie returned with packages for Billy and Ned. Maggie was teaching the girls how to sew and they'd made stuffed bears for the boys out of scraps of flannel.

"Thank you, thank you, thank you!" Neddie hugged each of the girls, but Billy went to Anna and said, "Well, now, thank you very much, Love." He kissed her on the cheek and sat down on the floor next to her.

Everyone laughed at Billy's imitation of his parents. But Anna surprised them all by returning Billy's affections. "You're very welcome, dear." She kissed him on the cheek. More laughter erupted and filled the whole house until Anna got up and stomped her foot.

"It's not funny! Someday Billy and me are getting married."

"It's Billy and *I*, Annie; Billy and *I*." Solemnly, Maggie corrected her.

"Someday I and Billy are getting married."

"Yeah!" said Billy and put his arm around her shoulders.

Before there could be anymore fussing with the two little love-birds, Will gave out the packages he'd brought in from the truck. The girls each received a doll bed he'd made to fit their new dolls. Maggie had shown them to Bernie and Bernie took note of their size, so they fit perfectly. Each doll bed came with a lace edged pillow and a patchwork doll blanket, all made by Bernie.

Lizzie and Anna were overjoyed, said many "thank yous," hugged both Will and Bernie and ran upstairs for their dolls.

Will handed a soft package to Karl. "Now before you go opening this, I want you to know it used to be your Daddy's. I found it on the boat a few weeks ago and took it home so Bernie could wash and mend it. I hope it will keep the sun out of your eyes like it did for him."

Maggie started to laugh. "Oh, William, I thought I'd never have to look at that ugly thing again. Some friend you are!"

Karl knew exactly what it was. "Oh, boy!" He laughed and tore the paper off an old fishing hat, made from brown felt with a red band that still sported the remains of a seagull feather. At least two sizes too big for Eddie, the big floppy brim looked like ruffles when he wore it; in fact, that's what everyone called him whenever he put it on.

"*Ruffles...* I forgot all about *Ruffles.*" Karl put the hat on his head. If it looked ridiculous on his father, it was even more so on him, since his head was that much smaller than Eddie's. When he pulled the hat down, his eyes were lost in the crown. "Yep, it'll keep the sun outta my eyes, that's for sure." Everyone laughed. "Thanks Will, thanks Bernie."

"You're welcome, Ruffles."

"*I bought it for looks now; ain't I pretty?*" Exactly the words his father used whenever anyone teased him about the hat. Karl smiled the same crazed grin he'd seen his father make hundred times.

Will, Bernie and his mother all laughed at him. After she caught her breath, Maggie said quietly, "You look just like him, Karl." Tears filled her eyes. "I miss him so much."

Bernie went to her friend and held her. "O'course you do, Love. We all do, but you sure have it worse than anyone, now don'cha?"

Karl took off the hat and stared at it, remembering what his father looked like when he wore it. His eyes filled with tears, too. "I wish he could come back."

Will sniffed and cleared his throat. "All right, now, I still have one more gift."

"It's for you, Maggie, and it's very special." Bernie smiled. "Now wipe your eyes and see what it is."

"You two have already done enough, you shouldn't go spending your money on me."

"We didn't." Will grinned but sat motionless, looking at Maggie. Except for the noise of younger children playing upstairs, it was quiet.

"Oh, for the love o' Pete, Will, give it to her."

Will reached into his pocket, pulled out a long envelope and gave it to Maggie. "Merry Christmas. And I can almost guarantee the New Year will be better than the old."

She took it from him. Karl stood next to her.

"Open it."

Carefully, she lifted the flap and took out a letter written on fine stationery, with the words *Denver Mills, Jacob Denver, Proprietor* printed on the top. When she unfolded it a check fell out and landed on her lap. She picked it up without looking at it and read the letter. Her face didn't change in expression, but she shook her head and said, "Oh, my." She looked at the check and said it again. "Oh, my..."

"What does it say, Mama?"

"You read it. Out loud." She handed him the letter.

"*Dear Mrs. Stern,*" Karl read. "*My brother informs me that* *you are looking for someone to purchase your late husband's share of the fishing boat, 'The Maggie O'Keefe.' I have looked the boat over and have spent time on board with William. I am impressed with the care with which it has been maintained. I would like to make an offer to buy your share of the vessel and be William's partner. Please accept this check for $100.00 as earnest money until I am able to visit Tomos Bay and present my offer to you in person. I extend my deepest sympathies to you and your children in this time of loss. Sincerely, Jacob H. Denver."*

Stunned, Karl felt like someone slapped him for no reason. "What? What is this? I thought we weren't gonna sell!" He shook the letter in front of him.

"I never said that, Karl," answered his mother. "This will help us; now there's no reason we'd have to live with Uncle Melvin."

"But the boat is my future! Now what am I gonna do?" Karl dropped the letter on the floor. This was too big, *way* too big to shove into his cave; he knew it wouldn't all fit. He fled into the kitchen, went halfway down the basement stairs and sat down, his elbows on his knees, chin resting on the heel of each hand. He stared at the bottom step, at the place where the gray paint was nearly worn off.

Maggie called after him. "Karl, come back, please?"

He didn't answer or go back. His stomach burned from swallowing the lump in his throat. If he didn't let something out of the cave, he'd explode.

"Let me." Will's footsteps crossed in the kitchen. He came down the basement steps and sat next to Karl, carefully draping his arm across Karl's tender shoulders.

That was all it took. They sat without talking until Karl stopped crying.

"Better? Can we talk now?" Will handed him a handkerchief.

"Yeah. I don't want to sell the boat. It's like selling my Daddy."

"Let me tell you something, son." Will took his arm off Karl's shoulders and turned slightly to look at him. "I'd have to sell the whole thing—my half, too—if Jacob hadn't offered to be my partner. Then the boat would be gone forever. I can't afford to run the business on my own. My brother is a good man, Karl, he's a *good* man; he's got a big heart and is doing this because—well, because he cares about me. He has a fine business sense and there's no doubt he'll be able to teach me a thing or two."

"Is he going to live here and fish with you?"

"Oh, no; heavens, no." Will laughed. "He's a lumber man, runs a big sawmill down in Wakelin. He has the money to pay a fair price to your mother up front, which is what she needs. No, he won't be moving to Tomos, but he is making it possible for the *Maggie O'Keefe* to stay with us. The fishing will go on. I think that's what your Daddy would want."

"But what about me? I wanted to work with him as soon I'm done with eighth grade."

"You know, your daddy always bragged about how smart you were, every little thing. New fathers do that, but he never stopped. He wanted you to finish high school and go to college. He wanted you to have a chance at the things he missed out on."

"But what if I want to fish?"

"I'll tell you what. After you finish high school, if you still want to be a fisherman, I'll help you get started. I'll teach you everything I know, and maybe we'll even work together again. I'll help you, I promise."

"It feels so sad."

"I know it does; for me, too. Your daddy and I worked together since before you were born. But now my brother is giving me a new start. If your father can't be here, having Jacob is prob'ly the next best thing."

"When is he coming to talk to my mother?"

"He'll be here for New Year's."

As Karl stared into the basement, he felt like he was looking down a long dark tunnel. He used to think he knew what his life would be like, but not anymore. Closets and nightmares and Uncle Melvin and snakes; going insane, and now this.

He leaned against his father's friend. "Will?"

"Yeah?"

"I'm scared."

"Aw, don't be. I'll be here." He put his arm back across Karl's shoulders.

"Will?"

"What?"

"If I could pick anyone for a new father, it would be you."

"Why, thank you. I take that as a real compliment."

Maggie called from the kitchen. "Come on up for dessert, fellas. We've got pound cake and blackberry pie and whipped cream. If you don't get up here soon, there might not be any left."

Will took his arm back, turned and looked at Karl again and grinned. "Whaddaya say, Ruffles? Dessert?"

In his mind, Karl saw the *Maggie O'Keefe* in the water, his father piloting it through the harbor and away. He opened his cave to swallow the boat and watched them glide in, smooth as satin.

"Sure, I guess, why not?"

Chapter 14
An Unexpected Possibility

Jacob opened his eyes and checked his watch as the train slowed toward its stop. They were on time. Out the window he could see Will waiting for him on the platform. He picked up his satchel and followed the other passengers down the aisle and out the door.

Will smiled at him. "Happy New Year, brother!"

"William!" Jacob put out his hand, but Will did not extend his in return.

"You don't want to touch me." He'd come from his foundry job and was so dirty that even the lines in his face were caked with black dust.

"I guess not!" Jacob withdrew his hand and backed away. He looked toward the boxcar where men were unloading trunks and crates. "Where's your truck?"

"Other side of the station."

"You'd better bring it around. The trunk Mother sent weighs more than she and Hilde combined; it'll take both of us to load it."

Will left with Jacob's satchel and returned in the truck. They each took a handle and lugged the thing from the boxcar, weaving their way through the milling crowd, finally hoisting it into the back end.

"Good, grief, what's in here?"

"Gifts. Christmas presents, for you and Bernie and the boys. Mostly the boys."

"Does she ever do anything without overdoing it?" They both climbed in.

"After the load she sent at Thanksgiving, I told her that whatever I brought this time would have to fit into one trunk. One. Anything else would have to stay home. Or she could mail it."

"How is she?"

"Fine. Bossy. I can't tell you what a relief it was to get on the train."

"Yeah?"

"She's been trying to turn me into a socialite again, dragging me to every *faaabulous* Christmas dance and party she could find." Jacob imitated his mother on the word *fabulous*. "She had a different woman waiting for me at each one. Or a different girl, I should call them girls."

Will looked at him, grinning. "And?"

"And what?"

"Any luck?"

"No! You think I'd give her the satisfaction?" Just thinking about his mother irritated Jacob. "They're all so forward; they giggle at everything and the only thing they can talk about is themselves."

"You've set your standards pretty high," laughed Will.

"I'm fine by myself. Hilde takes care of the house, she's good company for supper, then she cleans up and goes home. It's perfect."

"I have to tell you, Jacob, a wife is a whole lot better than a housekeeper. More fun, too. Say, would you mind if I made a quick stop? There's someone I need to see. It'll only take a minute."

"Sure."

Jacob watched the town go by as Will passed by his own neighborhood and turned onto another road. He read the street sign. "*Blight Street?* What kind of name is that?"

"The story goes it was supposed to be *Bright Street* but some sign painter tried to get his revenge by changing one letter. I guess no one cared enough to fix it."

Jacob chuckled. "Some revenge."

They pulled up to a house that looked almost like Will's, except the shingles on the sides were tan instead of brown. "Wanna come in?"

"Whose house?"

"Maggie Stern's. Eddie's wife. There's been trouble and I stop by every day to make sure everyone's safe and sound."

"I could stretch my legs a little."

Will got out of the truck, and Jacob followed him. A snow shovel scraped against wood in the back of the house. "'Z'at you back there, Karl?"

The scraping stopped. "Yeah. Will?"

"Come meet my brother."

A boy came loping around from the back, almost as tall as Jacob and all arms and legs. He wore a red wool stocking cap and a brown jacket that hung loose around his middle, so loose, thought Jacob, that two boys his size could have fit inside. In the dusky light, he looked ghostly with darkened eyes against pale skin. When he came close enough to shake hands with Will, Jacob saw the bruises.

"Hey, Will!" He laughed when he saw Will's dirty face. "Boy, do you need a bath!"

"An honest day's work, still on my face. Karl, this is my brother, Jacob."

"Is he the one—?"

"Yeah, but we'll come back for that later. Jacob, this is Eddie's son, Karl Stern."

Jacob extended his hand. "Karl, nice to meet you."

"Well, you look clean enough, anyway." Karl took his hand, but only briefly, his eyes moving from Jacob's head all the way down to his feet. He turned back to Will. "Are you here to see my mother?"

Will nodded. "How is everything? Has Melvin been around?"

"She doesn't know it, but I saw him drive by twice today. Both times, Aunt Kathleen was in the car, so he probably wouldn't have tried anything."

"Dog-gonit," said Will, "he's supposed to stay away from you."

"I don't suppose there's a law against driving by someone's house."

"Make sure your mother bolts the doors from the inside, every night, and when nobody's going in or out during the day."

"Okay, yeah, I will. Gotta clean the back stoop and make a path to the trash barrel before supper." Karl went off to the back of the house again.

Before Will knocked, a girl came to the door and let them in. She looked to be eight or ten or eleven; her hair was the most unusual and beautiful color he'd ever seen, not really red, but not really blonde either.

"Hi, Will. Mama said to let you in. Who's he?"

"This is my brother, Jacob Denver. Jacob, this is Karl's sister, Elizabeth."

"Lizzie," she corrected him.

"Hello, Lizzie." Jacob nodded and smiled.

A woman with hair the same color as Lizzie's came from the kitchen. She wore it pulled back and fastened with combs; a few stands in front had come loose, forming a soft frame around her face. She wore a plain green house dress with an old gray sweater and had a dishtowel flung over her left shoulder. Her nose was delicate and slender, her eyes turned upward at their outer edges, and although they were watering, she smiled at Will. She was magnetic, she was beautiful, she was exquisite. Jacob began to feel all jittery, like he'd been drinking too much coffee.

"Will, you don't have to come over here every day— not that I don't like seeing you." She used the back of her hand to wipe her eyes.

She turned her head and that's when Jacob noticed the bruise under her eye and the stitches above her ear. Shocked, he wondered what kind of trouble had befallen these people.

"I want to see for myself that you're all okay" said Will.

"Well, we're all fine." She turned to Jacob. "Hello. I'm Margaret Stern." She held out her right hand, but quickly took it back, laughing. "Oh, no, I'm sorry; I've been chopping onions. You don't want to smell like onions."

Will interrupted. "Maggie, this is my brother, Jacob Denver."

Jacob nodded his head, smiled and said, "I happen to like onions." He hated raw onions; why did he say that? He put his hand out to Margaret and she took it. Her hand was small compared to his, and cold.

"Your brother has been our white knight for the past few weeks, Mr. Denver."

"Is that so?" Jacob looked at Will and chuckled. "I

think he needs to polish his image."

As Margaret turned to look at Will, another little girl came from the kitchen. This one had fair, curly hair.

"Mama!" The girl held her right hand in her left. Blood dripped from one of her fingers into the hand the cupped beneath it.

"Anna, what did you do?" Margaret crouched down and took her daughter's hands into her own. "What did you do?"

The little girl started to cry. She looked at the floor. "I wanted to finish cutting the onions for you."

"What have I told you about knives?" She took the towel off her shoulder and wrapped it around the hand with the bleeding finger.

"Not to play with them. But I was *helping*."

"I told you to leave them alone."

"I'm sor-sorry. Are you going to punish—" Anna looked up at the side of her mother's face where the stitches were, and froze for a second before screaming. "*No stitches*, I don't want stitches!" She wrapped her arms around her mother's neck; Margaret held her. "Please, please, no, *please*, Mama!"

"Hush, now. Let me look at the cut again." Margaret peeled the little girl off her neck and unwrapped the bloody hand. Anna stopped screaming, but sobs still wracked her body. The tip of her thumb still bled, but only a little. Margaret smiled slightly and looked up at Will. "Well, what do you think, Will?"

Will bent down to look. "Oh, I think we can let Dr. Lyman eat his supper tonight."

"I can take care of it for you." Margaret stood up. "Go up to the bathroom and rinse it off. I'll be there in a minute."

"*No iodine.*" Anna started to panic again, that same raspy cry. "No iodine, Mama, please, please, *please!*"

"Anna Mary!" Margaret scolded her sharply. The little girl quieted. "Do as I say, or you will be punished."

Anna turned and went up the stairs, still crying, but not screaming.

Margaret turned back to Will. "See, everything is fine, except for my children playing with knives. I think you'll have to excuse me now, so I can tend to our latest crisis. Mr. Denver, nice to meet you." She looked into his eyes.

Jacob felt like he'd drunk another cup of coffee.

"Now I can't shake your hand." She smiled at him and held her palms up; they were bloody from the little girl's cut.

"That's all right."

"We'll be back on Sunday afternoon," said Will, "after dinner, to talk about the boat, is that all right?"

"It's fine. I'll see you then." She turned to go upstairs.

"Hold it!" Now Will spoke sharply.

She turned around. "What?"

"After we leave you're supposed to lock the door and throw the bolts."

"I refuse to make my home into a prison, Will." Her quiet defiance impressed Jacob. "If I do that, it means Melvin gets what he wants—for us to live like a bunch of scared rabbits. I will lock up at night and be careful the rest of the time."

"Aw, come on, Maggie, don't take any chances."

"I don't intend to. Now I must see to Anna. But just so you don't worry, I'll wait until you go so I can lock the door behind you."

Jacob opened the truck door and got in. He tried to

act unaffected by what he'd seen. "So, what happened to them?"

"Melvin Straus, her sister's husband, has been hounding Maggie and threatening the boy for weeks. He thinks it's his job to take over for Eddie—in every way. He tried a few things with Maggie and scared her half out of her wits."

"What kind of things?"

Will looked over at him and shook his head. "Jeez, Jacob, you *have* been alone too long. You saw her, what do you think?"

"Oh. Yeah."

"I've had friends sleeping by her front door for the last two weeks to make sure he didn't come back and try anything else. Spent a few nights there myself. And then, a week ago, he came to 'discipline' Karl." Will raised his voice. "And beat the *shit* out of him!" He let out an angry sigh. "In the process, the sonofa—he hit Maggie, too. I stayed half the night helping the doctor put 'em back together. They had a miserable Christmas."

"What about her sister?"

"Oh, he takes *real* good care of her. She stays shut up inside her house for weeks at a time, according to Maggie; she thinks Kathleen's recovering from whatever he does to her."

"Any children?"

"No, thank God." Will pulled up in front of his own house. He looked out the window and smiled. "Speaking of kids, look."

Two little smiling faces, Billy and Ned, peered out the front window, jumping up and down. Here we go again, thought Jacob. "It must be nice to have someone who's happy to see you."

"It's called family. Mother has a point, you should listen to her."

"Right." Jacob scowled at his brother and got out of the truck.

After supper, Jacob offered to wash the dishes so Will and Bernie could get the boys settled down and into bed. They'd been wild with excitement when he opened his mother's treasure chest of gifts and it didn't end with the opened presents. They giggled and squirmed all through supper, making any meaningful adult conversation impossible. Being around them made Jacob jumpy and irritable.

Later, after Bernie and Will went to bed, Jacob delayed climbing the stairs to the frigid attic as long as he could. It was still warm in the living room, so he stayed up to read the newspaper. He looked for a story about a woman and boy being beaten, but didn't find one. Well, that happened a week ago.

He put the paper down and went to the window. A light snow fell to earth, reflected in the lamplight shining from his window, clean and fresh and new. He watched the movement of the flakes and was captured by the beauty of it. It took only a little wind to make the snow blow one way and then the other. He gazed at it, such a simple thing, yet so beautiful.

The thought of his mother's schemes to find him a wife intruded and made Jacob frown. Lately she'd been pulling him this way and that, choking him, suffocating him, trying to make him happy the way *she* wanted him to be happy.

Then he saw that with a little more power, the wind could lift the snowflakes and draw them upward. Amazed, he watched them rise from the ground and float in the air.

He knew they had to come down again somewhere, but he wanted to believe they would keep going up and up and up, not stopping until they finally reached the peace of heaven. What a wonder that would be, those fragile, little snowflakes defying gravity and the laws of the universe!

The beauty of Margaret Stern, her strength, her confidence—her vulnerability—had added a new current of air to his life. Jacob began to breathe again. He was free; floating, flying, rising into the sky, looking down at the sorry snowflakes bound to stay on earth

Chapter 15

Remember Me

At half past noon on New Year's Day, Jacob put on his good suit and said good-bye to his brother's family. He kissed Bernie's cheek and hugged Billy and Ned, who'd become more entertainment than aggravation to him. His train left at three, so there would be plenty of time to visit Margaret Stern and present his offer. His jitters returned as he climbed into Will's truck.

"Now listen," said Will, "you should know the boy is plenty upset about selling his father's boat. He may be a bit ornery; remember he's hurting. He's been acting strange lately, I think it's all been too much for him."

"All right. I'll be my usual charming self. Anything else I should know?"

Will chuckled. "You? Charming?"

"I told you women have been flocking for my attentions." Jacob smiled and pulled a comb from his pocket and ran it through his dark hair, his hands shaking slightly.

"You told me Mother was behind that."

"I did not."

"Right. Now quit your primping, Princess, you're gonna

— 184 —

make me look bad. Anyway, we're here."

Jacob followed his brother up the walk and waited while he went to the door. After he knocked three times, the door finally swung open.

Will howled with laughter. "Ruffles! Howareya?"

"'Now ain't I pretty?'"

"You sure are, darlin'. Jacob, come meet my friend, Ruffles." Will entered the house and held the door open.

Jacob stepped inside. He felt it immediately, subtle at first, then nearly bowling him over until he wanted to weep with longing. Whatever it was awakened within him a yearning he'd put away years ago, catching him square between denial and desire. The mixed aromas of coffee, sweet spices and baking apples; the stately, worn furniture; the warmth that went far beyond temperature all cast a spell over him. But he knew there was more to it than that.

"How do you do?" said the boy under the hat. "I am Ruffles." He bowed slightly.

"Ah, nice to meet you, Ruffles," replied Jacob. Will said the boy had been acting strange, but this wasn't at all what he expected.

"Karl, take their coats, please. I'll be there in a minute." Margaret's voice came from the kitchen.

Her voice is part of it, thought Jacob.

"Your coats, please." Ruffles took Jacob's coat first and hung it on a peg by the front door. "Nice. Heavy. Must be warm."

"It is." Jacob tried to keep from laughing.

"William, give me your ratty old jacket. A little thin, don't you think?"

Karl's antics were part of it, too.

"You don't like my jacket?" Will acted insulted, but his

eyes twinkled.

Margaret came from the kitchen, more lovely than before. Spellbound, Jacob nearly gasped. Even with the fading bruise under her right eye, her simple beauty outshone all the powdered, rouged, and perfectly coiffed young ladies who'd been seated across from him at the countless dinner parties he'd endured at his mother's insistence. When he looked at her, his whole world began to shift. *She's* the source, he thought. He wanted to cry out.

Margaret laughed at her son. "Karl, take that thing off, now."

"My name is Ruffles."

"Ruffles, you'd better let Karl come out, otherwise he won't get any apple pie." Still smiling, she looked at Jacob and extended her hand. "Hello, again, Mr. Denver. No onions this time."

She had no idea she was an enchantress.

Jacob took her hand, felt her firm grip, the softness of her skin. A current ran from her fingers into the palm of his hand, feeding his jitters.

"I understand you've already met my son, Karl."

"My name is Ruffles," came the voice from under the hat.

"Yes, we've met already."

"Karl, please take the hat off, I don't want to have to ask again."

The boy removed the hat. He had white blond hair, curly like the little girl's and a bit too long. The bruises under his eyes were faded to a greenish yellow. "Hello."

"Nice to see you again, Karl."

"Yessir."

The little girls watched them from the kitchen door. Jacob smiled when he saw them.

"I believe we have some business to do." Margaret seemed to have no problem taking charge, but not in a bossy way. "Come in; let's sit in the dining room. Karl, I want you with me for this." She took the chair at the head of the table, motioned for Jacob to sit at her left. Karl sat at her right, and Will sat on the other side of Jacob.

Lizzie came and whispered in Margaret's ear. She smiled. "That's a wonderful idea. Lizzie, this is Will's brother, Mr. Denver."

"I know, I met him last time."

Jacob nodded. "Hello, Lizzie."

She nodded, before disappearing into the kitchen.

He cleared his throat. "Mrs. Stern, I want you to know how impressed I am with the *Maggie O'Keefe*. It's a fine vessel. Your husband and my brother have taken good care of it."

"Yes, well," she paused, looking at the tablecloth. "It's how they made their living."

The boy kept his eyes on his mother. Jacob saw him lean toward her slightly.

The brothers laid out the plan. Jacob tried to remain business-like even with all the strange emotions rolling around inside him. He reached into the breast pocket of his suit coat, pulled out the contract and unfolded it.

She reached for it. "Please. I want to read it before I sign anything."

"Of course."

Margaret held the papers so her son could read them, too. Suddenly she gasped. She'd read to the bottom line. "This is way too much. The boat's only worth half of that, isn't it, Will?"

"We had the boat and all the equipment appraised, Mrs. Stern, and I'm offering you a fair price."

"Then give me half; my husband only owned half."

"You don't understand," answered Jacob. "This *is* half of what it's worth. If you look at the next page, you'll find a copy of the appraisal."

Margaret turned the page, glanced at it briefly, then looked at Will. Karl took it from her and read what it said. He raised his eyebrows.

"Will, tell me this isn't charity for a poor widow with three hungry mouths to feed."

She trusts him, thought Jacob.

Will grinned. "It isn't charity. Take it, Maggie, sign the paper. Come spring, the fishing will go on; you know Eddie'd want that. And you and the kids will be taken care of; he'd want that, too."

Margaret's eyes locked onto Karl's. They stared at each other for a few seconds; neither blinked. Something passed between them. A shared pain? Some kind of mutual comfort? Embarrassed, Jacob glanced away.

"Do you have a pen, Mr. Denver?" She said it without moving her eyes from her son.

He reached into his pocket and gave her his best fountain pen.

Margaret signed the papers; so did Will and Jacob. There were several copies, one for each of them and one for Jacob's lawyer. When they finished, he gave her an envelope containing a check for the full amount.

Karl put the hat on again and pulled it down over his eyes.

Margaret sighed and looked across the room to the clock on the mantle. "Mr. Franke let us borrow the boat before you and Eddie bought it, Will. Did he ever tell you that we spent the first few nights of our marriage there? Our honeymoon." The corners of her mouth pulled down and for a second her eyes got red, but there were no tears.

The boy got up, tripped on the leg of his chair, and ran upstairs.

Margaret stood up. "Karl?"

"Let him be, Maggie," said Will. "I'll go after him in a minute."

Jacob felt bad for the boy.

Margaret held her hand out to him and he took it. His hand easily surrounded hers.

"Mr. Denver, thank you so much."

After witnessing the barely disguised grief of the boy and his mother, Jacob could hardly speak. He felt like an intruder. He cleared his throat again. "Please, call me Jacob," he said, hoping she'd ask him to call her Margaret. He looked into her eyes and saw a miracle.

She looked away. "Now would the two of you like some coffee, and maybe some apple pie?"

"Do you really have to ask?" Will grinned again.

Jacob smiled. "That would be lovely." *Lovely*. He sounded like his mother.

"I'll get Karl." Will took the stairs two at a time.

Margaret excused herself to the kitchen. Jacob heard her talking to her daughters. "Did you draw that all by yourself, Annie? Why, it's your best picture yet. Now move your papers and crayons so we can cut the pie." Dishes rattled, silverware clanged.

Somewhere above him, Jacob heard his brother talking to Karl. He couldn't make out the words, but Will spoke with great tenderness. These were the sounds of a family, so ordinary, so real. His own big house stood still and lonely, like a tomb, except when Hilde had her Ladies' Guild over or he sat moping at the piano, using scales and sonatas to ward off the long evening. He wanted *this,* not some blue blooded rich girl and a houseful of servants.

Careful, Denver! He tried to push away the feeling that he was standing at the end of his life looking back, watching the beginning of something important, but it wouldn't leave him.

Lizzie came from the kitchen with six forks. She put one before Jacob, then one at every place, shyly glancing at him once and again. Anna came next, with the napkins. She stopped in front of him.

"My name is Anna Mary Stern and I'm six years old," she announced with a broad smile. There were two, no, three empty places where her front teeth used to be and a white bandage on her finger. "I know who you are. You're Billy's Uncle Jacob."

"Yes, indeed."

"Billy's my boyfriend."

"Oh, I see. Well, Anna, I'm pleased to meet you." They shook hands. "Tell me, how is your finger?"

She held it up for him to see, pouting. "Mama says it'll get better, but I'm not allowed to use knives until I'm ten years old."

"I suppose mothers know best, don't they?"

Anna nodded. She put the napkins under the forks and went back into the kitchen.

Will and the boy came down the stairs together; Will had him laughing. They sat at the table with Jacob.

"So, you're the young man who saved my brother's life." Jacob knew the whole story.

"I don't know if I'd say that," answered Karl. "I had a lot of help. Anyway, Will did the same thing for me a week ago, so we're even."

Jacob saw how the boy admired Will. A stab of envy

pierced his heart. Did anyone admire him like that? "And what did my brother do to save your life?"

"He got Uncle Melvin away when he was beating me. You shoulda seen it, Will took care of him with my mother's wooden spoon." Both Karl and Will laughed.

"Oh?"

"He stuck it in Uncle Melvin's ribs and made him think it was a gun, so he backed off."

"Clever, William. I thought maybe you'd taken up cooking."

Will shrugged. "Just making do."

Lizzie came out of the kitchen carrying two fancy china plates, each with a large slice of pie. She set one before Jacob and one before Will. With both hands, Anna came carrying a third plate and set it in front of her brother. Margaret came with coffee in a china coffeepot, while the girls brought out more pie for their mother and themselves. Jacob thoroughly enjoyed the procession.

Finally, Margaret came and sat down again. The pie tasted better than anything he'd ever eaten—or did he think so because she made it? It didn't matter, he savored every bite.

As they ate, Karl recited statistics about Lake Superior. "Do you know Lake Superior is the deepest and the coldest of the Great Lakes, with an average yearly temperature of only forty degrees? It's cold enough to kill a person, even in summer."

Will looked down at this plate. "We know all about that, Karl."

Nobody spoke for a moment.

"I just want to make sure your brother knows what he's getting into."

"Karl received a set of encyclopedias for Christmas

and has been reading them all week," Margaret explained.

Jacob didn't know how he should respond, but he looked at the boy and hoped his words sounded kind and not sarcastic. "Well, thank you for enlightening me. I do appreciate it. You've inspired me to read up on it myself when I get home."

After that, the conversation became easy and light-hearted; even Karl laughed. Margaret got up more than once to refill their coffee cups and each time she did, Jacob watched her go into the kitchen and eagerly waited for her to return. He relaxed and thought this felt more like a home than any place he'd ever been.

Before Jacob and Will put their coats on, the girls came from the kitchen holding their hands behind their backs.

"Will," said Lizzie, "I made something for you." She held out a picture of the *Maggie O'Keefe* floating on a lake of blue with a slice of yellow sun shining down from behind a single cloud.

Will sat back down. "Well, now, isn't that nice? You're a fine artist." Two figures stood on the boat, one with yellow hair and one with brown. "Tell me about these people."

"That one's you, and that one's my Daddy. I drew it so you'd always remember him."

Will hugged her for a long time. "Oh, I promise you, Lizzie, I will always remember your Daddy." After he let her go, he dug in his pocket for a handkerchief and wiped his nose. "Thank you. I think I'll hang this in the boat. What do you think?"

Lizzie nodded and smiled.

Anna had a drawing, too, but she came to Jacob. "I

made you a picture, too, Mr. Denver." She held it out to him.

"Oh, my goodness." He had no idea what to make of it.

"See, here's the boat and there's Will and there's you. And those down there, they're fish."

"Well, I like to see all those fish. But tell me, why is Will the only one on the boat?"

"See, you're on the shore and you're waving for him to come home for supper."

"Oh, yes, I see it now. Thank you."

"Turn it over. See, there's a picture of me."

A smiling face surrounded by yellow curlicues filled the whole page. Jacob's heart melted. "I like this very much, Anna. Do you think you could autograph it for me?"

She looked puzzled.

Karl chuckled. "Put your name on your paper."

Anna hurried into the kitchen and came back a few seconds later and gave the paper back to Jacob. Underneath the face, in beginner printing, were the words *Anna Mary Stern.*

"I am going to hang this in a special place. Thank you very much." He wanted to hug the little girl or kiss her cheek, but he bent and shook her hand again instead.

"Jacob, it's getting late." Will handed him his coat. It was almost two-thirty, the train left at three.

"I guess we were having such a nice time we forgot to look at the clock."

Margaret followed them to the door. Before Jacob put on his gloves, he took her hand again. The current was still running; its energy went straight to his heart. "Thank you, Mrs. Stern, for your hospitality."

"I should be thanking you, Mr. Denver."

"It's Jacob."

She smiled at him. "It's good to know I have money for emergencies now."

"My privilege." He wanted to kiss her hand but didn't dare. "I hope our paths will cross again."

"You never know, perhaps they will." Her smile was like the sun rising after a long, dark night.

Will jingled his keys. "Let's go, Jacob, if you miss the train I'll have to put up with you for another whole day."

"My, we wouldn't want that to happen, now would we?" He winked at the girls, shook hands with Karl, and took one more look at Margaret to fix her face in his memory.

"You're awfully quiet." Will glanced over at Jacob. They were halfway to the station and he hadn't said a word.

"You didn't tell me she was so beautiful."

"Who? Maggie?"

"Who else? But not just the way she looks." Jacob shifted in his seat. "The way she talks and the way she treats her children and the way she was with us. And not just her. Her house, her kids, her coffee, her pie..."

"I won't argue with you on that."

Jacob didn't speak again for a long minute. He knew his voice would sound tight, but he couldn't make the feeling go away. "She was... it was so... I dunno, Will, I feel like... "

"Aw, Jacob!" Will raised his voice. "Come on now, *jeesh!* She's still mourning her husband, for Pete's sake. It's only been a couple of months." He took his eyes off the road and looked at him. "Don't *do* that now."

"Don't do what?"

"Don't go blubbering all over my truck. And don't

go after Maggie, she's got enough on her mind without a lumberjack boyfriend pestering her."

"I'm going to write to her. I'm going to write and ask if I can see her when I come back in February."

"Why are you coming back in February?"

"To see her and sleep in your attic." They'd arrived at the station. Will stopped the truck and Jacob jumped out. He retrieved his satchel from the back and stopped at Will's door. Will rolled down the window.

"Thanks, Brother." Jacob took Will's hand. "It was a great New Years. The best ever, and I mean it."

"Glad you came. Thanks for the boat deal. Say hello to Mother, tell her we'll write."

"*Call* her. You've got a telephone. She loves hearing from your boys."

"We'll try." Will started to roll up the window.

Jacob nodded and turned away.

"Jacob, wait."

He turned back.

"Be careful. Please. They're all real breakable, Maggie especially. They've had enough suffering."

"Who's going to make them suffer? I'm just going to write her a letter." The train whistle blew and he had to run to board it.

Jacob leaned back in his seat and closed his eyes, wondering at the events of the past few hours. He'd given up the idea of ever loving a woman again, yet from the moment he saw her, he felt something—something *big*. Was it pity? He remembered what hit him as soon as he walked in her door, the way he felt when he first looked at her, the electricity running from her fingers into his hand. He felt sorry for her grief, that was for sure; if he had the power to make it disappear, he would. He felt sorry for the boy, too, he knew that. But no, it wasn't pity. Strong, confident, and dignified, Margaret Stern was anything but pitiful. She seemed to know what she wanted for her family, what she needed. But would she want *him?* The question burned in Jacob's heart.

He pictured her face. She wore no rouge, but she didn't need any; even with the nasty bruise, her cheeks reminded him of those pale apricot roses Hilde planted last year. Her eyes enlivened her smile and her smile lit her entire face. Her fair hair, that beautiful mixture of blond and red, hadn't been bobbed like nearly every other woman he passed on the street; it must be quite long if she kept it pulled away from her face like that. He wondered what she looked like with it loose around her shoulders.

Her body was rounded in the right places, not thin and shapeless like so many young women these days. She was no longer a girl, but she was still youthful. Never in his life had he seen or met anyone like her.

Surely, his mother would not approve of this, but then he didn't approve of her meddling, either. He could see her shocked face, hear her disbelieving voice. He smiled. What a delicious thought!

Jacob looked out the window as the train passed trees, fields, barns and animals. And houses where real people lived—where *families* lived. He wondered if any of them were as warm and welcoming as Margaret's.

He decided it was time to hire the carpenters to come back and finish the second story of his house; he'd call them tomorrow. Just in case.

Chapter 16
Ink, Pencil and Paper

When Karl went back to school on the day after New Year's, he thought he'd resume his usual place as the seventh grade outcast, but Susan, Rebecca and Ella met him at the door, giggling. They all wore the familiar Holy Angels' blue plaid uniform, each girl's hair in either one braid or two.

"Hi, Karl!" they said, almost in unison.

"Hi." Karl wanted to thank them for what they did, but they made him nervous. He looked at his shoes. "I have to go hang up my coat."

They followed after him. "Did you know that Jimmy and Elmer are supposed to apologize to you today?" Rebecca caught up and walked at his side.

"So I hear."

The five minute bell rang and students disappeared into classrooms, including the girls. Sister Mary Anthony came flying down the hallway, on her way to some important place, but Karl called out to her anyway.

"Sister?"

She slowed down and almost stopped. "Yes, Karl."

"Thank you for the cupcakes you sent home with my sisters. It was very nice of you."

She smiled, but warned, "You'd better get to your seat before the bell."

"Yes, Sister."

A few minutes later, as the seventh grade class followed the sixth graders into the church, Jimmy and Elmer turned around in the line and looked at Karl, whispering back and forth. Karl wished sister Mary Anthony would let the whole thing drop instead of making his former friends "apologize" to him in front of the whole school.

After chapel devotions and the weekly announcements, Father Cunningham called Karl forward.

"Karl, I understand that the fuss you made during Mass wasn't entirely your fault. Regretfully, you alone were punished twice for things other boys had a hand in."

Karl nodded. "It's all right, Father." He certainly didn't expect an apology from *him*.

"While we can't undo what happened to you, we can try to make things right between you boys."

Sister Mary Anthony stood and called Jimmy and Elmer to the front of the church. They had composed a letter of apology to read to Karl. She made Elmer read it out loud.

> *"Dear Karl,*
> *We are very sorry for making you fall on your face. Sister is making us tell you this as an apology. A long time ago we were pals. Maybe we can be still be friends.*
> *Sincerely, Jimmy and Elmer."*

Elmer handed the note to Karl. Karl didn't say anything, but extended his hand to each of them. They took it, but didn't really shake it. Neither one of them looked sorry for anything, with those little smirks hiding in the corners of their mouths. Karl appreciated Sister Mary Anthony's efforts, but he didn't trust Elmer or Jimmy.

Later, before math class started, Karl looked at the note. Some of the letters were darker than the others, like they'd been traced and retraced. Puzzled, he scanned the note for a clue. At the bottom of the page, in minuscule handwriting it said, "Read the dark letters, stupid."

Yourestillapansystern. *You're still a pansy, Stern.* Karl chuckled. Clever. He folded the note and put it in his pocket. He looked up to see Elmer and Jimmy laughing at him. He smiled at them and nodded his head. Elmer rolled his eyes and looked up at the chalkboard. Jimmy stuck out his tongue like a little kid. That's about what Karl expected of them, but it didn't matter. He had no use for friends like those two.

That night when he was supposed to be doing his homework, Karl took the note from his pocket and smoothed it out on his desk. He took out his colored pencils and drew a snake all along the sides and the bottom of the paper. He drew a side view of the cobra's head around the names of his former friends, its long tongue underscoring the word *sincerely*. Up at the top he drew a giant foot, this one with a boot exactly like his. Satisfied with his work, Karl opened his drawing pad and laid the note inside, closed it, and slid it back under his mattress. Now he could concentrate on his history lesson.

The cream colored envelope, addressed to *Mrs. Margaret Stern,* was still cold from its journey in the postman's sack when Maggie brought it into the house. She knew she'd seen the even, measured handwriting somewhere before, but couldn't quite place it. Inside, on crisp, sharply folded stationery was a letter from Will's brother.

She thought they'd finished all their business about the boat, but as she read what he'd written she had to turn away from her children so they wouldn't see her face. Heart pounding, she slipped it back into its envelope and put it in the pocket of her apron. When she was sure the children were asleep, she reread Mr. Denver's letter before hiding it under the mattress of her bed—her bed and Eddie's.

> ...*I know your husband has only been gone a few short months, so I hope I am not being too forward to ask if I might see you again the next time I come to visit my brother? I, too, am alone, and not by choice. I would greatly enjoy sharing your company. I hope to hear from you soon.*
> *Sincerely, Jacob H. Denver*

Day after day, Maggie read Jacob's letter, each time thinking how she should respond. Every morning she tried to write an answer, and every morning she put the letter back under her mattress without writing a thing. She had a good idea what he had in mind—no, she *knew* what he had in mind and it scared her. There hadn't been a single night when she didn't cry herself to sleep longing for Eddie, not *one*, so how could she think about another man? What would the children think, what would her mother think if she allowed him to court her? She knew for a fact he wasn't Catholic; that would be a problem, too.

On the other hand, although the boat brought far more money than she'd expected, she knew it wouldn't last forever, even if she watched every penny she spent.

Even though she hadn't seen Melvin since Christmas Eve, she knew he wouldn't stop hounding her unless there was another man in her life. And who would take care of her children if she should die before they grew up? She shuddered. She'd do whatever it took to keep Melvin from getting his hands on them. For weeks, she weighed these things in her mind. Jacob seemed to be likeable, a good man, if reserved and a little sad. Being Will's brother and all, she thought she might be happy with him.

"Oh, stop it," she said out loud. "He only wants to visit. What harm could there be?" So as soon as the house was quiet, she sat down and wrote with as little emotion as possible.

> *January 24, 1929*
> *Dear Mr. Denver,*
> *Thank you for your kind note. The children and I enjoyed meeting you on New Year's Day. I am grateful that Will needed to look no further than his own family to find a new partner. My son and I would have hated to see the boat sold off to someone else.*
> *You are welcome to come visit us any time you are in Tomos Bay.*
> *Yours Truly, Margaret Stern*

Karl knew the girls in his class talked about him all the time and it made him uncomfortable. He was finished with Elmer and Jimmy, that was for sure, but none of the other boys wanted to have anything to do with him, either. At lunchtime they never left room for him to sit at their end of the table, but the girls always saved him a spot, usually in the middle of a bunch of them. He didn't have much to say, but listened to their silly giggling and smiled politely. Of course, if any of them asked him a question, he'd answer. Then they'd all be quiet and listen, like his words were special or golden or something. He appreciated how nice they were being to him, but it was embarrassing, too.

When he started his math homework one night, he found an envelope stuck in the pages of his book. Someone must have put it there when Sister Marguerite called him to the chalkboard to do long division. He opened the envelope and looked at the end of the note before he read the rest of it. *Yours truly, Ella.* He sighed. Oh, brother, now what?

> *Dear Karl,*
>
> *How are you? I am fine. I liked having you sit next to me at lunch yesterday. I wish you would talk to us more, all the girls know how smart you are, and how lonesome you must be since the boys started ignoring you. I can't figure out why they are so mean to you, but I will always be your friend.*
>
> *One thing I want to ask you is, how come you had bruises on your face on Christmas Eve? You looked like someone hit you. I'll bet you showed them, didn't you?*
>
> *And another thing we were wondering is what happened to you at Mass on Christmas Eve? Some of us saw you sit down real fast, and you had to lie down. Did you get sick? Are you okay? Please write back.*

Karl got up from his chair and flopped on the bed, face down. He didn't want to tell Ella that Melvin beat him for punishment. And why did she have to know what happened to him in church? Nobody needed to know he was going insane. When he closed his eyes, he saw the snake trying to take over the whole altar. He got up, shivering.

He pulled his drawing pad out from under his mattress, found his pencils and set to work. He drew Father Cunningham as best he could, and the altar and the cobra on top of the altar. Father had a surprised expression on his face, his eyes and his mouth all in the shape of the letter O. Karl thought about putting a foot in this picture, but didn't.

"Karl, bedtime. It's late." His mother knocked on the door.

He flipped the drawing pad over, gathered up the pencils, and threw them in the desk drawer. "What time is it?"

His mother opened the door. "It's nine-thirty. I'm going to bed. Do you still have work to do?"

"Ahh, yeah, I do. I have my math yet."

She came over to the desk and put her hand on his back. "What have you been doing in here all evening? You haven't come out of your room once since supper."

Karl saw her eye the drawing pad, still on his desk.

"I have lots of homework." He remembered the history quiz tomorrow. He hadn't reviewed anything yet. He yawned.

"Well, finish up and get to bed." She kissed his forehead. "Good night."

When he heard her door close, he got up and pulled his own shut again and slid the pad into his school bag. If she saw what he'd been drawing, she'd know for sure he was going crazy. Better hide it from her as long as he could.

Every evening when he came home from the mill,

Jacob flipped through the mail looking for a letter from *her*, hoping she would see fit to write to him. But day after day, week after week, he received nothing. What if she never answered his letter? What if she had found him repulsive? He made himself quit thinking of her as *Margaret*; the name carried too many hopes, too many dreams. *She* and *her* would work much better. Discouragement grew like a noxious weed within him.

"Chacob, you are moping around here like you lost your best friend. What's gotten you?" Hilde, his housekeeper, didn't miss a thing. In ten years, he'd had little success keeping anything from her.

"Nothing, I'm fine. See?" He smiled—brightly, he thought.

"You are a fraud. You sooner or later will tell me."

"There's nothing to tell, Hilde, nothing at all." How could he explain to her the long, slow demise of possibility, the disappointment of an affection born only to die untested, undeclared and unrequited? He wouldn't allow himself even to think the word *love*.

Finally, at the end of January, he received a letter from Tomos Bay. Hilde still bustled around the kitchen preparing their supper, so Jacob put the envelope in his pocket and climbed the stairs to see what the carpenters had accomplished that day.

Savoring the anticipation of reading Margaret's letter, he breathed in the smell of cut wood and sawdust, the sweetest fragrance he knew. The workmen had already framed in walls for four smaller bedrooms, not the three he'd first planned for. There would be a small bath at each end of the hall and a private bath in what would be his room, not the two he originally thought he wanted. All this cost him plenty, but he didn't mind. Besides, the work needed to be done sooner or later.

Jacob stepped into the master bedroom, took out the letter and opened it. His heart sank when he saw how short it was. *What were you thinking, Denver?*

He read the note. Pleasantries, pleasantries before the let down. Then the last sentence. *You are welcome to come visit us any time you are in Tomos Bay.* Any time. He smiled, laughed, heard music in her name. "*Maar-g'ret*," he chanted, like a mother calling her child.

"Chacob, wash up your hands for supper. And close that door, cold air is coming down here."

He put the letter back in the envelope and the envelope back into his pocket. "Right away, Hilde."

The girls at school started to ignore Karl and one day "forgot" to save him a place at the lunch table. He had to eat with the sixth graders, which wouldn't have been so bad except none of them would talk to him, either. When he opened his history book that night, another note from Ella fell out.

> *Dear Karl,*
> *Why are you so rude to me? I sent you a letter two weeks ago and you didn't answer. You hurt my feelings. My mother says in order to have a friend you have to be one, and Karl Stern, I can see why you don't have any pals. You don't know how to be one!*
> *We all still want to know what happened to you at Christmas. Like who beat you up and if you got sick in Mass. You know, all the girls care about you, so you should answer our questions. We're the ones who told Sister Mary Anthony what really happened with Jimmy and Elmer, you know. So please write back.*

Karl sighed. He knew he should thank the seventh grade girls for having the gumption to stand up to Sister Mary Anthony for him and for being so nice when his best friends turned on him. He probably owed them an explanation. He tore a page from his writing tablet.

> *Dear Ella,*
> *I'm sorry I never wrote back. I know I should have done it sooner, but I didn't know what to say. My uncle hit me as punishment for leaving school that day. He is mean and I think he was just waiting for a reason to do it. The police told him he has to stay away from me and my mother, so we're okay now.*
> *What happened to me in Mass on Christmas was—I fainted. I passed out and fell over like a big baby. My mother made me stay in bed the next day, but as you know, I am all over it now. I want to thank you and all the girls for standing up for me in the lunchroom. My sister, Liz, told me all about it. Now I think she wants to be like you: brave.*
> *Sincerely, Karl Stern.*

Karl folded the note into a little package that would fit into his pocket. He'd give it to Ella on his way out of school the next day so he wouldn't get in trouble for passing notes in class. He looked at her letter again and thought about drawing on it, but decided not to. His pencils didn't have any snakes for the seventh grade girls.

Ella smiled at him the next day when he tossed his note to her as they left school. He hurried out the door and across the playground where he stopped to wait for Lizzie and Anna. When he turned around and looked back, all the seventh grade girls were bunched up around her like a swarm of honeybees.

On February 14, Maggie received another envelope in the mailbox from Jacob Denver. He'd sent her a valentine, a pink heart edged with paper lace and a bouquet of roses in the center. Underneath the flowers it simply said *Valentine*. On the back he'd written *I will see you soon. Yours, Jacob.* Maggie felt funny when she read it the first time, like she was being unfaithful to Eddie. No, she couldn't let this happen. But the more she thought about it, the more she realized she had to. Her heart skipped a beat as she read his note a second time.

Thankfully, the mail had arrived before the children came home from school. After she read his note a third time to make sure he'd written what she thought he'd written, Maggie took it to the bedroom and hid it under her mattress with his first letter. Sitting on the bed, she gazed at the one photograph she had of Eddie, their wedding picture. Maggie took it from the night stand and held it to her breast, plunging into the deep and empty well of his absence, crying her heart out for him.

The older grades at Holy Angels School didn't make a fuss for Valentine's Day like the little kids did, but Sister Anne, who taught Karl's last class of the day, brought heart shaped cookies for her students.

"Now, I have something important to say to all of you. We sisters do not have families like you do, so we become one another's family and you become our children. I want to tell you that I care about each one of you and that you mean a great deal to me. Jesus told us to love one another, which means we should treat each other with kindness and respect and affection. I know some of you have cards or messages for your classmates, so I am giving you the last five minutes of class to hand them out. And you may eat your cookies."

While many other students got up to give envelopes and construction paper hearts to their friends, Karl stayed at his desk and took a bite of his cookie. He hadn't thought about giving valentines this year, although Lizzie and Anna had been making them for days.

As he sat at his desk, every girl came by and left him a card or piece of candy; he was glad they weren't mad anymore. He smiled and said "thanks" to each one. Then Elmer came by with a big envelope, and held out his hand to Karl.

"Hey, let's let bygones be bygones, huh, Karl?"

Karl shook his hand and said, "Okay, sure, I guess so," but he knew they were up to no good. He put all the cards in his school bag and waited for the bell to ring.

Later, in his bedroom, he looked at the cards from the girls. They said things like "Be Mine" or "Good looking" or "Please sit by me tomorrow." He smiled. Even though it embarrassed him, he had to admit he liked all this adoration.

Then he took the big envelope from his bag and opened it. He expected something to jump out at him, but instead found a nice card, the kind of card a person would send to a mother or grandmother, or maybe even a sweetheart. It had a bouquet of purple and yellow pansies on the front and underneath the flowers it said *Pansies for Thoughts*. Karl started to laugh. He turned it over and read, *Thinking of You, Valentine.* Underneath, in Elmer's handwriting it said, *We still think you're a pansy, Stern, so go kiss your Mama. XOXOXO.*

Karl laughed so loudly his mother heard and came upstairs. He showed her the card.

"Who gave this to you, Karl? This isn't funny, it's *mean*." Her eyes filled with tears.

"Don't worry about it, Mama, it's just from a couple of dumb boys. They think I'm a sissy."

"Who? Elmer and Jimmy?"

"Yeah."

"Sister Mary Anthony should know about this."

"No. If she finds out they're still doing stuff, they'll get in trouble and it'll only get worse for me. Forget about it."

"You poor boy." She pushed his hair away from his face. "Not only did your Daddy die, but your friends have all deserted you."

"Forget it, Mother. I'm perfectly happy without friends, I don't need 'em."

She shook her head. She seemed extra sad today.

"I've got a lot of homework."

When she left the room, Karl closed the door and took out his colored pencils. All around the pansies on the front of the card, and around the words on the back, he drew snakes with venom dripping from their fangs. When he finished, it was suppertime.

Chapter 17

Falling

Two days later, in the early afternoon, Jacob Denver appeared at Maggie's door, this time without Will. She was surprised when she saw him, not because he'd come to visit, but because she'd forgotten how much he resembled his brother with his dark brown hair and eyes, the shape of his face, his broad forehead. Jacob's hair was much neater than Maggie had ever seen Will's, except when he and Bernie got married and at Eddie's funeral.

Mr. Denver had a small cleft in the middle of his chin, and unlike his brother, was clean shaven. Silver flecks around his temples brightened his hair, while a thin scar stretched in a line from the corner of his left eye toward his ear. Maggie had forgotten how his eyebrows were like awnings over two sad eyes; she wondered where the sadness had come from—and what about that scar? He was taller and broader of shoulder than Will, who was wiry and sinewy, with the powerful arms of one who dragged in heavy nets filled with fish, like Eddie's arms had been.

On New Year's Day, he'd been dressed in a charcoal gray suit, a starched white shirt and a tie, but today he wore black pants, a simple white shirt and a brick colored sweater. Maggie noticed the intricate stitches and patterns in the wool. Whoever made it for him did lovely work. The only sweater she ever made for Eddie was thick and uneven, obviously the work of a beginner. He loved it anyway.

Jacob Denver sat at her table, drank her coffee and ate the plate of warm cookies she put before him, listening to every word she said as if it were the most important thing in the world, watching her every step as though he'd never seen a woman move around in a kitchen before. At first, Maggie wanted to hide from the intensity of his attention. *Doesn't he see what I am—simple, poor, and uneducated? How am I going to tell him if he can't see it?*

Their conversation began awkwardly, with moments of silence that begged to be filled. More than once, each would take the initiative to fill the gap and they'd both speak at once. Then they'd laugh, nervous and embarrassed.

But things changed when Mr. Denver asked Maggie about her children: how old were they, what were they interested in? "They were all well behaved and delightful when I met them," he said.

She shook her head. "Well, I'm afraid Karl with that ridiculous hat of his wasn't especially delightful."

"Oh, but I enjoyed him. He's an interesting young man. Anyone can see how bright he is. I hope he plans to continue in school."

"He wants to fish, like his father and like Will, but he's too young. Will told him he has to finish high school before he'll even consider helping him get started." Self conscious and a little embarrassed, Maggie paused and looked into her coffee cup. "Of course, I am completely against him going anywhere near the water, especially *that*

water. Losing him the way we lost his father—losing him
at all—would surely send me to my grave."

Mr. Denver sat quietly while she pulled a handkerchief
from her pocket and wiped her eyes.

"I apologize, Mr. Denver."

"There's nothing to apologize for, nothing at all."

Soft, like a whisper, he touched her hand, and then
withdrew his. The place where his skin brushed hers
burned, then ached. She covered it with her other hand
and felt her face get hot.

As Mr. Denver prepared to leave, he gazed away from
Maggie, as if he were trying to think of what to say. He
turned to her and said, "I think you are an extraordinary
woman, Mrs. Stern. I'd like to see you again. Will you write
to me?"

Maggie's face got hot again, but she smiled. "It would
be rude not to answer your letters, now wouldn't it?"
*Extraordinary? What on earth could a man like Jacob Denver see
in me, with my shabby home, my homemade dress and my plain face
and hair?*

"Somehow I can't imagine you being anything but polite." He hadn't taken his eyes away from her, not even for
a second.

She thought she should look away but couldn't, and
somehow, that didn't bother her. She offered her hand. "I
enjoyed your visit, Mr. Denver."

"Please—call me Jacob."

Maggie nodded; still not sure she was ready to use his
first name; not sure she was ready to let him use hers.
"Then you must call me Margaret."

He took her hand in both of his, surrounding it with
his warmth. "Until next time, dear Margaret." He smiled
when he said her name.

February 17, 1928   *Wakelin, Wisconsin*
Dear Margaret,

Thank you for another lovely visit. Your home is the warmest place I have ever been, but that has nothing at all to do with the temperature. You are so hospitable to a stranger such as me. I was sorry when it came time for me to leave.

It is not the way your home is decorated, the way you are clothed or even the wonderful aromas of sweets baking in your kitchen that drew me in and warmed my heart. It was you. The pride and love with which you speak of your children, the care you take to make me comfortable, your smile and your laugh: all these things are shelters, and a refuge against the bitterness of life. What makes you extraordinary, Margaret, is that you would impart them to a weary soul like me even as you suffer your own sorrow. You make me believe that while broken hearts may never be completely healed, it is possible that they might be mended.

I will be with my men in the woods, at lumber camp, for the next week or so. I will write to you from there and tell you about our adventures. I look forward to your next letter.

Yours, Jacob Denver

Maggie wept when she read Jacob's letter. He's such a nice man, she thought, how can I use him like this? Doesn't he realize how simple I am, that all I know in this world is taking care of my family?

The next morning after the children left for school, she washed the breakfast dishes and went to visit Bernie. After playing with Billy and Ned for a few minutes, she helped Bernie fold the laundry she'd taken off the line in the basement.

"So, now, what's on your mind, Maggie?"

"Why do you think there's something on my mind?"

"Because I know you. It's Jacob, isn't?" Bernie's eyes sparkled, but she didn't smile. "He came to visit only a few days ago, and by now you must have another letter from him."

"Someone's got to stop him."

"Don'cha like 'im?"

"Well, yes, but I don't know him very well and he's writing all these things about me. He thinks I'm something I'm not. What have you and Will been telling him?"

"Nothin'. In fact, Will's been tellin' 'im to leave you alone. He's afraid Jacob's going to hurt you."

"Oh, no, I don't think that will happen. No, I'm afraid *he'll* get hurt, or feel like a fool once he realizes what I really am. Then he'll be embarrassed because he has to tell me I'm not his type. The poor man."

"Jacob Denver, a poor man?" Bernie threw her head back and laughed. "Jacob knows how to get what he wants. Don't get me wrong, the man has a heart o' gold, but once he has somethin' in his head, why, he'll do whatever he has to. What did he write, if you don't mind me askin'?"

Maggie pulled the letter from her pocket and held it out to Bernie. "Here, read it yourself."

"No, Darlin', you read it to me. The letter's addressed to you."

"I don't know if I can."

"Try."

Maggie started to read, paused, swallowed, and went on. *You give me hope that while broken hearts may never be completely healed, it is possible...*" The tears in her eyes made the words all run together."...*That they might be mended.*" She looked up. "It's so beautiful. But why, how could he think all this? He must want it to be true, so that's what he sees."

"You silly girl." Bernie put her arm around Maggie's shoulders. "It's what he sees; it's how you make him feel, so it *is* true. He's taken a fancy to you."

"That's ridiculous. Look at me, a poor widow with three children. I ruined the only nice dress I had at the cemetery. Anyway," she said softly, "I still miss Eddie."

"Jacob knows all that, an' just between us, if anyone can understand what you're goin' through, it would be him."

A long silence followed before Maggie spoke. "Can you tell me why?" Her eyes searched Bernie's. "What happened to him?"

Bernie picked up the laundry basket and answered quietly. "I think the tellin' of that tale is better left to him, Love. Come on upstairs, now; you need a nice cuppa tea."

Jacob took his cup of coffee and sat at the makeshift table in the cook's tent. The camp was quiet, the rest of the men already buried deep in their bedrolls, keeping warm, sleeping up energy for a new day. He sharpened a pencil with his jack knife, opened his tablet and began to write.

> *February 19, 1928*
> *Dear Margaret,*
> *Greetings from the "Grub Master." This week it is my job to feed this unruly band of lumberjacks. My father made me learn every part of the business, including cooking for the men while we're at camp. It is nice to please them for*

once, instead of being the heavy-handed taskmaster out to make their work more difficult by enforcing something as tiresome and irrelevant as safety rules. And out here it isn't hard to please them, either, since we all work up an enormous appetite cutting trees, sawing, loading the timber and of course, trying to keep warm. We arrived this afternoon and set up camp. I fed them pork and potatoes for supper. Tomorrow the hard work will begin.

We are only about fifteen miles from home and will be cutting hardwoods, which we will mill for furniture. The virgin forests of White Pine are gone, thanks to my Grandfather's generation, so now I must be selective about what I cut.

There will be no way to mail this until I get back to Wakelin, so this will have to be a letter in chapters, like a book. I am thinking of you.

Good night, Jacob.

Jacob wrote each night from the camp; in all there were six "chapters." When he returned to his office at the mill, he put all ten pages in a large envelope, addressed it, put on more stamps than it needed, and dropped it at the post office on his way home.

He hoped there would be a letter from Margaret, and he wasn't disappointed. He took it with him into the bathroom, filled the tub with hot water and eased himself into the bath before opening it.

February 21, 1928
Dear Mr. Denver,
I hardly know what to say in response to your letter. Your sentiments are lovely, and they touched me more deeply than words can say. But you do not know me and I fear that

you have experienced something in my humble home that exists only in your eyes.

To be truthful, I have had no intention of creating a refuge for anyone. My home has been my own hiding place these past months and my only goal has been to take care of my children and live through one more day. Aside from that, I am ashamed to say I have had little thought for anyone but myself. So I cannot for the life of me understand what you see in me or in my home.

None of this is to say I find you unpleasant or that I do not like you. I could never say that. But I say these things to you so as not to deceive you. A friendship based on anything but the truth is not a friendship at all, but deception. If there is anything I have learned since my husband's death, it is that life is too short to waste on things that are not good and honorable and true.

Thank you for your visit. I hope to see you again. If you tell me when you'll be in Tomos Bay next, perhaps my children and I could welcome you for a meal.

Yours truly, Margaret Stern

Jacob leaned back and closed his eyes. How could she not know how warm and wonderful and comforting she was? He opened his eyes again, reread the last three sentences, dropped the letter on the floor, and slid down into the hot water, submerging even his head. A meal at her table; what a thought! He came up laughing. How soon could he go back to see her?

After Hilde went home, he sat at his desk and wrote a short note to Margaret. He'd gotten into the routine of "talking" to her at the end of the day, and rather liked it.

February 26, 1928
Dear Margaret,

Thank you for your letter. You underestimate yourself and the power of your kindness. I do appreciate your candor, but whatever I saw and felt in your home was real, indeed.

As much as I look forward to lumber camp, I am glad to be home and back to my own warm bed after a whole week in the woods. Day after tomorrow, I will be taking a smaller crew to the foot of Door County where we will harvest some cherry trees for the owner, an acquaintance of mine. Cherry is such a beautiful wood. These we will also mill for furniture. I will write to you from there, and hope to visit Tomos Bay again early in March. I will let you know for certain when, as the offer of a meal at your table is enticing, indeed.

Good night, Jacob.

March 1, 1928
Dear Jacob,

Thank you for your "chapters" from camp and for the letter you wrote when you got home again. I enjoyed reading about lumbering and your experiences with your workers. Reading your "chapters" was like reading a book, only I know the author and the book was written especially for me!

We struggle with snowstorm after snowstorm here. It is March already, but winter is not going to give up the ghost anytime soon. I kept all three children home from school yesterday and today because of their nasty head colds. Of course, these are not days of leisure for them. The Sisters sent home all the assignments they would have had in school, so I am teacher as well as mother, especially for the girls.

I have rambled on long enough. I hope your time in Door County is profitable and that you return home safely. I look forward to your next visit.
    Yours truly, Margaret

Jacob stood by the window of the new master bedroom, using the last bit of daylight to read Margaret's latest letter. Perhaps the longing he'd denied for years, the dream he'd released so long ago was about to come true. *I look forward to your next visit.* He smiled. She wanted to see him again. Jacob slipped her letter into his pocket and went downstairs to his library. He took out a piece of stationery and began to write.

March 5, 1928
Dear Margaret,
    It so happens that I will be visiting my brother next weekend and would love to see you...

Chapter 18

Spilt Milk

Maggie received Jacob's letter on Thursday.

> *March 5, 1928*
> *Dear Margaret,*
> *It so happens that I will be visiting my brother next weekend and would love to see you. I will arrive on Saturday, but will have to start for home again on Sunday morning. I'll plan to come by your house around 5:00, if your invitation stands. I am so looking forward to seeing you and your wonderful children again.*
> *Yours, Jacob*
> *P.S. If this is for any reason inconvenient, please tell Will and I'll come another time.*

Maggie felt a rush of excitement, then fear, then dread. He would be here for dinner, day after tomorrow. What would she serve him? He probably liked fancy food. And what would she wear? Everything she owned looked thin and tired. Well, she did have a nice lavender dress, but it wasn't warm enough to wear in March.

She looked around and saw peeling paint in the corner of the dining room; limp curtains that needed to be washed and ironed; windows that needed to be freed of their winter grime. How could she possibly have the house ready in only two days?

And how would she prepare her children for a strange man at the dinner table? Well, Karl knew she'd been corresponding with Jacob; he'd mailed letters for her on his way to school.

Her stomach churned. Whatever possessed her to invite Jacob Denver to dinner? She picked up the telephone receiver to call Bernie, then quickly put it back in the cradle. "But I want to see him," she said out loud.

Anyway, she'd been thinking about how to get rid of that cameo brooch ever since Melvin gave it back to her. Jacob seemed nice enough, trustworthy. Maybe she could ask him to sell it in some other town, where Melvin would never find out.

Even though the children would be home from school in an hour, she took down all the curtains in the living room, dining room and the kitchen and hustled them into the washing machine. After she'd washed them and wrung out the excess water, she took them outside and hung them on the line, hoping they would freeze dry before dark. Her hands turned red from the cold and she blew on them as she came back into the house. Tomorrow she would wash the windows, iron the curtains and go to the market. There wasn't a thing she could do about the peeling paint.

Before she went to bed, Maggie looked through her closet, trying to decide which dress might be good enough for company. She could wear her green flannel dress, but Eddie said it made her look matronly. If Eddie Stern thought it made her look old, she couldn't wear it for Jacob Denver, either. She sighed. It would have to be the lavender dress. She'd iron it tomorrow.

She lit the votive on her bedside table, turned off the light and knelt for prayers. She prayed for her children, for Kathleen, her mother and Aunt Mary, and then for Eddie's soul. Her loneliness for him overwhelmed her. How could she think about another man when her heart still ached for Eddie Stern?

When she could no longer keep her eyes open, Maggie blew out the candle, crawled under the blankets and gave in to sleep. She saw a pinpoint of light expand and take shape until it became a heart with a terrible, bleeding wound. Soon the bleeding stopped, and the wound, still raw, began to mend and scar over. As she watched, the scar grew, distorting the heart until it was unrecognizable. It made her feel sad. She tried to open her eyes, but couldn't.

"You have to watch this, Maggie, it's your life."

"Eddie?"

"Watch."

The blob split again and grew some more, then split and grew, layer upon layer of bloody red; wounds, scars, and growth, over and over. With each wound, Maggie felt a clutch in her stomach, but when it grew, she watched with wonder. Finally, it became a perfect red rose, glowing, lit from within.

"Your heart is big enough, Rosie."

Frantic, she cried out to him. "Eddie, stay; don't leave me again. Please, Eddie, *please...*"

Her eyes flew open and she sat up in bed, out of breath. A warm breeze caressed her cheek and was gone.

She threw back the covers and hurried down to the kitchen. She turned on the faucet and let the water run over her hands, cupping them and drinking from them again and again. When they quit shaking, she dried them off and started back to bed, stopping for a moment in the living room. Without turning on any lights, she stepped onto the rug and by memory found the place where Will and Rob laid Eddie's dripping body. She dug her toes into what little pile there was, expecting to cry, but instead she pictured her lavender dress. She remembered the fancy white sweater Mother Stern gave her a long time ago and smiled. They would go together nicely.

Maggie hadn't finished dressing when she heard Jacob's car at exactly five o'clock. She looked out the window, sliding her arm into the sweater from Mother Stern.

"Karl, let Mr. Denver in and tell him I'll be down in a minute," she called down the stairs. "And please, take his coat."

"Yes, Mother."

Maggie sniffed her arm. She'd forgotten to air the sweater out. She peeled it off, opened the bedroom window, stuck her arm out and waved the sweater around in the cold air. That would have to do. Why couldn't he be a few minutes late? She still needed to brush her hair.

Maggie slipped the sweater back on and shivered. She heard Karl open the door, then Jacob's voice.

"Hello, Karl, it's good to see you again."

"Hi. I can take your coat. My mother is still getting dressed."

"I see. Well, it sure smells wonderful in here."

"She's been cooking all day. She made us clean all day, too."

"Well, that sure is a rotten way to spend a Saturday."

"You better believe it. And she made us get up early."

"Really? All because of me?" Jacob laughed.

"Yeah. Most Saturdays she lets us have a little fun."

"Oh, stop it, Karl." Maggie whispered. "Please, please, be polite."

Lizzie ran up the stairs, yelling. "Mama, Anna, Mr. Denver's here."

"I know, Lizzie, you don't have to shout."

Anna went running from her room and bounding down the stairs. "Hi, Mr. Denver. I'm Anna Mary Stern, remember me?"

"Yes I do, Anna."

"Do you still have my picture?"

"I do. I hung it in my library at home. I look at it every day."

"You have a whole library?" asked Karl. "What kind of books?"

Good boy, Karl, keep him occupied. Maggie finished brushing her hair.

"Well, I have some books about trees and lumbering. A few history books and some biographies about men like Abraham Lincoln and Thomas Jefferson and some about musical composers, like Beethoven and Brahms and Chopin. I have the works of Shakespeare and some fiction, too."

"Do you have an encyclopedia?"

"As a matter of fact, I recently bought a new set."

"Have you read them yet?"

"Well, no, I use them as a reference tool, to look up specific information."

"You mean you aren't going to read them all the way through?"

"Do you think I should?"

"If you want to know everything, that's how to do it, I think."

Maggie pulled her hair back, twisted and tucked it, fastening it with her ivory combs. She slid her feet into her good shoes.

Lizzie stood in the doorway, watching. "You look pretty, Mama."

"Thank you, baby." Maggie leaned down to kiss her forehead.

Lizzie turned and ran back down the stairs. "Here comes Mama, and she looks real nice."

"Elizabeth!" Maggie whispered loudly enough for everyone to hear.

Mr. Denver stood up and smiled when he saw her. "Margaret, you *do* look lovely."

"Thank you. I'm glad you could come."

She held out her hand and he reached for it. While he held it, he sniffed twice and chuckled.

"Ahh... cedar. A wonderful aromatic wood."

Maggie felt her face get hot. Why didn't she think to air it out yesterday? "I hope you're hungry, Mr. Denver."

"It's Jacob, remember?"

"I hope you're hungry, Jacob."

"Famished."

When they gathered at the dining room table, Maggie asked her children who wanted to say the blessing.

Anna volunteered. "Bless us, Lord... and these gifts... that we are about to... eat... by thy... boundful... goodness, through Jesus Christ our Lord. Amen." Everyone crossed themselves except for Mr. Denver.

"It's *bountiful,* Anna," corrected Karl. "*Bountiful,* not *boundful.*"

"Shh, Karl, let her be. It was lovely, Annie, thank you."

"Mr. Denver, are you Catholic?" Lizzie squinted at him.

"Well, no, my family is Methodist."

"If you're not Catholic, you can't go to heaven, you know."

"Lizzie, that's a terrible thing to say to a guest." Maggie felt her face get hot again.

"It's all right, Margaret. I know there are many good things about the Catholic Church, Lizzie, but I don't happen to agree with that idea."

"Well, Sister said—"

"Enough." Maggie wilted inside. "To tell you the truth, that teaching has always bothered me."

Jacob smiled. "Now, I prefer to think of God as being merciful to all people, even to Methodists."

"Karl, pass the rolls," Maggie changed the subject. "Mr. Denver, you're company, you start the chicken."

"So, Mr. Denver, are you married?" Karl handed the dinner rolls to Anna. "Do you have any kids?"

Maggie wanted to crawl under the table and hide. "Karl, don't be so nosy."

"Well, if he's coming around to see you and he already has a family, don't you think you should know about it, Mother?"

"That's enough, now." She covered her mouth with her left hand.

"I think it's commendable that you're concerned about your mother, Karl. But I live all by myself. The only family I have is Will and Bernie and their boys and my mother.

And my housekeeper, Hilde. She's from Germany. She's not related, but she's family, all the same."

Anna reached for the butter and knocked over her milk. It ran down the side of the table and onto Mr. Denver's lap. "Oh, no!" She started to cry.

"Anna, give Mr. Denver your napkin." Maggie hurried into the kitchen for dry towels. She took a deep breath before returning to the dining room.

Jacob looked up and smiled at her.

Maggie sopped up the milk-drenched tablecloth around him, gave him a dry towel to clean off his trousers, and helped Anna move her plate and silverware so she could clean up the mess underneath.

"I'm sorry, Mr. Denver." Still in tears, Anna looked at Jacob then quickly glanced at Maggie.

"Anna, there's a saying where I come from. *There's no use crying over spilt milk.* No harm done, so you can stop fussing about it. I'd much rather see your smile." Jacob spoke to Anna, but looked at Maggie.

Maggie gave the wet rags to Anna and sent her into the kitchen. Anna stopped crying, but still looked plenty glum. When she came back, though, she wore a huge grin. She stood in front of Jacob with her hands on her hips. "Well, now, thank you very much, Love."

"You're very welcome, my dear," Jacob nodded to her, and laughed.

Maggie's heart melted. *What a sweet man.*

After chocolate cake with chocolate butter cream icing, Maggie excused the children to their rooms. She looked hard into Karl's eyes, and whispered in his ear. "No eavesdropping, do you hear me? If you do, I'll—"

"Yes, *Mo-ther.*"

Maggie and Jacob watched the children clamber up

the stairs. She sat down again, closed her eyes and let out a sigh. After her children's behavior, she wondered how wise it would be to ask Jacob to take the brooch. She took a deep breath, let it out and opened her eyes, trying to smile. "More coffee?"

"No thank you, Margaret. But I'd like to help you with the dishes."

"Oh, heavens, no, you're company, it wouldn't be right." She refolded her napkin. "I'll wash them later."

"No, let me. I wash dishes all the time, I don't mind. Hilde bawls me out if I don't clean up after my breakfast."

She looked away from him and fingered the edge of her napkin. "Listen, this meal didn't turn out quite as I'd planned. I wanted it to be nicer; I'm sorry."

"What do you mean? I loved every minute of it."

"My children usually have better manners than sending our guests to hell with milk all over their pants, accusing them of—"

Jacob leaned back and laughed. "But I liked it."

"No, this is too hard." Maggie looked at him for a second, then down at her hands, hoping her tears would land in her lap so he wouldn't notice them. "I don't think I'm up to this; it's too soon. Maybe it would be best to forget—"

"Do you want me to go away?"

"Yes—*no*. I don't know..."

"Margaret, look at me." He waited until she looked up. "Most things worth doing are hard, at least in my experience. I can't forget about you and I don't want to go away." He reached for her napkin, opened it, and dried her eyes.

She wanted to fall into his arms.

"All I want is to help you with the dishes."

Maybe she still could ask him. "There is something else you could help me with. I'm almost afraid to ask, though."

"I'm happy to do whatever I can for you."

Maggie reached into her apron pocket and took out the jewelry box. "I'd like you to help me get rid of this. I hope it won't be too much trouble." She handed it to him.

His eyes widened when he saw the brooch. "Do you need more money?"

Maggie shook her head, embarrassed. "It has nothing to do with money. I want that thing out of my house— out of my life."

"But you should keep it if your husband gave it to you." His voice softened. "Getting rid of it won't make you forget him, you know."

She shook her head again, a lump forming in her throat. "Eddie Stern never had money for such an expensive gift." She swallowed. "Someone else gave it to me a long time ago and now he thinks he has the right to... Please, will you take it? I never want to see it again. You're the only one I know who lives that far away. Please, throw it in a lake or a river or sell it and give the money to somebody who needs it."

"I assume there's more to it than what you're telling me."

Why did she decide to do this? Maggie held out her hand for the box. "This was a bad idea. I'm sorry, Mr. Denver." She stood up. "Thank you for coming."

Jacob also stood. He put the box in his pocket. "My name is *Jacob*, and I'll be glad to help you." He took Maggie's hand. "I only hope you'll be able to tell me all about it someday."

She thought she should move, but he wouldn't let go. She looked away, then back again. She didn't want to cry anymore, but his kindness drew it from her.

"But for now, I'd like to help you wash the dishes," he said again. Staring into her eyes, he took her other hand. Neither of them moved for a moment, and Maggie didn't look away. "I'll wash, you dry."

Dinner at Margaret's had been wonderful, even more than Jacob hoped it would be. When he awoke on Sunday morning, he knew he couldn't leave town without seeing her again, so after a quick breakfast at Bernie's table, he stopped at 617 Blight, to thank her once more.

She smiled when she opened the door and saw him on the porch. She had her coat on, but it was unbuttoned so he could see the beautiful soft green flannel dress she wore underneath. A gold necklace hung around her neck with a small mother of pearl cross resting above the valley between her breasts.

After the initial "hello," Margaret seemed distracted and ill at ease. The children were dressed up, too, and never left her side as she told him how they'd all enjoyed his visit. She kept looking at the clock on the mantle. "We're just leaving for Mass, otherwise we'd love to have you stay," she said.

"I would be happy to drive you; if you squeeze together there'll be room for everyone."

"I couldn't trouble you—"

"It's no trouble."

"Thank you for the offer, but we'll walk. We have to leave now, though, otherwise we'll be late."

It became so awkward Jacob wished he hadn't gone to see her unannounced and uninvited. All the way home, he worried and fretted. She'd been perfectly polite to him— but how could she be otherwise? He didn't think she could hurt a soul, certainly not intentionally. But maybe she already knew she'd never be able to return his affections. After all, she started to ask him to leave last night. Maybe she was just using him to get rid of that brooch.

The more he stewed about it, the more worked up he became. His stomach burned. He had to know—one way or the other—if he had a chance with her. So before he unpacked his travel bag, went through Saturday's mail or even checked to see if Hilde had left anything for his supper, Jacob sat down at his desk to write to *her*. He thanked her again for the wonderful dinner, praised and admired her children and closed the letter:

> *I think about you more and more each day, Margaret. I wait anxiously for your letters and whenever I leave you, I long to see you again. No other woman delights me as you do; you have even overtaken my dreams.*
>
> *You seemed to enjoy my company as much as I enjoyed yours last night, but this morning there was an awkwardness between us that troubles me greatly. I care for you, dear Margaret, but if you would rather refuse my attentions, please tell me now, before you capture any more of my heart. I will be sorry if you tell me to leave you alone, but if that is your wish, I will not bother you again.*
>
> *Will you please respond and tell me whether my hopes and dreams are futile or if there is a chance you might return my affections? I pine for you and anxiously await your reply. Please have pity and answer me without delay.*
>
> *With all my heart, Jacob.*

C. A. PETERSON

When he finished, he felt like he needed some air, so he put on his warm jacket and walked downtown to the post office. He didn't kiss the envelope like he wanted to; what if someone saw him do such a ridiculous thing?

Jacob thought it might be possible he'd have a letter from *her* by the middle of the week, but he received nothing on Wednesday or Thursday, either. On Friday, with no letter from *her* in his pocket, he climbed the stairs to inspect what the carpenters had done, but saw only a hollow attic filled with sawdust. Maybe tomorrow, he thought, surely tomorrow.

Chapter 19

Interfearance

Karl began feeling like the postman for all the letters his mother had been giving him to mail, almost all of them to Mr. Denver. He knew she got letters from him, too, nearly every day. He hoped they were writing about business, about the boat, but deep down, he knew the letters weren't about that at all.

"Why do you keep writing to Will's brother?" he asked as Maggie handed him one more letter to mail on his way to school.

"Because he's a nice man and we've become friends."

Karl scowled at her. "You've got friends around here, you know, Mother."

"Yes, I do. Take the letter and mail it for me, will you please?"

Karl took the letter, but he didn't mail it. He intended to—tomorrow—but first he needed to know what she was up to. After school he hid behind the neighbor's woodshed and opened it, thinking he'd reseal it and do as his mother had asked.

March 13, 1928
My Dear Jacob,

I was so happy to see you on Sunday morning, how thoughtful of you to come by again! I wish we hadn't been in such a hurry to get to Mass, then you could have stayed longer and had a cup of coffee before you started on your trip home.

You were so kind to offer to drive us to church, and I owe you an explanation as to why I refused. My neighbor watches us like a hawk and tells my mother about everything she sees happening here. She made false accusations about my honor a few months ago and I prefer not to fuel her imagination any further. Please forgive me for hurting your feelings, I never intended to hurt you.

Since you have not told me what your hopes and dreams are, I cannot say if they are futile or not, but I can tell you this. You have appeared out of nowhere at the most painful moment of my life and your letters and visits have come to mean so much to me. Even though I still miss my husband and will never get over losing him, I crave your attentions and your kindness. I believe you are an angel sent from heaven, come to ease my sadness. I do want you to be my friend or confidant or something more, if that is to be, but Jacob, please be patient with me. We are two different people with different ways and will need time to learn things about each other.

I hope this letter puts your mind at ease. I look forward to your next letter and hope I will see you again soon. Until then, I remain...

Yours, Margaret.

Karl couldn't believe his eyes. Traitor! What was she, in love or something? He put it the letter back in the envelope, folded the whole thing, and slid it into his back pocket. He would burn the letter with tonight's trash. She had no business being so friendly with that man, even if he was Will's brother.

When he went into the house, Karl set his face like a silent storm cloud; he didn't have one word for his mother. He did his afternoon chores angrily, heaving coal into the furnace as if he were feeding the fires of hell itself, dumping wood for the stove on the kitchen floor, without stacking it like his mother expected him to. When he finished, he went outside to mope on the front steps even though it was still cold out. With his bare hands, he touched the step he was sitting on. These were the same steps his father crossed every morning going to work; the same steps Will and Rob crossed bringing him home for the last time that day. Karl shivered and remembered being on these same steps when he heard that terrible noise coming from his mother.

This was still the same tan, shingle sided house he'd known all his life, like all the other shingle sided houses on the street. It was the same neighborhood, the same dreary winter, with the same frigid wind blowing across the lake. But even though nothing had changed, the letter in his pocket made it all strange and different. He spit into the snow, and looked up to see Melvin drive by. He jumped off the steps, threw a snowball hard against the side of the house and ran around to the back door. Lizzie was just coming outside with some papers for the burn can so he called her a stupid dummy and tormented her until she went in and tattled on him.

"What's gotten into you, Karl? Up to your room, right

now. Do your homework and think about how you're going to apologize to your sister, then go to bed. I'll get you up early so you can finish your other chores in the morning."

"No supper? I'm starving!"

"Sorry. You did it to yourself. Goodnight." She turned her back to him.

The mantle clock chimed five as Karl stomped up the stairs and slammed his bedroom door. His stomach had already been growling for an hour. He flopped on the bed, grumbling. "She doesn't care about anyone but *him*."

After ten minutes of bawling his father out for falling off the boat and dying, Karl took out his drawing pad and colored pencils. He thought about drawing Mr. Denver in a snake's mouth, but couldn't bring himself to do it. He didn't dare draw his mother, either; if he did she might die, and then they *would* have to live with Melvin. He rapped his pencil against the edge of the desk. He needed to draw something or he'd explode.

He pulled the envelope out of his back pocket, took out the letter and flattened it on the desk. All around the edges, front and back, he sketched curling, slithering snakes, black and tan, like the cobra he'd seen in church. He started to draw an enormous mouth ready to devour his mother's final words: "Yours, Maggie," but it felt too much like drawing her so he didn't finish. It was a stupid idea and didn't make him feel any better, so Karl put the letter back in its envelope and stuck it in his shirt pocket. He'd burn it tomorrow.

After rushing through his homework, he undressed and fell asleep trying not to think about his mother with anyone except his father, but he couldn't think about anything else.

Before she went to bed, Maggie looked in on Karl. He looked angelic, like he always did when he slept. The fair curls he'd inherited from Eddie made him look sweet and innocent, but tonight they surrounded a young man's face, where bits of fuzz had begun to grow above his lip, where angles replaced the soft curves of childhood. He usually hung his clothes on the back of his chair, but tonight he'd left them in a pile next to the bed. When Maggie picked them up to hang them on the hook behind the door, she saw her letter sticking out of Karl's shirt pocket. He'd opened it!

"Karl Edward Stern, how could you?" She turned on the overhead light and stood over him. "How dare you take my mail and read it?"

Karl sat up and blinked against the sudden brightness. "What? What's going on?"

"You didn't mail my letter; you kept it and read it, didn't you? Shame on you, *shame* on you. First thing in the morning, you will answer to me." Maggie left the light on, closed the door sharply behind her and muttered. "What am I going to do with you?"

As she got ready for bed, her eyes fell on Eddie's face in the wedding picture next to the bed. Karl's resemblance to his father only made her angrier. "This is all your fault, Edward." She turned the picture face down and slid the letter from the envelope. When she saw what Karl had drawn around her words, she gasped. "What on earth?" Heart racing, she went to his room with the letter in her hand. Light still came from under the door, so she went in without knocking. Lying on his back with his elbow draped across his eyes, he snored like a man. She dropped her hands in resignation and turned off the light. "First thing in the morning, Karl."

Back in her own room, the walls seemed to move in closer and closer, while the turmoil inside threatened to suffocate her. Shivering, she put on her threadbare housecoat and slippers, tore the patchwork quilt off the bed and went down the stairs, out the front door and onto the porch.

She wrapped the quilt around herself and sat down on the third step from the top. It was the same quilt they'd wrapped Eddie's icy body in five months ago, the same quilt that had warmed them both the night before he'd fallen in the water. It was the same quilt that had kept Karl warm, too, when he was a baby, when she brought him to bed to nurse.

She took a deep breath and let it out again. It was cold, but not that cold. The street was dark, but there were still lights on at the neighbors' house. She was alone, all alone, but inside were two little girls and Karl, as sad and angry and as confused as she was. She grieved for the man she'd known and loved since she was barely old enough to have such feelings, and now she had feelings for a man she'd met only a couple of months ago, whom she barely knew.

Out in the cold darkness, Maggie pulled the quilt over her head, held her stomach, and let the familiar, body-wracking sobs overtake her. That night she found no peace in her sleep.

Karl appeared for breakfast in a defiant, sour mood; even his fair curls couldn't make him look angelic today.

Maggie stopped stirring the oatmeal and turned around to face him. She stood with one hand on her hip and the other holding the wooden spoon up in the air, wielding it like a weapon. She did not say *Good morning* like she usually did. She'd deal with this before Lizzie and Anna were out of bed.

"You stole my letter and you read it and you drew ugly snakes all over it. It's a criminal offense to tamper with the U.S. Mail. If you *ever* open my mail again, I will call the police."

Karl laughed. "Sure you will, Mother."

Before the words were out of his mouth, Maggie slammed the wooden spoon on the table, cracking and splitting it, sending bits of oatmeal flying everywhere. It felt good, and it felt good to see Karl jump. She spoke without raising her voice. "I am still your mother, and you will continue to respect and obey me as if your father were here watching you."

"If he's watching me, he's watching you, too, and reading your love letters to that man."

Without thinking, Maggie reached out and slapped Karl hard across the face, something she'd never done before. She gasped and her eyes filled with tears. Karl's mouth hung open.

"You will *never* speak to me like that again. You will *never* snoop into my business again, do you understand? If you want to know something, ask. *Ask!* You were wrong to read my letter." She paused and moved the burning oatmeal off the stove. "I expect you to come directly home from school today and be prepared to write an essay about why it was wrong to do what you did. And be ready to explain why you drew snakes all over my letter to Mr. Denver. You have all day to think about it." She turned her back on Karl and wiped her eyes with the sleeve of her housecoat. "Now go downstairs and put some coal in the furnace then bring me some more wood for the stove. Your breakfast will be ready when you finish."

"I hate burnt oatmeal," he grumbled as he clumped down the basement steps.

"Be glad you're getting anything."

All day Maggie tried to compose a new letter to Jacob, but she could find no words for him, always imagining Eddie behind her, looking over her shoulder. She couldn't keep her mind on anything; she didn't eat her lunch until almost two o'clock because she lost track of the time.

After choking down a cheese sandwich, she stopped in the bathroom and looked at herself in the mirror. She looked terrible. Her eyes were the worst: bloodshot and inflamed from too much crying, dark circles below from too little sleep. She washed her face in cold water and combed her hair. Better, but still not good.

By the time Lizzie and Anna came home from school, Maggie managed to put a plate of warm ginger cookies on the table along with three glasses of milk, a piece of writing paper and a pencil. The cookies were Eddie's favorite; she hadn't made them since he died. They were Karl's favorite, too.

"Where's Karl? Didn't he walk home with you?" They both shook their heads. "Well, finish your cookies and go on up to your room and get started on your homework. I have some things to talk over with him when he gets here."

Lizzie got up and took her glass and Anna's to the sink. Anna picked up her book bag, then dropped it and went to her mother. "Mama, I wanna hug you."

Maggie crouched down and opened her arms.

"I wish you would stop being sad. It makes me feel funny."

Maggie held her youngest tightly, and kissed the side of her neck and her cheek and her forehead. "My sweet little baby, you're growing up."

Lizzie wanted the same thing. She put her arms out, and burst into tears. "Mama... Mama, please don't cry anymore, please?"

"Lizzie, honey, it's all right. I'm all right; we're all going to be all right. It won't be like this forever, it'll be better soon. Now, shhh." Maggie kissed her forehead, too, and wiped off her cheeks. Karl came in the back door and tripped on his way up the steps. "You two go start your homework. I'll come up in a little while to see if you need help."

Obediently, the girls left the kitchen. Before they started up the stairs, Anna said, "Golly, Lizzie, why'd you have to go and cry? That didn't cheer her up any."

"Couldn't help it."

Maggie smiled sadly when she heard them, before turning to Karl, now sitting at the table, stuffing cookies into his mouth and washing them down with milk.

"Where have you been? I thought I told you to come straight home."

"I did come straight home, but I stayed after school to help Sister Anne. Roddy Jeske threw another big fit in geography before school got out. He hit Sister Anne when she threatened him with the ruler, and then he threw his books and papers and stuff all over the room, and he dumped out the goldfish bowl and tipped over the plants. They had to call his father to come get him. Sister got pretty upset, so I stayed to help her clean up the mess."

"That was very thoughtful. I'm sure she appreciated—"

"He scared me, Mama."

"Roddy? Why? Did you think he would hurt you?"

Karl shook his head. "He scared me because I know how he felt and I wanted to do what he did."

"Why?" Maggie sat down.

"Ever since Daddy died, I get so mad. Sometimes I'd like to throw things and break stuff, and scream at people, like Roddy does." His chin sat on the palm of his left hand, his elbow on the table.

"I think I know what you mean. Sometimes I feel like that, too." Maggie sighed and slid the paper across the table. "You have some writing to do for me. Both sides. We'll talk about it when you finish."

After supper, Maggie left the girls in the kitchen to wash and dry the dishes while she went up to Karl's room to read what he'd written. She sat down on his bed and he handed her the paper, folded into a small package. Maggie unfolded it and read.

Why it was wrong to do what I did.
1. *Because I didn't do as I was told and mail the letter.*
2. *Because it wasn't my letter.*
3. *Because I didn't ask to read it.*
4. *Because it was private and I was nosey.*
5. *Because I didn't honor my Mother. (I broke a commandment.)*
6. *Because I embarrassed my Mother and hurt her feelings and made her mad.*

7. Because I interfeared with the U.S. Mail.

8. Because now Mr. Denver won't get his letter and maybe
he'll be mad at my mother for not writing back.

Maggie looked up at her son. "You didn't tell me why you drew the snakes."

"Yeah, I know." He began to draw faint lines in the margins of his math paper. "My pencil likes to make them when I feel... nervous."

"You must have been very nervous to make them so fierce. They scared me."

"It's only a drawing, Mama."

"I know. What frightens me is you getting so upset you'd draw them in the first place. I'm worried about you."

"I'm perfectly fine. Turn over the paper, there's more."

Maggie read Karl's note out loud.

Dear Mother,
I am sorry that I didn't mail your letter to Mr. Denver and I'm sorry that I read it without your permission. I apologize for being nasty to you this morning. I will try to do better in the future and promise not to open any more letters unless they have my name on them. I just have one question for you. Why?
Love, Karl.

"Thank you, I accept your apology, and I forgive you."

"But can you answer my question, Mama? Why?"

"Why Mr. Denver?"

"Yeah. And how can you do this when Daddy just

died? Don't you still love him? Do you love Mr. Denver more?"

"Oh, Karl. Is this why the letter got you all upset?"

Karl looked down and started to erase the lines he'd been drawing on his math paper. "I guess so. But don't you still love Daddy?"

"Yes, of course I still love your father. I would cut off my arm or my leg or both if it would bring him back. But the world doesn't work that way. Sometimes I wish it did." She folded Karl's paper and put it in her pocket. "I will always love him and I will always miss him, but he's gone." She swallowed the thickness building in her throat. "He's gone." It occurred to her that all this sadness had worn her out.

"Then how—"

"How can I do this so soon? I've asked myself the same question, but I don't think I'm doing anything. It's just happening. Mr. Denver is a nice man. He likes me; he likes all of us. He likes you."

Karl shook his head. "No, I don't think so."

"Yes, he does. He thinks you're smart and interesting, and he wants to know you better. I think Will has told him about you." She sighed again and smoothed the skirt of her dress. "I don't know if you can understand this, because I'm only learning about it myself. But when a person who loves you dies, you don't just lose that person. You lose all the love they had to give you. That's one reason why it feels so—so empty and sad. Because nobody can ever love you in that way again."

Karl nodded. The corners of his mouth pulled down a little.

"But that doesn't mean other people can't love you in big ways. They'll just love you in different ways." Maggie realized this herself as she said it. "I love you, Karl, even more than ever."

He left his chair at the desk and sat next to her. She put her arms around him. "You're my boy; I will *always* love you, no matter what."

Karl looked up at her. "So do you love Mr. Denver more than Daddy?"

"Now hold your horses, Karl. I don't even know if I love Mr. Denver and I don't know if he loves me. But if it does happen, it will be different from the way I love your father. Not more, not better, just— different. They're two different men. There's nothing else I can say about it." She smoothed some of Karl's curls off his forehead and kissed him. "You need a haircut again."

He pulled away. "I know, but not now. I have to do my homework. Thanks for talking to me." He went back to his desk.

"I like talking to you." Maggie got up and went to the door. "One more thing. I'm sorry I struck you this morning. I don't know how I could have done that. Your father and I agreed never to hit you children. Can you forgive me?"

"I prob'ly had it coming," he mumbled.

"But can you forgive me?"

He nodded. "Yeah."

That night, Maggie fell asleep while reading to Anna. For the first time in weeks, she slept peacefully.

Chapter 20

Death Comes Knocking

Early on Friday morning, before the children left for school, Maggie's mother called to say she didn't feel well and needed help. This alarmed Maggie because Isabelle rarely asked for anything. She slipped Jacob's letter into her pocket, thinking she'd rewrite her response when she had a free moment. In coat, scarf, gloves and boots, she made the half mile trek through the wind and blowing snow.

Maggie hung her coat on a hook and left her boots in the doorway. It felt nearly as cold inside as it was outside, so she shoveled coal into the furnace before doing anything else. Her mother usually kept her kitchen neat and tidy, but several days' worth of dirty dishes filled the sink. Alarmed, she took the stairs two at a time and rushed to her mother's bedroom.

Maggie found her in bed, teeth chattering, with a mountain of blankets piled on top of her. Isabelle's hair, once the same color as Maggie's, seemed to have faded nearly to white since Maggie saw her at Mass last Sunday. Her eyes were sunken, her face burned hot with fever.

"Good heavens, Mother."

"Margaret, you came."

"Of course I came." Maggie watched the shallow rising and falling of her mother's chest. "How long have you been sick?"

"Oh, I don't know. Since yesterday?"

Maggie laid her hand on her mother's forehead. "You're burning up; I'm going to call Dr. Lyman." She turned for the door.

"Wait." Isabelle grabbed at Maggie's dress. "Wash those dishes before he gets here. I don't want him to think I'm a lazy sloth."

"The dishes don't matter." Maggie started down the stairs.

"Please?"

"Don't worry, Mother." Maggie ignored the dishes and rang for the operator. Dr. Lyman said he'd come right away, to leave the back door unlocked.

When Maggie went back to her mother's bedside to wait for the doctor, Isabelle appeared to be sleeping. For all the nastiness her mother inflicted upon her over the years, the depth of her own dread surprised her. "She can't die yet," she thought, she prayed. "It's never been good between us, and there's Kathleen to think about. She can't go until we take care of these things, do you understand?" She looked at the wooden crucifix that hung above the bed, against the faded brown and blue wallpaper, and whispered, "Oh, God, that's not a very nice prayer, is it? I'm sorry."

"Did you wash the dishes, Margaret?"

"They're all taken care of."

Isabelle started to cough, but stopped herself. "I've got the devil's own headache; it hurts too much to cough."

"Hello, there." Dr. Lyman knocked on the door jam and stepped into the room, rubbing his hands together to warm them.

Maggie helped her mother sit up while the doctor put his stethoscope against her chest and her back. He felt her neck and let her lie down again, took out a thermometer and put it in her mouth. He took her pulse, waited a minute then read the thermometer. He raised his eyebrows and tilted his head toward the door. "Margaret?"

Maggie followed him out of the room.

"She's got pneumonia and her fever is at one hundred and three, almost four. We need to get her temp down and we've got to get her coughing."

"Pneumonia..."

"I'm going to give her some aspirin; that should help her headache and the fever. I'll leave some here so you can give her two every four hours. You'd better start sponging her off, too. How long has she been sick?"

"Judging from the dishes in the sink, she hasn't felt well all week. She just called me this morning."

Dr. Lyman pushed his glasses up the bridge of his nose with his left index finger. "I'll be back this afternoon, but call me if she has trouble breathing."

The gravity of her mother's condition hit Maggie hard, but she didn't have much time to think about it. All day long, Isabelle felt too cold then too hot; too hot then too cold. Maggie lost track of how many times she sponged her off and covered her back up again. She could see her misery and pitied her.

Dr. Lyman came back again around two o'clock. Isabelle's fever had gone down a little, but he said her lungs sounded worse. He brought along a homemade contraption: a two quart crock with a metal pie pan for a lid; the pan had holes punched through and a heating element affixed to the center. After Maggie filled the crock with water, he plugged in the heating element. Soon it made steam, which could help loosen the congestion in Isabelle's lungs.

Dr. Lyman helped Maggie make a tent over her with a sheet, hanging it over the high headboard of the bed, attaching it with safety pins and clothes pins, pulling it taut the whole length of the bed and fastening it to the footboard in the same way. They pulled the bedside table close and draped the side of the sheet over it so that she could breathe in the moisture.

After they'd set up the tent and the steamer, Dr. Lyman took Maggie into the hall again. "Keep her in the tent with the steam going, but sponge her down when the fever goes up again—which it will. It doesn't look good for her."

"Are you saying she could die?"

He nodded. "I'm sorry, Margaret. I think it's time to get Kathleen over here to help you. And you'd better find someone to take your children, because you're going to be busy all night, and tomorrow, too, if she lasts that long."

Maggie looked at the floor.

"Are you all right?"

"It doesn't seem real."

"It never does, does it?"

Maggie picked up the telephone after the doctor left. She asked the operator to ring Bernie's house, then Holy Angel's School. Sister Mary Anthony said she would keep the children until Will could pick them up. She rang Kathleen, too, but she didn't answer.

In between keeping water in the steamer and sponging her mother's fevered body, for the next two hours Maggie ran up and down the stairs to the telephone, trying to reach Kathleen. She never answered, and while the operator became impatient, Maggie became frantic.

When Will's truck pulled up in front of Isabelle's house, Maggie threw on her coat and ran outside to thank him for his help and to see Lizzie and Anna before he took them to his house for the weekend. She asked Karl to stay with her, and he agreed; having him nearby brought her great comfort. As they walked into the house together, Maggie tried to thank him for giving up time with Will to help her, but she couldn't because of the lump in her throat.

"Aw, never mind, Mama." He smiled at her. "It feels kind of good that you'd want me to stay." He put his arm across her shoulder and gave her a quick squeeze. "Grandma must be pretty sick, huh?"

"Yes, she is, and I need to get back to her. Go see if you can find yourself a snack."

Kathleen finally answered her telephone at four-fifty. She sounded like a frightened little mouse. "Hello?"

"Kathleen, where have you been? I've been calling all afternoon."

"I'm not supposed to answer the phone when Melvin isn't here. What's wrong?"

"Mother's sick... It's pneumonia. Dr. Lyman says she might not... I need you, Kathy, do you think you could come?"

"Ooh, noo, he's home early."

Maggie could hear Melvin's angry voice in the background, saying, "What have I told you about using that thing?" She heard the earpiece fall, a scuffle and a slap.

"Kathleen!" Maggie yelled into the mouthpiece.

Kathleen didn't answer, but Maggie heard her talking to Melvin. "Mother's sick. I need to go help Maggie."

"I'll just have to see about that."

Click.

Horrified, Maggie placed the earpiece back in its cradle.

Karl came from the kitchen. "What's wrong?"

"Aunt Kathleen..." She took a deep breath, not wanting to think about what could be happening to her sister at that very moment. "Listen, would you please make sure the furnace has plenty of coal tonight? That's your main job. And bring in some extra wood for the stove, I think we'll need to keep the coffee pot on. I have to get back up to Grandma." She turned and went upstairs, calling over her shoulder. "I'm sorry I don't have time to fix supper for you. Look through the ice box and see if there are any leftovers." She wondered if she'd done the right thing by asking him to stay.

Isabelle's fever had gone up again when Maggie returned to her room. She lifted the sides of the steam tent, uncovered her mother and began sponging her off for what seemed like the hundredth time. The fever was so high that as soon as she finished, she had to start all over again. A door opened downstairs and she heard Karl talking to someone. Maybe Melvin had allowed Kathleen to come after all. As she rolled her mother's naked body onto her side for the second time, something moved in the hallway. She leaned over the bed, her back to the door. "Good, you're here; I could use your help, Kathy."

No answer, only the sound of one footstep.

"Please? I've been doing this all day."

When Kathleen didn't appear at her side, Maggie turned around. Melvin stood in the doorway, watching. She gasped, quickly covered her mother with a sheet, and grabbed one of the flannel-covered bricks that Isabelle used as a bed warmer. Shaking, she held the brick shoulder high. "Get away!

He laughed. "Now, that's a fine welcome."

"What are you doing here?"

"I came to see about your mother."

"Where's Kathleen?"

"Oh, dear, she's under the weather, too." He bounced the tips of his chubby fingers against each other. "So I came to help instead."

"You can't help; it has to be Kathleen or no one. What's wrong with her?"

"Oh, you know how sickly your sister is."

"You hit her."

"I don't think she's strong enough to come over here."

"What did you do to her?" Maggie took a step forward.

"Why, nothing, Margaret, I'm only looking out for her best interests."

"If you didn't do anything to her, go and get her!" Maggie made her voice as rough as she could. She stomped her foot like a child. "I need her help."

Melvin leered at his mother-in-law. "I'm not sure I should allow it."

"Mother needs her." Maggie's wrist began to tremble from holding the brick up.

Melvin didn't move his eyes from Isabelle. "Well, maybe I'll let her come after supper, we'll see." He started to laugh as he went down the stairs, calling to Karl. "My, goodness, your Mama's a feisty one," he laughed. "I like that in a woman, yes I do!" The front door closed.

Maggie shouted into the hallway. "Karl!"

Karl came running, but didn't come within view of his grandmother's bed.

"How did he get in?"

"He walked in like he lives here."

"Well, for heaven's sake, go lock the doors, and bring in the key Grandma keeps under that rock."

"Are you all right, Mama?"

"Yes, yes, just go get the key and lock all the doors." Maggie shivered. She didn't know what was worse: her anger, her fear for her sister, or the fact that Melvin had seen her mother's naked body.

Karl's anger bubbled inside him; he wished he could punch Melvin in the stomach. He found the key and locked all the doors, then pulled his drawing pad and pencils out of his book bag. He drew Melvin, exaggerating the roundness of his belly and the size of his nose. He drew a straight line for his mouth, with the edges turned up just enough to give him a sinister smile. He held a broken bottle in his right hand, wore shoes with pointy toes and big heels, an undershirt with chest hair poking out of the neckline, and black pants that gaped open in the front. Karl surrounded him with snakes, with a few of them wrapped around his ankles, not in a threatening way, but like a puppy adores his master. Each and every snake wore a smile like Melvin's. He thought about putting a pair of horns on his head, but decided he wasn't good enough to be the devil. On the top of the picture, he wrote the words, in big block letters: "Who has a foot big enough to crush this wicked man?"

Kathleen came by herself after dark. A red mark crossed her cheek. "Melvin didn't want me to come over, but his team is in the dart tournament in Ashland so I left after he did. He won't be home until supper tomorrow."

"Are you sure you want to do this?" asked Maggie. "What will he do to you when he finds out you came over anyway? I heard him hit you once today, and I can see where he did it."

When Kathleen looked away, Maggie could see a bruise forming.

"Listen, Maggie, it's just his way, I can handle it. Besides, he doesn't need to know I'm here; I'll go home before he gets back." Kathleen glanced into her mother's sick room. "Anyway, I only have one mother; he'll have to understand that."

"How much longer are you going to take this?" Maggie couldn't hide her disgust.

"Forever. I married him. Now forget about it. We're here for Mother now. How is she?"

Maggie shook her head. "Someday he's going to go too far and—"

Isabelle stirred.

"Not now, Maggie. Put it out of your mind."

Dr. Lyman came back again at eight thirty. His shoulders slumped under the weight of his own fatigue; his eyelids drooped and he didn't smile at all. "You girls are doing a good job, but I think we're fighting a losing battle. She's still too hot, and her breathing is labored. If you prop her up with a few pillows, she might be more comfortable." He packed up his bag, and called the sisters and Karl into the hallway. "If she lasts the night she probably won't make it through tomorrow."

"Oh, no..." Kathleen twisted her handkerchief.

"I'm sorry. It's time you called Father Cunningham. Karl, could you do that?"

Karl nodded and went downstairs.

Dr. Lyman followed him. "Keep doing what you've been doing. I'll be back in a few hours. There's a baby trying to come into the world, so I won't be home if you call, but Mrs. Lyman will know how to find me."

Maggie and Kathleen went back into their mother's sickroom and stood by the bed. Kathleen whispered, "Do you think she can hear us?"

"Of course she can." Maggie lifted the flap of the tent and moved the steamer out of the way. Once more, she uncovered her mother's fevered body.

Isabelle opened her eyes a little. "Please, please... can't you help me?" She barely had enough breath to talk.

"We're working hard to keep you with us, Mama." Surprised at the depth of her own sadness, tears ran down Maggie's face; Kathleen cried, too.

"Nobody cry," croaked Isabelle. "I'm not worth your tears."

Maggie wiped her own eyes and turned her mother on her side to sponge her back. "Yes, you are." Her tears fell on Isabelle's fevered body and evaporated away with the rest of the water. "Oh, yes you are."

Karl brought Father Cunningham to his grandmother's room and stood in the hall watching. Maggie caught sight of him, pale, his brow creased, looking worried, like an adult. Having him here was almost like having Eddie standing by.

The priest put his hand on Maggie's shoulder. "This has to be too much for you, child."

"I'm all right, Father."

"May I come in, too?" Karl asked from the doorway.

"Of course." Maggie held out her arm for him so he would come and stand next to her. She kept her arm around him, but now she leaned on him and he supported her. What would she do without him?

Isabelle opened her eyes when Father Cunningham began to pray. She kept them open through all the prayers, watching his every move as he brought out the sweet smelling oil for anointing and marked her with the sign of the cross.

Father took her hand, looking sad. "Isabelle, I've known you for so many years. I will keep praying for you. God bless you, my dear." He looked at Kathleen then Maggie. "Call me again if..."

"Yes, Father," said Kathleen

Before he left the room he took Kathleen's hand, then Maggie's. Karl followed him down the stairs.

Maggie touched her mother's forehead. "Oh, dear, Mama, we just had you cooled off." If they didn't keep up with her, she'd burn up before morning came. "Kathy, come here—"

Isabelle shifted in the bed, her eyes opening as wide as quarters. Breathless, she pleaded with Maggie. "Help... I'm so... scared."

"It's all right, dear, don't be afraid." Maggie brushed her cheek. "We're here."

Kathleen took her mother's hand, but Isabelle pulled away and began to strain, trying to cough but not having enough strength to do it. She rolled onto her side, her hands in fists; her fists over her heart. She drew up her legs, her knees and elbows nearly touching.

Maggie took charge. "The tent—put the sides down, get the steamer going again. We left her out of there too long." She realized she sounded like her mother, bossing her sister around.

Kathleen lowered the sides of the tent. Terrified, Isabelle clutched Maggie's arm and wouldn't let her go.

Maggie peeled away her mother's hand. "I'm right here." She hurried to the other side of the bed, lifted the tent wall and crawled in. Steam began to fill the small space they shared.

"Take it easy, now; try to keep breathing." Maggie stroked her mother's arm.

Although Maggie's heart beat wildly, Isabelle seemed to relax a little. Maggie reached over and brushed a strand of hair from her mother's eyes. She tried to smile at the old woman lying next to her. "Please, please, God," she whispered, "please, help her." Like raindrops falling hard on rock, she started to cry in painful spasms, her tears wetting the sheet beneath her.

Suddenly, Isabelle sat up, her arms flailing in the damp air. Bending forward, she gagged and choked. Maggie watched her naked chest and stomach expand and violently contract as they expelled the rot that was making her so sick. She gasped and wheezed, air rushing in, resuming its rightful place. Isabelle worked hard, coughing, gasping, spitting. She looked at Maggie.

"I'm sorry," she whispered, her voice weak and hoarse. "I wet the bed."

Maggie rubbed her hand gently across her mother's hot back. "It's okay, Mama, don't worry about the sheets."

"Is she all right?" Kathleen voice sounded far away.

"I think so, she coughed up a big mess, but—"

"What's going on in here?" Dr. Lyman had returned. He lifted the side of the tent where Maggie sat. "What in the blazes are you doing in there? Are you crazy? Get out, this instant!" He took her arm and pulled it.

Overcome by another fit of choking and coughing, Isabelle's eyes widened.

Maggie jerked her arm away from the doctor. "Don't, you're scaring her."

Dr. Lyman bellowed. "Are you trying to turn your children into orphans, Margaret?"

"We need to get these sheets changed." Maggie ignored the doctor, touched her mother's cheek and smiled. "She's still hot, but she's breathing better. Here, lie back and rest." Isabelle closed her eyes, exhausted.

"Get out of there!"

Maggie lifted the flap and climbed out of the tent. "I don't know what I did wrong, but you can chew me out later. First we need to wash her up and get some clean sheets and a blanket." She opened the other side and started to pull the dirty bedding off her mother.

"Wait, let me see that." Dr. Lyman looked over her shoulder. "That's from the infection, all right. You've got to keep her coughing."

"What do you think we're doing?" Maggie couldn't hide her irritation. "Would you mind giving us a minute to clean her up?"

Dr. Lyman backed away, went into the hallway and paced. Kathleen didn't have the stomach to help Maggie with the mess, so she went for soap and water, more towels and clean sheets. When they had Isabelle all cleaned up and between fresh sheets, propped up on her pillows like a queen and wearing a summer night gown, they allowed Dr. Lyman to come back in.

He listened to her breathe and took her temperature again. "Nearly one hundred and three degrees. Still too hot. Not out of the woods by a long shot, but her breathing does sound better. Keep sponging her off, keep that fever down. I think you can get rid of the tent, but keep the steamer going next to the bed. Put the tent back up and call me if she has more trouble breathing."

"Thank you so much, Doctor Lyman." Kathleen turned to her sister. "Maggie, you should have a break. Why don't you go put on a pot of tea?"

"No." Dr. Lyman took a firm hold on Maggie's arm. "She's coming with me." He led her out of the room and to the end of hall, where he stood blocking her way, one hand on either wall.

He glared down at her. "What were you thinking?"

Maggie glared back. "You scared her!"

Kathleen stepped out of the bedroom with her finger over her lips. "Shh."

Dr. Lyman lowered his voice. "How long were you in that thing with her?"

"I went in to calm her down."

"You could have held her hand from the outside."

"She was confused and scared."

"Do you know how this kind of disease is spread, Margaret? I'll tell you how it's spread: *through the air!* Anyone's at risk just from being in the room with her, but that's to be expected. But you, you've almost guaranteed that you'll be sick in a few days, as sick as she is. For the love of Pete, what am I going to do with you?"

As the doctor ran his hand through his hair, Maggie saw him shake.

"You didn't tell me how the disease is spread. I did what I would have if she'd been one of my children."

Dr. Lyman leaned toward Maggie. She couldn't escape his anger. "Let me give you a little advice, young lady. Get something in writing about who should take your children if you die, because if you get this sick, you could."

"You should have told me."

Maggie saw Karl come up the stairs. She knew he'd heard everything.

The doctor whipped around. "Yes, Karl, what can we do for you?" He pushed his glasses up the bridge of his nose.

"I need to go in here." Karl went into the bathroom and closed the door with a bang. Immediately, water began running, loud and hard.

"Look, now you've scared him, too."

"I'm trying to scare some sense into *you.* There's nothing I can do to keep you from getting sick, nothing. Make arrangements for your family. And for God's sake, get that boy out of here; he shouldn't be exposed to this. Now, listen." He shook his finger at her, like her father used to. "If you start feeling bad, stop what you're doing and go to bed. If you get a fever or a headache or a cough, or anything, call me right away. Do I make myself perfectly clear?" His eyes got red and he pulled out his handkerchief and blew his nose.

"Are you all right, Dr. Lyman?"

"No, I don't suppose I am. There was one more orphan born into the world tonight, a beautiful little boy whose mama didn't survive his birth. Your children have already lost their daddy; they shouldn't lose you, too."

"I'm sorry." Maggie looked down at her hands.

"You've got me all worked up, Margaret. You people are special, I've watched you grow up; I've seen your babies born and watched them grow, too." He put his hand on her shoulder and squeezed it.

The toilet flushed and the water stopped running. Karl came out of the bathroom and started back down the stairs, but stopped when Maggie called after him.

"Everything's okay, honey, don't worry."

"You have a quite a mother, Karl; a little foolish, but courageous. She's got a good heart, you're lucky to have her."

"Yessir, I know that."

"Time for me to go home. Karl, get your things, you can't stay here. I'll take you to Will's house." He turned to Maggie. "Try to get some sleep, you look exhausted." He started down the stairs, but stopped and spoke without turning around. "Just so you know, Margaret: you did exactly what I would have done for my own mother, or my own child." He went down two more steps, then turned back to face her. "If I'd thought of it."

Chapter 21

Love Me!

Jacob didn't bother pulling the window shade when he
went to bed. A street lamp cast silvery light against the
wall, giving a ghost-like glow to the white shirt he'd left
hanging on the back of his chair. He listened to his alarm
clock beat out the rhythm of seconds, minutes and hours;
his life ticking away, each second, each minute consumed
by the one that followed it. Would it always be like this,
sleeping in a half-cold bed, never needing to pull the shade
against voyeurs who sought a slice of his happiness for
their own thrill?

He sighed, tried to relax, sat up and looked at the clock.
Twelve-fifty. He'd been rolling around in the bed for an
hour, almost two, now. Why hadn't Margaret answered his
letter? Day by day, his need to know how she felt about
him increased, until the not knowing had thrown him all
out of joint.

"Patience, patience, Jacob." He imitated his mother's
voice. "It's been less than a week, dear."

"Well, I'm no good at patience." Jacob answered himself, shifting angrily in bed. He took a deep breath, let it

out again. "So here's the plan, Margaret. If there's no letter in the morning, you'll find me on your doorstep by supper. I have to know. I *have* to know." He stared at the shadows on the wall and felt his eyelids grow heavy. "Please love me. Please... love me."

He rose before six; washed and dressed in the white shirt from the chair and a pair of gray trousers. For some reason he put on the navy sweater Lana sent him the Christmas before she and her mother came from Pennsylvania. She'd knit it herself; her needlework always drew compliments from women, making him feel like he had to explain where it came from, so he rarely wore it.

He tried to eat breakfast, but nothing tasted good, so he cleaned the kitchen and paced the floors until the mail came at ten minutes before nine. He took it into the library, set it on his desk and stared at it. "You're acting like a fool, Denver." Quickly, he flipped through the envelopes. Nothing. "Damn!"

He pulled his valise out of the closet, threw in a clean shirt and few other essentials and left a note on the kitchen table for Hilde: *Gone to Tomos*. He drove north, past a few farms, around the lakes and across the stump-studded wasteland that used to be forest thick with virgin pine, but saw none of it. Even though he rarely prayed, he said over and over again, "Please don't let me be a jack-ass. Don't let me be a jack-ass, please don't let me be a jack-ass."

He knew, however, that he very likely *would* act like a jack-ass. It's what he did when he got all riled up.

Three hours later, in front of 617 Blight Street, Jacob got out of his car. He pounded on her door, but nobody answered. He went around to the back door, but no one answered there, either. He peered in the kitchen window: nothing, no sign of anybody. Back in the car, he noticed that no smoke came from the chimney. Where could she be?

He stormed into Will's house without knocking or even saying, *Hello.* "Bernie, where is she? There's no one at Margaret's house. What's going on?"

"Well, that's a fine *how d'you do* if I ever saw one. Suppose *you* tell *me* what's goin' on?" Busy baking, Bernie wiped her flour coated hands on the front of her apron then rolled them into loose fists and plunked them on her hips.

"I came to see her. Margaret. But there's nobody at her house. Something's wrong."

"Is she expectin' to see you today?"

"No, but—"

Anna bounced into the kitchen with Billy behind her. "Hi, Mr. Denver."

"Hi, Uncle Jacob."

"Hello, Anna. Billy." Without smiling, Jacob turned back to Bernie. "Where is she?"

"Her mum's sick with pneumonia. She's been takin' care of her. The girls are with me, and Will and Karl went off to the hardware store. Would you mind tellin' me what's got you so worked up that you'd drive all the way up here without tellin' anyone you were comin'?"

"Ahh..." Jacob looked at the children and back at Bernie. "I can't."

Bernie shooed Anna and Billy out of the kitchen. "You two go see what Lizzie and Ned are up to."

"Ned's crying again," said Anna. "Lizzie's reading to him."

"Go tell them I'll come up in a minute. Now off with ya both. Go."

Anna and Billy giggled and ran out of the kitchen and up the stairs.

"Now can you tell me what's goin' on in that head o' yours, Jakey?"

"I have to see her. I need to talk to her. I haven't heard from her all week. Tell me where her mother lives so I can go—"

"She's like to be awfully busy."

"That's all right. Where—"

"Mrs. O'Keefe lives on Oak Street, white house with green trim, I don't know the number off hand, but there's a fence out front with an arbor over the gate."

Ned started to howl. "Mummy!"

"I've got to see to my boy. Behave yourself, you hear me, Jacob?"

Jacob turned to go and bumped into Neddie, who'd come looking for his mother, his left hand over his ear.

"Hey, pal. I'll see you later, gotta go." Jacob called over his shoulder.

Ned cried louder. "Unca Jacup, come back!"

Jacob could still hear him wailing after he closed the front door.

He drove around for fifteen minutes and finally found Oak Street, not far from Margaret's house. He pulled up in front of the white house with green trim, arbor over the gate. Without turning the engine off, he sat looking at the house, trying to decide what to say when he saw her. He shook his head; it was a little late to be making up a speech. He sucked in a deep breath, and held it for a few seconds. "Please, Margaret..." He got out and tried to look confident as he went to the front door, as if visiting at her mother's was the most natural, everyday thing he could be doing.

Jacob rang the door bell, waited, and rang again. A woman came to the door; she resembled Margaret, but seemed much older.

"Yes?"

"Jacob Denver. I'm here to see Margaret. I'm a friend of hers."

The woman opened the door. He stepped inside; she locked the door behind him. "I'll see if she can come down."

She disappeared up the stairs while Jacob stood by the front door, shifting his weight from one foot to the other. He could hear two women talking, but couldn't make anything out until Margaret said, "Jacob? Oh, dear."

Just as he'd feared: she wasn't going to be happy to see him. He crossed his arms.

He had to wait a long time before Margaret descended the stairs. She wore a rumpled house dress that had once been either blue or green, now faded to a dingy gray. She'd combed her hair, but her face was drawn and her eyes were puffy with dark circles underneath. She didn't look much like the beautiful woman he had dinner with only one week ago.

"Jacob? I didn't expect to see you today. I'm a mess, but—"

"You never answered my letter, Margaret."

"I'm sorry. I did write back, only I couldn't mail it."

"Why not?" *Second thoughts?*

"I meant to write the letter over again, but Mother got sick and I haven't had a moment to myself since then."

"Why couldn't you mail the first one?"

"I can't tell you, it wouldn't be right."

He stepped toward her. "Margaret, I've been waiting and waiting to hear from you." He knew he was being *pushy-pushy*, as Hilde would say.

"I'm sorry. Listen, my sister has to leave soon, so I'm going to make something to eat while she stays with Mother. Are you hungry?" The clock struck three thirty. "I haven't eaten since breakfast."

"Please, can't we talk first?"

"Take off your coat and come into the kitchen."

Jacob took off his coat and gloves, flipped them onto the davenport in a huff, and followed her across a worn out blue rug. Why couldn't she give him a few moments of her undivided attention?

"Sit down." Margaret opened the icebox and looked inside. "There isn't much here, except for some cheese. Would you like a cheese sandwich?"

"I'm not here to eat, I'm here to talk."

She slapped the cheese on the table. "Is whatever you have to say so important that I have to go without eating? Kathleen has to go home, and I'm pretty sure she won't be coming back. This could be my only chance to eat for the rest of the day. Would you mind terribly?"

"No. Go ahead." He crossed his arms again.

"Shall I make something for you, too?"

Jacob sighed. "Oh, all right." *You're already acting like a jack-ass, Denver!*

"Would you like some coffee? I should make some coffee."

"Don't make it on my account."

"I need it." She filled the coffee pot and put it on, but the stove had gone cold. "I'll be right back." She went out the back door and came in again with an armload of wood.

"You could have asked me to do that for you."

She gave him a brief glance, then put the wood in the stove and cut four thick slices of bread. "Would you like your sandwich grilled? The bread's gone dry."

"Only if you're going to grill your own."

She pulled a griddle out from one of her mother's cupboards—pine—Jacob noticed, not painted and chipped like her cupboards were. She buttered the bread, sliced the cheese, assembled the sandwiches on the griddle and put the griddle on the stove. The coffee started to perk. She stood with her back to him, tending the food. "Speak, Jacob, I'm all ears."

"You didn't answer my letter."

"I told you I did answer it, but something happened and I couldn't mail it."

"What?"

She turned around. Her tired eyes flashed with anger. "I told you, it wouldn't be right for me to say. It sounds like you care more about why you didn't get a letter than about what I wrote to you."

"You know how important this is to me."

She turned back to the stove. "Coffee, Mr. Denver?"

"Please." *Mr. Denver.* That stung.

Margaret flipped the sandwiches then stepped around him to take some dishes from the cupboard. She set out plates, cups, and saucers for each of them.

He stared at the little baskets of fruit that decorated the edges of the white plates. They were old, their glaze checked from use and age.

She poured into his cup, then into hers. "It's hot."

"I can see that."

When the sandwiches were done, she cut them both with the spatula before putting them on the plates. She went to the sink and rinsed off her hands, came to the table and sat down. "I say grace before I eat."

"I know."

She bowed her head and crossed herself, sitting very still for a minute. "O, Lord, bless these gifts which you give to us from your gracious providence and please bring Mother back to health and guard Kathleen and help me be patient and merciful with this man. Amen."

Jacob stared at his plate.

"Go on, eat while it's hot, before it turns hard like a doorstop."

"Margaret," he traced and retraced the handle of his coffee cup with his finger and looked up at her. "Will you please tell me what you wrote?"

She swallowed the bite she'd taken and took a sip of her coffee. "Eat."

Jacob took a bite of his sandwich, then another. He wondered how could she do such wonderful things with dry bread, butter and a bit of cheese, but didn't tell her how good it tasted.

Margaret ate in silence, too. She finished her coffee and got up for the pot. "At the moment I don't know what to say to you. More coffee?"

"Please."

She refilled both cups. "No, Jacob, I *do* know what to say to you." She set the pot down hard on the stove. "It seems to me you're wanting to be the center of my life. Is that right, do I have that right?"

Jacob shifted in his chair and cleared his throat. "Well, I... I guess you could say that." Stunned and embarrassed that she'd perceived the truth even before he did, he felt like a little boy caught sneaking candy from his Grandma's purse. "But Margaret, I only want your—"

"Now hear this, Mr. Denver: I have family depending on me." Her eyes blazed. "My babies have no one but me, and now my mother might as well be one of them. Kathleen is going home in a little while so she's there when her husband gets home, since he forbid her to come to her own mother's deathbed." Margaret choked a little on the word *deathbed*. She covered her face with her hands. "Sooner or later she's going to die from what he does to her." Her eyes filled with tears which she quickly wiped away with her sleeve.

Jacob touched her arm. "Margaret—"

She pulled away from him. "No, I'm not finished. You can't come around and think you can force your way into the middle of all this. I can't drop my responsibilities to them just to make sure you feel—"

Someone began pounding on the back door and cursing, breaking Margaret's tirade. "Oh, God, no, it's Melvin." She hurried to the stairs and called to her sister. "Kathleen, Melvin's here. Don't come down."

Margaret came back and stood in the kitchen doorway, eyes wide in terror. "I forgot to lock the door when I brought in the wood. Be careful, Jacob."

The knob turned and the back door flew open. A heavy man in a red hunting jacket stomped up the four stairs from the back door. Sweat dripped from his greasy brow. "Where is she? That stupid bitch, she ought to know better than to defy me! This is all your doing, Margaret."

Just in time, Jacob stepped between Melvin and Margaret, one arm on each side of the door.

The man glared at him. "I see Margaret is taking advantage of her poor mother's illness to do a little business—again."

Jacob couldn't believe what he was hearing. The muscles in his jaw tightened. "Be careful what you say—"

Melvin interrupted, yelling past him. "You tricked Kathleen into coming over here and doing all the work so you could turn a few bucks, didn't you? Now she's gonna pay and it's all your fault!"

"Kathy, please," cried Margaret. "Go back upstairs! Don't—"

"You're home early, Melvin. How was the tournament?" Kathleen didn't sound frightened at all.

Jacob turned slightly to see what was happening behind him; Melvin pushed him aside and pounded across the dining room.

"Why, you little..." He grabbed Kathleen by the back of her hair, ripping it from the neat bun she wore at the nape of her neck. He used it as a leash, dragging her around the living room with him. "What did I tell you about coming over here?"

Kathleen didn't wince or whimper or fight her husband, rather, she seemed resigned, even bored with it all.

Margaret, still crying, tried to stop him; Melvin pushed her away with his free hand.

Quickly, Jacob stepped toward the man, raising his fists. "Let go of your wife before I—"

"Who the hell d'you think you are?" As Melvin glared at Jacob, he twisted Kathleen's hair until she looked like a corpse hanging from a gallows. "You come any closer and she'll pay." He shook her and watched her face turn red. "When are you gonna remember who's boss, Kathleen? I keep having to remind you. I guess it's time for another lesson."

"Fine, Melvin." Kathleen's voice was tight, like she had no air. "But first let me say goodbye to Mother."

Melvin twisted Kathleen's hair some more, until her cheek touched her shoulder.

"Stop it, Melvin!" Margaret's voice wavered with hysteria.

"Come on, she's an old lady, and she's s-sick..." Miraculously, Kathleen remained calm. "Remember how she always makes you Irish potatoes for your birthday?"

"Irish potatoes!" Melvin spat out the words. He let go of her hair and kicked her behind, making her stumble toward the stairs. "One minute, Kathleen. *One!*"

Jacob couldn't stand it anymore. His heart beating hard and fast, in two strides he was behind Melvin, his left elbow around his neck, his right hand on Melvin's right wrist, jerking it up behind his back.

"Get your hands off me!" Now Melvin's voice sounded tight.

"Not on your life."

Margaret ran to pick up her sister's hair pins, then caught up with her on the stairs. Kathleen moved gingerly, in obvious pain.

Jacob turned Melvin around and walked him through the kitchen, down the steps and pushed him out the door. He resisted the urge to spit on him. "Don't even try to come back in here!"

Melvin turned back and glared at Jacob, rubbing his neck. "She's *my* woman and she's coming home with *me!*"

"We'll see about that."

Jacob slammed and locked the door and hurried into the dining room. He called up the stairs. "Do you want me to call the police?"

He heard them talking quietly before Kathleen came floating down the stairs with dignity and grace. She'd combed her hair and coiled it back into a bun. Margaret followed, her eyes red, her face mottled from crying.

Kathleen looked at Jacob and smiled. "No, thank you,

Mr. Denver."

"Are you sure you want to go home with this man, because I can—"

"It's my home, too. But thank you. I see my sister has found a good friend in you." She turned to Margaret and they embraced.

Margaret clung to her, sobbing. "Please, don't go."

"I have to."

"He'll k—you're going to—"

"Then I'd be with God, wouldn't I, Magpie? And God is good."

The conversation became muffled. Kathleen said, "You'd best go see to Mother. She's feverish again."

"No."

"Maggie, let go, now. I have to go home; Melvin needs his supper." Kathleen straightened her sleeves and held her hand out to Jacob. "It's nice to meet you, Mr. Denver."

Melvin began to pound on the back door. "Come on, Kathleen!"

Kathleen slipped on her coat and looked first at Margaret, then at Jacob. "Take good care of my little sister. And please—will you pray for me?"

"Let's *go*, Kathleen!"

She hurried to the door. Before she even stepped outside, Melvin grabbed her arm and dragged her to the car.

Jacob followed and closed the back door behind her. His heart slowed and his breathing began to return to normal, but he was still angry. How could that man be so brutal to his own wife, and how could she accept it like it was nothing? Margaret came and stood next to him. He put his hand on her shoulder, but she rested her forehead against the glass and watched Melvin drive away.

"Good bye, Kathy," she whispered. Her lip quivered

and more tears fell.

"I can stay in case he comes back."

"He won't. He'll be too busy with her."

"When can we talk?"

"Another time." She didn't look at him.

"Later?"

"That depends on Mother."

"Please?"

"We can try."

He went to the living room for his coat and gloves and put them on. She followed; there were no pleasantries or small talk.

"Thank you for the lunch. You've given me a lot to think about." He didn't think she'd heard him. He opened the door.

She shivered and crossed her arms. "Jacob? If it helps, the letter I didn't send... you would have liked it."

He nodded, but didn't feel happy about it. "I'll come back later with some supper for you."

She didn't answer, but looked at him as if she were seeing someone else. He stepped through the door and she closed and locked it without another word.

Chapter 22

Worthy

Karl sat cross-legged on the dirt floor of Will's basement wielding a large needle; he and Will were mending fishing nets for the new season. The odor of old fish and the dusty, damp smell of the basement made one unforgettable stink that Karl always associated with net mending. He'd helped his father and Will with the same job over the last two winters and never liked it. This year he *hated* it, knowing his father wouldn't be there to cast out the nets come spring.

But today, Karl had other things on his mind. "I don't understand why I couldn't stay at Grandma's with my mother. She needs my help."

"Sure, she needs help, but your Aunt Kathleen is there." Will spoke without looking up. "You've given your parents plenty of sleepless nights with that cough you get. Your mother is right and so is Doc Lyman. There's no sense in exposing you to pneumonia."

"Then, my mother shouldn't be around it either." Karl's arm rested on his knee, the cord in his hand dragging in the dirt. "If she gets sick, she could die, and what'll happen to us?"

"Don't go borrowing trouble. She's a strong woman, she'll be fine."

"That's not what I heard Dr. Lyman say. He got mad at her and said she'd get sick for sure and she might die from it. He said she should *make arrangements for her family*, whatever that means. He told her she should write it down."

Will looked up from his work. "He did, huh?"

His response only validated Karl's fear. "Yeah. So what happens to us if she dies?"

Will scratched his beard and turned his attention back to the net. "That's not for you to worry about."

"Well, of course I'm going to worry about it!" As Karl shouted, his voice cracked. "She can't die, too."

"Seems to me you were eavesdropping on somebody else's conversation."

"I didn't mean to. I needed to use the bathroom and they were in the hall talking. What am I gonna do, Will?" The more Karl talked about it, the more scared he became.

Will stopped again. "Right now, you're gonna help me with this net. You're gonna do what you need to do every day; go to school and do your homework and help out at home as much as you can. And you're gonna trust the people who care about you to work this out."

"I won't go live with Uncle Melvin and neither will my sisters. We'll run away if we have to. I'll get a job and take care of them."

"That's enough, Karl. If it comes to that, *I* will make sure you have a good place to live with people who care about you. But it's not gonna to come to that." Will smiled. "Come on, you're too young to have this big worry on your shoulders. You should be having fun. Say, I oughta teach you how to play chess. You'd like it."

"Maybe." Sulking, Karl picked up his needle and finished tying the knot he'd started. As he wrapped and pulled and tied, he pushed the fear of his mother's death as far into his cave as he could.

When Jacob left Mrs. O'Keefe's house, his throat felt tight. He thought his collar might be pinching him, but when he opened the top button of his shirt, the feeling didn't go away. He didn't understand. Margaret said he would have liked the letter, but he wasn't happy about it, he was confused and worried.

He went into town and checked into the Grand Hotel, then asked if the restaurant would pack up a dinner for him. He found his room and stretched out on top of the bed, studying the pressed tin ceiling. Sure, he could have slept in Will's attic like he usually did, but tonight he needed peace and quiet. He couldn't shake the image of that bully dragging Margaret's sister around by the hair and kicking her backside. He wondered how she got tangled up with a creature like him. She seemed to be proper and refined, like Margaret.

He knew there were men who threatened and mistreated their women and children to get their own way. Selfish bastards, they were, thinking the whole world revolved around what they wanted or thought they needed. He'd never do that to a woman.

He got up a little before six, washed his face, combed his hair, buttoned his shirt, and went down to the restaurant to pick up the food he'd ordered. A few minutes later, he knocked on Mrs. O'Keefe's door again, this time carrying a huge picnic basket. He waited on the front step for nearly five minutes before he tried the knob. It was locked. He trudged through the snow to the back door, knocked again, waited, and tried the knob. It turned.

He let himself in, wondering if he should scold Margaret for leaving the door unlocked. He set the basket on the kitchen table and checked the stove. A few coals still glowed inside, so he set all the hot food on top: the mashed potatoes and gravy, the whole chicken and the pie. The cabbage salad went into the icebox; it would be a feast for the two of them with plenty of leftovers for her meals tomorrow. When Margaret saw what he'd brought for her, Jacob knew for sure she'd take the time to talk to him.

"Jacob! How did you get in?"

He jumped, nearly dropping the chicken on the floor. "I knocked at the front door, but you didn't answer so I came around to the back. I'm sorry about before."

"Well, I'm glad it's you and not Melvin." She looked at all the food on the table. "Are you expecting company?"

Jacob thought he saw the beginning of a smile. He smiled at her. "No, this is all for you. I hope you're hungry."

"As a matter of fact, I am, but I have to get back to Mother, she's burning up again. Keep the food warm, I'll come back as soon as—oh, look, you brought me a whole chicken!" She beamed. "Thank you so much. Would you mind doing something for me?"

Her weary smile made him go all weak kneed. "Of course, anything."

"Would you please start some broth? She hasn't eaten for a couple of days, but I think she might take a little soup." Maggie disappeared into the small pantry adjacent to the kitchen and returned with a large pot.

"But I don't know how."

"Easy, anyone can do it. Put the chicken in the pot, cover it with water, add a little salt and put it on the stove."

"But—"

"And you'll find carrots and onions in the root cellar. Two carrots and one onion, chop them fine."

Onions? "But Margaret, what about our dinner?"

"Oh, just take some meat off the bones for us." She took a clean glass from the cupboard and filled it with water.

"I need a knife."

She called from the stairway, glass in hand. "Look through the drawers; I'm sure you'll find one."

Jacob took off his sweater, rolled up his sleeves and got to work, ripping the legs off the chicken and cutting meat from the breast, wondering when he'd get to eat any of it. After he put the rest of the greasy bird into the pot and filled it with water, like she said, he went looking for the vegetables. Chopping onions was the last thing on his mind when he told her he'd do anything. He was tempted to quarter them, like he'd seen Hilde do when she made soup.

He chopped the carrots first, no problem there, but chopping the onion was a different story. He tried to stand as far away from the cutting board as he could while he chopped, but his eyes still watered and his nose still ran. He thought he might gag. He sensed a movement in the room and looked up, face wet, needing his handkerchief. "Margaret, I can't do this; I can't stand raw onions."

She stood in the doorway with a crock in her hands, looking at him. "You told me you liked onions, otherwise I wouldn't have asked you. Put them in the pot as they are." She took the crock to the sink and filled it with water; turned and went back up the stairs without another word.

When did he say he liked onions? The strange feeling in his throat came back. She'd been less than happy to see him, and now it seemed like he could only make her angry. He felt like going back to the hotel and trying to forget about her and her crazy family, but he needed to see this through to the end. He sat down at the table to wait.

After nearly an hour she reappeared, went directly to the stove and stirred the broth. She looked exhausted.

"Margaret." Jacob stood.

"So what other blarney have you fed me? Do you always tell lies to get women to like you?" She spoke into the pot.

"I don't lie. I don't know what you're talking about. Sit down and eat, I brought all this for you."

"I've only got a few minutes. Mother's sleeping, but not very soundly." She started bringing food to the table.

"No, sit down." He pulled out a chair for her. He filled two plates and sat down across the table from her. "Are you going to say grace?"

"I'm too tired," she sighed. "You do it."

Jacob cleared his throat, looked at her, then down at his plate. He considered asking God to help him be patient and merciful with her, like she had of him, but even he knew prayer wasn't the place for sarcasm. "Well, I don't know if I remember any. Hmm... Hilde says something like, *O give thanks to the Lord for he is good and his mercy endureth forever. Amen.* He looked up. She'd fixed her eyes on him with an icy stare.

"You said you liked onions."

"When?"

"That first day you came by with Will. I said I couldn't shake hands because I'd been chopping onions, and you said you happened to like onions."

Jacob remembered. He also remembered not knowing why he said it. "Well, I... I didn't mean to lie, I'm sorry. What I meant was—I liked *you*. I still do. That's why I need to know—"

She started to cry. "How can I believe what you say if you lied about the onions?"

"I brought you supper and I started the broth like you asked. Please don't cry. I do care for you, Margaret, and I hoped we could talk about how you feel—"

Her fork clanged as she dropped it on her plate, making Jacob jump. "Your pestering me like this isn't helping any." She stood up and leaned close to him, balancing herself with her hand on his upper arm, looking into his eyes. "Here's how I feel about you: I love getting your letters. I like your visits—well, most of them—and I like you. You might even say I care for you. At least I think I do."

Jacob's heart skipped a beat. He covered her hand with his. But she went on, her fury building with each word. He wished he understood why she was so angry.

"I assume those hopes and dreams you wrote about involve a family, maybe with me, so you'd better listen. I believe in telling the truth, no lying allowed, otherwise how can anyone trust? I believe when you're in a family and one person is sick or weak or hurt, everyone else works for the good of that person, no matter what it takes, because if that person isn't well, no one else in the family is, either." Her eyes filled with tears again. "If you don't like that, Jacob, if you can't live with that, then you're not the man I thought you were, and you can forget about me." The tears escaped and went rolling down her face. She let go and backed away. "Thank you for bringing all this food, and thank you for chopping onions and putting the soup on, but now I've lost my appetite. Finish your supper and be on your way. We can talk some other time if you still think so much of me." She turned and disappeared up the stairs.

Stunned, Jacob stared at the doorway. "Margaret? I'm sorry." He wanted her to come back, but he knew she wouldn't. How was he going to fix this?

He tried to eat, but the strange feeling in his throat choked him and kept him from swallowing more than a few bites. He took Margaret's plate, covered it with a towel and set it in the icebox in case she got hungry later. He cleared the rest of the food and washed the dishes, wondering again if he should give up on her. He felt like a stinking pile of rotten sawdust.

Karl and Will sat in the kitchen with the chessboard between them when they heard a knock on the front door. The door swung open before anyone could have answered it.

"It's my brother," Will said, getting up. "He always does that."

Karl got up, too, and followed Will into the dining room.

"Well, well, Jacob, I heard you were in town." Will shook his brother's hand.

"I came up to see Margaret." Mr. Denver didn't seem to put much into the handshake.

"Hi, Mr. Denver. My mother's staying at my Grandma's; Grandma's sick."

Mr. Denver nodded at him. "I know, I just came from there."

"How is she? My mother, I mean."

"Tired, but all right, I guess. I took her some supper."

Mr. Denver didn't smile like he did before.

"That was real nice of you, thanks." Karl could tell he wanted to talk to Will in private. "I'm going upstairs to see if I can find that book Bernie told me about at supper." He looked at Will, and Will nodded.

"Shush, please, all of you." Bernie scolded. She sat in her rocking chair in the corner of the living room holding a flushed and sleepy Ned on her lap, scowling at them. "This boy's had an earache all day, and now he's almost asleep. Will, you two go on back to the kitchen, an' mind you, keep it down. Karl, don't go wakin' up any of the others, you hear me?"

"I won't," he whispered as he climbed the stairs. He went into Will and Bernie's bedroom and looked through the pile of books next to the bed. He didn't remember the title of the book she told him about, so he pulled one from the stack at random. He returned to the living room and tried to get comfortable on the davenport, hoping he'd be able to hear what Mr. Denver said to Will. He pretended to read, holding his breath so he could hear better.

"Jeesh, Jacob, did you think at *all* before you came rushing up here?"

"Well, I waited all week to hear from her. I had to know."

"She has family responsibilities. Did that ever occur to you?"

"I know, I know, she made that perfectly clear."

"So did she answer your question?"

Karl sat up straight. Did he ask her to marry him?

"Yes. I think so. I think she likes me, but now I feel bad about it. What's wrong with me?"

Karl let out his breath. Must not have been that.

"You're pushing her too fast."

No answer.

"Aren't you?"

"You know what kind of jack-ass I can be."

"Aw, cut the jack-ass talk. The old man thought it was funny—*Jack*—but I don't. You aren't a jack-ass, you're a man; so quit using it as an excuse."

Neither of them said anything for a few seconds, then Will spoke again. He sounded mad. "Grow up, Jacob. You run this big company and all your other enterprises, you take good care of your workers, but you can't see what she needs because you're too worried about yourself."

"That's not true, it isn't."

"Then why'd you come?"

"I came because I'm crazy. For her."

"If you hurt her—or any of them—I'll have your neck!" Will growled almost like an animal.

"Why can't you trust me?"

"What are your intentions? D'you love her?"

"Yeah, I do."

"Then let me tell you somethin'. Loving someone is a whole lot more than goin' off all goo-goo eyed. You gotta help 'em when they need help, take care of 'em, too."

"I know, I know."

"So how does she feel about you?"

Karl already knew the answer from the letter he didn't mail; he didn't want to hear it from Mr. Denver. In a voice loud enough to wake Ned, he turned and called out, "Hey, Bernie, this is a great book."

Angry, Bernie scolded him. "Karl, shush!" Ned started to cry, holding his ear. "You woke 'im up."

"Oh, no, I forgot, I'm sorry." Karl felt awful and thought he might cry, too. He knew how miserable Ned had been all day. "I'm really sorry, Bernie."

"Oh, it's awright, he's gettin' restless again, anyway."

"I can rock him for a while." He put down the book. "Neddie, wanna sit on my lap and let your Mum stretch her legs?"

He held his arms out. "Play horsie, Karl?"

"It's too late for horsie," said Bernie. "It's time for sleep."

Ned started to wail. "I wanna play horsie with Karl."

"It's okay, I can be a slow horse. I'll take him." Ned climbed into Karl's arms and Bernie stood up and stretched.

Bernie wagged her finger at them. "No roughhousing." She felt Ned's forehead and went into the kitchen.

Karl walked around the living room holding Ned for few minutes, dipping every so often and making soft clip-clop noises with his tongue. When Ned rested his head on his shoulder, Karl sat in the rocking chair and rocked slowly, back and forth, back and forth, still making the same noises.

His throat tightened, but it helped to have this warm little body next to him. Holding Ned reminded Karl of how he used to hang onto his stuffed bear when he felt sad or scared or all alone. He didn't need to be reminded about sad, scared and all alone, though; they were all over him tonight.

Karl listened to Bernie, Will and Mr. Denver as they talked in the kitchen. He could hear Bernie making a call to Dr. Lyman and he could hear the brothers laughing quietly. Things must have settled down between the two of them. He wondered how Mr. Denver answered the last question.

A chair scraped on the floor. "You want a cup of coffee, Jacob?"

"No, I should go. Didn't sleep well last night. I've got a room downtown."

"You coulda stayed here."

"I'd be in the way."

"Suit yourself. See you tomorrow?"

"No. I'm heading home first thing." Another chair scraped the floor.

Will and Mr. Denver came from the kitchen. Will stopped and watched Karl rocking Ned, tilting his head and smiling. "You'll make a fine father someday, Karl," he said softly.

At the word *father,* Karl's eyes began to burn. "Yeah, maybe." He fought to keep the tears from leaking out.

Mr. Denver came close and squatted down, whispering, "Time for me to go." He put his big hand on Karl's boney knee and squeezed it, before moving it to Ned's back.

Ned looked up at him. "Bye-bye, Unca Jacup."

Mr. Denver kissed his nephew on the forehead. "Bye, Neddie." He turned to Karl. "Take good care of my little pal."

"Sure thing, Mr. Denver."

"Goodnight, son."

Son. A bolt of lightning cracked through Karl's chest, into his heart and beyond, stirring up all the things he'd been throwing into his cave. He took a deep breath and swallowed them back down.

Mr. Denver stood up and went to the door. He turned around before he went out. "I'll call you next week," he said to Will.

"Goodnight, Jacob." Will closed the door.

Bernie came with a compress in one hand and a glass in the other. "You want me to take 'im again?"

"Naw, we're doin' fine, aren't we?"

Ned sat up when he heard his mother's voice.

"How 'bout a little drink, Ned? Dr. Lyman said this would help." He drank from the glass Bernie held for him and then leaned against Karl again. "Here, he said this should help, too." She placed the warm, moist compress between Ned's aching ear and Karl's chest. Bernie looked at Karl. "You sure you don't want to finish your game with Will?"

"Yeah. You go on to bed."

"Thank you, Karl, you're a good boy." Bernie patted his arm. She turned off all the lamps but the smallest one and covered the boys with a red quilt, kissing each of them. "One of us'll be down in a couple hours to take over for you. G'night." She turned and went up the stairs

"'Night."

Karl rocked Ned in the dark. *Goodnight, son.* Son. That must mean Mr. Denver is going to marry Mama, if she doesn't get sick and die first. The idea of someone wanting to fill the empty place left by his father's death made the hole feel bigger than ever. He felt Ned's little body begin to relax; he felt the rhythm of his breathing slow and deepen. He remembered how Will said *You'll make a fine father someday.* A roaring in his ears began as his cave emptied in a rush, a flood of tears spilling down his face. He tried to be still and silent, like the rocks that took a beating from the waves along the shore, but he wasn't made of stone and couldn't do it.

Suddenly Ned sat up. "Don't cry, Karl. Here." He took the compress, and put it against Karl's ear. "All better, now." He stuck his thumb back in his mouth, rested his head against Karl's chest and went to sleep.

"Thanks, pal," whispered Karl. He found solace in the

warmth of the compress, which he slid back between his heart and Ned's ear, where it belonged. He found solace in the steady back and forth movement of the rocking chair, but most of all, he found solace in little Neddie. Karl held him closer and rocked into the night.

Jacob found some writing paper in his hotel room and sat down to write a note to Margaret. He knew he wouldn't be able to sleep if he didn't do something to make things right again.

Dear Margaret,

I came here to assure myself that I mean something to you and then acted like a pig-headed oaf. Please, I beg you to forgive me for thinking only of myself at a time when you have so many serious worries and responsibilities. I am also sorry about the onions. If I could turn back the clock, I would do many things differently, but, alas, time only moves forward, so I am at the mercy of your forgiveness.

I can see how much you need help caring for your mother, and perhaps help with your sister as well. Please write to me or tell Will what you need, and I will make sure you get it. I can hire a nurse for your mother so you can rest, I can have groceries brought in, I can hire someone to wash your clothes and your mother's, if it would help. I will do whatever I can for you. Anything, Margaret, anything.

I've learned many hard lessons today, and if you agree to see me again, you will see that I am greatly humbled in your presence. I admire your dedication to your family. I hope and pray (yes, pray) that someday I will be like you and worthy of your affections. You will always have mine.
Jacob.

Jacob folded the paper and slid it into an envelope, but did not seal it. He wanted to read it again in the morning so he'd remember what he wrote. He pulled the shade, undressed and crawled under the heavy wool quilt on the bed. He fell hard asleep hanging onto the extra pillow.

Maggie drifted awake when she heard the chugging of an engine in front of Isabelle's house. She'd fallen asleep in the chair next to her mother's bed a couple of hours ago, after she'd calmed her down from a violent fit of coughing. She got up and stretched the kinks from her neck. She pulled the curtains aside slightly and saw Jacob's car in front of the house and immediately felt guilty. In the dusky light of dawn, she saw him get out and walk toward the front door with something white in his hand. Even though she wanted to, she decided not to answer the door; she knew she looked frightful in her mother's old bathrobe with her hair down, not even braided for sleep. She sighed, then noticed exhaust coming from the tailpipe in the cold air. He hadn't turned off the engine. She watched him get back in the car, empty handed, and drive away.

She whispered his name and started to cry. He must have left another letter, which probably meant good-bye forever, since she'd been so cranky and rude last night. Without a sound, she crossed the room and went downstairs, opened the door and took the envelope from the mailbox. Hands shaking, she opened it. Cold from the tile floor in the foyer spread from the soles of her feet to her ankles as she read, leaning against the wall. *...I hope and pray (yes, pray) that someday I will be like you and worthy of your affections.*

Worthy? Maggie clutched the paper to her breast, crumpling it as she did, and slid down the wall until she sat on the floor. *Of course you're worthy, Jacob.* She pulled her feet close, wrapped them in the bathrobe, and hugged her knees to her chest. She rested her head against them, realizing how much she missed having someone's arms around her. She'd been a terrible shrew last night, and now *he* was begging for forgiveness. She began to weep until she fell into a teasing sleep that offered no cure for her exhaustion.

Chapter 23

In Sickness...

"Your mother's alive thanks to you, Margaret." Dr. Lyman snapped his bag shut. "You've given her some fine care; you'd make a good nurse."

Maggie shook her head slightly. "I have all I can handle here, thanks." She'd been at her mother's side non-stop since Friday morning: six days away from her children, her house, her bed.

"How are you feeling? You look a little washed out."

"You're just waiting for me to drop, aren't you?" She smiled. She didn't tell him about the ache in the back of her neck, across her shoulders and down her spine.

"No, I'm concerned. You look awfully tired. Are you getting any sleep?"

Maggie didn't answer. It wasn't just her mother keeping her up. She'd been fretting about what she should say to Jacob in the letter she had no time to write.

"Do you remember what I said to you? If you start to feel sick, I want you to call me right away—"

"*And go to bed, without waiting to see if it gets worse. How could I forget?*" She didn't mention the dull headache she'd had for the past couple of days because it went away as soon as she took one of her mother's aspirin pills.

"Why isn't Kathleen here helping you?"

"Melvin pushed her around the other night because she'd come here against his wishes."

Dr. Lyman scowled. "Have you tried calling her?"

Maggie nodded, then winced and rubbed the back of her neck. "He won't let me talk to her. I finally gave up."

The doctor shook his head. "What's wrong with your neck?"

"Nothing."

"I'm going to get some help for you. You can't keep this up all by yourself."

"No, you don't need to do that. I have a friend who of-fered. I should call..." Maggie did not want to say *him*.

Dr. Lyman stepped out the door and into the March sunshine and slush. "Then what are you waiting for? If you don't have something arranged by tomorrow, I'll do it for you."

Maggie closed the door behind him and leaned against it for a moment, tears in her eyes. "Oh, stop it," she said out loud. "No more of this." But she knew she was *in a state*, as her mother called it, where even the smallest thing would elicit either crankiness or weeping. She'd been moving around the house all day like a tired old woman with jumbled thoughts; Dr. Lyman was right, she did need help.

The telephone rang. She looked at the clock as she went to answer it. Three forty-five. She smiled. The chil-dren called her every day after school.

She answered as brightly as she could. "Hello. Did you have a good day today?"

"Why, yes, thank you, and now it's even better."

Maggie almost dropped the earpiece. "Jacob?" She heard him laugh and imagined him throwing his head back like he did.

"You were expecting my call?"

"The children call every day after school." She felt her face get hot. "But I'm glad it's you."

"How are you?"

"Mother's getting better."

"That's good news, but how are you?"

"I hope you can forgive me for being so out of sorts... and I'm sorry I haven't written to you yet."

"How *are* you?"

She took a deep breath. "Jacob, I hate to ask, but I need help. I'm so tired."

"I didn't think you'd want to ask for anything, that's why I called. Tell me what you need."

"Sleep."

"I'll send the sandman right over."

Maggie smiled. "Tell him to wait until Mother's asleep."

"I'll call around and see if I can arrange a private nurse for the night."

"Who will you call?"

"Don't worry, I'll figure it out; it's the least I can do."

"No, it's not; you're very kind."

"Margaret?" He paused. "I have a lot to learn, I know, but can we start over? Can you forgive me?"

"Yes..." She whispered then cleared her throat. "We should talk, you're right. When do you think you'll come back?"

"Soon. Easter?"

"But that's a week and a half away."

"Sooner?" Jacob sounded surprised.

"I'll try not to be such a shrew."

"You were worn out and I pushed you too hard. I'll come as soon as I can. I'll let you know when."

"I'd like that. Good-bye, Jacob, and thank you."

As she hung up, Maggie closed her eyes and leaned against the wall, remembering their last encounter. He'd been insufferable, barging in at the worst possible time with only one thing on his mind. Bernie was right, Jacob Denver knew what he wanted and insisted on getting it.

Still, Maggie sensed something about him, something like the skin of a person's inner arm, tender and prone to pain, something in need of succor and soothing. Whatever it was, she yearned to touch it. Wise or foolish, her heart was drawn to him.

When Maggie opened the door a few hours later, Dr. Lyman stood on the doorstep with a large woman at his side. Her brown coat hung unbuttoned, revealing a white and blue nurse's uniform underneath.

"Margaret, this is Ethel Iverson, she's here to take care of your mother tonight. Your friend, Jacob Denver, has arranged to have someone come every night, as long as you need it."

"How did he know to call you?"

"I suppose he called his brother first. I told him I thought you could use help for more than one night. I'll wait while you show Mrs. Iverson around, then I'll take you home."

"Thank you, Dr. Lyman, but you don't need to stay. I think Will would give me a ride when he brings the children home."

"No children tonight. You need rest; no helping with homework or getting up before daylight to make their breakfast. If they come home you'll keep working. Maybe tomorrow."

"But—"

"Doctor's orders, dear." Mrs. Iverson had already taken off her coat. She patted her hair and smoothed her skirt. Her wide bosom looked like it wanted to escape from the white apron over her uniform. "I'd like to meet my patient."

Isabelle complained about Maggie abandoning her to a stranger until Mrs. Iverson asked if she was, by any chance, related to Michael O'Keefe the constable, because she'd known him years ago when he walked the beat near her home, and he was *such* a kind man. They had many friends and acquaintances in common and were so busy chatting that Isabelle hardly noticed Maggie's departure.

Maggie sighed and leaned her head back in Dr. Lyman's car. It would be good to be home, even if it was only for the night.

Before the last class began on Wednesday, Karl went looking through his school bag for an extra pencil to lend Brian Culligan when the bag slipped out of his hand and fell, dumping its contents all over the floor. His drawing pad, open to the picture of Father Cunningham and the snake, landed on top of everything. Sister Anne stood only one row over, chatting and laughing with Ella. Karl hurried to get it back into his bag, but Sister had already seen it. He felt his stomach rise to his throat.

"Karl, what is that?"

"Nothing, Sister, just some drawings I made."

"May I please see them?"

"Sister, they're nothing."

"Now." She held her hand out to him.

Of all the people in the world, he didn't want Sister Anne mad at him. He handed her the drawing pad without looking up. He had to swallow twice to keep his lunch down.

Her eyes grew big as she flipped through the rest of Karl's drawings. "You and I need to talk about this, Mr. Stern. After school." She tucked Karl's sketch pad under her arm.

Karl stood, knees shaking. "Sister? Please, I have to help my sisters get to Mr. and Mrs. Denver's house. We're staying with them because our grandmother is sick and our mother is taking care of her."

"Yes, I heard about that." Sister Anne turned around. She sounded angry, but looked worried. "Take them and come right back. It will give me time to look at all your artwork."

"Yes, Sister." He wished the floor would open and swallow him into the furnace below.

Brian started to laugh. "Oh-oh, teacher's pet's in trouble now."

Karl didn't respond, but pretended to turn his attention to the blackboard as class began. He had trouble concentrating on the topic of the day, the life of the Incas, so he wrote down nearly everything Sister said, word for word, in case she asked him to answer a question. As class ended he noticed he'd drawn a curly snake all around his notes. He flipped his paper over and took a deep breath.

After walking the girls to Will and Bernie's, Karl returned and found Sister Anne sitting at the table in the front of her room studying pages from his sketch pad. She rested her forehead on her left hand.

"Sister?"

She looked up at him. "Come in and close the door, Karl. Have a seat. I need a few more minutes, please."

Karl sat still until he couldn't take it any longer. "Sister, please let me explain." He shifted in his chair.

"In a moment." Sister Anne couldn't take her eyes off the drawing of Father Cunningham and the snake.

Sister Mary Anthony knocked once before opening the door. Sister Anne slowly closed the cover of the drawing pad. Karl didn't turn to face her. "You're late for our meeting, Sister, everyone's waiting."

"Go on without me, I'm not coming."

"What have you done now, Karl?"

Without turning around, Karl slunk down in his chair, remembering the strength in Sister Mary Anthony's hands.

Sister Anne stood. "Karl isn't here for discipline."

"Then take care of it tomorrow and come to the meeting."

"I'm sorry, Sister, but this can't wait." Sister Anne sat down again.

Karl heard Sister Mary Anthony click her tongue. "We'll talk about this later!" She closed the door with a bang and Karl could hear the soles of her shoes slapping the wood floor as she walked away.

Sister Anne sighed and muttered, "I'm sure we will."

Karl sat up straight again. "Sister, I'd hate for you to miss your meeting because of me."

"At this moment, you are more important than any teachers' meeting."

More important? "But you said I wasn't in trouble."

"I said you weren't here for discipline. I think you are in trouble. These are terribly frightening drawings."

"I can explain all of them, Sister, if you'll let me."

Sister Anne got up and moved to the chair next to Karl's, turning the drawing pad so they could look at it together. Karl could smell the starch from her wimple. "All right, I'm ready to listen." She turned to the cobra he'd copied from Volume C of his encyclopedia. "Why snakes?"

Karl sighed. "Because I saw one in church."

"The one carved into the floor?"

"Well, not exactly." He grabbed hold of his thighs to prevent himself from running away. He knew she had her eyes locked on him even though he stared at his drawing. "At Mass... on Christmas Eve."

"Didn't you become ill during Mass?"

"No, I passed out." He glanced at her for a second and looked away. "Well, I didn't feel well because my uncle beat me pretty good the day before. My mother, too."

"Melvin Straus?"

"Yes, Sister."

She sighed. "Tell me about the snake."

Karl told her how he saw the snake come up out of the floor and wrap itself around Father Cunningham, how it got on the altar and looked at him with its fiery red eyes. He told her how the snake shattered into a million pieces then blew away.

"That's when I fell over and fainted."

Sister Anne reached in her pocket for a handkerchief. "Oh, my."

"Umm, Sister, I need some water. May I get a drink, please?"

Sister Anne put her warm hand on his arm. "You stay

right here."

The gesture was so like her, a gift of comfort and understanding. Karl released his thighs and let himself sink into his chair.

She went to her closet and took a clean glass from the shelf, then filled it from the drinking fountain in the hall and brought it back to him.

"Thanks." Karl knew his voice sounded weepy, like a girl's. He took a drink and cleared his throat. "I think I'm going insane like my grandfather did. Do you know if he saw things that weren't there?"

"I have no idea what he saw. But you are not going insane. I believe you had a vision."

"Sister?"

"A message from the Lord."

"What does it mean?"

"The answer has to come from inside you. You have to figure it out."

"All I know is I've never been so afraid, even when they brought my father home before he died. The room spun around and everything went dark. It got into me, Sister; it... it took me."

"No, Karl, it most certainly did not!" She slapped the table for emphasis.

Sister Anne's sharp voice wound its way into Karl's cave, chasing everything else out. Talking about that awful night brought everything back and now her anger made it feel worse than ever: all the weeks of pretending he hadn't really seen anything in church, all the weeks of having snakes leak out of his pencil, all the bad dreams, all the hours of missing his father, all the times he begged a deaf God to send a foot down to crush Melvin Straus. In a rush they all came back, swirling around him like a great

C. A. PETERSON

storm out on the lake with him going under. His head began to pound like it did on Christmas Eve.

"Nobody else knows about this, Sister." He whispered, afraid that anything louder would make his head explode into a billion tiny bits, like the snake. "Please don't tell my mother, or anyone. Please don't make me show her my drawings."

She put a warm hand on his shoulder. "That would be too much for her, now, wouldn't it? I won't say anything unless you give me permission."

Somehow, Sister Anne always made Karl feel like he was more than a stupid kid. "I appreciate that, thank you." Thank God, she wasn't still mad at him.

They sat together for another hour, looking at the rest of Karl's drawings. He told her everything: about Jimmy and Elmer's letter of apology and the valentine they sent, about all the things Uncle Melvin did, about his mother's new friend and how much he still missed his father. When they finished, Sister Anne went to her desk and began to page through her Bible. Exhausted, Karl put his head on the table and drifted off.

He opened his eyes and sat up when he felt Sister Anne's hand on his back.

She smiled at him. "Did you have a nice nap?"

"I'm sorry, Sister."

"Don't be, I liked having you here, even if you were asleep."

They both chuckled, remembering how she'd fallen asleep while Karl washed the floors under the pews.

Sister Anne became serious. "Karl, I have an assignment for you." She handed him a slip of paper. "I want you to study these verses and draw something that represents what you think the Lord is telling you. Or you may write about it, if you wish."

Karl looked at the paper. There were four passages written out, the first one being the verse from Genesis that Sister quoted while they were scrubbing the floor. Karl had already memorized it, but didn't think it would help him any. "But, Sister, I'm afraid I'll never figure it out."

"You will. I have faith in you, Karl. The evil one cannot hold you; you are a child of the light. You have to believe that with all your heart."

"But, what if I can't?"

"Good Friday is next week. The worst, most evil thing that could ever happen took place when the Lord was crucified. Nothing that bad can ever happen again, so don't be afraid. And then Sunday—well, Sunday after next is Easter, Resurrection Day." She smiled.

"Sister, I have too much homework to do this tonight."

"I don't expect you to finish this by tomorrow. Read the passages and think about them; read them every night before you go to bed, especially during the holy days. Your assignment is due when you come back from Easter break."

"I'm still afraid I won't be able to figure it out."

Sister Anne bent over and looked directly into his eyes. "You will. You *have* to." She locked her eyes onto his the same way the snake's had.

Karl held his breath, wishing she'd look away.

She looked up at the wall clock. "Goodness, it's nearly supper time. You'd better be on your way. I hope I didn't get you in too much hot water, Karl."

"Thanks, but you don't need to worry. Bernie—I mean Mrs. Denver—has been taking care of us, and she's swell."

Sister Anne smiled. "We've been praying for your grandmother."

Karl slipped the drawing pad in his school bag, and put on his coat and hat. "Thank you, Sister." He stopped before going out the door, smiling slightly. "I hope you don't get in hot water with Sister Mary Anthony."

Sister Anne smiled and laughed, clasping her hands together over her heart. "Oh, Karl, you're worth it."

After a hot bath, Maggie crawled into bed and fell asleep before she could revel in the cool sheets, her own nightgown, her own pillow, her own house. Eddie was making a racket building a bookshelf for Karl's room, and irritated, she was about to ask him if he could please wait until morning for all that pounding. When she sat up, though, she realized she'd been dreaming. The clock read 9:15 and someone was at the door. She should have been at her mother's hours ago!

When she jumped out of bed, the cold bedroom air came at her like a blizzard. Shivering, she tied her housecoat around her waist and started down to answer the door. The hallway spun around her as she started down the stairs, but the pounding prodded her on. She tried to call out, but her breath caught and she started to cough. She stumbled at the bottom step and staggered to the front door. *What is wrong with me?*

Dr. Lyman stood on the porch in his winter coat and gray fedora, frowning.

Maggie opened the door for him. "I'm sorry, I overslept, I'll get dressed and be right back," she said hoarsely, turning too fast. The room started to go in circles again.

"Hold on there, Margaret. Sit down."

Coughing wildly, she bumped into the ottoman. "I have to get to Mother's," she croaked.

"Not until I have a look at you. Sit down." He leaned over her and felt her forehead. "Wait right here, my bag is in the car."

When he opened the front door, the March sunshine came splattering across the gray rug, brightening the faded maroon flowers, bringing with it a March chill. Maggie's teeth were chattering when the doctor returned a few seconds later. "If I'm sick, who's going to take care of Mother?"

"Here, under your tongue." He thrust a thermometer in her mouth.

She took it out. "What about Mother?"

"Keep it under your tongue." He took out a stethoscope and listened to her breathing, and took her pulse, keeping an eye on his watch. "Your heart's going a mile a minute."

She took the thermometer out again. "Because your pounding on the door startled me out of a sound sleep."

"Give me that."

"I have to get dressed."

"No, you don't." Dr. Lyman read the thermometer. "It's over a hundred and two degrees." He squatted down and felt her neck and looked into her eyes. "When you didn't show up this morning, Mrs. Iverson called me. Your mother's asking for you, but you're too sick to go back."

"Then who's going to take care of her?"

"Not you. Mrs. Iverson said she'd stay until noon. How's your head, any headache?"

She pressed her fingers to her temples. "Not until you asked." Resigned, she leaned back in the chair, sighing. Her head pounded fiercely whenever she coughed. Her neck still ached and so did her back. Her arms and legs felt like logs.

Dr. Lyman brought her a glass of water and two aspirin then went to the telephone. Maggie drifted in and out of sleep while he talked.

"Margaret?" He shook her shoulder a little.

Maggie opened her eyes. She tried to get up, but he gently pushed her back into the chair.

"I talked to Melvin Straus and convinced him to allow Kathleen to go over to your mother's."

"How is Kathleen?" Maggie sat straight up. "Will you go see her and tell me if she's okay? Please? He's mean, he hits her."

"You're always worried about someone else, aren't you? Yes, I'll see if I can talk to her in private."

"Thank you."

"You shouldn't be alone, either, so Mrs. Lyman is coming for the day and I'll see what else we can arrange for you."

"I can take care of myself; you don't need to trouble her. It's only a chest cold."

The doctor frowned. "It's pneumonia."

A cough way deep in Maggie's chest begged to come out, but she stifled it. "But I don't have anything in writing about my children yet." She started to cry. "I want you to know… they are *not* to go to live with Melvin Straus. Ever."

Dr. Lyman rubbed her back as she coughed. "I don't think you're in much danger of dying, but I'll ask Will to help you write something up, all the same."

"What about Karl?" Maggie buried her face in her hands. "He's going to be so upset after what he heard you say."

"Margaret!" He spoke so sharply that Maggie looked up, holding her breath. "Listen to me. Until you are well, you are not to worry about anyone but yourself. You can't do anything anyway, so let us take care of things. Your kids will be fine with Will and Bernie, I'll talk to them myself. This is only a little bump in the road, life is full of them."

"My daddy used to say that. You remind me of him."

Dr. Lyman smiled. "I'll take that as a compliment. He was a fine man." He held out his hand and helped her to her feet. "Let's get you back to bed before I go for Mrs. Lyman."

"Chacob, your supper is on the table." Hilde, Jacob's housekeeper called from the foot of the stairs.

"Have you been up here yet?" Jacob inspected the window the workers enlarged that day.

"No, it's too cold."

"Well, put on a sweater and come up, I want to show you what I'm doing."

"Oh, for heaven sakes, just a minute."

Jacob heard her footsteps before he saw her. As she stood in the shadows at the end of the hall he caught a glimpse of the one he'd built the house for in the first place, the one who'd never come to live here. She had the same nearly black hair—Hilde's now peppered with gray—the same blue eyes, the same nose with the slightest hook, the same ready-for-anything stance, the same feisty nature. But Jacob had stopped crying over his spilt milk a long time ago. Every once in a while, though, Hilde would remind him of what he'd lost by the way she tilted her head or the way she smiled or stood waiting for an answer. Then he would feel a little stab of something he didn't want to name. Usually, he ignored it.

"What do you want me to see? Wood and sawdust? I have already plenty of dust downstairs from all this cutting and hammering."

"Come on, I want to show you around." Jacob felt like a little boy with a secret. He took her by the elbow and walked her around the debris on the floor. He showed her the bedrooms and the big new bathtub that had to be hoisted up on the outside of the house and brought in through the enlarged window.

"What about closets? You can do better than pegs on the wall, Chacob. And where is the linen closet? Where are we going to put towels and sheets?"

"I don't think about things like that, that's why I need you." He squeezed her elbow before she pulled away.

"And what about a chute for the laundry?"

"What's that?"

"A tunnel to the basement between the walls for dirty clothes. You put a door in the wall, or a trap door in the floor, then you throw in your dirty socks and *whoosh*, they go to the basement. And then I don't have to carry all that down to wash."

"Hilde, you're amazing." He grinned at her.

"Better you should make it a door in the wall. A trap door little kinder could fall through."

Embarrassed, Jacob bent over to pick up a bent nail. He squatted down and brushed some sawdust away, searching for another one.

"Aha—it's a woman, isn't it? You found yourself a woman!" She clasped her hands over her heart, leaned her head back a little and looked down at him with her twinkling eyes and her pinched little smile. "I knew it, Chacob,

I knew it!" She laughed, the pitch of her voice raising almost an octave. "I know you get letters from her all the time. Come wash up your hans for supper and you tell me all about her."

"Now, Hilde—"

The telephone rang before she'd reached the bottom of the stairs. "I get it for you."

Jacob heard her answer. "Chacob Denfer residence." She flipped the *r* on the word *residence*. He smiled; he'd always liked the sound of it.

"It's your brother." Hilde stood at the foot of the steps waiting for him. "Make it quick, supper's ready."

Mildly concerned, Jacob thumped down the stairs. He and Will had just talked yesterday. "Hello, William."

"Jacob, I don't want you going off all half-cocked, but you should know Maggie's got pneumonia."

"What?"

"She woke up sick this morning. In her own house, in her own bed, thanks to the nurse you got for her mother."

"Why didn't you call me?"

"What do you think I'm doing?"

"I'll be there as soon as I can." Jacob disconnected the call, his heart pounding away in his chest. He stared at the wall. No. *No!* He wasn't going to let it happen again, not with him so far away. He started for his bedroom to pack a bag, but he'd barely turned around before the telephone rang again. He grabbed it and snapped, "Denver."

"Now Jacob, I told you not to get all worked up over this."

"You knew I would."

"Yeah, I did, but listen to me. We've got everything under control. One of the sisters from the hospital is with her tonight, Doc Lyman has someone set up for tomorrow, and we'll see what she needs after that. She's not as sick as her mother was. The kids are still with us; the girls are fine and Karl will be, too, once we get him calmed down."

"I'm still coming. Maybe I can help."

"You've got a business to run."

Jacob raised his voice. "For once I don't care about that." He ran his trembling fingers through his hair.

"It's too late to start out tonight. Sleep on it, why don'cha?"

He sighed. "Tell her I'll be there tomorrow."

"I will." Will's voice softened. "Don't worry, she'll be fine, Jacob."

"I hope you're right." He hung up. Even though he took a deep breath, his knees started to shake.

Hilde came to the door of his library. "Wash up your hans, now, and come sit down, before your supper gets cold." She started back to the kitchen.

A flood of memories threatened to drown Jacob. Was history about to repeat itself? He followed her, feeling like a helpless child. "*Mutter?*" He didn't know why he'd said it, and in German, knowing how it would affect her.

Hilde stopped, one foot in the kitchen, still as death. She did not turn back to face him. "*Was sagten Sie?*" She whipped around. "What did you say?"

"She's got pneumonia."

"Your woman?"

He nodded. "Margaret."

"Oh, Gott im himmel." Hilde opened her arms to him slightly, a rare gesture from the only person who knew the immensity of the sorrow he'd worked so hard forget.

They clung to one another as they hadn't years ago,

Jacob depending on Hilde's common sense to tell him it wouldn't, no, *couldn't* happen again. She pulled away, brushing away tears she hadn't let him see before.

She pulled an embroidered hankie from her pocket and wiped her nose. "Your woman, is her heart sick like Lana's?"

"I don't know—I don't think so."

"Then she be okay."

Karl shifted his overloaded school bag from one hand to the other as he waited for Lizzie and Anna outside Holy Angels School. He could have been halfway home by now, but he knew the girls shouldn't walk to Will and Bernie's without him. They'd have to cross too many busy streets by themselves.

First Anna appeared. Her curly hair blew all over the place in the wind. Apparently, Bernie didn't know how to get it into a proper braid like his mother did. Lizzie finally came out the door, scowling.

"What's wrong with you?" he asked, as they started walking.

"Helen and Audrey said we're orphans because our father is dead and we aren't living with our mother. They said we're *pitiful* and that the school should take up a collection for us."

"Aw, why do you listen to them?"

"Because they're popular and good students and said they're gonna be friends with me because they feel sorry for us."

"Sounds like a couple goody-two-shoes to me."

"So are we orphans, Karl?" Anna tried to take his hand.

Karl jerked his hand away and looked around to see if anyone had seen it. "Not by school, Anna, only when we cross the big streets."

"You didn't answer my question."

"No, we're not orphans. *Orphan* means both your parents are dead, and Mama isn't dead." He shuddered inside as he said it.

"I wonder how she is," said Lizzie. "Remember when Daddy died? When we went to school he was sleeping, and when we came home, he was *dead*."

"That was different."

"No, it wasn't." Lizzie's lip trembled.

Anna reached for Karl's hand and this time he held on to it. He might as well tell them about his plan. "Okay, listen. I'm gonna get you two across the busy streets, then I'm going home to see Mama."

Anna jerked his hand. "But, Karl, Dr. Lyman said we're supposed to stay with Will and Bernie."

"Yeah, I know, but if I go home, I can find out how she really is and then I can call and tell you the truth."

"You're gonna get it, you know." Lizzie squinted because of the sun when she looked at him.

"From who?"

"From Will."

"I'm not afraid of him. Anyway, so what if I do? At least we'll know how she is." Karl had no intention of leaving his mother again; he knew he could help out. He already had his speech prepared for when they tried to get him to leave.

Anna needed a hug before she would let go of Karl's hand, and Lizzie wanted to know what to tell Bernie when she asked where he was.

"Tell her the truth." He watched as they set out the

last two blocks without him before turning for home. It would be good to sleep in his own bed again.

Despite being nervous about how he'd find his mother, Karl felt lighthearted as opened the back door of 617 Blight. He'd be the hero, taking care of everything she couldn't do until she got well. Smiling, he pushed the door open, but stopped short when he found Mr. Denver coming up from the basement, wiping coal dust off his hands.

Chapter 24

More Winter

"That's my job," snapped Karl.

"Karl!" Although worry lines ran across his wide forehead, Mr. Denver smiled. His big hand reached out and squeezed Karl's shoulder.

"I can take care of the furnace from now on, so you don't have to bother anymore."

"Well, the house felt cool and you weren't here, so I got it going again. Here, come in and close the door." Mr. Denver backed off the landing and stood on the first step down. "I sure am glad to see you. I didn't think—"

"I still live here, you know." Karl closed the door and hung up his jacket. Mr. Denver followed him up to the kitchen.

"Do you drink coffee? I just made a pot."

"No, I don't."

"Well, have a seat anyway. We can talk." Mr. Denver sat down. He slouched over, resting his forearms on the table.

It was bad enough that he'd come at all, but now he acted like he belonged here. Karl scowled. "I'm going up to see my mother. That's why I came home."

"Good luck. Sister Mary Somebody is guarding her pretty good. She said I could go up in a few minutes, and that was over an hour ago. I've been here all afternoon, but I still haven't seen her." He knocked on the table three times with the knuckles of both hands.

A short, squat little nun with thick eyeglasses came into the kitchen. "It's Sister Mary Regina, sir." Her frighteningly huge blue eyes peered through the glasses at Karl. "And who are you?"

"Karl. I live here and I want to see my mother."

Sister Mary Regina started opening drawers until she found the silverware. She pulled out a serving spoon. "Not now. Her fever is too high again, so I'll be busy with her for awhile. Then you can see her."

"What do you need that spoon for?" asked Karl.

Sister Mary Regina looked at Karl like he didn't know anything. "To give her medicine."

"That's an awfully big spoon, isn't it?"

"She's awfully sick. Too sick for visitors."

"I'm not leaving." Mr. Denver stood up and crossed his arms. He looked annoyed.

"Me, neither." Karl crossed his arms, too. "I live here."

"I don't have time for you two." The nun walked off in a huff.

Maggie wondered how much longer she'd have to put up with Sister Mary Regina. She'd been in and out of her room all day, waking her every hour, forcing her to drink water or cool tea so she'd have to make trip after wobbling trip to the bathroom. When Maggie complained of a pounding headache, Sister Mary Regina refused to give her the aspirin Dr. Lyman ordered, saying it was part of the earthly suffering she had to endure, being a sinner and all. "It's good for your soul," she said.

Despite Maggie's best efforts to keep her eyes open, she was floating across town with her father when Sister Mary Regina nudged her awake. She stood at the edge of the bed with a basin of water in her hands, towels draped over her arm. Again.

Maggie groaned. "No, please, not again. That's torture."

"Don't act like such a child. Now take off your nightgown." Sister Mary Regina swung the washcloth like a paintbrush, splattering Maggie's fevered body with icy water. "There are two people here to see you. I told them you were too sick for company, but neither one of them will leave."

"Who?" Her teeth began to chatter.

"A Mr. Denver."

"W-will Denver?"

"No, he said his name was *Jacob*. And your son is here. I thought he was staying with friends, but from the looks of things, he's not going back. Do you want to see them?"

Maggie nodded. "P-please stop, I feel much cooler now."

"If you want to see your visitors, you'll have to let me wash your back, too."

Maggie gave up and rolled onto her side. When Sister Mary Regina finished, she asked her for a towel so she could dry off, but the nun left to empty the basin. "Air dry!" she commanded from the bathroom.

Weak and shivering, Maggie sat on the edge of the bed, dried off with the towels that had been underneath her, and pulled her nightgown back over her head. Sister came back with a bottle of castor oil and a big spoon.

"Please, Sister, will you help me brush my hair and braid it again?" Maggie tried to ignore the bottle.

"After you take a good dose of castor oil. We don't want you getting all bound up, now, do we?"

"I can't swallow castor oil; it makes me sick. It's horrid."

"Nonsense. It's good for you. Do you want to see your company?"

"Yes, but—"

She filled the spoon. "Then open up."

When Maggie tried to say *no* Sister forced the spoon into her mouth. It banged against her teeth and cut into the corners of her lips. Quickly, Sister tilted it up. Half pooled in the back of Maggie's mouth while the rest of it went dripping down her face and onto her neck. She choked and gagged before it went down.

The nun poured another spoonful. "That wasn't enough to oil a squeaky gate. Again."

Maggie pursed her lips and shook her head. She felt like a child.

Sister raised her voice. "Open up, or I won't allow that man come up here. It isn't proper anyway."

Maggie sighed, squeezed her eyes shut, opened her mouth and swallowed the slimy liquid, shuddering. She willed herself not to gag and swallowed again, wiping her face and neck with the towel. "Please help me with my hair, now." Her voice sounded thick and oily. She wanted to spit.

Karl sat in the kitchen with Mr. Denver, waiting. He decided to try a cup of coffee, which wasn't too bad once he mixed in two spoonfuls of sugar. Mr. Denver said it would be even better with milk or cream, but there wasn't any in the icebox. They didn't have any cookies, either.

Mr. Denver looked at his watch every five minutes and asked him so many dumb questions Karl thought he must have made up a list beforehand and memorized it. "You're in eighth grade, is it?" "Do you have a girlfriend?" "When's your birthday?" "What's your favorite food your mother makes?"

Finally, Sister Mary Regina came back into the kitchen and rescued Karl from all this senseless talk. "You may both go up now, but make it short. My patient needs her rest."

Mr. Denver looked like he couldn't get upstairs fast enough, but Sister Mary Regina quickly stepped in front of him, blocking his way. "And, *Mr. Jacob Denver*, the bedroom door stays open, do you understand? I shouldn't allow this." She glared and shook her finger at him. "Don't you go trying anything with her."

"No, Ma'am."

"It's no, *Sister*."

"Yes, Ma'a—yes, Sister."

Karl looked up at the ceiling. This guy doesn't even know the proper way to talk to a nun. He led the way upstairs and dumped his school bag on his desk while Mr. Denver stopped outside Maggie's door.

"Margaret," he whispered, and stepped in the room. Karl took his place at the door.

His mother was as white as the sheets around her. She reminded Karl of the way his father looked the morning he died. He took a deep breath and shoved the urge to scream deep inside his cave. *Please God, not her, too!*

She opened her eyes and slowly turned her head to Mr. Denver. She smiled. She didn't even notice Karl. He crossed his arms again, scowling, pouting. If she was going to die, he should be in there, not this... this *stranger*.

"Jacob, you didn't have to come all this way."

"Oh, yes, I did. I couldn't be anywhere else."

Karl rolled his eyes.

Mr. Denver pulled a chair next to the bed, sat down and reached for her hand, but she pulled it away.

"You have to be careful, Jacob, I don't want you getting sick, too."

"Don't worry. I have the constitution of an ox." He dared to lean over and kiss her forehead.

Karl thought about calling Sister Mary Regina. *Hey, Sister, he's trying something!*

"I came to help take care of you, and I'm not going home until I'm sure you're well again."

Suddenly, Karl saw his mother inhale sharply, her eyes opening wide. "Get me the basin—in the bathroom—and a towel. Hurry!"

She's gonna puke. Karl moved out of the doorway. So he wants to take care of her, does he?

Mr. Denver jumped up and found the basin then grabbed a hand towel. The instant he put it on her lap, she sat up, gagging and retching, holding both sides of her head. Karl thought Mr. Denver looked like he was about to puke, too. He felt his own stomach turn, but only a little.

His mother groaned. "I hate—that—stuff."

"What stuff?"

"Castor oil. She made me take castor oil." She retched again, but there was nothing left in her. Exhausted, she leaned back against the pillows, handing the basin back to Mr. Denver. Her eyes fell closed and she covered them with her hand. "Oh, my poor head. Please, get that out of here."

"Ah, sure." Mr. Denver walked out of the room holding the basin at arm's length.

The bathroom door shut and the lock turned. Mr. Denver ran a lot of water, but even so, Karl could hear what he was doing. *Some help he's gonna be.*

Karl sat down in the chair. "Hi, Mama."

She moved her hand and opened her eyes. She smiled when she saw him, then frowned. "Why aren't you at Will's?"

"I came to see you, to see how you *really* are. And to help out. Anyway," he lied, "I've got a lot of homework this weekend, and Billy and Ned make too much noise. I need some peace and quiet."

"We'll see what Dr. Lyman says. But it's good to see you, anyway."

Karl leaned over and kissed his mother's fevered forehead, just like Mr. Denver did. "How do you feel?"

"I've never had such a terrible headache and this coughing only makes it worse."

"Are you going to d— Are you going to be all right, Mama?"

She reached for his hand. "It'll take a little time, but I'll get over this. Don't worry, baby."

Karl couldn't remember the last time she'd called him *baby*. He'd always hated it, but today it comforted him.

The bathroom door opened and Mr. Denver stumbled back into the room. The normally robust color of his face must have gone down the toilet. "I'm going out for some air. I'll be back in a little while." He turned and went down the stairs without waiting for anyone to answer.

Karl called after him. "Don't worry, Mr. Denver. I'll stay with my mother."

But Mr. Denver wasn't gone half a minute before

Sister Mary Regina returned. "It's time for you to leave, too, young man. Your mother needs her rest."

Karl stood up. "Yeah, I'd better call my sisters."

"Tell them I miss them. And I love them." Maggie closed her eyes. "And tell them I'm going to be fine. And thank Bernie for me."

"I will." He kissed his mother's warm forehead again. *The score is two to one,* he thought.

Still a little shaky, Jacob sat on the front porch and sucked the cool air into his lungs. He hadn't considered that taking care of a sick person might mean doing nasty, disagreeable things, or that it would wrench his stomach quite so badly. He wanted to escape; to go somewhere else, maybe not all the way home, but somewhere away from the sounds and smells of sickness. He could get a room downtown and come back in a few days when she felt better.

Then the image of a train barreled into his memory and wouldn't leave the station without his acknowledgment. He shivered, remembering: it was winter, windy and cold, so cold that spit froze into pellets almost before hitting the ground. A leftover Christmas wreath, encased in ice, banging against the door of the station; the crazy worry of waiting; Hilde stepping from the passenger car all alone, her face frozen in disbelief, bad news coming from her mouth in short bursts of German. His heart wailing as he stood silent and motionless, watching bundled figures unloading freight cars, the icy wind stinging his eyes until they watered. The creaking sound of pine being pried loose, the feel of frozen flesh, the nightmare of a surprise gone bad. Stomach lurching, running and gaining no ground, slipping on ice, taking cover behind an outhouse, turning inside out, the sight of his own guts freezing on the ground.

"Lana, no. No," he whispered. Chilled from the memory, he hugged his arms across his chest, warming his hands underneath them. He'd been able to keep this at bay for years. Why did it decide to jump up and bite him today?

Jacob shook his head to get rid of the images. His heart had frozen that day, and now, after all this time, it was beginning to come to life again. The thawing hurt, but he couldn't turn back. As long as Margaret needed him, he'd stay and take whatever came with it. This is where he wanted to be, where he needed to be.

He stood up and blew on his hands to warm them. The temperature had fallen again. Thick, gray clouds hung low overhead and he thought he saw a few snowflakes drift through the air. He sighed. "Just what I need, more winter." He opened the door and went in. He'd try to cook some supper. Even if he didn't feel much like eating, the boy was bound to be hungry.

Chapter 25

Ghosts

Will showed up less than ten minutes later, loaded down with a box filled with food from Bernie. Jacob let him in, but Will didn't even say hello before he let Karl have it.

"What in God's name has gotten into you? You've got no business bein' here; didn't you hear what Doc Lyman said last night? You wanna get sick, too?" Will handed the box to his brother and took Karl by the arm. "I should drag you back! What do you have to say for yourself, boy?"

Jacob stood clear, remembering his own encounter with an angry Will.

"Sorry Will. I don't mean to be disobedient but I'm staying with my mother no matter what." He didn't wince or whine or try to pull away.

Jacob was impressed. Karl acted more like a man than a boy.

"You can make me go home with you," he continued, "but you'll have to tie me up, 'cause I'll come back here first chance I get."

Will leaned close to Karl's face. "Well, I got lotsa rope!"

He let him go.

Karl took a couple steps backward. "Come on, Will, have a heart. I was here when my Daddy... An' what if she... I have to be here, that's all there is to it."

Karl didn't sound like a rational adult anymore. He looked like he might cry. Poor kid, he'd been through enough. Listen," said Jacob, "I don't know if it makes any difference, but I'd like Karl to stay. I could use the company."

"Oh, yeah?" Will turned on him. "Well, you shouldn't be here either!"

"I'm not leaving until I know Margaret's going to be all right."

"You're fools, both of you. We'll see what Doc Lyman has to say about this." Will turned to leave, then came back to Karl. He reached into his pocket, producing some sheets of paper folded in half. "Give these to your mother, they're from the kids. What Doc Lyman says, goes, d'you hear me? If he says you can stay, you stay, if not—"

Karl interrupted. "I'm staying with my mother, Will."

Will squinted at him. "You're just like your father, you know that? Stubborn as a wet knot." He stormed out the door.

Jacob called after him. "Tell Bernie thanks for the food."

Will growled over his shoulder as he stomped down the steps. "The soup is for Maggie, so you two stay out of it." He got in his truck and drove away.

Jacob closed the door and looked at Karl. Karl shrugged. Jacob took it as a sign they were allies.

When Dr. Lyman came with a new nurse, Karl scowled

even before he got up to answer the door. Jacob saw his determination and hoped Dr. Lyman wouldn't be too hard on him. Once the doctor had been upstairs to see Margaret, he let loose a tirade on Sister Mary Anthony for not following his orders, but seemed only mildly irritated with Karl. He told the boy he could stay only if Jacob agreed to keep him from spending too much time in his mother's room. "He's in charge, Karl; whatever he says goes." Jacob sat up straight. He was used to being the boss, but being responsible for Margaret's son—well, that gave him goose bumps.

Thankful that Dr. Lyman brought a more sympathetic nurse, Jacob crept into Margaret's bedroom, not wanting to wake her. No longer did he need to know exactly how she felt about him; sitting next to her sickbed was enough. A beam of light from the hallway stretched into the dark room, crossed the foot of the bed and cast itself from there to her face. Her eyes were closed, her brow smooth. Like flecks of pale copper, little wisps of hair surrounded her head, catching the light, almost sparkling. He followed the curve of her face with his eyes; from her forehead to her perfect nose, over her lips, down her chin to her perfect neck. He stored it all in his memory so he'd be able to take it out and gaze on it again and again when he was away from her.

He wished he never had to be away from her.

As he shifted in his chair, Margaret opened her eyes. When she reached for his hand, the same electricity he felt before raced from her fingers straight to his heart.

He spoke softly. "Ohh, I'm sorry."

She smiled and touched the back of his hand to her warm cheek.

"I didn't want to wake you. You looked so peaceful."

"I'm glad you came back."

"I'm sorry, Margaret. I needed some air."

"Please don't call me that anymore."

"What?"

"*Margaret.*" She reached for her water glass. Jacob gave it to her; she drank then took his hand again. "I want you to call me *Maggie. Margaret* is for my mother and for Father Cunningham and people who aren't close to me. But you, Jacob... I know what happened when you took the basin from me. Do you feel better now?"

He looked at their hands, embarrassed. She's the one who's so sick, and here she's concerned about him. "I'm fine. *Maggie.*" He smiled. He felt like he'd been given a treasure chest filled with gold and precious jewels.

She squeezed his hand and let go, clearing her throat. "Will you please get me a towel?"

Jacob jumped up and hurried to the bathroom. *Not again!* He found a fresh bath towel hanging by the tub. He grabbed it and flew back into the bedroom. Maggie took it from him, buried her face in its folds and began to cough. She coughed so long and so hard that Jacob started out the door to get Mrs. Iverson.

"No, wait," she gasped. "I'm all right. Dr. Lyman said it might keep you and Karl from getting sick if I coughed into a towel."

Jacob sat down again and spread a cool washcloth across her forehead. "Do you always worry about other people?"

"Mmm..." Maggie's eyelids closed. "I'm so tired."

He kissed her forehead and whispered. "Sweet dreams, Maggie."

Karl sat at his desk and sighed. Although he was glad

to be home, nothing felt right with his mother being so sick. He missed her cooking and he didn't like having strangers in charge of everything. Will said not to worry about what would happen to him and his sisters if she died, but he couldn't help it. If she did die, there would always be strangers in charge, unless they had to live with Aunt Kathleen and Melvin. He shuddered, suddenly cold both inside and out.

He pulled his colored pencils from the desk drawer and tapped the brown one against the edge of his desk, wondering how to draw pneumonia. There were fevers, coughing, and very sick people. He remembered his father lying on the cot in the kitchen, burning with fever, trying to cough out all the lake water he took in. Did he have pneumonia, too?

On the upper left corner of the page, Karl began to sketch his father on the cot, rosy cheeks underneath his beard, eyes closed. He made a little balloon above his head, coming from his mouth, like in comic books, and wrote the word *cough* inside. He made little red marks coming from the word. He erased the smooth line around the balloon and replaced it with a zig-zaggy line.

Underneath, he drew his father again, this time all laid out in his Sunday best with a lily in his hand. They hadn't really put a lily in the coffin with him, but it was a nice touch for the drawing. It surprised him that he could draw his father without getting a lump in his throat. He still missed him like anything, that was for sure.

On the right side of the page, next to his father on the cot, Karl drew his mother in bed, propped up on pillows with her eyes only half open. He made a zigzag balloon coming from her mouth, too, with the word *cough* inside it. He drew a second balloon, a smooth one, and wrote,

"Oh, Karl, I can't believe you came! You will help me get well." He didn't have anything to draw underneath her, so he scribbled in that space with every color he had to make sure he wouldn't have to draw her coffin, too.

All along the edges of the page, like a frame, he drew the winding body of a cobra. Its head bent down smiling at his dead father, its tongue encircling his body. Then, with a very light touch, he drew a huge foot on top of everything, its lines and curves crossing but not covering the pictures of his parents. He wished there really *was* someone who could make all this bad stuff go away. Suddenly, Karl felt a catch in his throat. The world had become a dark and dreary place where nothing was right anymore.

Maggie thought of Jacob when she closed her eyes. She remembered the sound of his voice, his deep brown eyes, soft and warm. He'd come all the way from Wakelin to be with her, *all that way*. She smiled, until Eddie's voice came from far away.

"So, marry him."

"Eddie? Where are you?" She felt a warm breeze blow across her cheek.

"You know where I am, Rosie."

"Please, please don't leave me again," she whispered. Her throat ached in its tightness; she squeezed her eyes shut, but tears came anyway. Her heart raced; it wanted to go to him. She almost tried; but, no, there were the children to think about. And now Jacob, too.

"You're gonna marry him."

She couldn't tell if he was about to scold her or laugh.

"But I love *you*, Eddie, I want *you*."

"I'm gone, Rosie." He sounded farther away with every

word. "Marry him."

"No, don't go, please? I need you."

"Goodbye, Maggie."

"*Nooo!*"

She woke up in a fit of coughing. Hot, she was *so* hot. She kicked the blankets off and started to pull her nightgown over her head when she realized her bedroom door was open. She got up to close it, but lost her balance and fell to the floor. Another round of coughing overcame her, leaving her with little strength to get up again.

The night nurse, Mrs. Iverson, appeared out of nowhere, her body blocking nearly all the light from the hallway. Gently, she lifted Maggie and helped her back to bed. Heat seemed to roll over her body in wave after wave, but Mrs. Iverson's hands were cool and soothing as she drew the warmish, wet washcloth over her fevered body. She hummed softly as she worked. "Margaret," she said, "Mr. Denver is such a nice man, you have truly been blessed. Heaven smiled on you the day he came into your life."

Karl went down to the kitchen looking for a glass of milk before bed. Mr. Denver and the nurse sat at the table, talking quietly. They stopped as soon as they saw him.

"I need some—" he opened the ice box. "Oh, that's right. No milk." He found the package with Bernie's oatmeal cookies, took one out, gave the package to Mr. Denver and got a glass of water instead.

"You're up kind of late, Karl." Mr. Denver took a cookie and gave the package to Mrs. Iverson.

Karl looked at the clock. Ten-thirty. "I know. I'm going to say goodnight to my mother and go to bed." He saw them glance at each other and didn't like the looks of it. "What's wrong?"

"You can talk to her in the morning, dear, she's sleeping now."

"Something's wrong." He stopped chewing. "What? What is it?"

"Her fever's gone up again; that often happens at night. She'll be fine."

Mr. Denver rubbed his bloodshot eyes. He looked real tired.

"I have to say good night to her. I won't be able to sleep if I don't."

Mr. Denver stood up. "I'll come with you, then."

"I'm not going to wake her up, don't worry." Karl hurried up the stairs and opened his mother's door. She looked peaceful enough. He slipped into the room; Mr. Denver followed and stood at the foot of the bed.

"Good night, Mama," he whispered. "Hurry up and get better. I love you."

As he turned to leave, she took his hand. "Where are you going, Eddie?"

"Mama, I'm Karl." His heart went galloping out of his chest and across the room. "Come on, you know me."

"Would you go look in on the baby?" She smiled sweetly.

"Mama, I'm *not* Daddy." He raised his voice and heard it waver. "I'm not Eddie, I'm Karl. Your son. *Karl.*"

"Oh." She frowned. "Then where's your father?"

"Mama, don't." Karl turned and ran across the hall to his own room, slamming the door behind him. He pulled off his clothes, turned out the light, yanked the quilt back and threw himself into bed. What was wrong with her? Was she dying? Was *she* going insane? He covered his face with his quilt and curled up into a ball. How much worse could this nightmare get?

Maggie looked at Jacob, confused. "Will? When did you get here?"

Jacob wanted to run away, just like Karl, but he couldn't do it. He moved around the bed and took her hand in both of his. "Maggie..."

"Where's Eddie?"

"I'm sorry." He swallowed the lump in his throat. "I'm so sorry. He's not here." He swallowed again. "He's gone. Remember?"

"Oh." She closed her eyes and nodded slightly. "I'm all mixed up." One tear ran down the side of her face.

"I'm Will's brother. I'm Jacob."

She opened her eyes and smiled sadly. "I know who you are. I'm sorry, Jacob." She squeezed his hand.

"I think you'd better rest now. I'll be here when you wake up." He kissed her hand and set it on the bed.

Mrs. Iverson poked her head in the room. "Everything okay?"

Jacob shook his head.

She felt Maggie's forehead. "I need to cool her down again." She switched on the lamp. "I'll be back in a minute, then you'll have to leave. Maybe you could find a blanket and a pillow and stretch out on the davenport. You look mighty tired."

Jacob nodded. He hadn't thought about sleeping. As he watched Maggie's breathing, he wondered if Lana asked for him before she died. He wondered if she'd been confused, too, or if she just went to sleep and faded away.

He listened to Mrs. Iverson humming softly as she

filled the basin with water. Turning to leave, his eyes fell on the framed photograph on the bedside table. A wedding picture. He picked it up. Even with the yards and yards of veil cascading from her head, he recognized Maggie. He studied it closely. She'd been little more than a child; much too young for marriage, he thought.

When his eyes moved to the groom, Jacob had to blink twice before he understood what he was seeing. No wonder Maggie got confused. Eddie Stern stood stiffly next to his bride, the grin on his face clashing with his formal stance. And he looked exactly like Karl.

Chapter 26

Lucky

On Monday after school, Karl walked Lizzie and Anna across the busy streets so they could go back to Will and Bernie's. He stood and watched as Melvin drove by, but when his car turned toward Grandma's house, he figured his uncle wasn't out to bother them.

Mr. Denver was waiting for him in the kitchen. "Where've you been? I thought you got home at three forty-five; it's four-twenty."

"I promised to walk my sisters across Walnut and Main Streets before I came home."

"Oh, I forgot." Mr. Denver pulled his jacket on.

"How's my mother?"

"Better. Her fever's under control, so Dr. Lyman said she doesn't need a nurse to come at night anymore. Mrs. Iverson came for a while this afternoon and helped her take a bath." He smiled. "Your mother said she felt like a new woman."

Karl pulled a bottle of milk from the icebox. "You're going home, then?"

"Oh, heavens no, not yet. Just out to see if I can buy a

few things to wear. I packed in such a hurry I only brought one extra shirt. Where do you suppose I should go?"

"There's *Beastrom's*, that fancy new store in Ashland. But we still have all my father's clothes. You look to be about his size."

Mr. Denver tugged at his collar. "Oh, I don't know, Karl; that doesn't seem right."

"Why not? Nobody else is using them. They're packed away in the attic, I know right where they are." He poured the milk into tall glass and took a gulp. "Someone might as well use them."

"What would your mother say?" He reached into his pocket and jingled his keys.

"I dunno. Ask her. Do we have any cookies or bread or anything?"

"Your Aunt Kathleen brought a basket over this morning, look in there."

"I wonder how she got out of Melvin's prison."

The telephone rang. "You answer it," said Mr. Denver. "I need to go before the stores close."

Karl moved too fast and bumped the glass with his elbow. Milk went all over the table and onto the floor. "Ah, nuts."

Scowling, Mr. Denver sidestepped the milk and went to the telephone. "Stern residence."

Karl could tell it was Bernie. She was loud enough that Mr. Denver had to hold the earpiece away from his head. Even though she yammered so fast Mr. Denver couldn't get in a single word, Karl could make out most of what she said.

"The girls... late... Did Karl..."

"Slow down, now."

"I'm not gonna slow down until..."

"Hold on, Bern... Karl, you *did* see your sisters across the street?"

"Yeah, that's why I got home late, I told you." He finished wiping the milk off the table, but there was still a puddle on the floor.

"Talk to Bernie, I'll take care of that."

Karl took the earpiece. "Hi, Bernie. I walked them across the street, they should be there by now."

"I *know*, Karl! So where are they?"

"I don't... Oh, no." Karl felt his hands get clammy.

"What?"

"Uncle Melvin drove past us when we crossed Main, but he didn't stop, so I thought he was going over to Grandma's." He suddenly felt sick.

Bernie yelled in his ear. "Lemme talk to Jacob again!"

Mr. Denver took the earpiece, put it next to his ear then held it away from his head again. "You go right over to his house... Karl knows..."

"Let's go, Mr. Denver." Karl went for his coat.

"Calm down, Bernie."

"Not until... safe'n sound! Promise you'll call me as soon as..."

"I promise." He hung up.

Karl took one deep breath, then another. *Who has a foot big enough to crush this evil man?* He thought he might explode.

"I'll tell your mother we're going out."

"I should tell her, this is my fault."

"No, you'll upset her, you look like a ghost. Finish wiping up the floor, I'll go."

As soon as Karl finished, he bounded up the stairs. "Come on, Mr. Denver."

His mother clutched a pillow like a baby. "Melvin is

behind this."

"Now, Maggie, we don't know that for sure. Maybe they stopped off to play somewhere."

She shook her head. "They know better than that."

Karl stuck his head in the room. "Mama, I'm sorry."

"Go find your sisters, Karl."

His mother's panic tied a knot in Karl's stomach.

"Go on, both of you!"

As soon as Maggie heard the back door slam, she slipped out of bed and took the votive from on top of her dresser. When she tried to make a place for it on her bed table, she saw the picture of Eddie and burst into tears. She turned it around so she wouldn't have to look at it, then changed her mind. With shaking hands, she slid it into the drawer where she still kept some of his things. She lit the votive, knelt by the bed and crossed herself. "*Not—my—girls!*" Something in her wanted to make the same keening noise she'd made at Eddie's deathbed, but a fit of coughing overcame her.

Karl told Mr. Denver how to get to Melvin and Aunt Kathleen's house, but he didn't have much else to say. He bit his lip and opened and closed his fists, wishing he could slug Melvin, remembering the satisfying feel of his foot sinking into his belly before Melvin beat him on the coal pile. If Melvin hurt Lizzie and Anna, he'd get more than a foot in the stomach, that's for sure.

They turned onto Melvin's street. "Wait a minute, Mr. D, pull over."

The car stopped. Mr. Denver leaned over to look out

the passenger's window. "Is this the house?"

"No it's down there a ways." Karl turned to face him. "Listen, I gotta tell you, my uncle is crazy. He beats my aunt, he hurt my mother and me, too, and he's got this closet in his house where I think he... He's evil, like a snake. You better be careful of him."

"I gathered as much. I made his acquaintance last week, at your grandmother's. You're right, he's dangerous. Thanks for the warning."

"So shouldn't we have a plan?" Even though he'd been able to tough out the beating he got from Melvin, the thought of confronting him again terrified Karl.

"Well, we'll have a lot more power if we're both calm. I know Melvin's type; I've hired and fired quite a few of them. He *wants* you to get all riled up, because it makes him feel like a big man."

Karl closed his eyes and saw Melvin's face. He opened them again and let out a big breath.

"That's it, take a deep breath when you feel like you're going to blow up. It helps. We'll find them, but we have to be able to think clearly when we do." Mr. Denver reached over and squeezed Karl's knee. "Hold on."

This guy seemed to know what he was doing, much to Karl's surprise. "I'll try, Mr. D."

"Say, that's all right." Mr. Denver smiled but kept his eyes on the road.

"What?"

"*Mr. D*"

"My mother would say it's disrespectful."

"Well, I happen to like it." Slowly, he drove to Melvin's house. It looked dark inside, but there were tire tracks in the driveway. "See that?"

"Yep." Karl took another deep breath.

Jacob parked the car across the street from the house. They got out and ran around back. Karl looked in the window and saw Lizzie's book bag on the floor.

"That's Lizzie's bag," he whispered. He took another deep breath and tried the door. The knob turned. He looked at Mr. D.

"Go on. They're here."

Silently, the two entered the kitchen. Three dirty bowls and spoons littered the table, an empty ice cream carton sat in the sink. Karl heard Anna wailing upstairs.

"I want Mama, I want my Mama!"

"Don't believe him, Anna; he's lying."

"Shut up and sit down, Elizabeth, or I'll have to teach you who's boss in this house. Hush, Anna, never you mind. See, now you can play with the dollhouse whenever you want, and Uncle Melvin will be here to take good care of you."

Karl and Mr. D looked at each other and started up the stairs. They stopped for a moment in the hallway, watching. Melvin and the girls were in the spare room, the room with the creepy closet. He sat on the bed with Anna on his lap straddling his leg. His eyes were closed, like the way a person would close his eyes when he took a bite of really good chocolate cake. Anna sobbed, her head bowed against his chest, her arms folded against her stomach, her little body convulsing with some horrible sorrow. With one hand Melvin held her knee tight against his crotch while his other hand disappeared under her blouse, rubbing her bare back. He shifted her on his lap, pushing her knee harder against himself. Lizzie sat on the floor on the far side of the bed, pale as death.

"What are you doing with that child?" Mr. D's booming voice filled the room.

Melvin jumped and pushed Anna away. She stumbled and ran to Karl. Still sobbing, she clung to his arm, her face mottled, her school uniform disheveled, the blouse pulled out of her skirt. Lizzie scrambled to her feet, followed Anna and hid behind her brother. Mr. D shoved Melvin against the wall, both his big hands around Melvin's neck.

"Did you think no one would come looking for them?"

"We were having a nice time together, weren't we, girls? Remember, I bought you ice cream."

"Go call the police, Karl; and then your mother, let her talk to Lizzie and Anna. Stay with your brother, girls, he'll take good care of you."

As he left the room, Karl looked back at Mr. D. That's when he noticed how big his feet were.

Jacob felt like throwing something. He watched the police car leave with Melvin Straus in the back seat. The officers didn't share his outrage; they'd probably let him go with a slap on the hand. Karl had his uncle pegged, the man was crazy. Was Melvin stupid enough to think he could keep Maggie's girls like they were a couple of stray puppies?

Lizzie and Anna told the police the whole story. Uncle Melvin stopped them on their way to Bernie's and said they were supposed to come with him. He said he'd buy them ice cream if they were good, whatever kind they wanted. They went to his house, and after he'd given them big bowls of peppermint ice cream, he told them the real reason he'd come for them. Their mother wasn't really sick, but she was *playing the whore*—they quoted his exact words—and she didn't want them anymore. She ran away and left them, he said, so now they had to live with him and Aunt Kathleen. Jacob's anger almost got the best of him while he listened; he looked at Karl and saw him squeeze his hands into fists.

When Jacob climbed into his car, Maggie's kids were waiting for him. Karl sat in the back with the girls, grinning from ear to ear. He had one arm around each sister, and each sister sat as close to him as they could. At this moment, they obviously adored him. Jacob remembered Will's words to Karl: *You'll make a fine father some day.* The picture of Eddie Stern crossed his mind and Jacob felt like a colossal intruder.

Maggie brushed her hair, rebraided it, and with a coughing towel in her hand, made her way downstairs to wait. She cried when she heard Lizzie's voice on the telephone, then fell into another fit of coughing. Karl came on the line, saying nobody was hurt, Melvin got arrested, and they'd be home as soon as they finished talking to the police.

"Bring the girls home—here—Karl. They should be with their Mama. I'll call Bernie."

Maggie sat on the edge of Eddie's easy chair, waiting. She felt all the muscles in her neck tighten and her head started to hurt again when she coughed. She thought she ought to have a hot meal ready for her family, but when she stood up to go into the kitchen, the room spun around again.

After exactly thirty-eight minutes, a car pulled up outside the house. Wobbly but determined, Maggie got up and opened the door. Lizzie and Anna ran into her arms.

She held onto them and kissed the top of their heads.

"Mama, I didn't believe a word he said," Lizzie announced.

Anna replied, "Yes, you did, Lizzie; you cried, too, and you know it."

"Come, sit with me." Anna and Lizzie cuddled up to her on the davenport. "What did Uncle Melvin say to you?"

"He said you were playing the whore and you ran away because you didn't want us anymore, so we were going to live at his house from now on." Lizzie squinted up at Maggie. "What's *playing the whore?*"

Disgusted, Maggie shook her head. "It's not very nice. We can talk about it another time."

Anna started to cry again. She crawled onto Maggie's lap and wrapped her arms around her neck. "Do you still want us, Mama?"

Maggie couldn't keep tears from her own eyes. "Why wouldn't I want you? You're my precious babies. I will always want you. Uncle Melvin told you a bad lie. I love you; and Lizzie, you, too. And Karl." She looked at her son, who stood watching from the door. He still had his coat on. "Thank you, Karl. Where's Mr. Denver?"

"He went for a walk. He said he'd be back once we had some time together."

"Oh, for pity's sake. Go find him. After all he's done, he should be here." Her heart filled with happiness. Her world was in this house, safe and sound. She wanted him here, too.

Jacob shoved his hands into his pockets and started down the block. He couldn't figure out why he felt so

C. A. PETERSON

unbearably sad. Maybe because predators like Melvin Straus would tell such despicable lies to little girls so they could use them for their own perverted pleasure. Maybe because he had to decide whether or not to tell Maggie what he saw Melvin doing to Anna. What good would it do? Did she really have to know?

"Hey, Mr. D!"

He turned and Karl almost ran into him, all arms and legs. "Hey, we sure did it, didn't we?" He grinned. "You were right about not getting all riled up in front of Melvin. Come on, my mother wants you to come back. You're a hero, you know."

Jacob smiled. "Well, if I am, you are, too." He threw his arm across Karl's shoulders and the boy didn't seem to mind.

After supper, Jacob sent Karl and the girls to help their exhausted mother upstairs and back to bed while he washed the dishes. He'd barely started when he heard wild giggling and Lizzie's voice calling him upstairs. He found them gathered around Maggie's bed. Karl had on that dumb hat of his father's. He held out an old suitcase.

"Here, Mr. D. You don't need to buy new clothes. It was Ruffles' idea and we all voted on it. These are Daddy's and you can use whatever you want."

Jacob couldn't say a word. He looked at Maggie.

She smiled at him. "Go ahead, Jacob. You deserve it."

Everyone agreed. As he reached for the suitcase, he wondered how he'd gotten so lucky to be part of all this.

Chapter 27

A Reckoning

Karl turned up the collar of his jacket as he waited for his sisters outside Holy Angels School. The wind blew from the east, gathering cold air from the ice-caked shores of Lake Superior and spewing it over the town. He remembered his father saying that a wind from the east meant they'd have bad weather in a day or so. Even though there'd already been a few days of sunshine and warmth, Karl knew winter wasn't finished with them yet. The overcast skies made the day downright gloomy.

As he crouched beside the gnarly old oak tree trying to keep warm, a car pulled up in front of the church. He got up, thinking Mr. D had come to give him and his sisters a ride home, but he stopped short, stunned, when he saw Melvin Straus get out. All hunched over in the wind and holding onto his brown fedora, Melvin scurried across the church yard and went in the side door, the door where you were least likely to run into another person.

They hadn't even kept him in jail for twenty four hours! Karl's clenched jaw began to ache. He took a deep breath. Although he didn't know what he was going to do, he knew he couldn't just go home and do his homework like any other day.

Lizzie and Anna came running toward him, the edges of their coats flapping in the wind. At almost the same moment, Mr. D arrived. Karl helped his sisters get into the car, and said, "I think I'll walk, Mr. D." He tried to act normal despite his anger.

"In this wind?"

"Yeah, don't worry. I need to talk to somebody. I'll be along in a little while."

"Everything all right?"

Karl smiled, knowing it looked phony. "Yep."

"When should I start to worry?"

"Nothin' to worry about. I'll be home before supper, for sure."

Mr. D looked Karl in the eye without saying anything for moment. "Breathe deep, boy."

"Yessir, I remember."

Karl watched the car drive away. Soon his mother would be well again and Mr. D would go home. He realized he'd miss him, then thought of his father and felt guilty.

He leaned against the tree, shivering. He watched a few leftover oak leaves break free of their branches and sail away like little brown boats in the air. The cold wind made it feel like forever before Melvin came out of the church, and when he did, the sight of him made Karl wish he could knock him over and beat the daylights out of him. But he knew he'd only get in trouble for doing something like that, and anyway, it was about time Father Cunningham found out what his favorite parishioner did to Lizzie and Anna. Maybe he could keep Melvin from doing anything else to hurt them. As Melvin drove away,

Karl entered the church using the same side door.

The corridor, with its floor polished to a mirror-like shine, smelled of beeswax and the same soap Karl used when he had to scrub the church floor with Sister Anne. He almost expected to see her waiting for him. If he hadn't been on a mission, he would have lingered for a few minutes to see if he could find the peace and comfort he'd known that afternoon.

He hurried partway down the hall and stopped at the door marked *Father David Cunningham*. Although his teachers sent him to deliver messages to Father every so often, he'd never noticed the carvings in the wall on either side of his door. He stopped for a moment and stared. On the left was a cross with points at the end of each arm, like they'd been sharpened or something. On the right was a fierce looking eagle, perched but ready to fly, its head turned to look at the cross, its wings spread wide. Karl shuddered. They seemed like omens. Why hadn't he ever paid attention to them before?

He took a deep breath, rubbed his jittery hands together and knocked on the door.

"Yes?"

"Father Cunningham, it's Karl Stern. May I come in? I'd like to talk to you, please."

The door opened and the priest stood there wearing a rumpled rabat over a white shirt. His glasses sat halfway down his nose, like they always did when he was reading something. He lifted his chin to examine Karl through the lenses before pushing the glasses up. He extended his hand toward the one extra chair in the room. Karl stepped in and Father closed the door.

"Have a seat." The priest sat down heavily, his chair creaking at the insult of his weight. He looked like he'd been wrestling with someone. "Now, what can I do for you?"

"Well, Father, I just saw my Uncle Melvin coming from your office." Karl took a deep breath. "Um... I know he's a friend of yours, and I know he gives a lot of money to the church and all, but I think you should know he's been hurting my family."

"In what way?"

"Well, one time he got too friendly with my mother, and another time he hit her, and me, too. The police took him away."

"That happened some months ago." Father Cunningham leaned back in his chair, took off his glasses and cleaned them with a wrinkled handkerchief.

"I know, but yesterday after school, he stole Lizzie and Anna while they were on their way to Mr. and Mrs. Denver's. That's where they were staying because my mother is sick. He lied to them, and said she wasn't really sick, but she didn't want us anymore so we'd have to come live with him. He's so mean, Father, and we didn't know where they were and we were all so worried and scared."

"Well, they were in school today. They seemed fine. He didn't harm them, did he?"

"He was doing things to Anna when we found them." Karl felt his cheeks get hot. He took a deep breath and let it out again.

"What kind of things?" Frowning, the priest leaned toward Karl, both elbows on the desk.

Karl cleared his throat. "She was sitting on his lap and he was..." He burst into tears. *Not in front of Father Cunningham, stupid!* Quickly, he wiped his eyes on his sleeves.

"Go on."

"And he... He was shoving her knee against his crotch and... he stuck his hand under her blouse."

Father Cunningham closed his eyes and sighed.

"The police took him away, but now he's out again." It was easier for Karl to talk when Father wasn't looking at him. "I'm afraid he'll come back and hurt us some more. He's evil, Father."

"We're all sinners, Karl." He opened his eyes and looked into Karl's.

"I know, but I think he's dangerous." Karl saw some cloudiness in Father's left eye. He had to concentrate to keep from staring at it.

"Let me tell you a thing or two, son."

Father Cunningham never called him *son* before.

"Melvin Straus has done some bad things, but he wants to do better. Certainly you know how much good he's done in this community. Did you know he and your grandfather were good friends?"

"Grandpa O'Keefe?" Karl didn't understand. Aunt Kathleen said her father didn't approve of Melvin.

"No, your father's father, Karl Stern; you're named for him. They were neighbors. Melvin is the oldest of eleven children. His father beat him silly, so when Melvin was about your age, your grandfather, being the kind of man he was before... Well, he took him in and started to teach him the newspaper business. Melvin showed a lot of promise."

"I didn't know that."

"But when your grandfather went mad—got sick, I mean—something happened to Melvin. Nobody knows what, but he clammed up tight and wouldn't say a thing about it. He had to go back to live with his parents again."

"Oh."

"So maybe you can be a little more understanding, now."

"But Father, he can still hurt us. He hurts Aunt Kathleen all the time. Why are you friends with him?" He wiped his sweaty palms on his pants.

"I'm his priest." Father Cunningham removed his glasses, got up and opened the door to the tiny washroom behind his desk. Without closing the door, he ran the water and washed his hands for a long time, soaping and rinsing them twice. He splashed water on his face, then dried off and sat back down, replacing his glasses. "The judge released Melvin this morning under the condition that he report to me twice a day and I know of his whereabouts at all times. I can't say anything else, Karl, the confidentiality of the confessional and all."

"But what about *us*? Don't you care about *us*? What if he comes back and does something worse?"

"Have you heard from your Uncle George?"

"He sent me a letter at Christmas. I answered it, but he never wrote back."

"If you are so worried about Melvin hurting you, maybe you should apply to the abbey school where George teaches. You'd be safe there. I'm sure he'd help you get in."

Anger bubbled up from deep inside, but Karl pushed with all his might until it stayed in his cave. He took a deep breath. "But, Father, what about my mother and my sisters? And Aunt Kathleen? Anyway, I don't want to be a monk."

Father Cunningham stood and went to the door, moving like he had a heavy vestment draped across his shoulders. "You must trust in the Lord for protection. I pray for your family everyday," he said. "Thank you for coming to visit."

Karl's mouth fell open. He remembered Father's prayers when his father lay dying. Some help they were! "But, Father—"

"I'll see you in chapel tomorrow." The priest put his hand on the doorknob.

"Yes, Father."

As Karl slouched through the doorway, Father Cunningham reached out and squeezed his upper arm, holding on like he didn't want to let him leave. He tilted his head slightly, brows furrowed. "Take care out there, son. That wind is wicked."

Karl didn't even think to take a healing breath of the clean, sweet air outside Father's office. He stormed down the hallway and tried to slam the outside door, but it was too heavy and swung closed of its own accord.

All the way home, Karl stewed about his conversation with Father Cunningham. Was the priest on his side or Melvin's? He would have said Melvin's, except for the way Father held his arm in the doorway. He wondered if talking to the priest would change anything for his family.

After supper, Karl read through the passages from Sister Anne again. *And he hath put all things under his feet and gave him to be the head over all things... For he must reign till he hath put all enemies under his feet. The last enemy that shall be destroyed is death...* He stared at the words, and for the first time he really thought about them. If all things were under his feet—*his* must mean the Lord—wouldn't that include Melvin? Wouldn't that mean God would keep Melvin from hurting them anymore? And if Father Cunningham was like a stand-in for God, didn't that mean he'd keep

Melvin from doing anything else to them? And to Aunt Kathleen?

But what if Father Cunningham *didn't* help them? What if he didn't *want* to?

Karl took out his drawing pad and pencils and sketched the cross he'd seen carved in the wall next to Father Cunningham's office, with its four sharpened ends. It looked like a sword, maybe for punishing sinners. Above the cross, he tried to draw the eagle, too, but couldn't get it quite right. He knew it would be a sin to draw a snake around the cross, but he drew one around the eagle, making it so the snake and eagle were staring at each other, face to face, the snake's tongue flicking under the eagle's beak. He stopped and scratched his head, remembering when Daddy said that eagles often eat snakes if they can't get fish.

He turned the page and drew Father Cunningham washing his hands, a deep frown on his face. He drew lots of bubbles rising from the soap, with water splashing in a mess from the sink. Underneath he wrote *Friend or Enemy?* He framed the drawing with another snake, staring at the priest. This one didn't smile or flick its tongue, it just watched.

Mr. D knocked once and opened the door. Karl flipped the drawing pad closed.

"Your sisters want you to say bedtime prayers with them. Your mother's already sleeping."

"Sure thing."

Karl was glad they had memorized prayers and didn't have to make anything up themselves. After today, he didn't know *what* to say to God.

Chapter 28

The Big Empty

Maggie opened her eyes. The last thing she knew, the room had been bright with sunshine, but now the light coming from outside was dim and dusky. She'd slept the whole afternoon away again. She sat up and coughed, working hard to clear as much sickness from her lungs as she could.

She'd become accustomed to Jacob appearing at her door the moment he heard her coughing or moving around. She looked forward to the sight of his face, his smile, his laugh. She sat still and listened for his footsteps coming up the stairs, but the house was silent. Disappointed, she leaned back to rest against the mountain of pillows he'd bought for her. She couldn't remember ever being the sole focus of anyone's tending, and she liked it.

So where did he go? He wouldn't have left for home without saying good-bye, would he?

Maggie looked at the clock; it was nearly four. He must have gone to get the children from school. She smiled. They were beginning to like him, she could tell. Last night Anna climbed on his lap, asking for a lumberjack story, her eyes growing wide when she heard his tall tales about cooking for "six hundred men who were as hungry as six hundred grizzly bears." Even Lizzie, always the skeptical, serious one, laughed at his silliness. And Karl, who seemed to resent Jacob at first, had warmed to him ever since they rescued the girls from Melvin.

Sick of her bedroom, sick of her nightgown, sick of looking like an invalid, she got out of bed and opened her closet door. Jacob Denver had seen enough of her at her worst; tonight she would bathe and dress for supper. She pulled out her newest house dress, the green and white one; its hemline was a little long, but the color favored her.

The back door opened then closed loudly, followed by the clamor of feet on the stairs. Lizzie and Anna met her at the bathroom door, still in their coats and hats.

"Mama, you're up!" Lizzie hugged her mother's waist, nearly knocking her over.

Anna jumped up and down. "Are you better yet?"

Maggie smiled and reached out so she could hug both of them. "Yes, I'm up, and yes, I'm getting better." She sent them downstairs to see if Mr. Denver had a snack for them, then ran the bath water. She'd barely slid into the tub before Lizzie came knocking at the door.

"Mama, I have to come in and watch you. Mr. Denver said you shouldn't be taking a bath all by yourself."

"I'm okay, Lizzie. Tell him I can manage alone."

"But Mama, he's not going to like that."

"Tell him I'll call if I need help."

Maggie could hear Lizzie tripping down the stairs. She leaned back in the warmth and closed her eyes, imagining all the sickness being washed off her body, circling with the water and tumbling down the drain. "Tomorrow I will

be well," she said to herself, realizing that she was still awfully tired. "Or maybe the day after."

Another, louder, knock broke into her thoughts. "What
do you think you're doing in there, Margaret?" Jacob's
words were frantic.

"Taking a bath. Is there something wrong with that?"

"Two days ago you needed help; what makes you think
you can do it alone today?"

"Because I'm feeling better today. I slept all
afternoon."

"I don't care; you shouldn't be in there by yourself."

"Are you angry with me, Jacob?" Maggie smiled.

"Either Lizzie comes in to watch you or I do."

"And wouldn't you love that!" Maggie laughed.

Jacob stumbled over his words. "No, I wouldn't. Well,
yes, but... I just don't want to see you fall."

Maggie laughed again. "You won't see me fall if you
stay out there."

"Come on, Maggie, you know what I mean." He strung
his words together with an impatient whine. "I'm sending
Lizzie back up here and you *have* to let her in; I insist."
Now he sounded like the boss.

"You're not going to give up, are you?"

"No, I'm not, it's not safe—"

"Oh, all right, send her back. Jacob?"

"What?"

"I'm coming down to the kitchen for supper. I'm tired
of crumbs in my bed."

The aromas of beef and onions floated through the
house. Maggie smiled to herself, wondering how Jacob
managed to cut the onions. Maybe Karl helped him. He

must have known that roast beef would taste terrible without them. When he met her at the bottom of the stairs, she noticed his dark eyes; they weren't simply brown but a warm brown, like the fancy velvet coat Grandma O'Keefe made for her when she was a little girl. Looking into them made her feel like she did then: safe and treasured. Maggie's heart quickened when his eyes searched hers for a moment before abruptly turning away.

Even though the chatter of the children was lively, with more tall tales from Jacob followed by laughter and silliness, conversation between the two of them was awkward and self conscious. Maggie regretted teasing Jacob; no wonder he seemed ill at ease. How could she have done such a thing when he'd been so good to her?

While they were eating, Jacob kept looking at Maggie when he didn't think she'd notice. After sitting at her sickbed, he knew he loved her, knew it better than he knew how to spell his own name. He longed for the day she'd tell him she loved him, he ached for her touch; he'd even dreamt of her beautiful hair spread out on the pillow next to his, the bed still warm from their love.

When he went to scold her for taking a bath alone, her teasing tempted him sorely. The idea of her unclothed body on the other side of the door lit his desire to white hot; it hit him out of the blue like a bolt of lightning after a storm. After Maggie allowed the girls in to help her, he said he needed to go out for firewood, but he really needed the cold air.

Standing out on the back stoop, he reached into his jacket pocket and felt the little box he'd been carrying around for weeks like a good luck charm, the ring inside an unseen talisman whose power might draw her to love him. But he knew the ring had nothing to do with it. He had to ask her himself. Tonight.

Maggie offered to help with the dishes, but Jacob refused to allow it, telling her to go sit in the living room. Karl built a fire for her, making the room rosy and warm. Lulled by the warmth, she fell asleep in the easy chair, but not before looking around the room. Her eyes moved from the green-globed lamp in front of the window to the captains' clock on the mantle to the worn rug with the water stain where they'd laid Eddie. In one way or another, they all bound her to him forever. Her eyes filled; she hurried to wipe them dry, in case Jacob came from the kitchen. For fifteen years, she and Eddie shared one heart, one bed, one flesh. Now she felt like she was waving to him across a vast open sea, knowing that the pain of losing him would never disappear as he had. But she was getting used to the hurt, aware that it, too, bound her to him, even with Jacob in her life.

Jacob knelt before the fireplace, adding more wood to the pile of glowing embers. He rearranged the logs with his bare hands and poked around with a stick he'd found out in the backyard. Before long, flames licked the edges of the logs; their flickering golden light filling the dark room and dancing on his beloved, who slept peacefully in the chair, her feet resting on the ottoman.

After brushing a few pieces of bark from his shirt, Jacob stood and held his hands out, warming them. For a long while, he gazed into the fire, awed at how life could take such a turn and offer him a new chance at happiness. Nervous but excited, he turned to look at Maggie, so still and quiet in the easy chair. Maybe he should let her be and ask her tomorrow; maybe he should just sit and watch her sleep by the fire. Tentatively he whispered her name.

She opened her eyes, stretched without coughing and smiled. "Oh, Jacob, this is bliss."

He smiled, too. "What?"

"This. The fire is lovely. I'm getting better. And you're here." She reached out to him. "Come, sit with me." She moved her feet off the ottoman so there would be a place for him. "You've been babying me shamelessly, rescuing and feeding my children and now you're keeping me warm. Saying thank you isn't enough, but I don't have any other words."

Jacob sat down and took her hand. "No thanks are needed. I want to be here. I want to take care of you." Suddenly he had an idea. "Just a minute." He pulled the davenport closer to the fireplace. "There's room for both of us over here."

"No, I have something to say to you first."

"What's that?"

"I'm sorry about teasing you this afternoon. I know I embarrassed you. I hope you can forgive me."

"Well, I have to admit you got me thinking." He chuckled. "Not that I wasn't already."

"I'm sorry."

He sobered and shook his head. "If you want to apologize for something, tell me you're sorry for getting in the bathtub by yourself. You could have gotten hurt."

"I apologize, but I knew I didn't need help. You're starting to act like a mother hen, Mr. Denver." Her eyes twinkled.

"And why shouldn't I? I love you, Maggie." The words slipped out of his mouth, no thinking required. He held out his hand to her. "Come here, now."

Maggie stood, wobbling slightly. In an instant, Jacob steadied her with one hand on each of her elbows; bending to her until they were nose to nose, eye to eye, separated only by the firelight. He hadn't planned this, either. Then his lips were on hers, so sweet, so tender—one completely perfect kiss. The fire crackled as it devoured the wood he'd kindled, lavishing upon them the garnered warmth of the sun, as if the tree it came from existed for this moment alone. They sat close on the davenport, watching the fire, holding hands, listening to the mantle clock measure out moments that were here and gone, here and gone. Jacob wanted to grab them and make them stop so his time with her would never pass away.

He took a deep breath and let it out. *Oh, please...* He turned to face her, kissing her hand before releasing it. "From the moment I met you, Maggie—in this very room, with onions all over your hands and that terrible bruise on your face—my life started to mean something." He put his hand where the bruise had been and Maggie covered it with her own. "I'm in love with you, and I'm wondering if... if you think you could love me?"

"I don't *think* I can love you, I *do* love you." She smiled, the sweetest sight he'd ever seen.

"Then marry me. Will you? All I want in this world is to make a life with you and make you happy; I want you by my side, always."

Maggie looked away a little too quickly. She wrapped both arms around his neck and whispered, "Jacob, you're the most wonderful man."

Alarmed, he peeled her arms from his neck and held

her hands. "*You're the most wonderful man*, but..."

"I can't give you an answer yet."

"Why? Why not? You said you loved me."

"I *do* love you. But I want you to understand what you're getting with me. I'm giving you the chance to think about it some more."

His heart fell into the pit of his stomach. "I don't need to think about it anymore. I know what I want. I want *you*."

Maggie's eyes scanned the room and came back to Jacob. "If I say *yes*, I'll be bringing three children with me. I love them with my life, and God help the man who tries to make me love them less."

Relieved, Jacob smiled again. "I would never expect you to do that."

"The father they've known all their lives is dead. They miss him, especially Karl, but they need a man who will be patient with them and love them anyway. They'll test you, Jacob."

"I can love them; I can give them whatever they need. I want to, Maggie."

"You know we're Catholic."

"I know. We can work it out." His mother would disapprove, but he didn't care.

She smiled, touched his cheek then sobered. "Melvin will always be after us. I angered him when I refused his offer to bring my family to live in his house. And he's got something against Karl." She looked down, her voice nearly a whisper. "The brooch you took to get rid of for me... he gave it to me when I was very young. He thinks he should have me. It's an ugly story."

"All the more reason to marry me. I can protect you— all of you."

Smiling, she cradled the sides of his face in her hands. A current of love ran from her fingertips to his heart. "There's more."

"Tell me, I can take it." He'd do anything so she'd say *yes*.

Maggie leaned close. "I want to kiss you first."

They kissed, slowly, three, four, six times. Jacob could tell that she wanted him, too. His heart raced.

She pulled away. "Jacob... There's a hole in my heart. A big empty place." Her eyes filled with tears. "There are still days when I can't believe he's dead. It still hurts more than I ever would have imagined."

He'd been afraid of this.

"Sometimes, for a few seconds, I forget, and I wait for him to come home because I want to tell him about something you've said or done. And when I remember he's gone, I feel like I'm betraying both of you." She looked down at her hands. "I'm sorry," she whispered.

Jacob took the handkerchief from his pocket—Eddie's handkerchief, Eddie's pocket—and caught a tear running down her cheek. "I want to make up for the sadness, for everything. Please let me. Let me fill the empty place."

"But I don't think you can. The hole is permanent." She reached for his hands and held them.

Jacob considered pulling them back, but held on.

"Eddie's dead. It happened to us. It's our story, our history. It won't ever go away and it can't be undone."

Jacob jerked his hands away. "Then how can you say you love *me?*" He knew he was on the verge of acting like a jackass, he could feel it coming on.

"Because I *do*. I *do* love you. I don't understand it, either, but I *know* I do." She wiped her eyes. "One day I was absolutely riven with grief for Eddie and the next day, you were in my heart, too, visiting and smiling and sending me letters; making me watch for the mailman." She smiled and took his hand back, holding it to her heart with both of hers. "One of you didn't go away just because the other was here. There's room for both of you. I *want* you here, you *belong* here."

He scowled. "Well, that sure is nice to know." *Be careful, Denver.*

"Jacob, listen to me. You've taught me that even if a heart gets broken, it still can love, because a new place starts to grow, and it gets bigger and bigger. I had this dream once about a heart breaking and growing new places." She leaned forward, pleading. "*You're* in that new place. It's there for *you*. But I don't think it could grow, and I don't think I could ever love again if I tried to make the big empty go away. Do you understand what I'm saying? I love you, Jacob. But the big empty has to stay. I can't pretend it's not there. It has to stay because it's part of me."

"You're making me compete with a dead man, Margaret. How can I possibly win?" Jacob knew his voice betrayed his resentment. "*He* can't do anything wrong anymore."

"It's not a competition. No one can win and no one can lose, and no one can compete with you for my heart, no one. But I want you to understand that in some ways, Eddie's still with us. It's like you're brothers."

Jacob looked into the fire. She still held his hand to her heart. He wanted to move it a few inches to hold her perfect breast, but that would only confirm he was the king of all jackasses. He took it back. Finally he spoke. "I think I understand you. I'm trying to understand. But I haven't changed my mind. I still want to marry you."

"Please, think about it for a while. I've told you the truth the best I can, I've tried to be honest because I care for you." Her eyes filled again. "I'm giving you a way out now if you decide you can't live with all this."

"I don't *want* out!" Jacob felt like stomping his foot like a child.

"Ask me again when you know for sure."

"I am sure." He leaned back and looked at the ceiling, resting his neck on the back of the davenport. "Why do you question my love for you?"

"Sleep on it. Give it till tomorrow."

Jacob sighed. "All right, tomorrow. But please don't do this to me and then say *no*."

Disappointment filled his heart, made his joints ache. He didn't answer, but stood and kept his back to her so she wouldn't see his face, contorted with the threat of weeping. He hadn't planned on *that* either. He swallowed and tried to make his voice sound normal. "I'm tired and you're sitting on my bed. Goodnight, Margaret." He busied himself with his bedroll, which he'd been keeping in the corner of the room.

Partway up the stairs she stopped and began to cough. It sounded so violent and went on for so long Jacob almost went to her. He wanted to, but didn't.

Slightly out of breath, she cleared her throat and croaked out the words, "I'm so sorry for hurting you... my dear."

Jacob thought she said *my dear* as if she had to think about it first. He didn't turn around or say anything but waved his hand to dismiss her. He waited until he heard her door close before he pushed the davenport back, away from the fireplace. The flames mocked him. *Ask me again when you know for sure.* Did she think he'd only been playing around with the idea?

He stretched out, covered up with his blankets, and

rolled onto his side. The velvet covered jewelry box in his pocket jabbed him in the hip. Angrily, he sat up and dug it out. He felt like throwing it into the flames. He opened the box for the first time in weeks and saw how the firelight made the diamonds sparkle. He sighed and shoved it under his pillow. The death of Eddie Stern turned Will's world upside down, it nearly destroyed Maggie and her kids, and now it was getting in the way of his own dreams. "*It's like you're brothers!*" He muttered, imitating her. "Sure we are."

Chapter 29

What a Man Must Do

The morning sky matched Jacob's mood; it hung low and gray, the air heavy with mist. He made breakfast for Maggie's kids and took them to Holy Angel's School, all without waking her. He didn't want to see or talk to her until he'd taken enough time to *think about it*. He left a terse note telling her where he was going, that Bernie would bring soup for her lunch and that he'd be back by mid-afternoon. *P.S.* he added, *I'm not going to change my mind!*

Bernie's invitation to "come on over so we can chat" didn't seem appealing on the telephone, but Jacob found himself knocking on her door, anyway. Billy and Ned let him in, overexcited and wanting to play, as usual. Did they always have to think he'd come just to play with them? He gave them airplane rides for a few minutes, and tried to be a good uncle, but he couldn't put his heart into it. Thank God Bernie finally rescued him by telling the boys they were allowed to make a tent with blankets and dining room chairs.

Bernie led Jacob to the steamy kitchen, where the smoky aroma of a simmering ham bone filled the air. She slid a pile of chopped vegetables from the cutting board into the soup pot with the back of a knife. "How is she doing? Up and around yet? She must be getting better if you can leave her alone for a few hours."

"She is better, but not as well as she thinks she is. She got dressed and came to the kitchen for supper last night, then fell asleep in the chair." Jacob crossed his arms and leaned against the door jam. "Thanks for taking her lunch today. She'll be glad to see you."

"Ah, well, you deserve some time off, after all you've done. It's a wonderful thing, you taking care of her, keepin' an eye on the children, too. You should be proud o'yourself."

"Why? I care about her—and the kids. It's the right thing to do." He sighed. "I don't want to go home, Bern. I wish I could be with her every day."

Bernie raised her eyebrows and smiled slightly. "Is that so?"

"I asked her last night."

"Asked her what?"

"You know what I mean."

"You don't look too happy about it, Jakey. Did she turn you down?"

"She told me to ask her again after I thought about it some more. She seems to think she'll be some kind of liability for me, with her family and her past."

"What past?"

"Eddie. She still misses him. She says she'll never stop."

"Now what'd you expect, Love?" Bernie's voice softened. "They were married nearly fifteen years and he hasn't even been gone six months."

"I expected her to say yes. She knows how I feel about her."

"Does she know about Lana yet?"

"What does *that* have to do with anything?"

"You know you have to tell her."

"I'm over it. It's in the past, I don't think about it and I don't want to talk about it, either." Jacob raised his voice slightly. The boys stopped playing and looked at him.

"Seems to me you'd be willing to talk about it if you really were over it. Anyways, I don't think a person ever gets over losin' a husband or a wife, even if someone new comes along."

"Yeah, well..."

"It'll do nothin' but hurt things between you if you keep it from her."

"What would you know about it?"

In a huff, Bernie put one fist on her hip and wagged her finger at him. "Plenty! An' I know you too well to keep my mouth shut. You've got a big heart and a big lot 'o pride to go with it. You want to support her and take care of her family; that's good, an' they need it, but it's not love. Marriage means letting her support you, too. You've got to forget that pride o' yours and admit you need comfort and understanding as much as she does." She picked up the spoon and stirred the soup. "Lord knows you've needed it for as long as I've known you."

"I'm over it, I'm fine. Forget about it; I have." Jacob protested but knew she was right.

"If you truly love her, you'd better respect her, or you'll turn out like Melvin Straus."

"I resent that, Ber*nice.*"

Bernie went on like she didn't hear him. "An' if you're gonna respect her, you have to be honest with her. Quit being so tough and let her into your life, for heavensakes. She knows she's not the only one who's had sadness. She'll understand yours better than anyone."

Jacob shoved his hands into his pockets, jamming his middle finger against the little jewelry box. "What makes you such an expert?" He didn't know why he said that. Of all the people he'd ever known, Bernie was among the wisest.

"Six years livin' with your brother, that's what."

"I've gotta go look at my trees." Jacob put on his hat and started for the door.

Bernie grabbed his sleeve and poked his rib with her finger. "You know I'm right, Jacob Denver. She'll find out sooner or later and she'll never trust you if you're not the one doin' the tellin'."

Jacob pulled away and strode through the house to the front door. "'Bye, boys. Have fun in your tent." He pulled the door shut before they could answer him.

Jacob drove out of town, south toward the Tannin River, where he'd planted a new batch of white pine a few years back. Walking the rows of seedlings would give him something to do while he thought. He knew he'd acted like a jackass in front of Bernie but getting mad was safer than letting himself feel bad about Lana.

He'd barely left Tomos Bay when the wind started to pick up. It blew droplets of water against the windshield and made steering hard work. How could Bernie compare him to Melvin Straus? He remembered meeting the man for the first time, watching him drag Maggie's sister around by her hair; he remembered the way they caught him playing around with Anna the other day. Jacob clenched his teeth. As soon as Eddie Stern died, Melvin Straus, in his twisted, despicable way, tried to take over for him. Bernie was wrong if she thought he wanted to do the same thing. He loved Maggie, loved her enough to clean out her basin of vomit, loved her enough to stay even though it made him sick, too.

But the *big empty* in Maggie's heart troubled him. He didn't believe it would "never go away" like she said. Sometimes *he* could go a whole day without thinking about what happened to Lana. His throat tightened, but he swallowed the lump away. It made his stomach burn.

Less than an hour later, Jacob turned off the highway and followed a washboarded gravel road until he reached his seventy five acres of pine trees. He pulled his hat over his ears and had barely set his foot on the snowy ground when a gust of wind caught the door and slammed it against him, smacking his right side with a stunning shot of pain. He leaned against the car for a moment with both hands on the screaming rib. It felt like the same one he'd broken in Pennsylvania, the time Lana's horse threw him off. She'd been there to tend it with cool compresses and warm kisses, made it better in no time. This hurt like hell, just like it did back then.

The pain subsided after a few minutes, in fact, it practically disappeared, so Jacob began to walk the rows, reaching down every so often to caress the soft needles of the little trees, noticing where deer had browsed on a few of them. Could he live with Eddie Stern in the background of everything, seeing his face whenever he looked at Karl? He wished he'd never looked at that wedding picture.

Out of nowhere, Lana's face came to him, all surrounded by lace. A warm sensation rose from his rib; pleasant at first, it grew into a fire inside of him. He stopped walking and took a few shallow breaths until it settled down. "It's broken again, that's all," he said out loud.

As he walked, Jacob heard Maggie's laugh on the wind, felt her hands cradle his face the way she did last night, remembered the taste of her lips. He wanted her, he wanted her by his side, he even wanted her children for his own. Forget everything he owned: his land, the mill, the house. If he had Maggie's love and nothing else, he'd be happy forever. He stopped walking and looked absently into the distance.

So. If he wanted her to marry him, he'd have to be willing to share her heart with Eddie. It might bother him for a while, but he could get used to anything. He'd help her get over Eddie, and someday she'd thank God Jacob Denver came along when he did.

Now he could honestly tell Maggie he'd thought about it. He started walking again.

He was glad he didn't have to ask her to live under Lana's shadow. She didn't need to know that once upon a time he had a wife and hopes for a family. *Wife.* Good Lord, he hadn't let himself think about Lana as his wife in years.

Suddenly, pain sprung from his insides like lightning, the burning in his stomach pushing out that one rib, all heat and power. Jacob found himself flat on his back in the wet snow, not remembering how he fell, twisting in agony, screaming and yelling—for Lana.

Like lightning, here and gone in a flash, the pain disappeared. Well, almost. He sat up and rubbed his eyes, out of breath. For God's sake, why didn't he call for Maggie?

Chilled from sitting in the wet, sloppy snow, he got up, watching the mist thicken into watery pellets of ice. He made his way back to the car only to find the whole thing glazed over. The sight made him stop in his tracks; made him remember the day he waited so happily for Lana and Hilde to arrive; made him remember another storm that coated the hood of his new Model A with a slick and shiny layer of ice. Poor fool! He had no idea that his hopes, his dreams—his whole world—was about to unravel.

The instant Jacob reached for the door handle, the angry, burning pain returned. This time it wasn't only his rib; it spread up his arm and down to his hip, too. Troubled and afraid, he waited for it to pass, resting his head against the icy door, blessing the cold, waiting and waiting. "Please, help me," he whispered.

Fear ripped through him. Something was terribly wrong. He didn't want to die, not without seeing Maggie again. He took a painful, shallow breath and shut his eyes. Once more he saw Lana's face, her dark hair, her sparkling eyes, her teasing smile.

That's when it came to him.

His heart had a hole in it, too, an empty place, just like Maggie's. Bernie was right, he needed to tell her everything. But what would Maggie say when she found out he'd meant to keep something so important from her?

Then a deeper worry came and filled his heart with greater dread. He realized he'd never in ten years told the whole story to anyone, start to finish. What would it do to him when he did?

Maybe he should reconsider.

The pain crescendoed as it rolled from his rib and down his arm; his fingers throbbed and burned until he plunged them into the snow. "All right," he gasped. "I'll do it. I'll tell her."

Chapter 30

Shelter the Wayward

Karl knew he wasn't supposed to hate anyone, so he preferred to use the word *detest* when he thought of Melvin Straus. Deep down he knew that was wrong, too, but he couldn't help it. He'd been waiting for his sisters in the schoolyard when Melvin got out of his car and hurried through the wind and sleet into the church for his required meeting with Father Cunningham. When their eyes met, Melvin grimaced and spat on the ground like he'd tasted something bitter. Karl clenched his fists and released them. He wondered if he really had to bring his feelings about this into the confessional. Again.

Lizzie and Anna came running out of the school and were disappointed that Mr. Denver hadn't come for them. As the three of them slipped and slid all the way home, Karl listened to them debate whether or not their mother would marry Mr. D.

Anna grinned. "If she does, we'll have a Daddy again."

"No, he'd only be our *step*father," said Lizzie. "I want

a real father."

"Just pretend he's our real father."

Karl envied Anna. Things were so simple to her.

Lizzie pouted. "Our real Daddy knew all our secrets."

"Yes, but Mr. Denver will protect us from monsters and robbers and Uncle Melvin, won't he, Karl?"

"Prob'ly." Karl figured his mother would marry Mr. D sooner or later.

"So do you like him?" Lizzie slipped and grabbed Karl's jacket to keep from going down.

"Hey, watch out, you want us both to fall?"

"Sorry. So *do* you?"

"Yeah, I guess so."

Lizzie squinted up at him. "It feels funny to think of Mama being married to anyone else."

"It's probably going to happen so you better find a way to like him, Liz."

"I *do* like him. He got us away from Uncle Melvin, didn't he?" Lizzie sighed. "I wish we could have our real Daddy back, that's all."

Anna started to skip. "Well, *I* am very, very, very happy." She slipped on the ice, falling on her behind. She giggled. "Whoops!"

"Come on, Annie, you're getting all wet." Karl took her hand and pulled her up. "Anyway, it's not a day to skip and be all happy like that."

"Yeah, it's Holy Thursday and tomorrow is Good Friday," reminded Lizzie, "the saddest day of the whole year."

"When we put Daddy in the ground was the saddest day. Now it's getting happier and happier!" Anna beamed.

Karl decided to let her be happy. She'd find out about

sad tomorrow.

Maggie put Bernie's soup on the stove and sliced the bread she'd brought along with it. It was after five o'clock and Jacob hadn't come back yet, even though his note said he'd return by mid-afternoon. She fretted as she stirred the soup. Either he'd gotten stuck somewhere because of the ice storm, or he'd given up on her and decided to go home. She didn't like either possibility.

She'd been foolish to say those things to him. She knew he loved her, knew he'd do his best for her, but then she went and threw Eddie in his face. How could she have been so stupid?

No, she'd been *honest*, not stupid. If he didn't come back, well, it probably wasn't meant to be. She'd cry herself to sleep tonight and feel sad, but if he couldn't understand about Eddie, then it was for the best. She'd have to think of something to tell the children, though.

Maggie moved the soup and went to look out the window for the hundredth time. The sleet had turned to snow and darkness had fallen, thick and deep. "Jacob, please come back," she whispered. "Please be all right."

The children were working on their special Holy Week projects, all due tomorrow. She called them to wash their hands and come down for supper. She'd look at their projects after they ate; it would put her in the right frame of mind for Good Friday. And keep her mind off Jacob.

Jacob inched his car to a stop in front of 617 Blight Street. Cheery lights shone through the windows at him, a beautiful sight, indeed. He felt like he'd finally come home.

The journey from Tannin River was wretched. No one in his right mind took a car or a truck out in weather like this, but what choice did he have? Even though he could have walked faster than he drove, all of his concentration went into keeping the car on the road. He didn't let himself think about anything but getting to Maggie's in one piece. He didn't have any more spells along the way, although his side never stopped aching.

He gazed at the house, hoping Maggie would be her usual kind and understanding self. "I'm a little late, but here I am." He half walked, half slid around to the back door and paused for a moment before he knocked. He heard the family around the supper table. In a minute, he'd be with them. He wanted to weep with joy.

As he waited on the back porch, a chair scraped on the floor and he heard Maggie say, "No, sit down, I'll get it." He heard her footsteps come down the four steps to the landing. The light above the back door came on. She peered through the window, raising her eyebrows when she saw him. The locks turned and the door swung open.

He grinned at her. "Could you offer shelter to a wayward soul tonight, Ma'am?"

"Jacob, come in here! What happened, where have you been, are you all right?" She threw her arms around him. "I thought maybe you'd gone home."

"I've been trying to get back here all afternoon." Jacob looked over her embrace at the three kids gawking at them from the kitchen door, smiled and winked at them, "but I left my ice skates at home."

Maggie let go of him and backed away. "Look at you, your lips are blue, you're freezing." She turned to the children. "Karl, go get that big heavy sweater for Mr. Denver and Lizzie, you find him a blanket. Annie, get some dishes and set another place at the table."

"Can Mr. Denver sit by me?" Anna clapped her hands and started to jump up and down.

"Yes, just give him enough room."

Lizzie and Karl left and returned almost immediately. "Hi, Mr. Denver." Lizzie smiled at him. "What took you so long?"

"Ice and snow and my own stupidity." He smiled back at her.

As soon as he'd taken off his jacket, Maggie gave him a heavy wool fisherman's sweater. Eddie's, he assumed. He pulled it over his head and followed her up the stairs to the kitchen, rubbing his hands together.

Anna grabbed his sleeve and led him to the table. "Come on, you should eat some soup to get warm."

He put his hand on her head, ruffled her hair and sat down. Fatigue overcame him. He sighed. "I went to look at some trees near Tannin River and stayed too long. The rain started to freeze and it took everything I had to stay out of the ditch. The heater in the car is no good and I wasn't prepared for the cold." He turned to Maggie. "I'm sorry I didn't get back in time to fix your supper."

"Nonsense." She touched his hand. "It feels good to be out of bed and doing something again. Anyway, I slept all afternoon."

Jacob looked at Karl, Lizzie, then Anna, his eyes finally resting on Maggie again. "I can't tell you how beautiful you all look to me." He shivered and rested his chin in his hand. "Lizzie, I'm still cold, do you suppose I could have that blanket?"

She brought it and draped it over his shoulders. "Don't you get sick, too, Mr. Denver."

Hungrily, he ate the hot pea soup Maggie set in front of him. It warmed him from the inside with a good warm, not the burning like he'd felt this afternoon. "Thank you, Maggie."

"Thank Bernie, this is her meal."

"No, I mean thank you for... You're a wonderful family to come home to." His eyes filled with tears.

Aw, come on, Denver, cut it out!

He looked down and rubbed his eyes. "Listen," he said without looking up, "I'm beat. Would anyone mind if I took a little nap? I'll wash the dishes later."

"Nothing of the sort," replied Maggie. "The girls will help me and we'll be finished before you know it. Karl, will you put a fire in the fireplace, please? Come, Jacob, we'll move the davenport closer to the fire so you can stay warm. Nobody will disturb you."

He got up, pulled the blanket tighter and went into the living room. Maggie followed with Karl. The easy chair with the ottoman looked inviting, so he sat down. "I think I'll nap here, if that's all right."

Maggie put his feet on the ottoman. "Are you getting any warmer?"

He nodded.

She leaned over him and touched his face, kissing his cheek. In her hazel eyes he saw the whole earth and a hint of heaven. He took her hand as she began to move it away.

"Wait. Don't let me sleep all night. Wake me when everyone's gone to bed. There's something I have to tell you." He kissed her hand and sank deeply into the chair, deep into sleep.

Sounds of the family's evening routine drifted into

Jacob's consciousness until he was awake enough to listen. From upstairs he heard Maggie's voice congratulating someone for doing *a very nice job;* the harmony of recited prayers; Karl's deepening voice; water running in the bathroom. Jacob rested in the easy chair with his feet on the ottoman, reveling in such ordinary noises. He loved it. No, he loved this family and he wanted to be part of all their routines.

Only, he hoped he wasn't about to ruin his chances.

After what seemed like hours, the woman of his heart came gliding down the stairs, golden and lovely in the firelight.

"I've been waiting for you."

She jumped. "You were supposed to be asleep."

He laughed softly. "I'm sorry; I didn't mean to startle you." He got up and went to her. "Come here." He held her close until a jabbing pain took hold of his rib. He winced and stepped away. The pain got worse and he held his hand right on top of it.

"What is it?"

"Can we sit down?"

"Wait." Maggie pushed one end of the davenport toward the fireplace and then the other.

He came around and sat facing the flames. "I have a lot to tell you, and I'd like to get it over with." The pain eased up.

"It wasn't only the weather today, was it?"

He shook his head.

She sat next to him. "What?"

"I got hurt. I had these spells. I was afraid I wouldn't make it back."

"I *knew* something was wrong." Maggie stood up. "I'm calling Dr. Lyman, he'll come right over."

He reached for her. "Come back here; no one should be out in this weather, not even a doctor. The wind blew the car door into me, that's all."

"Unbutton your shirt and let me look at it."

He did as she asked, revealing a purple bruise on his right side, almost as big as Maggie's hand. "It feels better than before. It only aches now, but before, the pain came so sharp I didn't know what was happening." *Well, yes he did.*

Tenderly, Maggie put her cool hand on the bruise.

"Ohhh..." He leaned back and closed his eyes.

"Let me get you a cool compress." She moved away and got up again.

"No, I need you." He reached for her. "You. You'll make it better."

"But—"

"Please, sit down, will you?"

She touched the bruise and then bent to kiss it. "All better, now?"

Her motherly action only fed his desire to have her with him every moment, every day for the rest of his life. He smiled at her then looked into the fire. "I haven't exactly been honest with you, Maggie. There are some things about me... I thought if I could forget about them, it wouldn't matter." The center of one log burned through, sending both ends crashing into the ashes. "I had no intention of telling you anything, but Bernie made me see different." He felt her eyes on him, but continued to stare into the fireplace.

"Whatever it is," she said quietly, "it doesn't matter."

"Yes it does. I've never told the whole story to anyone except for the little bit I knew that night." Jacob cleared his throat. "And then only to my father."

He took Maggie's hand and held on to it. The room around him spun and stopped in a slightly different place from where it started. He turned sideways so he could face her, but couldn't look her in the eye. He started to stroke the top of her hand with his thumb, looking at it, instead.

"The truth is, I was married before for a short time." He looked up briefly, to see how she'd reacted. She didn't look angry or hurt or even surprised, so he went on, his eyes returning to her hand in his.

"When I was a young man, my mother sent me on a trip to New England. Her family tradition said it should be Europe, but the war made her nervous so I stayed in the states. My father disapproved, but she was more stubborn about it than he was, so I went. I traveled by train, saw all the sights, and after a few weeks, got bored and decided to go home.

"On my way though Pennsylvania, I visited a charming little village at the foot of the Blue Mountains. I stayed in a tourist inn, kept by a German woman and her daughter." He paused to think about what words to use next. "They were wonderful, both of them." He stopped for a minute, swallowed.

"I fell in love with the daughter right away; her name was Lana. So young, with dark eyes. Beautiful." Jacob's own eyes burned. "They didn't have any other family, only the two of them, so they liked having me around." He stopped and chuckled. "They thought I could do all the handy-man repairs that men are supposed to do. I knew about trees and lumber, not pipes and doorknobs, but I learned fast because I wanted to impress Lana's mother. I'd never been so important to anyone except for being Henry Denver's son. I couldn't bear the thought of leaving either one of them."

He sighed and tried to breathe deep, like he told Karl to do, but he couldn't because of the pain. "So I asked Lana to marry me and come to Wisconsin and she said yes, if her mother could come along. Of course, I wanted her to come, too. So we got married in a little chapel up in the hills." He stopped talking for a few seconds. His thumb, still on Maggie's hand, stopped moving.

"A few weeks after the wedding, I came back to Wisconsin to build a house for us. Hilde had to sell the inn before she could move and needed Lana's help. Everything took longer than we'd thought, but six months later they'd sold the inn, and I was nearly finished with the first floor of the house, so I sent them money for the train. They were to come at the end of January." Jacob looked up at Maggie for an instant, then back down. His throat felt dry and tight. He began stroking her hand again with his thumb.

"It's all right, you don't have to hurry."

The mantle clock struck half past nine. Finally he could speak again. "When I went to the train station... their train was late, but when it got in, they weren't on it. I waited for the next train, which came hours later and was the last one for the day but they weren't on that one, either. I didn't sleep all night.

"Early the next morning I went back to the station; sat there all day again. Finally, late in the afternoon, Hilde got off a train that came from Chicago, all by herself. She looked so helpless and confused until she saw me. I knew it was something terrible. *Where's Lana?* I kept asking her, and at first she would only shake her head and say *tott.* Eventually, I understood: Lana was dead." Jacob stopped abruptly, swallowed hard and tried to take a deep breath before he spoke again.

"Oh, no, Jacob. I am so sorry," Maggie whispered.

"Please, no sympathy, I have to finish this." Jacob tightened his grip on her hand, afraid she might run away.

"Lana didn't feel well when they left Pennsylvania, but she got on the train anyway. As the day wore on, she became sicker and sicker. The next morning, Hilde couldn't wake her in the berth they shared. She died in her sleep— of pneumonia. When you got sick, I was afraid, so I came as soon as I could."

Maggie sniffed and reached into her pocket for her handkerchief.

"Hilde got off the train in Chicago to find an undertaker, that's why the extra day." Jacob cleared his throat. "We waited in the freezing wind for them to unload the coffin. Even though Hilde begged me not to look, I opened the coffin; I had to see her one last time." He made a hiccupping noise.

"For months she'd been writing about a surprise. That's when I found out she was expecting. Our baby." He hiccupped again. "I put my hand on her stomach; I don't know what I thought it would feel like, but she froze solid in the box car—hard, like a block of ice. Her face was so puffed up; she didn't look anything like the girl I married. I ran away behind the depot and got so sick I thought I'd never eat again." Jacob hiccupped and shivered, cold from the remembering and from the telling. "Later, Hilde told me that Lana had rheumatic fever when she was little. The pneumonia was too much for her weak heart. It's why she died." He hiccupped again.

Maggie reached for his face.

"No, don't, please." He pulled his head away from her, still not looking her in the eye. "I stayed in my room and stared out the window for two whole weeks before my father got mad and forced me to go back to work. That's when I started acting like nothing happened, and pretty soon I'd convinced myself. I haven't spoken of it till now. By the time I went back to the mill, everyone already knew, so I didn't have to say anything." The pain in Jacob's rib flared then faded away. He finally looked into Maggie's eyes and saw her tears.

"What happened to Hilde?"

"She keeps house for me. She will always have whatever she needs, and when she's too old to work, she will come live with me so I can take care of her. I'll *never* go back on that promise, no matter what."

"That's the way it should be. She's your family."

"I didn't think you needed to know about this. I never even cried for her, but today I found out she's still with me. Like you and—" He stood up abruptly and started for the kitchen. "I need water."

"Sit down, I'll get it for you."

"No." The lid was off the jar of sorrow he'd hidden in his heart and he had to do something to keep the mess from spilling out.

He ran the faucet for a long time, leaning, resting his forearms on the edge of the sink, splashing his face with water. He'd told her, but dammit, he didn't feel any better for it; no, he felt worse.

He straightened up when he felt Maggie's hand on his back. He turned to her, water dripping from his face onto his open shirt. He knew he was in shambles.

"Look at me, Margaret, I'm a liar wearing someone else's clothes. I thought it would all be better if I told you, that you would forgive me and everything would be fine, but now there's all this—this—*emotion*." The words tasted like sour milk. "I'm about to explode with it. I'm sorry;

I'm not the man you think I am."

"Shush, now. The only person you've hurt is yourself." She pulled a clean dishtowel from a drawer and gently dried his face with it.

If he'd been able to keep his anguish contained before, Maggie's tenderness cracked and shattered the jar where it had been moldering away all those years. The long denied tears and cries rattled his lumberjack body and the mess poured out all over. Maggie's arms surrounded him, kept him from drowning in it.

"You've kept this shut up for too long, my dearest. Don't you know you've poisoned yourself?"

No, he didn't, but he knew she was right.

She held him until the spasms of grief finally let up, then made him sit down at the kitchen table. He felt like a child, but it was a good feeling. His side no longer hurt, not even a little.

Maggie put the kettle on, found him a real handkerchief and stood behind him massaging his shoulders until the water boiled. After she brewed and poured the tea, she sat around the corner from him, so close that her knees touched his thigh. He liked that. No words were spoken, none were needed. Sipping from his steaming cup, Jacob wondered how he could be the recipient of such sweet love.

Chapter 31
Set Me as a Seal Upon Your Heart

Karl finished his essay and pulled out the note from Sister Anne, thinking he'd read the Bible passages again, but the disturbing sounds coming from the kitchen kept him from concentrating. Someone was crying, but it didn't sound like his mother. The longer the noises went on, the more they troubled him. He stood up as quietly as possible and made his way down the hall. He'd be punished if he got caught, but what if something was *really* wrong and his mother needed his help?

He inched his way past her room and down the stairs. At the bottom of the steps, he heard her murmuring, just like she did when he cried the night before Daddy died. Carefully, he crossed to the far edge of the dining room and craned his neck to see. She stood at the kitchen sink with a white dishtowel in her hand, all close and hugging Mr. Denver. Good grief, it was him—*he* was crying! Karl spun on his heel to get back upstairs, his heart pounding in his ears. He didn't dare get caught spying on this.

He'd always felt uncomfortable, even scared, when he saw his mother cry. Seeing Mr. D bawling like that shocked and embarrassed him even more. He felt like he did that morning he accidentally walked in on his parents, still in bed, kissing, breathing hard; they never even knew he'd opened the door.

When he got to the top of the stairs, Karl turned into his mother's room. She'd left the bedside lamp on and he looked for the one photograph they had of his father, their wedding picture. He wanted to remember his father's face, the cut of his chin, the shape of his nose, but the picture was gone, just like the real flesh and blood Eddie Stern was gone. The familiar tightness in his throat set in. Did his mother put the picture away so she'd forget about him?

In his own room, he turned off the light and sat at his desk, leaning on his elbows, his forehead in his hands. Soon the crying stopped and he could hear his mother moving around in the kitchen. He dozed until he heard their hushed voices in the living room. He thought she would come up to bed any minute—she'd been too sick to stay up so late—but she and Mr. D kept talking. His desire to know overcame his fear of getting caught. Again, he crept to the top of the stairs to listen.

A fire in the fireplace was too nice a thing to waste, even though it had died down some. Jacob stirred the coals and added a couple more logs, then came and sat on the davenport close to Maggie, his arm around her shoulders. Light from the fire bounced off the walls, the furniture, and their faces; the darkened edges of the room cocooning them in a world of their own. Although he was worn out from all those painful memories coming back to him, he couldn't tear himself away from her. If there was any comfort for him in this world, it came from her.

She looked weary, too. She'd been up and about doing things for too long; he shouldn't have left her alone all day. Neither of them spoke for a long while, *the question* hanging between them like an unopened present.

Jacob stared into the fire. "Maggie, I am a man of many faults, but I love you more than I can say. And after tonight, I know I need you, too, like I need air and water and the woods." He turned to her. "I never thought I needed anyone before you. You're like... like life itself to me."

She took his free hand and touched it to her cheek; kissed it and held it close.

"I've done some thinking, like you wanted me to, and I know I can share your heart with Eddie. You say there's room for both of us, and the way you're so good to me, I have no doubts. I will honor him as long as I live, because without him I wouldn't have you." He winced. "No, I didn't mean... That sounded terrible, like I'm glad he died."

Maggie smiled. "Don't worry, I understand."

He nodded. "Do you think you can love someone who meant to deceive you? Can you forgive me?"

"Of course I can love you. I *do* love you."

"But can you forgive me?"

"There's nothing to forgive. You *told* me what happened. You need to forgive yourself."

"No, I need it from *you*. Please? It has to be from you."

"Then I forgive you."

"Thank you," he whispered. They were both still and quiet for a few seconds. "Do you think we could make a good life together?"

"It *is* a good life, Jacob, and we'll keep making it good. I will love your Hilde, and I hope you'll come to love my children—"

"I already do."

"And we'll be patient with each other, and we'll keep forgiving each other, and we won't keep secrets or tell lies, and we'll keep trying to understand each other. And we'll love each other, always. Yes, we *will* make a good life together." She smiled at him and when she did, the sun and moon and stars shone like jewels in the sky, all at once.

"Then you'll marry me?"

"Yes, I will."

Except for the crackling fire and the ticking clock, silence blanketed the room. The moment was plain, simple, ordinary. No trumpet blasts or violins or crowds of people shouting *hurrah for Jacob!*

Just to be sure, he asked again. "Will you marry me, Margaret? Soon?"

Maggie laughed softly. "Yes. As soon as school's out."

"And will you come to Wakelin and fill up my big empty house with your family?"

"They'll be your family, too." Despite the fire, she shivered. "And you'll keep me warm?"

He chuckled as he pulled her closer. "Of course." She sighed and he felt her relax in his arms. Her breathing became deep and rhythmic.

"Maggie?"

"Hmm?"

"Don't fall asleep." He still had the ring in his pocket.

She stirred and pulled away. "I'm sorry, Jacob. I wish I could stay here all night, but I need to go to bed."

He'd give it to her tomorrow. "One more minute?

There's something I've wanted to do from the first moment I laid eyes on you."

"Jacob!"

He laughed. "No, no, just this." He pulled the combs from her hair and ran his big hands through it until it fell around her shoulders and framed her face with pinkish gold in the firelight. "Ohhh..." He kissed her once, deep, long and slow, then a second time. When she pulled away, they were both breathless. Despite his exhaustion, every inch of his body was alert, infused with desire.

Smiling, Maggie got up and stood over him. "I love having you love me, Jacob Denver." She bent to kiss him again. "Good night, my dear. Sleep happy."

He watched her ascend the stairs like an angel. A few moments later, all wrapped up in his bedroll, Jacob Denver gave in to sleep and slept happy all night long.

When he heard his mother come up the stairs, Karl rolled onto his side, turning his back to the door. He knew she would come and look in on him; she never went to bed without making sure he and his sisters were safe in their beds, covered and sound asleep. Sure enough, his door opened and he felt her hands pulling his quilt over his shoulders. She kissed him on the cheek and whispered, "Good night, my darling boy."

Oh, brother.

As soon as she left, he sat up, hugging his knees to his chest. He'd heard enough to know she was going to marry Mr. D, and they'd be moving to Wakelin. He couldn't stomach any more. Even though he pretty much knew Mr. D was going to ask his mother to marry him, and that she'd probably say yes, it didn't occur to him that they'd leave Tomos Bay.

Well, of course they would, Mr. D's sawmill was in Wakelin, it only made sense. But it scared him. If they moved away from this house and Lake Superior and Will and the boat and the cemetery, how would they ever be able to remember his father?

Karl lay on his back and stared at the ceiling. He didn't need the light to know how dirty and smudgy it was. Mr. Denver's house had to be in better shape than this old dump.

No, but this was home; he and his sisters were born here and Daddy lived here, too. And died here, down in the living room where Mr. D slept, between the davenport and the fireplace.

If they went to live with Mr. D, Karl thought for sure everyone would forget about Eddie Stern. Maybe even *he* would forget, God forbid. Sadness overcame him. He wished he could talk to his father, his real father.

He drifted into a fitful sleep, waking when he heard the mantle clock strike one, then two, then three. After that, he couldn't sleep anymore. He felt like a rubber band stretched too far, pull him any tighter and he'd snap. He tried to close his eyes and relax, but his heart raced every time he did, and it would take forever to calm it down again. He had to talk to his father.

When the clock struck three-thirty, Karl got out of bed and put his clothes on. He left his mother a note: *Dear Mama, Don't worry. I couldn't sleep and went out for a walk. Be back in time for chores and breakfast, I promise. Love, Karl.* He left it on top of his essay, which she wanted to read, anyway.

Forgetting to turn off the lamp, he tiptoed down the stairs in his stocking feet. Mr. D didn't even twitch when he went by. Soundlessly, Karl pulled on his boots, coat, hat and gloves and let himself out the back door.

Big wet snowflakes fell around him, adding to the three or four inches that already covered yesterday's ice. All the houses in his neighborhood were still dark and there were no cars or trucks on the streets, not even the snowplow. It felt sad to see the town like this, abandoned, like nobody was alive except for him.

And here he was, Karl Edward Stern, kicking along in the wet, clumpy snow, going to pay a call on his dead father in the dark of night. Going to the cemetery—alone. He laughed at himself. Once he would have been terrified to do such a thing, but not anymore. No ghost or bogeyman was going to jump out of the shadows and get him; he'd be as safe as when he used to cling to his father's sleeve or his sea-worn hand. Even so, he was glad to discover that someone left the yard light on at the rectory.

His eyes scanned the cemetery as if it were a new frontier. It was blanketed with the falling and melting of a whole winter's worth of snow, the latest accumulation undisturbed and perfect. Some of the headstones were topped with pointy snow caps which, in the dark, might be mistaken for witches' hats, but he knew better. The falling snow softened the hardness of the place, making it park-like and friendly.

Karl shuddered when he remembered how greedy his father's grave was, how it wanted to devour Will Denver right along with Eddie Stern. If it hadn't been for his mother, he might have offered himself in return for Will. He stopped and shook his head. Ridiculous, thinking of a hole in the ground as a monster to be bargained with. It was nothing but a soggy sink hole, for pity's sake.

Finally, along the eastern border of the cemetery,

Karl found his father's grave. *Edward Stern 1895 –1928.*
He pushed the snow away from the gravestone, squatted down, pulled off his glove and traced the letters and
numbers with his bare finger. He thought it should say
something more, that Edward Stern was a good man, a
good father, *the best.* That should be carved into stone,
too, so everyone who passed by would know, forever and
ever.

"Daddy," he whispered. "I wish you could come back."
At that moment, Karl wanted his father more than anything in the whole world. His throat got thick. "It sounds
like we're moving away from here and I'm afraid we'll forget you. I know Mama still loves you but now she's..." He
swallowed. "I still love you, too, but I like him, and I..."
He couldn't stop the tears that came, and for once, didn't
want to.

He leaned against the stone, buried his face in his
elbow and gave it up. No sense shoving this into his
cave anymore, if Mr. D could cry, so could he. The
wet snow seemed to muffle his baby-like wails, so he
felt safe; nobody was going to come around and say
"Everything's all right, Karl," or "Grow up and take it
like a man, Karl."

When he looked up again, the snow had stopped and
the eastern sky brightened with the new day. A light shone
from the rectory window. He'd better get on home before
someone caught him here. He wiped his nose and stood
up. "Don't let us forget you, Daddy, please. Never let us
forget." That vain wanting rose up again and made him
feel so terribly empty. He sighed. Oh, well, it *was* Good
Friday, the perfect day to be miserable.

Then, as he lifted his arm to wipe off his face, Karl
sensed someone nearby. Like the day of the Lord coming

as a thief in the night, his knees were whacked hard from behind and then buckled, sending him headlong into his father's gravestone. The pain blinded him and everything went black, the dead of night.

Chapter 32

Melvin's Idea

Maggie awoke to the smell of frying bacon and smiled, remembering the feel of Jacob's hands in her hair, the taste of his kisses. For a moment she felt like she did on her birthday when she was a girl, knowing that there were surprises and presents waiting for her at the breakfast table, except that now Jacob was the surprise and the present. He'd gotten up early to make breakfast again, something she should be doing.

Then she remembered: it was Good Friday. Karl should have told him not to fix bacon; they weren't supposed to eat meat today. She opened her eyes and looked at the clock. Six-thirty. He must have overslept.

Maggie threw the covers back and padded barefoot across the hall to his room. A line of light shone out from under the door. She knocked once, waited, and went in. His bed was empty and unmade; his school clothes still hung from the peg on the wall. She checked the bathroom; no Karl there, either. When she went back to turn off the lamp, she found his note with a pencil sitting on top. *Don't worry, Mama. I couldn't sleep and went out for a walk. Be back in time for chores and breakfast, I promise.* The pencil sat under the words *Love, Karl* as if to underline them. She noticed his Holy Week essay underneath the note, written out in his neatest handwriting, all ready to be turned in. At least he'd finished his homework.

In the mysterious way love sharpens a mother's intuition, Maggie sensed that something was very wrong. Without thinking or allowing herself to imagine what the trouble might be, she turned off the lamp, closed his door and hurried to the bathroom to wash and get dressed. As she twisted her hair and fastened it back, she pulled herself in, steeled herself against whatever this day would bring. "Oh, don't go borrowing trouble," she said out loud. She took deep breath, plastered a smile on her face, woke Lizzie and Anna, and went to find Jacob.

He stood at the stove with a fork in his hand, turning the bacon.

Maggie smiled and kissed his cheek. "Good morning, Jacob." Before he could answer or kiss her back, she added, "Where's Karl? Did he bring the wood in for you? Did he feed the furnace?"

"No, Ma'am, *I* did it all." Jacob grinned and reached for her, still holding the fork. "I let him sleep. I hoped you'd come down first so I could do this." He kissed her lips.

Maggie pulled away, eyes scanning the dining room and living room. "You haven't seen him?"

"No."

"He's not in the basement?"

"No"

"Then he's gone." Her voice went flat.

"What?"

"He's not in his room." She went to the back door and

looked out the window.

"I didn't hear him go out."

"I didn't either."

Jacob handed the fork to Maggie. "I'll go look for him."

She put her hand against Jacob's chest. "No, eat your breakfast first. Maybe he'll come while we're eating."

Lizzie and Anna scrambled down the stairs. Anna came into the kitchen, but Lizzie stopped at the door with her hands on her hips. "Don't you know it's Good Friday, Mr. Denver? We aren't allowed to eat meat on Good Friday."

"Oh. I didn't realize that. I'm sorry."

"Elizabeth, that's no way to talk to your—your elders. Whatever happened to *good morning?*" Maggie didn't intend to sound so harsh.

Lizzie lowered her eyes. "Sorry, Mama."

"Apologize to Mr. Denver, not to me."

"I'm sorry, Mr. Denver."

"That's all right, I can put it in the icebox; maybe we can warm it up tomorrow."

"Well, I'd like some, if you don't mind, it smells wonderful," said Maggie. "You should have some, too, Jacob."

"But Mama, it's a sin to eat that. God will punish us!" Chastised, Lizzie's brow wrinkled with fear. "We have to be good today."

"It's more of a sin to insult this nice man who cooked your breakfast. You may eat the bacon or not, but you'd better sit down and eat your oatmeal. You don't want to be late for school, today of all days."

Anna sat down at her place. "Where's Karl?"

Maggie scooped oatmeal into Lizzie's bowl. "He's not here. I'm sure he'll be back soon."

Anna gasped, her eyes wide. "He'll get the ruler if he's

late for school!"

Maggie looked at her youngest, the one with curly white-blonde hair—just like Karl's—the one who adored her older brother. "Don't worry; he'll be back."

No one spoke during breakfast. Maggie ate her bacon, but nearly gagged on the oatmeal. The salty, burned crunch of the bacon seemed more fitting to the day than the sweetness of the cereal. Fear rose up from the back of her throat and she had to keep swallowing it back. After she sent the girls to brush their teeth, she turned to Jacob.

"You've done so much already, and I know you need to get home, but could you stay?" She stopped abruptly. No crying, she thought. Today I have to be strong.

Jacob put his hand on her arm. "After I take the girls to school I'll drive around and look for him, if you can tell me where to go."

She shivered. "The water. The marina. I'll call the school. And Bernie. And Mother, although I can't imagine why he'd go there."

"Don't worry; I'm sure there's a perfectly good explanation for this." Jacob moved his hand to her shoulder and started to lean close, but Maggie stood up.

"Please, don't baby me. I have to be strong today. He's in bad trouble, I know it. We have to find him."

Jacob stood up, too. "That's right, Maggie: *we* have to find him. *We* have to be strong. You're not alone anymore, remember?"

His earnestness touched Maggie beyond words. Her heart swelled with love for this man. She touched her finger to his lips and tried to smile. "Thank you, Jacob." She turned and started to clear the table, then went back and kissed him quickly, before the girls returned. "And thank you for the bacon, it was perfect."

After the shock of his father's gravestone smacking him in the head, Karl awoke to a disgusting smell and the rough chugging of an engine. His arms and legs were cramped into some kind of a box; at first he thought it might be a coffin, but no, they laid a person out in a coffin. His head ached like anything, then a painful spasm told him what the smell was as he puked all over himself.

The engine idled and died while the driver got out and unfastened buckles above Karl's head. A lid came off and he could feel cold air on his face.

"Holy shit, boy, you stink!"

As soon as Karl heard Melvin's voice, he knew he'd been crammed into that big old steamer trunk he kept lashed to the back of his Model T.

"What's wrong with you, pukin' all over my mama's nice trunk? It's an antique and here you go and spoil it. Shame on you. Now get your filthy stink outta there."

Karl tried, but he couldn't move. Melvin's hands grabbed the back collar of his coat and yanked him up, and held him, one hand at the collar and the other on his belt. With some difficulty, he pulled him out of the trunk and dropped him onto the ground.

Karl saw an explosion of color behind his eyelids when he landed.

"Get back, get over there, boy; over to the wall."

Karl realized his hands and feet were bound together. "I—I can't."

"Then I'll do it for you." Melvin grabbed him by the

hair and dragged him.

"Owwww!" Karl's back hit the wall. He toppled sideways and threw up again.

"Jesus, Mary and Joseph, now you're gonna stink up my garage, too." Disgusted, he kicked Karl's behind. "We've got a few rules here and the first one is: *shut up.* Shut up, do you hear me? Any more noise comin' from your mouth and I'll tie it shut so you can drown in your own mess."

Karl looked up and started to shiver. "Why are you doing this to me? Why do you hate us so much, Uncle Melvin?"

Melvin kicked Karl's butt again. "You're a Stern, aren't you?"

Melvin left. Karl heard him run up the back steps and open the door. "Kathleen, honey, I've got an idea." A few moments later, he came back, started the engine, and drove the car out of the garage. Karl heard him talk to Aunt Kathleen in a nice way before he pulled the garage door shut with a bang. He locked it from the outside, leaving Karl as alone as he'd ever been.

After Maggie called Sister Mary Anthony and Bernie, she filled the sink and washed the breakfast dishes. "Why are you doing this to me, Karl? And *you,* if you'd been more careful, Eddie Stern, you'd still be here and this wouldn't be happening!" She stopped and stood still. No, she couldn't say things like that anymore. Eddie died; that was part of her life now. It was time to stop being mad at him and let him go. If he was still here, Jacob wouldn't be and she wouldn't be getting ready to be his wife, and she wouldn't be saying *I love you* to this wonderful, sweet man, and he wouldn't love her and—

"Jacob," she whispered.

As she turned to wipe off the table, Maggie's stomach twisted inside of her. Karl must have heard them last night; he heard Jacob ask her to marry him and he heard her answer. He couldn't sleep and had to get away from both of them. Stricken, she sat down in his chair and covered her face with her hands. "That was none of your business, Karl!"

Melvin and Kathleen came by a short time later. "Margaret," said Melvin, "we need to talk, may we please come in?"

Maggie opened the door, cautiously.

Kathleen stepped in and hugged her. "Sit down, Maggie; we have something to tell you."

"No, I'm fine. What's going on?"

Melvin plopped himself into the easy chair. "Where's Karl? Do you know, dear?"

"He's not here. Why do you need to know?" Maggie hated it when Melvin called her *dear*.

"Melvin saw him early this morning," said Kathleen. "He was walking the train tracks."

"About five o'clock," continued Melvin, "headed toward Ashland."

"Ashland?" Maggie felt the floor move underneath her. Karl wouldn't do such a thing.

"I should have stopped him, but I had an early appointment with Father Cunningham and I couldn't be late. When I went back to find the boy, he was already gone."

"Where's Mr. Denver?" Kathleen put her arm around Maggie's shoulders.

"He's out looking for Karl." Maggie pulled away. She made her way to the door and opened it. "Thank you for the news. As soon as Jacob comes back, I'll tell him."

Melvin stood. "I have important meetings all morning at the bank, and I'm taking Kathleen and your mother to church at noon. If he's still missing, I'll come by later and help with the search." His voice was syrupy, too sweet.

"Never mind, Melvin. I'm sure Jacob and his brother will find him." Melvin was the last person she'd want to find Karl.

"Melvin is taking me to Mother's for the day so I can help her get ready for Easter dinner. She isn't very well yet." Kathleen looked at her husband and smiled slightly. "It was his idea." She turned back to Maggie. "Call us if you find Karl, all right, Magpie?"

Maggie nodded and opened the door. Melvin leaned down and kissed her cheek. "There, there, Margaret, I'm sure we'll get him back for you."

After they left, Maggie went upstairs and washed her face. Somehow, Melvin was behind this.

After making Karl's bed and her own, Maggie sat on the davenport, hands folded in her lap, trying to think of something she'd offer to God in place of Karl's life, but she remembered the time Father Cunningham said trying to bargain with God was the same as tempting him, so she gave up. She already felt tired and wanted to rest, but doing nothing made her chest feel tight and heavy.

From out of nowhere, she smelled the aroma of baking bread. She got up and quickly measured out flour and yeast and salt and mixed together a double recipe of bread dough. She set the bowl next to the stove and went out to the back porch for firewood. As she went out for her second armload, Jacob walked around from the front. Her heart beat a little faster. "Anything?"

He shook his head. "I went to the marina, but didn't see any sign of him. Then I stopped to see Bernie. He hasn't been there, either. Will gets off work at noon and she promised to send him over to help." Jacob frowned. "Here, let me do that." He took the logs from Maggie's arms, but she stooped over and picked up two more. "What are you doing? The wood from breakfast isn't gone already, is it?"

"I'm baking bread."

"You go on in the house now; you're not even wearing a coat."

Maggie went in and put her two logs in the stove. "Melvin and Kathleen were here. Melvin says he saw Karl walking on the railroad tracks to Ashland."

"When?"

"About five o'clock this morning. Melvin was on his way to the church to see Father Cunningham and couldn't stop. He's lying. I think he has Karl. And he told Kathleen she could spend the day with Mother; that's not like him. I *know* he has Karl." Maggie pulled out another mixing bowl and started to make dough for ginger cookies. It felt good to attack the butter and smear it into the grainy sugar.

"Maggie, will you please stop for a minute?"

"I can't." But she did stop. "I think I know what happened." She looked up at Jacob, then stared at the sweet mess in the bowl, trying not to cry. "He has this bad habit of sitting on the steps, listening to adult conversations. I've punished him, scolded him, but he still does it."

"You think he heard us last night?"

She nodded. "I'm sorry, Jacob. I think he might have

gone to the cemetery to visit Eddie. To his grave. He's been talking about doing that. Maybe Melvin found him there and took him."

"Does Straus have to work today?"

"Just this morning. Then he's taking Kathleen and Mother to church. He said he'd go out looking for Karl later this afternoon." She broke two eggs into the bowl and offered no mercy as she beat them into the butter and sugar. "I told them you and Will would find Karl."

Jacob finished stacking the wood in a neat pile by the stove. "Call your mother's house and talk to Kathleen. If Melvin's at work, maybe she'd let us into the house while he's not there. Call her now; tell her I'll come get her."

Maggie set down the spoon and went to the phone.

Kathleen refused her request. "How can you blame Melvin for Karl running away? He's the one who saw him, and we came right over to tell you about it. He even offered to help look. You have no reason to accuse him except for not liking him. Besides, you know he doesn't allow me to carry a key."

"You're an adult, Kathleen; you should have a key to your own home." Maggie's temper flared. "Why did he want you to be at Mother's today? Isn't it possible he wanted you out of the house?"

Kathleen's voice softened. "Please, Maggie, don't ask me to do this. He's been nice to me all week. I don't want to spoil it by turning against him."

Maggie hung up, fighting back tears. "She said she can't help us."

Jacob put his hat back on. "I'm going to the cemetery, and I'll ask around at the train station. If he really ran away—"

"He *didn't* run away."

"Well, if he *did*, someone other than Melvin Straus must have seen him."

Maggie wiped her hands on the same towel she'd used on Jacob's his tears last night. "I'm coming with you."

Jacob put his hands on her shoulders. "No, you're not. You just filled the stove with wood and you've got bread to watch and cookies to get in the oven. Besides, you should be here in case he comes home."

"I can't just sit here!"

"You're not, you're busy. I'll be back as soon as I know anything, or I'll call. Settle down, will you? You'll make yourself sick again."

"No, I won't, I'm fine."

Jacob came back and held her for a moment. "Call the police. Tell them what we suspect. Ask them to look for Karl at Melvin's." He kissed her cheek in nearly the same spot Melvin did. "We'll find him, don't worry."

Maggie watched him drive away, her hand on her cheek, as if the kiss might run away, too. She took a deep breath, picked up the telephone and asked for the police station.

Chapter 33

Via Dolorosa

The garage door banged open and Karl struggled to sit up. Backlit by the bright sunshine, Melvin's silhouette made him look like a giant. Karl squinted so he could see him. Melvin chuckled as he came in, holding his hunting knife in his right hand. "You look like a rodent, with those beady little eyes of yours. I should get out my rat poison, that'd take care of you." He bent over and reached for Karl's hands, sawing through the ropes that bound him. He grabbed Karl's face with his right hand and squeezed his cheeks so hard Karl thought he felt his skin tearing.

"Now, you listen to me, boy. I've got a job for you and you'd better do it right, or else"—he held the knife to Karl's throat—"someone could get hurt."

The odor of cigars on Melvin's breath made Karl want to throw up again. He let go of Karl's face and slid the knife into the leather sheath he wore on his belt, then handed Karl a pencil and paper.

"Write what I say. *Dear Mother.*"

"I can't. I need something hard to write on."

Melvin threw a scrap of wood at him. It hit him on the

forearm, sudden pain smarting all the way to his fingertips. Karl rubbed his arm.

"Write."

Karl took the pencil and wrote. *Dear Mama.*

"I said Mother, dear *Mother,* but leave it." Melvin paced
the garage floor, bouncing his fingertips together. "*Now
that you are well and have*—what do you call him?"

"Who?"

"Your mother's boyfriend."

"Mr. Denver."

"Write this: *Now that you are well and have Mr. Denver, you
won't want me around anymore.*"

Karl hesitated.

"Write!"

Karl knew it wasn't true, but the possibility hurt terribly. "That's not true, Uncle Melvin."

"I'll cut you if you don't write it. Do it." He reached
for the knife, keeping his hand on the hilt.

Karl wrote.

"Let's see... *Everything is different since Father died. I'm old
enough to make my own way now. By the time you read this, I'll be
long gone.*"

Karl wrote exactly what Melvin said. He wouldn't have
written *Father,* he would have written *Daddy.* Maybe his
mother would realize these weren't his words.

"*I'm sorry if I hurt you. Your son, Karl.*"

Karl wrote the words. He'd never sign a letter to her like
that; he'd say "*Love, Karl.*" He hoped she would notice.

He began to shake. "What are you going to do to
me?"

"Oh, we're going to have some fun today." Melvin
laughed. "*Lots* of fun." He snatched the paper away, folded it and put it in his breast pocket. "I need a drink, and

I'm such a nice uncle that I'm gonna share with you."

Melvin reached behind the stack of firewood in the back of the garage and produced a bottle filled with brown liquid. He pulled the cork, sipped, then took a couple of slugs before he gave it to Karl. "You must be thirsty. Here you go, drink up."

Karl took a sip. It burned his throat and his insides, so he handed the bottle back to Melvin.

"Shame on you, boy. Don't you like my hospitality?"

"It's whiskey. I don't like it. It's illegal, you know."

Laughing, Melvin took hold of Karl's hair and pulled his head back.

Karl thought if he got out of this alive, he'd ask Mr. D to take him to a barber for a real haircut—a real *short* haircut.

Melvin forced his mouth open and poured the fiery liquor in. Karl spit it out at him.

"Why, you little son of a bitch! You think I'm gonna let good whiskey go to waste?" Melvin came after him again, pulled his hair, shoved the bottle into his mouth, and tilted it till the whiskey ran in. He pushed Karl's chin upward and held it. "Swallow it!"

Karl choked and swallowed.

Melvin held out the bottle, laughing. "Take it, take it."

Karl took the bottle and started to pour it out.

Melvin snatched it then hit Karl's jaw with his fist. "Oh, dear, so sorry; that was an accident." He put the bottle on the hood of the car.

The garage spun in circles and darkness spotted Karl's vision. He began to fall, but Melvin grabbed his hair again and jerked his head back. "Look at those blue lips." He pushed Karl away and grabbed his knife.

Karl's heart raced. *Here it comes*, he thought. He

squeezed his eyes shut and bent to shield his chest with his arms.

But Melvin went after the rope around his feet. "Never let it be said that Melvin Straus doesn't care about little children."

Karl opened his eyes.

"I'm taking you in the house, but you can't wear those filthy rags in there, you smell like a sewer rat. Take off your clothes. All of them."

"But it's freezing out here." His lips and tongue felt thick.

Melvin laughed. "You sound like a drunk, Karl Stern."

"I'm cold."

"I'll find you something to wear, don't worry. You're right, you're freezing, I can't leave you out here. Take everything off."

Karl pulled off his coat. It *was* pretty disgusting. "It's only on my coat."

"Look down."

His pants were a mess, too. Karl tried to unbuckle his belt, but his hands were so cold he couldn't manage. He wondered what happened to his gloves.

"Here, let old Uncle Melvin help poor widdle Karly-boy." Melvin put the knife in the sheath and used both hands to feel around Karl's crotch. He laughed. "Now where *is* that buckle?"

"Cut it out!" Karl tried to kick Melvin's belly, but missed.

Melvin backhanded him across the face, throwing him onto the gravel. "Rule number one, Stern: *shut up!*" He smiled and groped Karl again. "Oh, my, you're quite the man, now, aren't you?" He undid the buckle and ripped Karl's pants open, sending buttons flying. "There. Now take 'em off."

Shaking with fury, Karl fumbled to untie his boots. Melvin pulled out the knife again, sliced through the laces and pulled them off Karl's feet.

"Proceed."

Karl took off his pants and put them with his coat.

"I said everything."

"But there's nothing on my under shorts, and there's nothing on my shirt."

Melvin pulled out the knife again and with no pressure at all, drew the tip along Karl's outer thigh. As a thin line of blood appeared, he leaned close to Karl's face and whispered, "Ev-ry-thing."

Melvin's hot breath on his face made Karl feel sick again. Without another word, he obeyed, then cowered on the gravel floor like an animal. Painfully, he moved as far away from Melvin as he could.

Melvin followed, bottle in hand. He held the knife to the soft tissue between two of Karl's ribs. "Now you're gonna drink up till I tell you to stop."

"I don't want anymore."

Melvin made a clean slice in Karl's flesh, about as long as his thumb. "Do it. I wanna get Eddie Stern's boy loaded, just like his Grandpa did to me."

Karl tried to move away.

Melvin made the slice longer. "Drink it, damn you, or I'll tell the whole world your mother's a whore with that Denver fellow sleeping over."

"No!"

Melvin knocked him back and held him down with his knee, squeezed his mouth open and poured the rest of the whiskey in. Karl refused to swallow and held it in his mouth. He'd never tasted anything so vile. His eyes began to water.

"I've got all day, Karl. I can stay on top of you as long as I have to."

Karl did nothing.

"Swallow the damn whiskey!" Melvin pushed harder on Karl's chest.

Involuntarily, Karl inhaled. Some of the whiskey got sucked into his windpipe; the rest went snaking down to his stomach, burning all the way. When Melvin released him, Karl rolled onto his side, coughing and choking. His guts felt like they were on fire.

Melvin laughed and backed away. "That should keep you warm for a while." He tossed the bottle behind the wood pile, then wadded up all of Karl's clothes, taking his boots, too.

"Where're you going with my clothes?"

"To burn 'em. They're all ruined, Karl, you know that."

"Not my father's boots."

"Oh, *especially* the boots."

Karl's feet had finally grown enough that they fit. "Not my boots!"

"What did I tell you? *Shut up!*"

Melvin left, slamming the garage door with another bang.

Clothes or no clothes, Karl knew he had to get out of there, but when he tried to stand, his pounding head made the garage spin around him like a sickening merry-go-round. He noticed a place along the bottom of the sliding door where the ground dipped, leaving a gap that might be big enough for him to slide through. He lay down on his belly and stuck his head and shoulders out into the snow. He shivered for a moment then didn't feel the cold anymore. Pushing with his feet and pulling with his hands and forearms, he got out as far as his buttocks, but all the moving around made his head feel worse than ever. The whole world tilted to a funny angle and wouldn't straighten itself out no matter what he did. He could smell the roasting and burning of his father's work boots in Melvin's fire. All the sadness and longing of the past six months condensed into that one moment, into one nearly lethal drop of sorrow.

"Daddy," he whispered, "come and get me." If he gave up, he could be with his father forever and it would be Melvin's fault he died, not his.

When he tried to move again, the whiskey came up, making his arms and legs weak and tired and unable to move another inch. Everything he'd done today was a bad idea—*ev-ry-thing*. He put his head down in some clean snow, tried to cross himself, tucked his arms underneath him, said his bedtime prayers, and closed his eyes.

Karl woke up when Melvin grabbed his feet and dragged him back through the gap and into the garage. Icy snow crystals and gravel scraped his stomach, thighs and private parts. Melvin propped him against the wall and slapped his face until he opened his eyes. He held out a woman's nightgown with little pink rosebuds on it and told him to put it on and get into the house. A seam ripped in the sleeve when Karl pulled it over his head.

Amused, Melvin laughed and slapped his butt. "Hey, there, Beau-tee-ful."

Like a table with one leg too short, Karl wobbled to his feet. He stopped and steadied himself against the side of the door.

"Keep moving, you idiot."

Karl reeled and crawled up the steps to the back porch.

Opening the door, he felt the warmth of the kitchen on his face before he collapsed into darkness.

After Maggie called the police, two officers came to the door. She expected concern, but they asked question after question about Karl: what kind of student was he, did he have any friends who were also truant from school, was there any money missing from her pocketbook, had he ever been in trouble with the law before?

"It sounds like you're more interested in catching a juvenile delinquent than in finding my boy. He's in trouble somewhere, maybe hurt—or worse—and you're looking for a way to blame him."

"Sorry, Mrs. Stern, but we need the whole picture."

"Here's the whole picture: He's a good boy; he's taken on a lot of responsibility since his father died. He looks out for his sisters. He did all his homework last night. Would a boy who's planning to play hooky do all his assignments the night before? I'm sure Melvin Straus has him. He hates Karl; why can't you go over there and get him? "

"Mr. Straus is your sister's husband, isn't he? This sounds like a family feud, Mrs. Stern, and we don't like to get involved unless absolutely necessary. Besides, Mr. Straus has done so much for this town; I doubt he'd do anything to hurt a kid."

Maggie opened her mouth to say *you have no idea what he would do* when the second officer cut her off.

"Don't worry, Ma'am. Your son is probably hiding somewhere until school is out for the day. Boys do it all the time." He tipped his hat and they were both out the door.

"Not Karl!" Fuming, Maggie slammed the door behind them and went to punch down her bread dough.

The new snow made it easy for Jacob to find Eddie Stern's grave. Footprints—*Karl's?*—led to and from the gravesite and the snow around the stone was trampled. Jacob stood silently before the man's grave. He thought he should say something, then noticed Karl's glove, mashed and frozen against the bottom of the stone. His heart pounded.

As he bent to pick it up, a groundskeeper came from behind, startling him and telling him he'd have to come inside and talk to Father Cunningham. Reluctantly, Jacob followed. Twenty minutes later, he sat bouncing his knee, waiting for the priest to show up. He didn't like wasting all this time sitting in this office like an errant schoolboy; he still needed to go to the train station and walk the tracks.

The image of Melvin Straus using Anna for his own perverted pleasure haunted Jacob. If he'd do such a thing to one so tender and innocent, what more would he do to Karl? He recalled the bruises on his face the first day they met, the bruises on Maggie's face, the picture of Melvin dragging Kathleen around by her hair. His hands balled into fists. *I'm not wasting one more minute in here!* As he got up to leave, the door flew open and a black robed priest entered in a hurry.

He was slightly out of breath. "And who might you be?"

"My name is Jacob Denver. I'm a friend of Margaret Stern's. I'm looking for Karl. He's missing."

The priest extended his hand. "So I hear."

Jacob took the priest's hand for a second and let it go.

"He came to visit his father's grave sometime during the night, and hasn't been seen since. I found his glove in the cemetery, so I have proof he was here."

Father Cunningham's chair squeaked as he sat down. He motioned to the other chair. "Please."

Jacob sat back down. "Margaret is worried. She thinks Melvin Straus has him."

"Mr. Straus kept his appointment with me this morning at the rectory at five-thirty, and he was on time. I see him every day, twice; he's coming back at noon for *Stations*. The judge released him to my supervision after the incident with Margaret's daughters. After all that, I don't think he would have kidnapped Karl." He leaned forward in his chair and put his elbows on the desk. "Do you think there's any chance the boy would have run off on his own?

Jacob shook his head. He thought he might yell if he opened his mouth.

"The loss of his father has been hard on him, and some of us haven't made it any easier, I'm afraid." The priest looked at the clock and stood up. "I'm sorry; I'm late for chapel with the children. I suggest you get some men together and go out on foot. Your brother has connections." He went to the door.

"Can't you call the—"

"Everyone here is praying for Karl; tell Margaret, will you? Tell her I have faith we'll find him." He held the door for Jacob, then disappeared down the hall.

That's all you're going to do? Surely a word from the priest would get the police to go over to Straus'. Jacob stormed down the hall. He had no trouble finding his way out.

After the cookies were cooled and put away, Maggie

called Kathleen again and begged for her help. Did she know if Melvin kept a key hidden somewhere outside the house, or was there a neighbor who might be able to let them in to search for Karl? Jacob could go over while everyone was at church and Melvin would never have to know.

"I can't help you, Maggie, I told you. Melvin has done some bad things, but he's been good to me all week and I feel like I have a real husband again. Besides, I don't know Jacob Denver very well. What's to say he wouldn't rob us?"

"That's right, Kathleen, you *don't* know Jacob Denver; he's wonderful, kind and helpful and he cares about Karl." Maggie swallowed the lump in her throat. "Please, please, can't you help us? I want my boy back."

Kathleen's voice became thin and distant. "I'm sorry, Maggie, I can't."

Maggie disconnected the call without saying good-bye. Karl being gone was bad enough, but Kathleen's unwillingness to help hurt her to the core. She sat in Eddie's easy chair and put her feet up. Her body ached with fatigue, but the more she tried to rest, the heavier her chest felt and the more her back hurt. She needed to do something.

She thought how she hadn't scrubbed the floor since before Jacob came to dinner, weeks ago, now. She got up and dragged the chairs into the dining room and got down on her hands and knees with a bucket of hot, soapy water and a scrub brush.

"Maggie."

Startled, she splashed water all over herself.

Jacob climbed the four steps to the kitchen. "What on earth? You're not well enough to be working this hard. Get up and let me finish."

"No, Jacob, I have to keep busy."

"You're all wet."

"Did you find anything?"

"I went to the station and talked to folks who just came from Ashland, but nobody saw him. I did find this, at the cemetery." He reached in his pocket and pulled out the brown glove he'd found mashed against Eddie's headstone.

Maggie gasped. "That's Karl's!" She got up and slipped on the wet floor.

Jacob took her arm and led her to the dining room. "Sit down and relax."

"I can't relax."

"Then just sit down." Jacob found the scrub brush and started where Maggie left off. "I met your priest."

"Does he know about Karl?"

"Yes. He said everyone there is praying for him. He said he has faith we'll find him."

"That's so kind of him." Maggie found comfort in knowing more important people were saying better prayers for Karl than she could.

Jacob stopped scrubbing. He seemed angry. "Isn't it his *job* to pray?" He looked down. "This floor isn't even dirty." He threw the brush in the bucket, making water splash onto the floor. "Did you know the judge released Straus to your priest's supervision after he took the girls? Don't you think Cunningham should have called the judge when he found out about Karl being missing?" He got up to empty the bucket.

"It's Good Friday. Father is very busy today."

Jacob whirled around, glaring. "Are you saying finding Karl is less important than parading around the church in long faces because a man was crucified nineteen hundred years ago?"

Maggie covered her mouth with her hand. "Be careful what you say."

He crossed the wet floor and stood in the doorway, facing her. His eyes were fierce enough to make her shrink away from him.

"Look, I'm not much of a church-goer, but did you ever think what Christ would have to say about this? I think he'd say, *To heck with Stations of the Cross* or whatever you call it; *to **hell** with it, let's go find that boy!* That's what I think."

"Jacob, that's blasphemy. You can't talk like that. Please stop or God will punish you."

"Whatever punishment we get is of our own making, Margaret." His voice softened. "God isn't going to strike me down for speaking the truth."

She looked away from him and focused on the puddle of water he'd left in the middle of the floor. His outrageous ideas scared her. She couldn't imagine God being more concerned about finding a lost boy than about being worshiped and adored, but she wanted it to be true.

"The truth is, Karl needs every bit of help he can get: God's, Cunningham's, the police, yours, mine."

Maggie burst into tears; the very thing she'd tried to avoid all morning.

He grabbed her, his arms all muscle and strength, and held her still, his body a shelter around hers. "What'd you tell me last night? It's poison to keep all that in."

She buried her face in the soft flannel of his shirt until he spoke again.

"We'll find him. We *will*. Cunningham expects Melvin in church at noon, so I'm going over to his house while he's gone. If Karl's there, I'll get him and bring him home."

Chapter 34

Prisoners

The smell of piss nearly took Karl's breath away. He didn't have to open his eyes to know he was in the closet. Melvin's torture chamber. He groaned. How much worse could this get? Carefully, he sat up and listened. The house was still. With his dry, croaky voice, he called for Aunt Kathleen. No answer; nothing.

He kicked at the door, but his efforts made only a dull thud. He pounded on it with his hands, but Melvin must have reinforced it with a slab of hardwood. His head hurt like it might explode, so he lay back down, resting it on his arm. Even with the odor of piss, he could smell lavender on Aunt Kathleen's nightgown. How could such a sweet lady live with that rat?

Cold air seeped into the closet from the outside wall and blew through the torn flannel nightgown. Karl shivered. He knew Melvin hated him. He didn't want to die, but he wasn't afraid of it either. "Let's get this over with, all right, God? If Melvin's going to kill me, the sooner the better," he prayed, "but please, I just want to go home."

His eyes filled with tears when he remembered 617

Blight Street; the warm kitchen, his room with the heavy quilt on his bed, the fireplace in the living room right near the place where his father died. For the first time all morning, Karl thought of his mother and sisters and even Mr. D. He knew he was in big trouble for going out in the middle of the night, but he'd rather face his mother's punishment than any more of Uncle Melvin. He knew she was frantic with worry, especially if she got the note Melvin made him write. He hated being the cause of more trouble for her.

"Please, if you get me home, I promise I'll behave and won't gripe about having a stepfather and I'll even love him so Mama can be happy." Remembering it was Good Friday, he groaned again and crossed himself. "Oh, no, Jesus, I'm sorry I can't make it to church, please forgive me. I know it's a big important day for you, but would you help me anyway? If you get me out of here, I'll go to church all afternoon, even if my head still hurts, and I won't complain about it, not one bit."

Karl began to drift off again but his eyes flew open when he heard banging and pounding coming from far away. He thought he heard someone calling his name—rescue! For once, God was answering his prayer and he'd never doubt again, *never!* His heart beat faster and faster with the hope that filled it. He sat up, kicked at the door and called out, "I'm here; I'm up here!" He shouted and shouted, but when he stopped, the house was silent again. The pounding stopped, nobody answered him and nobody came. He fell into despair, back to the foul smelling floor, back to the dark place where his head didn't hurt at all.

With Eddie Stern's hammer, pry bar, screwdrivers and

a small hatchet rolled up in an old piece of canvas on the seat next to him, Jacob parked down the street from the Straus residence. He'd left Maggie sleeping in the chair, but he knew she wouldn't rest for long, so he needed to hurry. He pulled his cap down over his forehead and ears and put on a pair of Eddie's work gloves before getting out of the car, tools under his arm. "I assume you'd understand about me using your things. Just looking for the boy. Give me a hand, will you?" For the second time in one day, Jacob felt connected to Eddie Stern. He didn't usually talk to dead men, but he thought the father-son link might somehow lead him to Karl.

If it hadn't been for the wrought iron fence, he would have gone along the side hedge to the back of the house, but there was no way except down the driveway. As he passed the front porch, he noticed a bolt up high on the outside of the front door. There was one on the back door, too. Straus must be in the habit of imprisoning people. A bitter taste set in on Jacob's tongue so that he had to spit.

Flattened and frozen into one of the tire tracks in the driveway, Jacob found a brown glove, the mate to the one he'd found in the cemetery. He picked it up, shook off the snow and slid it into his pocket, muttering. "Bastard."

Rubbish smoldered in a rusty old drum at the side of the garage; it's strong, pungent odor filled the air. Jacob looked inside and saw the toe of a man's work boot poking out of the ashes, smoke snaking upward. It looked like Karl's. "Damn!" His heart pounded in dread as he climbed the porch steps and turned the outside bolt, hoping the indoor lock would be open, but it wasn't. He cupped his hands on either side of his eyes and looked in through the back door. He saw no sign of Karl in the back hall.

He pounded on the door and called his name. No answer; nothing.

Jacob looked around and behind him at the two homes abutting the Straus property but he didn't see anyone. He tried sliding a small screw driver between the door and the jam, to jimmy the lock, but it wouldn't budge. He tried knocking on the door again, in case a neighbor was watching, then began turning one of the wing nuts that held the storm window in the frame, thinking he might find the inside window unlocked.

The sound of tires on gravel stopped him. Frantically, he rolled Eddie's tools in the canvas and hid them in the woodpile on the other side of the back door. He pounded on the door again, hoping no one else could hear the pounding of his heart.

"Can we help you? There doesn't seem to be anyone home." Two uniformed officers came around the corner.

"Yes, well, I guess not."

"A neighbor lady called, said you looked suspicious. Who are you?"

"Jacob Denver. I'm looking for a boy who's been missing all morning; Karl Stern. I believe he's in here." He took the glove out of his pocket. "Here, this is his. I found it in the driveway. D'you think you could help me? His mother called you people about it earlier, but no one would help."

"That glove doesn't prove anything; for all we know you could have brought it from home. Mr. and Mrs. Straus aren't the kind of people who would harbor a runaway. They are fine citizens."

Angrily, Jacob shoved his hands into his jacket pockets, the glove in one of them. *Bad move.*

One of the cops drew his gun. "Put your hands up."

Jacob raised his arms. "I don't have a gun; I'm here to find the boy. And he's not a runaway."

The second cop patted him down, then squeezed his big wrists into a set of handcuffs that were much too small.

He winced. "If you look in the burn can, you'll see Karl's boot. What's left of it."

The officer with the gun went to look in the can. He reached in and lifted it out. "This thing? It's so burned up; I don't know how you can say it was the boy's—or anyone else's." He threw it back in the can. Dusty ash and a few sparks exploded into the air then settled back down. "That doesn't mean anything. You're trespassing. You'll have to come with us." Each cop took one of Jacob's arms and led him to the police car.

"Are you aware that Straus assaulted Karl last Christmas, and he abducted Karl's sisters just a few days ago? Please, how can I get you to help us?"

They shoved him into the back seat. "You can tell 'em about it at the station."

Karl started awake when something rammed into the other side of the closet door. He opened his eyes to darkness, his heart knocking around in his chest, tripping over itself.

"Wake up, you lazy son of a bitch. It's time we had a little *man-to-man*." Melvin pounded on the closet door. "You awake?"

Karl didn't answer.

Melvin went on anyway. "You're the talk of Holy Angels today; hell, you're more famous than Jesus Christ, but I expect you already know that, Karl *Stern*. Thanks to you, Sister Anne looks like death and Father Cunningham's mind was anywhere but on *Stations of the Cross.* The old man kept losing his place. *He* ought to go to confession after that display of ineptitude." Melvin laughed.

Melvin went to church?

"Ineptitude. Your grandfather thought I was brilliant whenever I came up with a word like that. Your big, important grandfather, *Mr. Karl W. Stern, Editor in Chief* of the *Tomos Explorer.* He wanted to change my nasty little life for the better. He was gonna save me for the newspaper business."

Karl heard the pop of a cork being pulled from a bottle. More whiskey. He sat up.

"But that all ended when George and your grandmother found us behind the presses. They saw what he was doing to me. He said he was giving me something to write about. He said it would sell lots of papers. It was horrible, perverted, that's what—yeah, he was a perr-vert! He got me all liquored up, and then he made me..." Melvin choked and sniffled. *"Oh, God!"* Liquid sloshed in the bottle. He didn't say anything else for a while.

"I thought George was like my brother, so he shoulda helped me. I was sure your grandmother would. But they shooed me back home like it was all my idea, said I wasn't fit to live with them anymore. More like I wasn't fit to *live.* My old man came after me when I staggered home drunk like that. Beat me till his hands couldn't take it anymore, then brought out the strop. He wanted to make sure I felt it."

Melvin took another drink. His leather soles hit the hardwood floor, pacing back and forth, back and forth.

"I didn't see 'im again until the sheriff carted him off in a straight jacket a couple weeks later. That was bad enough. But you know what was worse?" Melvin started to yell. "Nobody said anything about what he did to *me*, not one word! Shit, even your old man acted like it was nothing!"

Karl thought he heard Melvin spit and cringed. He pulled his legs up under the nightgown and wrapped his arms around them to keep warm. Every inch of his body shook.

"And then George's brother went and married Kathleen's cute little sister. *Jeez...*" He kicked the door with one ferocious bang.

Startled, Karl's arms and legs convulsed.

"I couldn't escape that family. And when they went and named you after *him*, I..." He swallowed several times, caught his breath, and shouted loud enough to be heard across the street. "Did you know you were named after a crazy pervert, *Karl Stern?*"

On the word *Stern*, Melvin kicked the door again. Karl scudded to the corner of the closet, as far away from the door as he could get. Lies, these were all lies; didn't his mother say Grandpa Stern was a good man?

When Melvin spoke again, he sounded calmer. "I sure hope you heard every word I said, boy, 'cause someone's gotta pay for what they did. I waited twenty long years for this, and you're the one."

Karl's stomach jumped into his throat. He had to keep swallowing so he wouldn't throw up again.

Melvin laughed with glee. "After you gawkin' at me like that, serves you right. I couldn't believe my luck, finding you out in the graveyard all alone, bawling like a girl. *Oh, Daddy, oh, Daddy, boo-hoo-hoo, boo-hoo-hoo!* You're gonna be just like me, you little bastard!" Glass broke against the radiator; the radiator rang like a dampened bell. "I'm going for more re-*fresh*-ments." He laughed again. "We're gonna hava nice little party, just you'n me, *Miss-ter* Stern."

Karl wished he were dead, like his father. Then he could ask him why on earth they had to name him *Karl*.

Maggie pretended to be resting when Jacob left for Melvin's, but the minute she heard the engine of his truck fade off, she got up and stood at the front door, waiting for him to return. Will came by before one o'clock and went off to help Jacob, but came back with puzzling news. Jacob's car was parked near Melvin's house, but there was no sign of him anywhere.

"Not Jacob, too!" She wanted to cry.

"I'm sure he's fine," Will tried to assure her. "Maybe he went off on foot. Tell you what I'm gonna do."

Will's tenderness reminded her of Jacob.

"I'll call Johansen and a few others from the shop to go out on foot. We'll make sure someone walks every inch of the tracks between here and Ashland and we'll go off into the fields and woods, too. Once I get them busy, I'll go out looking for Jacob."

She didn't have any more energy to insist that Karl didn't run away. "Thank you, Will, you're a true friend."

"I'd say we're more like family, now, wouldn't you?"

Not wanting Will to know how right he was, she turned away from him. "I'll put some coffee on for your friends." As she waited, she sliced one of the warm loaves of bread, arranged the slices on a plate, then poured honey into a bowl and set out several spoons. She should show a little hospitality to Will's friends, it was the least she could do. When she'd finished, she remembered the cookies, so she put the bread and honey away and set cookies on the plate.

Will stuck his head through the kitchen door after making only a couple of calls. "The operator put Bernie through while I was talking to Wallis. She said Jacob's at the police station. I've gotta go bail him out. Johansen and Wallis are coming over, they'll organize the search."

"Bail him out? For what?"

"I have no idea, but you know Jacob; he doesn't do anything halfway."

Befuddled, Maggie watched Will drive away for the second time. She wished she didn't have to be alone.

The key moved clumsily in the lock and the door jerked open. Melvin's silhouette loomed over Karl, his hand around the neck of another bottle. When his eyes adjusted to the light, Karl saw he still wore his black banker's suit, his starched shirt now pulled out of his pants, his gray tie loose around his neck. Karl cringed, hugging his knees in closer to his chest, expecting Melvin to strike, but Melvin stood staring at him, motionless. His breath came faster and faster until he was breathing hard, like he'd been running.

Never had Karl known terror like this, not even when they brought his frozen father home, not even when he saw the snake coiling around the altar on Christmas Eve.

Melvin stepped into the closet. "Get over here, you little—" His hand came toward him slowly, like he had to think about what he was doing. He took Karl by the hair, dragged and yanked him to his feet. With the other hand, he shoved the bottle in Karl's face. About three inches of amber liquid sluiced around at the bottom. "I saved this for you, *boy*. You're gonna need it." Melvin's voice was quiet, his words slurred. "Drink it or I'll get out my knife and cut you in places a man doesn't wanna get cut."

Karl reached for the bottle, but was too dizzy to grab it. Melvin got mad and rammed him against the back wall of the closet, pinning him there with his body. He put the bottle in Karl's hand and backed away slightly. "I wanna see you drink that and beg for more. *Do it!*"

Karl managed to bring the bottle to his lips and took a sip. It tasted as bad as it did out in the garage.

"All of it!" Melvin pulled his knife from the sheath. He let go of Karl's hair and grabbed the neck of Aunt Kathleen's nightgown.

Karl put the bottle to his mouth again and swallowed half before he stopped, gasping and choking. His insides burned like the fires of hell. Melvin ripped the nightgown down the front and lowered the knife.

"Finishit!"

Karl downed what remained as if his life depended on it, ignoring the searing pain in his stomach.

Melvin grabbed the bottle and smashed it against the closet wall. Shards of glass flew everywhere. "Now get down on your knees and beg for more. Beg!"

Karl knelt on the glass. "Uncle Melvin, may I please go home now?"

Melvin tried to hit him but missed. "Beg for more, I said!"

Karl whispered, "May I please have some more?"

Melvin laughed. "What'sat you say?"

"May I please have some more?"

"I can't hear you."

This time Karl shouted. "Gimme some more!" His head rang.

"You don't have to shout, boy. All you gotta do is ask. *Poo-lite-ly.*" Melvin slammed the door and locked it again.

"I'm no perr-vert, but what he did to me, I'm gonna to do to you. It's only fair. You Sterns got it coming."

Melvin thumped unevenly down the stairs. Karl had heard about men doing it with other men, but he always thought it was showoff talk by the guys on the playground. He felt sick. He had to do *something* to get God's attention.

With shaking hands, he swept the glass together, then lifted the nightgown and knelt on the whole pile, moving around until he felt the sharp fragments dig into his knees. If he suffered, really suffered, maybe God would listen and get him out of here. He pressed his forehead into the glass, too, but it throbbed unbearably, so he lifted his head, spread the glass around, moved the nightgown aside and laid his bare body on top of it, shifting until he felt it dig into his flesh. "Please help me, please help me, please help me." He whispered the words over and over. Maybe if he said them a hundred times...

The whiskey took hold and Karl clutched his stomach. "Jesus, help me; Mary, help me; please, God, help me; *help me!*" The image of a bloody crucifix came into his head, threatened to suck all his breath out. He wept in despair. God had much bigger suffering to think about today.

Chapter 35
Between the Walls

On the street outside the Tomos Bay Police Station, Jacob breathed in the clean, cool air and watched Will climb into his truck. He followed, sure he'd seen a slight smirk on his brother's face.

"Any news about Karl?"

"Nope." Except for his eyes, Will's face looked grim.

They rode in silence for a time.

"My car is over by Straus'."

"I know."

"They said if I go back there, they'll throw me in jail, but d'you suppose you could take me over to pick it up? It's almost time to get Lizzie and Anna from school."

"Sure, whatever you want, Jacob."

They did not speak for a minute; the only sound was the engine.

Jacob looked at his brother. "Mother doesn't have to know about this."

"Of course not." At first Will didn't say anything else, then burst out laughing. "But I woulda loved telling the old man all about it."

Jacob saw nothing funny about any of this. "Listen, *William*, Karl's still missing and we still have to find him. I'm not afraid of spending a few nights behind bars if that's what it takes to get him back. I know Melvin's got him; I found his boot in the burn can and his glove in the driveway."

Will's eyebrows shot up. "Oh, yeah?"

"As soon as I get the girls home, I'm going back over there."

"Not without me, you aren't. Now listen, I've got some friends out looking on foot. I'm gonna call Swenson and see if he'll let us in the warehouse so we can look on the boat." He turned onto Melvin's street and stopped. "Then we can come back here."

"Why waste our time on the warehouse when we *know* Straus has him?"

"Because he knows the boat's important to Karl. If he has him, it's possible he could be hiding him there. Straus would have a perfectly legitimate reason to get in; say he's looking at a boat someone needs a loan for."

Jacob got out of the truck. "Okay, but as soon as we're done—"

"Just hurry up back to Maggie's. We don't have much daylight left and we're gonna need it."

Jacob got to Holy Angels just as Lizzie and Anna came out of school. They were stricken when they learned Karl still hadn't come home. Anna cried, but Lizzie's mouth made a tight line across her face. She had nothing to say until they stopped in front of 617 Blight. "You know this is all Mama's and your fault. You ate bacon on Good Friday and now God is punishing us for it. I want my brother back! I hate you, I hate you!" She opened the door and started to get out.

Stunned, Jacob yelled at her. "Stop!"

Lizzie's face blanched.

"You can blame this on me and you can hate me all you want, but don't you dare go saying such a mean and spiteful thing to your mother, do you understand?"

Lizzie stared at him, eyes wide.

"Do you?" Jacob didn't mean to sound quite so harsh. She was a little girl, not some errant lumberjack.

Her lip quivered. She nodded, her eyes filled with tears. "Yes, sir."

He softened his voice. "Go on in now, both of you, and give your Mama a hug. She could use it."

Jacob watched the girls run into the house and rubbed his eyes. "What have I gotten myself into?" He flung his door closed and plodded through the slush into the house.

Will and Jacob were leaving for the warehouse when Father Cunningham knocked on the door. Maggie thought he looked troubled and weary, just like he did the night he came to tell them her father had been shot dead. She began to shake when he told her to sit down. She saw Will and Jacob exchange looks. Will said he and the girls would go out for a newspaper. Everything seemed to move too slowly, even while her heart raced toward breaking. When they closed the door, Father sat down in the easy chair and Jacob sat next to Maggie on the davenport. She fought the urge to scream.

"Margaret, dear, after *Stations,* I found this paper on the floor of the sacristy. It's addressed to you. I'm afraid it's not good news." He handed her a piece of crumpled paper.

Maggie held it so Jacob could read it, too. He wrapped his arm around her shoulders and pulled her close.

On one side, it said *Mrs. Margaret Stern* in shaky, unfamiliar handwriting. On the other was a note in Karl's handwriting. *Dear Mama. Now that you are well and have Mr. Denver, you won't want me around anymore. Everything is different since Father died. I'm old enough to make my own way now. By the time you read this, I'll be long gone. I'm sorry if I hurt you. Your son, Karl.*

She turned the paper over and looked at the way it was addressed again. She sat still; scandalized by the thought of Karl running away because of Jacob, all the while knowing it wasn't true.

"He has seemed rather down in the dumps lately," said Father. "He still grieves for his father. We should pray to God for him." He began a long prayer, pleading for God to have mercy on this poor, misguided child and forgive him this grave sin.

When he finished, Maggie finally spoke. "You didn't ask God to protect him, wherever he is, Father. Please, pray for that, too."

"Don't make this any harder on yourself, Margaret. He's gone."

Jacob scowled. "Is it too much to ask?"

The priest prayed again.

"Thank you, Father." Maggie stood, holding the note. "Now look at this. I recognize Karl's writing. She turned the paper over. "But this is in someone else's hand." She handed the paper to Jacob. "Wait, I have something to show you."

She climbed the stairs and brought down the note

Karl left before he went out. She gave it to Father. "These *are* Karl's words." She took the paper back from Jacob. "These are not. I believe that Melvin Straus has kidnapped Karl, and if he is lost somewhere, it's Melvin's doing."

"Melvin came to church today, Margaret, with your mother and sister."

Jacob stood. "I found one of Karl's gloves in the cemetery and the other in the Straus driveway. And I found Karl's boot in Melvin's burn can."

"Then you should contact the authorities."

"We did. A word from you would be helpful, sir," Jacob spat the words.

"Well, I..." Flustered, the priest stood and put on his coat. "Really, I don't know what I can do."

Maggie opened the door for him. "Thank you for coming, Father. And thank you for your prayers."

"Bless you, child."

Jacob came behind her and shut the door with a bang.

Jacob and Will left shortly after Father Cunningham disappeared down the street. They found no sign of Karl in the warehouse or on the boat or anywhere else, just as Jacob expected. They drove by the Straus residence and found it dark. Weary from the day, Jacob walked boldly into the back yard and knocked on the door. When nobody answered, he and Will quickly turned the wing nuts on the porch window, removing the storm, but they found the inside window locked.

Jacob sighed. "I don't know what else to do, brother, aside from breaking a window to get in."

"We might have to do that, but let's go to Maggie's first

and make some calls," said Will. "Maybe Cunningham has contacted *the authorities* for us." They took the boot from the burn can and got back into Will's truck. He looked at Jacob, eyes narrowing. "When was the last time you had anything to eat?"

The police returned to Maggie's after Jacob called them himself. Since they weren't the same officers who'd arrested him, he showed them the gloves and the burned boot and explained where he found them. They took Karl's pillowcase, saying they'd search with bloodhounds in the morning. Maggie's eyes burned with anger and her voice cracked when she told them they should have done that hours ago; she knew Melvin had him and why couldn't they just look there, for God's sake? When they made an excuse about not being able to get a search warrant at this hour, she flew into a fury.

"Have either of you heard of Michael O'Keefe? *Officer* Michael O'Keefe? He was my father." Her eyes filled; tears ran down her face. "He gave his life in the line of duty, for the good of this town, so our children would be safe and you dishonor his memory! I want—"

"Maggie." Jacob tried to calm her.

"—my son back! It's your duty to protect him, so go out and do your job!" She fled to the kitchen while Jacob, the girls and the two officers stared after her. Lizzie and Anna came and stood close to Jacob.

"I'm sorry, she's upset." He didn't want them to take her away, too.

"Don't apologize, Jacob!" Maggie shouted from the kitchen. She banged pots and pans around as she started supper, even though nobody wanted to eat.

Jacob remembered when she was that angry with him and hoped it would never happen again.

Lizzie stared out the front door after the police left. Anna carried her doll around, announcing that she had a baby boy and she'd named him *Karl*. She fussed over him and refused to put him down even when Maggie called her to the table. After supper, Jacob washed the dishes and the girls dried, while Maggie let out the hem on Lizzie's Easter dress. When he finished, Jacob went out for a walk, saying he needed some air. In truth, part of him wanted to run away from all this. But as he stood on the front step, he realized he'd come to love Karl. After that, not even a walk in the fresh air could keep him from sharing Maggie's desperation.

Time didn't move an inch in Karl's dark prison as he waited for the inevitable. He had no idea if he'd been there a few minutes, hours or even a whole day. When he closed his eyes and opened them again, he couldn't tell if he'd been blinking or sleeping. He lay still and silent, breathing as softly as he could, listening for Melvin's return; listening, listening, waiting. He sweat like he had a fever, horror springing from every pore; he cupped his hands over his privates, knowing it wouldn't protect anything.

Once he thought he heard a door open and close. His heart raced but he didn't hear the sound of anyone walking around or climbing the stairs, so he relaxed a little. Soon, though, heavy footsteps crossed the hallway and he heard an animal grunt and the rush of Melvin peeing in the bathroom.

"Help me, help me, help me," Karl whispered, rocking on the glass as he lay facing the strip of light that came leaking in under the door. "Help me, help me, please, help me!"

"You ready for me, sweetheart?" Melvin laughed, lopsided and drunk. "Gotcha 'nother bottle."

A warm liquid filled Karl's hands. Disgusted, he realized he'd wet himself. The warmth spread, then quickly turned cold. He wiped his hands on the nightgown and shivered.

Melvin rattled the closet doorknob. "Aw, damn. Where'zat key?" He kicked at the door. In the darkness, Karl listened as he threw things around in the other room. "Where'zat goddamn key? Kathleen!"

If Aunt Kathleen was home, why didn't she come when Karl called her?

"Aww..." Melvin groaned. "She's at 'er Mama's."

Karl waited, hardly breathing. He didn't hear anything else until Melvin's drunken snoring rattled the walls. He sighed, wondering how long he had. His own eyes fell closed, lulled by Melvin's loud breathing.

Maggie clung to Lizzie and Anna after bedtime prayers, hugging and kissing them goodnight again and again. When their eyelids began to droop, she left them and went into Karl's room like she always did. She felt the chill of death as she sat alone on his bed, hugging his pillow and inhaling its sweaty boy-smell. Its feathers were badly matted; if Karl came home, she'd give him one from the pile Jacob brought for her sickbed.

She looked at the desk and picked up his essay. Every year the seventh graders were given the same assignment;

she remembered it from when she was Karl's age. *In the story of the Lord's passion and death, which character are you most like and why?*

Karl wrote: *In the story of Jesus' passion and death, I am most like Simon Peter. Not because I am great like Peter, who became the first Pope, but because I am a failure. Peter was a failure when he denied knowing Jesus three times after telling him that he'd even die for him. I am a failure because I was supposed to take care of my mother and sisters after my father died, and I haven't done a very good job of it. Whenever I try, someone else always has to take over for me. I only hope the Lord can forgive me like He forgave his close friend, Peter.*

"Oh, Karl, whatever put that idea in your head?" Maggie put the paper back on the desk. Dry eyed, she held the pillow again and stared at a crack in the plaster that ran from the ceiling all the way to the floor. That crack was here when Karl wrote his essay. It had been here ever since Eddie died, the whole time her boy believed he wasn't doing right by her. Even though she'd never noticed it until this minute, she thought it was probably here on the day she'd given birth to him, panting and crying only a few feet away from this room. She realized it would still be here whether or not Karl came home. It would be here as long as she lived in this house.

Losing Eddie was the worst thing that had ever happened to her, yet even with a broken heart, she'd surprised herself with her strength. But losing Karl, her own flesh and blood—*Eddie's* flesh and blood—was unthinkable. She couldn't imagine going on without him. She wanted to cry, but it wouldn't bring either one of them back, so why bother? Only vaguely aware of Jacob moving around downstairs and the girls sleeping in the next room, Maggie decided it was time to give up. The lump in her throat grew and tightened but she swallowed the grief until it took her lungs, too. She didn't fight the suffocating constriction and she ignored the darkness pressing in on her, focusing her eyes on the crack in the wall. Pain spread across her back and up her neck; her head began to pound.

In a flash it came to her that Karl was a prisoner, the studs and lath and plaster his jail cell. Eager to free him, she ran for her sewing scissors and began to chop away at the wall near the crack. These scissors had freed Eddie from his frozen clothing; surely they could free Karl, too! Gasping and gulping, she stabbed harder and faster until dry plaster covered her hands and littered the floor.

Downstairs, Jacob knelt before the fireplace arranging wood, stuffing old newspapers and sticks in between for kindling. He knew Maggie would want to sit up tonight and thought a fire might be enough of a comfort so he could tell her how he'd come to love her boy, how he'd willingly give up his house and even the mill if it meant getting him back alive.

At the same instant he struck the match, a piercing scream came from upstairs. He blew it out, tossed it onto the wood, and took the steps two at a time. Lizzie met him in the hallway, sobbing, the color gone from her face again.

"Something's wrong with Mama!"

"Where?"

Jacob followed her into Karl's room. He found Maggie holding her scissors like a dagger, stabbing and digging at wall, her eyes wild.

"He's in here." She was so winded she could barely speak. "We have to get him out!"

"He's in where?"

"Here. See the crack?"

Jacob took the scissors from her. "Now, why would he be in there?"

"Please, Jacob!" Her eyes were huge, pleading.

Jacob dropped the scissors, put his arm around her and led her to Karl's bed. They sat together; he pulled her close, until she rested against his chest. "It's okay, it's all right. Try to relax, now."

She panted, but didn't seem to take in much air. Her lips took on a bluish tinge.

"Do something, Mr. Denver!" The girl was about to scream again.

"Lizzie, come here." He tried to sound as calm and gentle as possible, which wasn't easy with his own heart pounding in his ears. She came close and he put his arm around her shoulders. "It's all right, sweetheart, it's all right. Can you help me? Do you know how to use the telephone?"

Lizzie nodded. "One time I called for help."

"Well, then you're exactly the person I need." Jacob smiled and rubbed her back a little. "Would you call Dr. Lyman for me?"

She nodded.

"Ask him to come right away. Say your mama is having trouble breathing, then wait downstairs and let him in."

Lizzie nodded again and ran out of the room and down the stairs. Jacob held Maggie, rocking her back and forth, telling her over and over that everything would be all right, but he said it as much for himself as for her.

When Dr. Lyman arrived, he told Jacob to take Lizzie down to the kitchen and fix her some warm milk so she'd be able to go back to sleep. She slipped her hand into his and didn't let go until he pulled out a chair for her at the kitchen table. Her childlike trust made Jacob's eyes water. He hoped he could bring her as much comfort as she'd given him.

She sat in solemn stillness, her eyes following him as he added a log to the stove and poured milk into a saucepan.

He cleared his throat before he could speak. "You want cocoa, too?"

Lizzie shook her head. "Mama doesn't allow us except on special days."

He almost said, *Well, today is special* because she'd taken his hand, but he thought better of it. "I'm sorry I shouted at you. I have to remember not to go scolding you kids the way I scold my lumberjacks."

"Are you going to be our stepfather?"

"I sure hope so."

"First it was my Daddy, then my brother and now Mama." Lizzie made all this sound so matter of fact. "If she dies, will we live with you?"

"Your Mama isn't going to die."

"I don't ever want to live with Uncle Melvin. We'll run away."

"I don't want you to live with him, either. I won't let that happen, I promise." All the more reason to marry Maggie as soon as possible.

They were silent as Jacob watched the milk so it wouldn't boil, then poured it into a cup and set it in front of Lizzie. "Don't burn your tongue, now."

Dr. Lyman came into the kitchen for a glass of water, frowning. Jacob followed him to the bottom of the stairs.

"What is it?"

The doctor pushed his glasses up and peered at him. "Her lungs are mostly clear, so the pneumonia hasn't set in again, which is what I feared. Hysteria does strange things to the human body, though."

"Is she still talking nonsense?"

"No, but she's embarrassed about what she did. I'm giving her something to help her sleep."

"I don't think she'll take it."

"I'm not giving her a choice. Anyway, she doesn't have to go to bed. Bring her down to sit by the fire. She'll relax and doze off; it doesn't matter where she does it."

A small hand took Jacob's again.

"Is my mother going to be all right?"

The doctor handed the glass to Jacob and sat down on the third step, cupping Lizzie's chin in his hand. "I think she'll be good as new very soon. She needs some sleep, and so do you, young lady. Go give her a kiss, then it's off to bed with you."

Lizzie yawned and looked up at Jacob. "Tuck me in, Mr. Denver? Please?"

Jacob handed the glass back to Dr. Lyman. "Of course."

While Dr. Lyman tended to Maggie, Jacob rubbed Lizzie's back until she fell asleep. He counted back the years and realized that Lana's baby—*their* baby—would have been about Lizzie's age by now, but he didn't shed a tear or even feel sad. Rather, he felt humbled by an immense sense of gratitude for this child.

Chapter 36

Peace at the Last

After Dr. Lyman left, Jacob watched the firelight paint Maggie a golden rose color as she rested in the easy chair. Her breath came deep and even, thank God, no more gasping or sputtering. He tried to tell her about Lizzie taking his hand, how he couldn't understand having such a moment of joy in the midst of all this darkness, but she'd fallen asleep before he could finish. He'd tell her again tomorrow. Maybe they'd have Karl back by then.

Jacob didn't know where else to look for the boy, even though he felt like he should go out again. Wearier than ever, his eyelids were heavy, but sleep brought no rest. He kept finding himself back in the police station, trying to explain himself with lips that were as stiff and dry as cardboard. He woke from this three times before he decided to keep his eyes open and watch Maggie sleep. He wondered if she'd still want to marry him if they didn't get Karl back alive. He thought there wouldn't be much joy in it; anyway, she probably wouldn't be up to it, even though he knew she'd need him more than ever.

Just as Jacob felt himself sink into the davenport once

more, the telephone rang. He picked it up before the second ring and answered it with a tongue thick with sleep.

"Jacob? This is Kathleen. Has Karl come home yet?"

"No."

"I'm still at Mother's and we've been up all night. I've been trying to decide what to do."

"Hmm…" Jacob yawned. The clock struck three.

"Melvin called at suppertime and said he got sick. He said I should stay here so I don't catch it, but if he really was sick he'd want me home to wait on him. I think…" she paused. "I think Melvin has Karl and I have a pretty good idea where he might be. Do you think Will would help us?"

Suddenly, Jacob felt like he'd been drinking coffee all night. He turned his back to the living room and kept his voice low. "Yes."

"There's this closet where he locks me up when he's really mad. He says it's so he doesn't kill me. Once he beat me and left me there for nearly three days."

"And you think that's where Karl is?"

Kathleen's voice became thin and far away. "Yes." She didn't say anything for a moment.

"Kathleen?"

"I know where Melvin keeps an extra key to the house. I can let you in. If we're careful, we might be able to get Karl out before Melvin wakes up."

"Why didn't you say anything about this before?"

"I was afraid." She started to cry. "But Karl shouldn't have to suffer any more because of me. If Melvin wakes up, I'll tell him to take me in place of Karl, and do whatever—"

"No, I won't let that happen. I'll call Will. One of us will come for you in a few minutes. We need your mother, too. I can't leave Maggie alone."

Jacob hung up and had the operator ring for Will.

Fifteen minutes later, when he let Isabelle into the house, Maggie still didn't stir. He added several more logs to the fire, leaned and kissed her forehead right in front of her mother, then hurried out the door. Kathleen and Will met him on the front walk.

"You'll have to drive, Jacob, my truck is almost out of gas."

Isabelle opened the door and called out in a voice too loud for three-twenty in the morning. "Mind you, boys, be careful!"

Jacob looked back to see her twisting a handkerchief and crying. He nodded at her.

"That's a first," Will muttered.

"No, it's not, Will," said Kathleen. "She's been up all night, too."

Will grunted.

They rode in adrenaline-charged silence for a moment before Jacob spoke. "Kathleen, we'll need some light once we get in the house. If we turn on the overheads, Melvin will wake up for sure."

"I keep a kerosene lamp by the back door."

"Good. Once we're in, you stay downstairs by the telephone and call for help as soon as you get the signal we've found Karl."

"The closet's in the spare room, top of the stairs, first one on the right. The key's on a hook in the molding. Be careful; Melvin's dangerous when he gets mad."

Jacob looked at his brother. "You stay with Kathleen. I'll get Karl. You've got a family to think about."

"And you *don't*? I'm comin' with you. It'll take two of us, especially if Melvin wakes up."

As they turned onto Kathleen's street, she crossed herself. "Eighteen years and I've never gone against him, not once." She took a deep breath. "This is all my fault because I wouldn't help my sister—"

Jacob interrupted her. "Forget it, Kathleen. It'll muddy your thinking if you don't." He glanced at her. "What matters is that you're helping now."

She nodded.

Two houses down, Jacob cut the engine, switched off the headlights and coasted to a stop in front of the Straus residence. "Here we go. God help us. Don't go slamming any doors."

Karl dug his toes into the warm sand as he stared at the hand painted road sign. It had markings like nothing he'd ever seen before in a green so full of life that when he traced them with his finger he felt a surge of something better than love, better than hope, more powerful than the strength of his father and Will combined.

He had no idea what the markings meant, so he bent down and copied them in the sand, returning to touch them again and again. If he ever got home, he'd draw them in his sketch pad and show them to Sister Anne. He drew a box with the upper right corner rounded off, a stick that curved slightly to the right from the top, a bent fishing hook and a slanted pitchfork. Whatever they were, he didn't want to forget them. He drew them over and over, until they were part of him.

In the distance, on the other side of the sign, stood a mountain the color of red bricks. The sun warmed his bare head and the breeze smelled of spring blossoms even though there were no trees or shrubs anywhere in sight. He didn't remember how he'd come to this oddly enchanted place, but he felt safe here, like when he was little and scared to death of a midnight thunderstorm and Daddy came and sat on his bed until he went back to sleep.

He still wore Aunt Kathleen's nightgown, ripped down the front and torn to shreds at the shoulder, a terrible reminder of Uncle Melvin and the closet. His knees began to shake, terror worming its way back into his gut. He wished he had a belt or a rope or anything to hold the nightgown closed and protect himself from Melvin. Then, as if he'd called for it, a length of green cucumber vine swirled by on the breeze, its leaves and tendrils fluttering and calling out to him.

Relieved, Karl smiled and caught the vine before it fell to the ground, but the moment he grabbed it, its leaves withered and blew away in a gust of wind. As he wrapped it around his waist, the vine twisted and cinched all on its own until he realized it had become a cobra, like the one he saw in church at Christmas. He untangled himself and flung it to the ground, screaming while the open nightgown billowed in the rising wind, exposing him all the more.

Suddenly a sword appeared in his hand. He swung it at the serpent, swooping it in a wide arc. The serpent reared its head and spit out a stream of brown liquid. Whiskey. Karl dodged it, but stumbled with the weight of the sword. The snake laughed at him with Melvin's voice.

Rage filled Karl's body and made him strong, stronger than he'd ever felt before. He would end this wickedness once and for all; he could do this! He stabbed the snake, impaled it to the ground, and left the sword standing in the sand.

But even before he moved his hand away, another sword came out of nowhere, which was a good thing, because he hadn't killed the snake at all, only divided it. Now two heads laughed at him, two tongues flicked at his bare feet, and two sets of red eyes bored into his soul. With trembling hands, Karl stabbed at one of them, again plunging the sword into the ground, leaving it standing. Now there were three snakes. Another sword, another stab, another serpent; another and another until he stood in a slithering mess of evil broken only by the countless swords which stood like crosses in a cemetery.

Although he despaired and grew weary, Karl knew he would die the moment he stopped fighting. Stab, thrust, stab again... Bitter disappointment filled him. He'd thought this was a place of goodness and peace; with all his heart, he wanted it to be. Stab thrust, stab. He couldn't keep this up much longer. He wanted to call for help, but who would come? Stab, stab, stab. This must be hell.

Without making a sound, Jacob and Will climbed the stairs to the second floor of Melvin's house. Will went first, carrying the lamp. When they got to the spare room Jacob moved past him and felt along the molding for the closet key, finding only a small hook that gouged the tender flesh under his fingernail. He winced and whispered. "No key."

"Shh, listen."

A soft whimper came from within the closet.

Jacob knocked quietly on the door. "Karl? Can you hear me?"

More whimpering.

Will handed the lantern to Jacob. "I'll tell Kathleen he's

in here. You keep looking for the key." But as he started through the doorway, he walked into Melvin, clad only in his undershirt and wrinkled black pants—unbuttoned.

"What in the *hell's* going on here?" His words were badly slurred. The smell of liquor came from his breath like a fog; it seeped from his pores. "How'd you get in my house?"

Will yelled, "Kathleen, call the police!"

"Don't you go telling my woman what to do!" Melvin grabbed Will by the collar of his jacket and shouted for Kathleen. "Get up here, you worthless bitch, or I'll kill you all."

"Where's the key, Straus? Where's Karl?" Jacob's voice was so loud and rough that Melvin jumped.

Will slammed his fist into Melvin's gut. Melvin lost his balance and stumbled then swung at Will and missed. He grabbed the lamp from Jacob and threw it across the room, where it hit the wall and exploded, kerosene soaking the old wallpaper and drapes. Flames spread across the wall.

"You're burning my house down, damn you!" Melvin pushed past Jacob, pulled a pillow off the bed and started swinging it at the wall, fanning the fire instead of smothering it. The pillowcase caught, burning his hands. He screamed and cursed.

Jacob pulled him away from the wall and threw him to the floor in front of the closet. His knee landed in the small of Melvin's back, his hands twisted Melvin's arms, holding his fat wrists behind him. "Where's Karl? Did you lock him in the closet?"

"We were only having a little fun. Owww! Lemme go!"

"Where's that key?" Jacob yelled through clenched

teeth. "Where is it?" With every ounce of his strength he had to fight the impulse to flip Melvin over and strangle him.

Melvin wailed. "I dunno. I lost it!"

Will pulled the quilt off the bed and tried to smother the fire, but gave up when he saw that it was already too far above his head. "We gotta get outta here!" He kicked at the closet door knob, trying to knock it loose, to no avail. He ran out of the room, calling over his shoulder, "We can pop the hinges if I can find a screwdriver."

"No, get my axe from the car! It's in the back."

Karl whimpered and coughed.

Never knowing such rage in his whole life, Jacob pushed his knee down harder on Melvin's back, meaning to cause him as much pain as he could. He wasn't about to leave Karl here alone, and he wasn't about to let Melvin go, either.

Meanwhile, the flames took the drapes and lapped at the ceiling.

The earth shook beneath Karl's bare feet as the red mountain convulsed and exploded. Huge boulders catapulted toward him while smaller rocks sped along the ground, kicking up a haze that made the air bitter to breathe.

Karl's heart jumped into his throat. He threw his sword into the fray of reptiles and began to run, snakes nipping at his heels and laughing behind his back. It's all over, he thought. Then he heard another sound; no, it was rather something he felt in the slam-pounding of his heart. *Turn around.* Terrified, he ran on and on, thinking the snakes had gotten into his brain and were trying to take over. The avalanche roared behind him while the snakes wrapped themselves around his legs, bit him, sucked away his blood, injected their poison. He felt his life fade away.

Turn around, Karl. Now the words were in the roaring of the earth.

He kept on running. "I can't!" But before the words left his mouth, he felt himself being lifted beyond the chaos. Serpents fell from his legs, his wounds healed, his life returned.

Watch, child.

All the sword crosses lay broken on the ground. The writhing snakes were crushed beneath wave after wave of rolling, bloody rocks. When the earth finally stilled, hawks and eagles appeared by the hundred, the mighty rush and flap of their wings drowning out the howl of the shattered mountain. Each bird began to dig, pulling snakes from under the debris, swallowing them whole and going back for more. When the snakes were gone, the birds flew away like overloaded fishing boats riding low in the water.

Karl realized his hand was clinging to the edge of a rough brown sleeve, just like he used to hang on to his father's sleeve when he was little. Something pulled him away and set him at the mouth of a cave carved into the high wall of a cliff. He looked over his shoulder, afraid of what might be behind him, but instead of the cold, engulfing darkness he expected, hundreds of votives flickered there like tongues. He knew in his heart that someone had lit them all for him. Astounded by their beauty, he stepped into the holy cave and crossed himself. He could almost see the prayers rising from the dancing flames. All that love nearly took his breath away.

"Karl! Karl!"

He returned to the mouth of the cave and looked down, past his own feet which now wore his father's boots. Down below, he saw another pair of feet, huge, bootless, and blazing like the sun. When Karl saw how horribly bitten and bloody they were, he wanted to turn away, but he could not. As his eyes adjusted to the brightness, he saw one last serpent writhing beneath the feet, crushed and twisting. As he watched, the snake became as still as death.

Another bird came riding on the wind, sleek and white, with ruby eyes and talons of gold. It took the last snake in its beak and flew away as quickly as it had come. Words filled Karl's soul; warm, peaceful words in a language he'd never heard before. *Shalom.* As he reached for the sleeve again, it all disappeared and he heard Mr. D calling his name.

His eyes flew open to see flickering light coming from under the closet door; outside was a roar and a ruckus. "I'm here, I'm in here; help me!"

Chapter 37
A Raging Flame

Karl kicked at the door with both feet. His voice was high pitched and squeaky, but he called out anyway. "I'm in here, Mr. D." The overpowering smell of smoke made him sneeze three times. What was burning? The house? He heard footsteps running, then Melvin's whining voice.

"It's not what you think. Can't you see I'm hurt?"

There were grunting noises, more footsteps, this time in a confused jumble.

Karl kicked the door again, afraid he'd been left behind. "Mr. D?" He couldn't manage much more than a whisper.

"Get away from the door, son; I've got my axe."

Thank God! Karl crawled to the corner of the closet, where cool air still seeped in through the cracks. He sucked in as much of it as he could.

Wham! Wham! Wham! The flickering light disappeared and the world became darker than closed eyes at midnight. Wham! Wham! With the complaint of cracking wood, the door jerked open. Thick smoke came billowing into the closet.

"Come on, Karl, hurry up."

"I can't see; give me your hand."

"I'm right here."

Karl reached, lost his balance and fell. Mr. D's strong arms found him and lifted him up. "Come on, now."

He coughed, got dizzy and stumbled. This time Mr. D picked him up and carried him.

"Wait, Mr. D, he took my clothes, I need a blanket or something."

"There isn't time."

Karl wrapped his arms around Mr. D's neck as they went down the stairs. It seemed easier to breathe in the living room, although smoke hung in a haze around the ceiling, getting thicker and lower by the second. "Please, I need a blanket."

Mr. D looked down at him. "Oh, good God, what'd he do to you?" He set him down on a chair, furious. "Take that thing off!"

Karl freed himself from Aunt Kathleen's nightgown, now torn and filthy. Mr. D ripped one of the red velvet drapes from the living room window and wrapped it around him. Karl held it closed and teetered, dizzy again. Mr. D carried him out the door and down the front steps.

Karl put his bare arms around Mr. D's neck and hung on for life. "Thanks for coming, Mr. D. I've never been so glad to see anyone." He started to wheeze and cough.

"Me, too."

The soggy snow reflected orange light from the fire. The window from the spare room blew out, flames escaping, licking the outside wall. Still in Mr. D's arms, Karl shivered, looked around and wondered what all had happened. There were police cars everywhere; sirens broke the quiet of the night, coming closer and closer; neighbors crept from their houses in bathrobes and slippers to see what the commotion was all about. Aunt Kathleen stood on the running board of one of the police cars, yelling wildly at someone in the back seat. It must be Melvin. When an officer tried to get her to move away, she turned on him.

"*No!* I've been waiting fifteen years to say this. Let me have just one minute, will you?" She turned back to the window and pounded on it, her voice rough with rage. "... did my best to love you... I tried... you hurt me... killed my babies... how *dare* you... to my family, to Karl!"

Aunt Kathleen had babies?

"You don't need to listen to that," puffed Mr. D. "I'm putting you in the car where you'll be warmer. Doc Lyman wants to see you right away."

"Aw, I'm okay. Just take me home." A fit of coughing overcame him.

"No, you're not okay, you need a doctor."

Exhausted, Karl closed his eyes and gave up. For a fleeting moment, he was a little boy in his father's arms again. When he opened his eyes, though, he saw the sooty face of Jacob Denver instead of the smiling face of Eddie Stern. Momentarily confused, the word *Daddy* came from his mouth, more like a question than anything else. Then he remembered everything that had happened and tears ran down his dirty face. He cried like a baby.

"Everything's all right, now, don't worry." Out of breath, Mr. D balanced Karl against the car door while he opened the latch.

Once inside, Mr. D fussed over him, trying to make him comfortable. His dark hair hung down almost to his eyes. "I'm going to find Kathleen. Don't you go off someplace and make me come looking again." His smile was forced and tight.

Karl wiped his face with his bare arm. "I won't, I promise."

After a little while, Aunt Kathleen climbed in next to Karl. She smiled when she saw him. "Goodness, those drapes look better on you than they ever did hanging in my window." She held out her arm to him. "Come here, you can use me for a pillow."

Karl leaned against her and they watched the pumper truck lumber across the yard. He thought he saw the outline of a cobra in the flames, but when he blinked, it disappeared. He started to shake. He could have died in there!

Aunt Kathleen stared out the window and whispered, "Goodbye house." She sniffed a little, and said, "I'm sorry it took us to long to find you, but everything's going to be all right, now. That monster won't ever hurt you again." She wrapped her other arm around him and kissed him over and over the way a mother would, stroking his hair, rocking him slightly.

"I didn't know you had any babies."

She gasped and pulled away. "You heard that?"

"Yeah." His head hurt too much to nod.

She pulled him close again. "I guess it's time to start telling the truth." She swallowed. "There were four of them, but none of them lived to see the light of day. He seemed happy when I first told him I was expecting, but after a few days he would get mad at me for something and beat me until..." She cleared her throat. "Each time was worse than the one before. I think he was jealous. That last time,

I waited too long to tell him and he got mad because I'd gone to the doctor without his permission. He threw me down the stairs and took me to a hospital in Duluth and told them I fell on the baby. It took us so long to get there, I almost died. They had to operate. They said I wouldn't be able to have any more children, so Melvin got his wish." She sighed. "After that he was nice to me for almost a year. I never told anyone what he did, but who would have believed me after he raised all that money for the orphanage?" She smoothed his hair away from his forehead. "I shouldn't be telling you, either. You've been through enough."

"We sure do have a lot in common, don't we, Aunt Kathleen?"

She nodded, then became stern, almost angry. "But don't be like me, d'you hear? Tell the truth when the police ask what he did to you. Don't hide a thing; don't leave anything out. You're smarter than I am. There's no sense in lying for him like I did. I mean it, Karl. Understand?"

Karl pulled the red velvet drapes tight across his middle. "I'll try."

"Don't just try. Do it. You're strong enough."

"Yes, Ma'am." He'd never seen Aunt Kathleen act this way before and it unnerved him.

Jacob scooped up handful after handful of snow, packed it hard, and pelted the front window of Melvin's house until it blew out from the heat. "Damn, *damn!*" He didn't remember ever being so hurt, so angry.

Will came up from behind and yelled at him. "You lookin' for a cold shower?"

Jacob hadn't noticed the pumper truck getting into position.

Will grabbed his arm and dragged him out of the way. "What's the matter with you, anyway?"

"I dunno. You know what he was wearing when I pulled him out? A nightgown! I hate to think what—" He stopped to catch his breath. Pain shot through his rib; he hadn't even noticed it since he rolled over on Maggie's davenport that morning. He winced and covered it with his hands. "And now he's crying for his daddy."

"But *you* got him out. You're his hero and he knows it."

Jacob groaned, weary in every possible way.

"What's wrong with your side?"

"Nothing. The car door hit it yesterday. He's heavier than I thought."

"Give me your keys. I'm taking you both to the hospital."

"I don't need any hospital."

"Yeah you do. Anyway, we can't leave him there alone."

"Oh, all right."

Jacob had expected wild joy when they finally rescued Karl, but now he thought he might cry if he wasn't careful—and wouldn't *that* be a fine thing to do right there in front of him? He held his side and stared out the window, miserable, watching lights come on in a few houses here and there. He wondered why he felt so dead inside, so sad. Karl and Will laughed and chattered away, relieved and excited, while Kathleen added a few subdued comments here and there, but he could only sit there like a chunk of dry wood.

Then they passed Holy Angel's Church. Even though it

was barely five o'clock in the morning, light shone through all the colored windows, glimmering jewels in the dark of this awful night. And beyond the church, across the cemetery, a sliver of pale orange brightened the horizon against a deep purple-blue sky, the promise of a new day. "Would you look at that..." Awestruck, he could barely croak out the words. This unexpected beauty released the tears he'd wanted to avoid. He dug in his pocket for a handkerchief and wiped them away before anyone noticed.

"Golly, yeah," said Karl.

Will stopped the car.

Kathleen craned her neck to see. "Oh, my! The Sisters have been up praying for you all night, Karl. Every once in a while they'll do that for someone, you know. They did it for your father."

Why couldn't everybody forget about Eddie Stern, if only for a few minutes?

"Really?" Karl spoke very softly. "I thought they were all mean, except for Sister Anne."

"They love you," answered Kathleen. "We all do."

Jacob wished he'd said that.

They watched the sun come up, letting the salve of love and beauty sooth the pain and ugliness of the past day.

Karl broke the silence. "Hey, Will? I sure appreciate your coming to find me."

"I wouldn't have done anything else, you know that."

"Well, thanks. And Aunt Kathleen, I'm sorry about your house. I'll bet you could come live with us."

"Thank you, Karl, but I'm going to be fine, don't worry." She reached under her coat and pulled out a bank bag folded over a three inch stack of money. "Our household funds. He didn't realize I knew where he kept it; he says I'm too stupid to handle money. It's all in twenties and fifties and even a few hundreds. I don't know why he kept so much at home, but now he thinks it's all burned up, so it's mine."

Jacob turned his head slightly and tried to smile. "If anyone deserves it, it's you."

"Mr. D?"

Despite his aching side, Jacob turned all the way around so he could see Karl's face. "Yes?"

"Do you think you could get me a real haircut today? A short one?"

"Sure." Jacob turned back so Karl wouldn't see his face; he moved too quickly and winced from the pain. *Sure. Thank Will, offer your sympathy to Kathleen and ask me for a haircut. I only carried you out of a burning building.* "Yeah, sure, I can do that."

Chapter 38

Reunion

The acrid odor of smoke made its way into Maggie's consciousness before she heard Will's voice.

"Maggie, wake up, we found him!"

It felt like a dream. She opened her eyes to see Kathleen and Will both leaning over her, smelling awful, but smiling. They had to explain things to her more than once before she understood. Melvin had Karl all along, but Jacob rescued him. Melvin burned the house down and the police took him away. Karl and Jacob were at the hospital waiting for her; they seemed to be fine. As soon as she got dressed, Will would take her to them.

Once it all began to sink in, Maggie noticed her mother sitting on the davenport. "Mother, when did you come?"

Isabelle laughed softly. "I've been here for hours, watching you. You've been sound asleep." She stood up. "I'll help you get dressed."

Kathleen followed Maggie and her mother up the stairs. "Would you let me borrow a dress, Magpie? I have to get rid of this smell."

Maggie opened her closet door. "I wish I had something beautiful to give you, but take whatever you need, anything."

Kathleen undid her hair and smelled it. "What I need is a bath."

Maggie hurried to find her a clean towel.

Isabelle sat on the edge of the bed. "Wait, I have something to say to both of you. I've been thinking. Examining my heart, like Father Cunningham said and I don't like much of what I see." She looked at each of them. "I hope you girls can forgive me. I've been a terrible judge of that man's character. Terrible. He's hurt you both, and now Karl, too. I'm sorry. Kathleen, you have a home with me for as long as you want. I'm going to make it up to you."

The clock downstairs chimed six times. Kathleen cried, her tears leaving tracks on her sooty face.

"And I never thanked either one of you for taking such good care of me when I was sick."

Maggie sat next to her mother and put her arms around her. "Oh, Mama." Her sleepy fog lifted. As anxious as she was to get to Karl and Jacob, she knew there might never be another moment like this one.

Isabelle pulled away. "Go on, now; get dressed, Karl is waiting." She blushed deeply and wouldn't meet Maggie's eyes.

Kathleen drew a hot bath. Isabelle helped Maggie with the buttons in the back of her dress. "My, my, Margaret, how long were you going to keep this Jacob Denver fellow a secret? He's very handsome."

Maggie smiled. "He's pretty wonderful, isn't he?" In a whole new way, life was good again.

Stiff from the bandage they'd wrapped around his ribs,

Jacob paced the foyer of the hospital, waiting for Maggie to arrive. He dreaded sitting or lying down, knowing that any change in position would hurt like hell. It would be better in a few weeks, they said. *Weeks!* He heard the truck before he saw it and watched out the window as Maggie got out, but didn't even try to open the massive oak door for her.

She rushed toward him. "Will told me what you did. How can I ever—"

He smiled at her and backed away. "Two broken ribs; careful, now."

"Oh, no..." She put her hand on his side, on the same place she'd touched him two nights ago.

If he had any doubts about why he'd put his own life in danger, they evaporated under the warmth of her tenderness. "Anyway, I'm a mess."

"I don't care. Where's Karl? How is he?"

He took her hand and led her across the foyer to a dimly lit green corridor. "He has to stay; he's got a nasty bump on his head. Dr. Lyman said that one knock on the head was bad enough, but two in only a few months could be very bad. He wants to keep a close watch on him. And he took in a lot of smoke. Other than that, he seems okay." He didn't tell her about the nightgown or that Melvin had been pumping whiskey down his throat.

Maggie stopped abruptly. "What else did Melvin do to him?" Her eyes got that wild look again. "What? Tell me."

"He's all right. Come on, he's been asking for you."

They stopped outside room 124, Karl's room. "Maggie, you should know he looks kind of rough."

A young nun approached them. "I'm sorry, you can't go in there, visiting hours aren't until ten o'clock."

"I can't wait until ten o'clock, I'm his mother!" Maggie left Jacob's side and flew into the room hitting the door-knob against the wall.

"I said you can't go in there."

"Sorry, Sister, she's been out of her mind with worry." Jacob followed Maggie, but stopped in the doorway when he saw the reunion between mother and son. Maggie sat on the bed holding Karl, the two of them almost as one; silent except for a few gaspy sobs and sniffles. They stayed like that for three whole minutes. Jacob leaned against the wall, but moved away when he remembered how sooty his jacket was.

She began to rock Karl slightly, held the back of his head close and murmured into his ear for the longest time. Jacob tried to make out her words but they were obviously for Karl alone. He felt like an intruder again.

So this is how it would be with these two. Karl had been here first; she'd loved him first. Who was Jacob Denver to come between them? Well, he didn't exactly want to come between them; he didn't know what he wanted. Maggie to love him the most? Karl to love him like he loved Eddie Stern?

Jacob couldn't take it. He crossed to the window and watched a horse drawn milk cart turn into the driveway. A lump grew in his throat but he willed it away. Finding his place in this family was hard work, harder than carrying Karl from a burning house, harder than taking care of a sick woman. He sighed. Maybe he'd feel more up to it once he had some rest.

The change in Maggie's voice caught his attention. Jacob turned around.

"What on earth were you thinking? Why did you go out in the middle of the night? *Why?* You had us all so worried, even your sisters and Grandma and everybody at the school and Father Cunningham and Will and Bernie... We were afraid you were gone for good!"

Karl coughed then leaned back on the bed. He avoided his mother's eyes. "I *was* gone, and I thought I'd never get home. I'm still afraid that I..." He shivered and pulled the sheet and blanket up to his chin, hiding his arms underneath. "I figured I'd be back before anyone woke up—and I *would* have, too, it if hadn't been for Uncle Melvin."

"Why did you go with him? What did he do to you?"

"He knocked me out and took away my clothes and locked me up in that closet and made me—"

Jacob interrupted. "We can talk about it later, remember?"

"Oh, yeah."

Dr. Lyman said that Karl needed to tell someone about everything Melvin Straus did to him—*everything*—or his spirit would be poisoned and he might turn nasty, too. *Get it off your chest, the sooner the better, but not to your mother, for God's sake. You've already caused her enough grief.*

"Aw, Mama, you know Uncle Melvin, that big bully."

Maggie pursed her lips.

Gingerly, Jacob bent and kissed her, right there in front of Karl. "It's time for me to go someplace and take a bath. I'll come back after lunch."

"*Parents*," Karl whispered.

"What'd you say?"

"Everyone around here's been asking about my *parents*."

"Well, I'm—" Jacob was standing in another man's territory and he didn't like it.

"I know all about it. I know you're getting married."

"You were eavesdropping again, weren't you?" Maggie

looked surprisingly calm, while Jacob's heart beat double time.

"I'm sorry, but I heard strange noises downstairs and I was afraid something was wrong. I heard what you said and then I couldn't sleep, so I went to see Daddy's..." Karl's face crumpled and he started to cry. This time Maggie sat with her arms crossed, as if she were thinking about whether or not to comfort him.

Strange noises. Good Lord, Karl heard him bawling about Lana! Jacob wanted to run away.

"What did I tell you before?" When Maggie raised her voice, Karl winced. "If you want to know something, ask me. *Ask!* You violated our privacy and you suffered for it and so did everyone who cares about you. Shame on you."

Karl pulled the sheet over his head and wailed like a two year old. "But I still miss Daddy!"

"I have to go." Jacob gave Maggie another quick kiss and went out the door.

Still angry, Maggie followed him. "Where are you going?"

"This is between the two of you, and frankly, I can't stomach any more of it."

"If you leave now he'll think you don't care."

Jacob stopped, but didn't turn around. "If he doesn't think I care after today, he never will. I'll see you both later." He started down the hall and called over his shoulder. "Tell him I'll bring a barber when I come back."

"No, wait; please, Jacob? We need you."

He turned around and saw the door of Karl's room close behind her. His legs were heavy and he longed for a hot bath and some sleep, but he followed.

Maggie sat on Karl's bed again, but now she spoke

softly and calmly. "I loved your father with all my heart. I still miss him and I know you do, too, but he's gone, and we have to accept that. And now God has given us a second chance. You of all people should understand how much we've been blessed."

Karl still hid under the sheet. He'd quit wailing, but he cried softly, sniffling every few seconds. "I don't want us to forget him."

"That's not going to happen. Ever. You have my solemn promise." She turned to Jacob, smiled, and held out her hand to him. "Come here, Jacob."

He stepped closer and took it. The electricity he'd felt the first time they touched surged with a greater power than ever.

With her other hand, Maggie reached for Karl's, put Jacob's on top of it, and held them in both of hers.

Without thinking about it, Jacob tightened his grip around Karl's hand.

"Look at me, Karl." Maggie waited until he let the sheet fall. "Eddie Stern gave you life. Jacob Denver saved it. Think of them as partners. Brothers. You belong to both of them now."

Karl stared at her, sniffed, and finally nodded.

Jacob couldn't take his eyes off her. *My God, she's giving me her son!* He put his free hand on top of hers and whispered, "Maggie."

Then, like a white bird coasting in from an unfamiliar place, Karl's other hand landed on top of Jacob's. The room was a blur, but the air was thick with promise. And love.

Chapter 39

Absolution

Later that morning, Sister Anne and Father Cunningham came to visit. Sister took Karl's hand, let it go, and hugged him. "We were so afraid for you, Karl. But God is good and here you are." Her eyes glistened but she looked like she did when one of her students gave her an apple.

Father Cunningham offered his hand to Karl, too, but he didn't try to hug him, thank God. "Good to have you back, young man."

Karl coughed and cleared his throat. "Well, when Uncle Melvin didn't let me go home, I asked God to save me and he finally did, but it took a long time." He looked over at his mother, remembering how she'd said *Eddie Stern gave you life. Jacob Denver saved it.* "Well, I guess it was really Will and Mr. Denver."

"They were instruments of the Lord, son."

Karl hadn't considered that. "Oh, yeah."

Father Cunningham said a prayer and blessed Karl, then took his mother's hand the same way he did the day his father died. "Margaret, I'm sure you don't want to leave Karl's side after everything he's been through, but I am wondering if you would allow me a few moments alone with him?"

She looked at Karl like he might disappear again. "Well, I—"

"I'll be okay, Mama."

Sister Anne's cheerful, musical voice cut through the awkwardness in the room. "Have you had breakfast, Margaret? I know the sisters who work in the kitchen and I'm sure they would be glad to fix you something." She put her arm around Maggie's waist and led her to the door.

"Sister? I have a lot to tell you and... that assignment you gave me..." He wished she would stay.

"Don't worry." She turned, smiling sweetly. "I'll be back in a little while."

Father Cunningham walked them to the door and locked it.

Karl had heard too many locks turn lately. "Father, what are you doing? I mean, can't we leave it unlocked?" He knew his voice sounded sissy, like a girl's.

"This is between us, just you and me, Karl." The priest stared out the window for a few seconds. Slowly, he turned back and looked into Karl's eyes. "I want to ask your forgiveness."

"Me? Shouldn't you go to another priest?"

"I did. He said I had to ask you."

Karl wanted to hide. Who was *he* to forgive a priest?

Father Cunningham took off his glasses and rubbed his eyes. "I have failed you. I've done you great wrong— your family, too, but mostly you."

"No, you haven't, Father. You're our priest."

Father Cunningham sighed. "Please be still and let me do this, will you?"

Karl gathered up the edge of the sheet in his sweaty hands, squeezed and wrinkled it.

"Before your father died, you wanted to know why I didn't pray for him to get well, but I lectured you instead. I was too harsh with you when those other boys made you trip and fall during Mass. I wouldn't listen to you and—"

Karl interrupted. "But washing the floor with Sister Anne was the best thing that happened to me since my father died. And Mrs. Buckley was playing the organ, and it was real nice, Father, honest."

Father Cunningham put his glasses back on and glared at him. "May I continue?"

Karl nodded. His head hurt a lot.

"I told you to tell your mother she was a fool to not move in with your aunt and uncle because Melvin Straus asked me to, even when I suspected he was hurting Kathleen. I called him to discipline you that day you stormed out of Mass. And after he beat you and your mother, I bailed him out of jail. And I did it again when he took your sisters. After you told me what he did to them, I should have called the judge, but I didn't. If I had, he wouldn't have been free to... And yesterday, if I'd been more helpful to your mother like she asked, the police would have found you sooner." He cleared his throat and looked down. "Can you forgive me for all that?"

"Father *you* didn't hurt us, Uncle Melvin did."

"I did you wrong, too, Karl." Slowly he raised his head and looked Karl in the eye. "I'm asking you to forgive me. *Please.*"

Karl hated having the priest he'd known all his life begging him for forgiveness; it felt like having to forgive

God or something. He pulled up his knees and wrapped his arms around them, resting his forehead on top, staring down at the white sheet. All the misery of the past months came flooding back. He remembered the pathetic prayer he said for his father as he watched the priest hurry away and the pain of it ripped through him like it was yesterday. He'd done enough crying to last a whole lifetime, but here it came again.

"I am so sorry, truly I am." Father's hand rested on his back, then slid to his far shoulder. "I don't want you to lose your faith or despise the Church because of me."

"You're a good man, Father." Karl leaned his aching head against the priest.

Father Cunningham started to move away, stopped, then clumsily put his other hand on Karl's shoulder so that his arms encircled him in an awkward, sideways hug. "Can you forgive me?"

"Yes," whispered Karl.

The priest squeezed his shoulder and backed away. "Thank you." He removed his glasses again and wiped his eyes with a wrinkled handkerchief. "You're an inspiration, son."

"But, Father, I don't know if I can forgive Uncle Melvin. I don't ever want to see him again."

"I can understand why you'd feel that way. I will pray for the Lord to help you."

"Thanks." Karl leaned back on his mound of pillows, all worn out. "Father? I don't know if I can come to Mass tomorrow. Would that be a sin, seeing how it's Easter and all?"

"Easter is about healing, Karl, and you need to get well. Come to think of it, we all do. What does Sister Anne always say? God is good? That used to irritate me, but now

I believe she's right."

Father Cunningham took Maggie home to get some rest after Sister Anne offered to stay with Karl. Sister settled into the easy chair one of the nurses found for her and told him how the whole school prayed for him.

"Did you stay up all night praying, too? We saw the lights on in the church."

"Why, yes, we did."

"Thanks. I sure appreciate it." Karl wanted to tell her how he saw all their prayers in his dream, but he didn't know how to describe it without sounding crazy.

Sister Anne didn't get all upset when he began talking about what happened, so he figured it was all right to tell her about Melvin getting him drunk and locking him up in the closet; he even told her about grinding his knees into the broken glass so God would listen to him. When he described the strange green symbols he'd seen, she found him a pad of paper and a pencil and watched as he drew them. She said they were letters in some ancient language and offered to show them to Father Cunningham.

"No, Sister, please. You're the only one who can know about this."

She nodded, so he went on and told her about the snakes and how he only made things worse when he tried to fight them. He described the candles in the cave, and the eagles and hawks, and he told her about finding himself in the hands of—she said it was the hands of the Lord!

"Sister, if that was the Lord, then I saw his feet and..." He felt himself getting all choked up again and had to stop for a moment. "They were hurt and so beat up, but they were beautiful, too, like the sun or something." He whispered. "What do you think it all means?

"It doesn't matter what I think. It matters what you think."

Karl stared out the window for a moment. "If *he hath put all enemies under his feet* then why didn't God stop Uncle Melvin from doing those bad things to me? And to Aunt Kathleen? How can that mean he cares?"

"God doesn't always keep bad things from happening to us, Karl. Of course God cares about you, your Aunt Kathleen, your mother and sisters and all of us. It's how God takes bad things and makes something good of them that matters, and how God never, ever abandons us."

He sighed, leaned back on the pillows and felt himself sink into the bed. "I guess I have a lot to think about."

"Yes, you do. I will ask the Lord to help you." Sister Anne's eyes got watery. "You're a special young man; you have so much to give the world." She took his hands in both of hers, shaking them slightly. "So much. Someday, you'll be able to share what you've been through, and you'll help someone else who asks these same questions." She let go of his hands and took out her hanky. "I am very proud to be your teacher." She smiled.

"God bless you, Sister." The words just came tumbling out of his mouth. He'd never said them before—to anyone. His face burned hot with embarrassment.

"Oh, you dear boy..."

The way she touched his cheek reminded him of his mother.

"I'll be glad to have you back in class, just as soon as you're well enough."

Dr. Lyman came at suppertime. He shone a light in

Karl's eyes and gave him permission to go to sleep, but said the nurses would be waking him every hour. If he made it through the night okay, he could go home in the morning.

"I'd like to keep you another few days, but Bernie and your Aunt Kathleen are planning quite a celebration for Easter tomorrow. You should be with your family. That's better medicine than anything I can give you—*if* you stay on the davenport and don't get too excited or go rough-housing with those little Denver boys."

Karl thought of Billy and Ned and laughed. Soon they'd be cousins.

"Then it's back to bed with you until I give you permission to get up and go to school."

"I think you and Mrs. Lyman should come for Easter, too; you're like our family."

"We'll see about that." Dr. Lyman snapped his bag shut. "Everyone's going to sleep better tonight knowing where you are. No more going out in the middle of the night, understand?"

Karl nodded and offered his hand. "Thanks for everything."

His head still hurt, but he felt better than he had in a very long time.

Chapter 40

Many Waters Cannot
Quench Love
June, 1929 Tomos Bay, Wisconsin

After tossing and turning for hours, Maggie threw back the covers and got up. She opened her cedar chest and removed the quilts she packed away yesterday, stacking them neatly on the bed. She had no need of a lamp or candle because the full moon shone through the window, casting its bluish glow into the far corners of the room. Anyway, she knew what she needed and exactly where she'd find it.

Before she married Eddie, she'd filled the chest with hopeful things, things she'd need for the future. Now, on the day before her marriage to Jacob Denver, it held precious items from her past: the white wedding dress she hoped Lizzie or Anna would wear one day; the christening gown her babies wore; her father's pocket watch wrapped in his handkerchief and tucked into a leather pouch; the long-johns she'd cut from Eddie's frozen body and dried without washing. One by one, she took each item from the trunk, reverently spreading them across the bed, an exhibit of sacred relics from her life.

Next, Maggie brought out a packet of cards and letters, the last year of her life gathered up and tied with a red grosgrain ribbon. On top was the sweet valentine from Jacob, then all his letters, then the cards and letters she received when Eddie died. Beneath it all she found the thing she hoped would help her make it through the coming day: the framed picture of Saint Andrew, patron saint of fishermen. Its glass was gone and the frame was dented, but the saint still stared solemnly out into the world.

Maggie shivered. These June mornings were cool enough that heat from the furnace would have been nice, but she'd let the coal supply run out, since they'd be moving to Wakelin soon; she and Jacob after the wedding tomorrow, the children and Mother Denver on the train at the end of the week.

At least, that's what they planned.

Before sliding her feet into her slippers or throwing on her housecoat, she crossed herself and said a prayer asking for Saint Andrew's help. Seeing him, touching the frame, hanging the picture back in its place by the door, adjusting it until it was level, all brought back the stunned grief she felt the day it got knocked from its nail, its glass shattering into a thousand tiny pieces. It couldn't happen again, could it?

The mantle clock struck three. In just over an hour, Jacob and Karl would leave for a day of fishing on the *Maggie O'Keefe* with Will. If she started now, there would be plenty of time to make them biscuits for breakfast. She'd lace them with honey and spices to make them sweet and fragrant so Jacob and Karl would still have the taste of her love in their mouths if they went overboard and... She shivered again, but from not the cold. This time, she'd be prepared.

At four o'clock, when the eastern sky began to brighten, the alarm rang in her bedroom; time to wake Karl. Jacob arrived moments later. "Do I smell breakfast?"

"You didn't eat at the hotel, did you?"

He followed her into the kitchen. "No, but I didn't expect you to do all this, either. Don't you know what time it is?"

"It's breakfast time for men who have a full day ahead of them. Besides, I want you to remember... I mean, this is the last meal I'll cook for Karl—and you—in this kitchen." The realization stuck in Maggie's throat.

Jacob pulled out the chair across from Karl, who grinned and spoke with his mouth full of biscuit. "You gotta try these, Mr. D, Mama makes the best—"

"Don't talk with food in your mouth, Karl!" She knew she scolded him more sharply than necessary. She turned to the stove and heaped Jacob's plate with eggs and bacon and stood still, staring at his breakfast. The anxiety that kept her from sleeping was working itself up to a real fright. If she didn't control herself, she knew she'd be *in a state* before long.

"Maggie? Are you going to let me eat, or do I just get to smell it?"

"Sorry." She set Jacob's plate down without looking at him and turned away again to wrap some biscuits for them to take along. Her hands shook. "Are you sure you have all your things packed, Karl? Remember, the truck comes first thing tomorrow morning and you'll have no time to finish later on today. Maybe you should stay home." Maggie had visions of tonight's fancy dinner—provided by Mother Denver—turning into another wake.

"Aww, Mama, you already said I could go. I'm going to miss the whole season as it is."

She turned and looked into his eyes. "Just be careful. *Please* be careful. Please."

Jacob, already finished eating, drained the coffee from his cup. "If we don't leave right now, we'll be late and my brother will be cranky all day."

Maggie followed them to the front door and waited while they gathered their jackets and gloves.

Karl noticed the picture by the door. "Well, hello, Saint Andrew. I haven't seen you for a while." He put Ruffles on his head and pulled it down over his eyes. "Not that you helped Daddy any."

"Well, he helped *me*, so never you mind."

"We have to go, Maggie." Jacob kissed her.

She hugged them both, forcing herself to smile. She knew how much Karl had been looking forward to this. "Have a lucky day." These were the same words she'd said to Eddie every time he went out on the boat for all those years. Saying them now made her face feel hard and tight.

Her smile vanished the instant she shut the door behind them; her chest and throat tightened, her knees trembled. Her heart begged her to stop them, to plead with them to stay off that boat. When she realized she'd forgotten to give them the biscuits, she flew into the kitchen for the package, then hurried out the door for one more kiss, one more look at their faces. "Wait!"

Karl rolled down his window and took the package from her, grinning. "Oh, boy, thanks, Mama!"

She grabbed the door handle to steady herself. Common sense told her they'd probably be all right but she feared the terrible grief of losing them.

"Margaret, come here." Jacob sounded more like a

lumber boss than a lover.

She kept her hand on the hood of his new Ford as she moved, afraid they'd leave her if she let go. She couldn't catch her breath, like when Karl was missing. Hot tears filled her eyes.

Jacob rolled down his window and put his hand under her chin. "Now you listen to me and stop your fretting. We haven't come this far just to have it end. I'm coming back and so is Karl."

"You don't know that." She almost didn't get the words out.

"I *don't* know it. I *believe* it. We're meant to be together; this is *supposed* to be. I believe it more than I've ever believed anything in my whole life."

Maggie felt the earth rock beneath her, like she was a baby in a cradle or a child being rocked to sleep. She could only stare at him: her dear Jacob, her dearly beloved.

"Come on, Maggie, *breathe!* Tomorrow is ours, it's our day. Everything will be all right." He kissed her through the open window.

As the rising sun warmed her back, her chest loosened. She wiped her eyes with the back of her hand.

Ruffles interrupted. "Let's go, Mr. D. Will said sunup and not a minute later."

Jacob let go of her chin. "See you for dinner." He smiled. "Wear that lavender dress. I love the way you look in lavender." He rolled up his window, and drove away.

Maggie waved until they turned the corner. She remembered the heart Eddie gave her in the dream, the heart that kept breaking, the heart that became a rose, blooming forever.

She clutched both hands to her breast, fingering the engagement ring on her left hand. "This is my life," she whispered, "this is my beautiful, beautiful life."

Karl should have known better, but he and Mr. D ate the rest of the biscuits before they got to the marina and washed them down with big gulps of water from the pump in the parking lot. Furious, Will barked orders at everyone until Mr. D said he sounded *just like Henry.* That shut him up but made him even madder. He chugged out of the marina and into the cold morning wind way faster than he should have, kicking up a furious wake behind them. The waters were choppy as always, but Will's anger turned them downright stormy. Before long, Mr. D hung over the bow of the boat, all green and wobbly.

Karl didn't feel much better, but was determined to keep his breakfast down and make this a good day. He stumbled into the steering house and found Will at the wheel, his brow deeply furrowed, his jaw set hard and his watery eyes straight ahead.

Karl took a deep breath and swallowed. "Sorry we were late."

"You woulda been on time with your father."

"Yeah, but my mother was all upset and worried about our coming so we had to—" he swallowed again, looked away from Will, and set his focus on the horizon. "We had to convince her we'd be okay."

Will grunted.

"So, could you take it a little easy? 'Cause he's out there really sick, and I thought this was supposed to be a fun day."

"What gave you that idea? We're out here to work, Karl; to *work!* Not everyone can afford to take the day off just b'cause his brother's getting married tomorrow."

"Oh. Well, sorry." He turned to leave, but Will grabbed his arm.

"I'm not sure I like him taking you off where I can't keep an eye on you."

Karl wanted to tell Will how much he'd miss him, but he had to dash to the side of the boat.

"Aw, jeez, not you, too!" Will backed off, slowed the engine and began a wide turn, nice and smooth.

Relieved of his big breakfast, Karl lifted his head. "What're you doin'? You know we'll both be fine in a few minutes."

"Uh-uh. Look at him up there, hangin' on for dear life."

Mr. D slouched at the rail, his face the color of death. His right armpit rested on the edge and his arm dangled over the side of the boat. He held onto the rail with his left hand and hoisted himself up every couple of minutes to hang his head over the side.

Will spit out his words. "He's pathetic. He's *nothin'* like your daddy. He doesn't even know he'd be better off at the stern."

"Well, tell'im, for petesake! We don't have to go back."

"Yeah, we do. I'm not gonna be the one to drag him home to your mother, half-dead, ice cold and soaked to the bone. I did that once." Will glanced at Karl, his voice softening. "Anyway, he *is* my brother."

Karl spit over the side and straightened up. "Someone should talk to him."

"Be my guest."

Karl led Mr. D back to the stern of the boat. "Just so you know, I've seen Will feed the fish plenty of times.

It happens to most everybody. You'll feel better if you watch the horizon."

Mr. D's words came out in little bursts through chattering teeth. "I'd rather lie down inside."

"That'll only make you sicker. D'you need another jacket or something?"

He nodded. "Are we going back?"

"Yeah. Will's worried about you."

"Oh, thank God."

"Wait here." Karl hurried into the cabin and dug through the storage boxes under the benches. He found an old brown wool jacket, moth eaten and too ratty to be worn anywhere but out in the middle of the lake. It had been his father's; he remembered seeing him wear it a long, long time ago. He felt funny draping it over Mr. D's shoulders, not like he was being disloyal, but like it was a coronation or something.

"You need a hat, too?"

"It might help, thanks."

Karl found Ruffles and put it on Mr. D's head. He chuckled. "It looks good on you."

"Jacob!" Will growled at him from the steering house. "What?"

"Come in here and sit down before you take a dive."

Karl helped Mr. D up the step and onto the extra seat. When he saw them, Will snorted, threw back his head and laughed.

"Well, look at you, Ruffles! Ain't you purdy?"

Mr. D scowled. "Yeah, look at me."

"You're supposed to say, *I got it for looks, now*," prompted Karl.

"I got it for *what?*"

"Ask Will; he'll explain." He grinned at the brothers,

so very different yet so much the same.

Karl made his way to the bow, squinting at the water that danced and sparkled in the sunlight. As he listened to their banter, his heart filled with an unexpected happiness. He passed his hand over the railing, knowing this was the last time he'd be on the boat for a long time, knowing how much he was going to miss it. But somewhere between the three of them and the *Maggie O'Keefe,* he knew his father lived on. And for now, that was enough.

Karl spread his arms and leaned into the wind. The sun was warm, and it sure felt good on his face.

The End

LaVergne, TN USA
01 August 2010
191623LV00002B/2/P